Love and War —
and Eternally Damning Prophecies

Love and War —
and Eternally Damning Prophecies

THE ANASTASIA EVOLUTION SERIES

River Eno

ISBN-10: 0-9966883-5-8

ISBN-13: 978-0-9966883-5-2

Freeze Time Media

Cover artwork by Jason Werner

Cover design by Di Freeze

To Frank, Frankie, and Austin,
because the things you do inspire me

Acknowledgments

This being my first book, I have a lot of people to acknowledge. First, a thank you to my family, both the one I was born into and the one that I made with the help of my husband, children, and friends. Thanks to Jason who offered words of support and of criticism that I probably didn't want to hear.

Thanks to Stace for reading the first manuscript and sending me a beautiful card that I still have pinned to my corkboard above the bits and bobs that tend to collect on an old ratty corkboard. And for her promising me she wouldn't let anyone else read the book and then letting her mom read it anyway, because she wasn't sure if it was good because it was good or because we were friends. Thanks to everyone who didn't say I couldn't do it.

Huge thanks to those who helped make an idea into something tangible that any human being could pick up and read at leisure. To my husband, Frank, for holding my hand through every doorway, down every hall, and around every bend in the road. Thanks to JJ McKeever for being the first professional to read the manuscript and actually liking it, and for introducing me to publisher, author, editor, and now friend, Di Freeze at Freeze Time Media. Thank you, Di, for listening to me rant and rave, prattle on, gush and be happy, prattle on some more, and become frustrated again all in the same email. I literally could not have done this without you.

Prologue

Location: The Genesis Territories of the Vampire on the eastern side of the States of America — the former United States

Philadelphia Territory — Military Headquarters

Date: Thursday February 22, 2056

Time: 22:41

ROMEO MARCHED INTO GENERAL Galen's chambers gripping the bottom end of the transfer papers given to him moments before.

"What the hell, Galen. Do I do my job like I need a partner?"

Slightly annoyed by the interruption, Galen looked up from what he was doing. He ran both hands over his dark hair, pulled back and clubbed at the nape of his neck, making sure any stray pieces were caught behind his ears.

"I can't stand it when you presume to know what I need." Romeo waved the official documents at him.

"I hardly presume to know what you need." Galen stood, picked a pile of workbooks off his desk, and moved to the presentation area of his room, arranged with black board and chairs neatly set for a seminar on domestic violence for new cadets coming into the academy. "She is who I want you to have."

"She?" Romeo pulled at the crumpled forms in his hand. "What? No, he's a he. His name is Andrew."

"Her name is Andru."

"That's not right. I saw it. His name is …" Romeo ran his finger along the information boxes at the top of the page. "Anastasia Drucilla Weber? Her commanding officer says she goes by the name

Andru." He looked at Galen, his brows pulled together. "That's dumb. What girl has a name like that? I already can't stand her."

"She will be good for you," Galen smiled.

"What the fuck does that even mean?" Romeo put his hands on his hips and his weight on one leg, wondering why every so often Galen decided he needed to be saddled with a neophyte or an old-timer headed for retirement. "I do just fine on my own."

Galen opened his mouth, only to be cut off by a hand gesture.

"I'm a first captain—your first captain, correct?"

Galen nodded, looking a little exhausted by Romeo's attitude.

"That makes me above all the other captains and their little lieutenant partners, correct?"

Galen nodded again.

"And you're my sire, right?"

Romeo knew how it angered Galen when he spoke of their relationship in that way.

"Yes," Galen agreed, "you are a part of me, and I would like you to—"

"We've been through this many times," grumbled Romeo. "I don't like partners. I don't like someone answering to me, and I certainly don't want to answer to someone. I don't like having to deal with the needs of a human during my shift."

"Vampires eat," said Galen accusingly. "You break for dinner."

"I stop at the bar, pay for a warm body, and leave. It takes me ten minutes—fifteen if the place is busy. I never have to piss. I never have an upset stomach." Romeo looked at the papers he was still holding. "And I never have to fix my makeup."

"Well, you are in luck," smiled Galen and he made his way to where Romeo stood. "She seems to be one of those 'goth' people. I think I have only ever seen her wear heavy black eyeliner. How long can it take to fix something that looks a mess already?"

"Are you kidding me?" Romeo slumped into the chair in front of Galen's desk more agitated than he was the moment before. "A goth chick?"

Galen put a hand on the back of Romeo's head and the other on the chair's arm. He kissed the younger man's forehead and then set a series of small kisses on his cheek.

"I think she will make a good captain one day. Will you teach her? For me?"

"She's a rookie," complained Romeo even as the feeling of Galen's hand in his hair drained the tension from his shoulders. "I mean literally. She's just stepped out of the academy. She's only been an officer for six months and three weeks. She has years to go before she can take the captain's test."

"I know," Galen whispered. He ran his hand down Romeo's chest until it was between his legs. "Please." He squeezed until Romeo squirmed in the seat. "For me."

Romeo turned his face so his lips touched the man that converted him—the man who could infuriate him and yet make him feel as no other person or vampire could. He kissed the vampire that would die for him, and he knew he couldn't deny him no matter how much he wanted to.

The soft touch of Galen's fingers on the back of his neck was so relaxing it sent chills down his spine.

"You owe me one," said Romeo softly, and when Galen drew back Romeo pulled his shirt to bring him in for another kiss. "And just so you know, I let you seduce me into doing this."

"Of course you did," said Galen as he straightened. "That would be the only reason you acquiesced with such ease. Not at all because you are weak to the pleasures of the flesh."

"Fuuuck you," said Romeo, trying not to smile.

The bell chimed and the door to General Galen's chambers opened. A woman—no, a girl—dressed in urban fatigues, a black long-sleeved button-down shirt, and tie closed the door and walked to the last row of empty chairs awaiting cadets. She looked around the room and then at the two men looking at her. She set her backpack on the floor and fell into military stance.

Romeo glanced at Galen and then back to the girl. He didn't

know her, but he thought she was attractive, even if a little odd looking. Her hair was a short, black mess, as if she hadn't combed it that day, or ever. Her ears were small, maybe slightly pointed, although it was hard to tell with so many earrings trailing the edge. She didn't have overly large eyes, but he could see them just fine. They were greenish and a bit wider set than average. Her jaw was strong, but not like a man's, and she had a ring in her nose and bottom lip.

"New cadet?" he asked Galen. "Your twenty-three hundred appointment?"

"Hello, Andru," said Galen. "I expected you half an hour ago. You knew to come here, yes?"

"Wait? Seriously?" Romeo scoffed and sat straighter in the chair. "This is her? She's tiny. She's not even five and half feet tall."

"I apologize, my Lord," said Andru, frowning at Romeo and then putting her eyes back to the floor, as is proper when in military stance. "I was told you wanted to see me the day before I went on vacation. That was two weeks ago. I just got back, and I forgot and went straight to roll call."

"Vacation?" asked Romeo, glaring in her direction.

"Yes, sir."

"Who takes a long vacation when they've only been at a job for six months?"

"It was planned a long time ago." She looked up, allowing Romeo to think more of her for disregarding the archaic rule of not looking a superior vampire in the eye, and mentally punishing her for thinking the rules didn't apply to her. "I told my group captain when I got out of the academy."

"I see," said Romeo, noting the slight tremor in her voice and enjoying it. "Where did ..."

Suddenly he smelled something so wonderful, but so strangely out of place it made him pause. It wafted around the room the way good cooking tends to move slowly throughout the house. Only this smell punctured its way into his brain the way the metallic odor of blood pushes aside most other thoughts.

It was a smell he loved. The scent of deep woods, of swamp oak, cedar, and the honeyed pine of cottonwood buds. It was a damp smell, as when the rain saturates the earth, matting the leaves to the ground in clumps. It brought back memories of childhood and family and young love.

"Romeo," said Galen, staring from behind his desk.

"Hmm?" Romeo startled as if poked. "What?"

"You were about to ask the lieutenant a question?"

"Oh." He looked at Andru, puzzled by what happened. "Where did you … where did you go?"

"Excuse me?" Andru looked around; she was standing in the same spot.

"Where did you go on vacation?"

"Oh, um, Baker Trail."

Romeo heard a faint cuckoo sound and rubbed his jaw, bemused.

"Near Pittsburgh," offered Andru.

"I know where it is." Romeo squinted at her. "It must have been freezing. Why would you do that in February?"

"It was really cold," she nodded. "My boyfriend likes to live outside no matter the temperature."

"You do everything your boyfriend wants?"

An unkind expression flashed across her face. She twisted her mouth and clinched her jaw. Romeo was fairly certain she'd bitten into her cheek. He wondered if it hurt or if she were used to it. He smiled to himself, thinking she was a feminist, and how he would have fun yanking her chain about it.

"I like it too," she answered with an edge in her voice.

Romeo got up, walked toward the lieutenant, and sat on the edge of his father's desk.

"Why do they call you Andru, Anastasia Drucilla?"

"It's a combination of —"

"Yeah, I got that. But why Andru? Why not Ana or …" He looked her up and down. "Shorty?" *Or pain in my ass*, he finished in his head, thinking loud enough for his father to hear it.

She looked at him, none too happy with the interrogation.

"Because that's what my parents called me."

He stared at her, deciding if he should acknowledge the chip on her shoulder, make her cry now and get this over with, or wait it out and slowly pick away at her over the next few weeks until she begged Galen to be transferred.

Another low cuckoo sounded.

"Well, it's a stupid name," he said, unable to keep his cool at her brusque tone.

"It's a nickname. I suppose my parents could have pulled a misnomer from ancient poetry and called it a day, but I wasn't so lucky."

Romeo frowned at the big smile on Galen's face.

"Did she just call me a misnomer?"

Galen put his hands up, not wanting to comment.

"How is my name a misnomer?" Romeo glared at the woman who seemed to grow larger with her attitude. "What do you mean by that?"

Andru stood quietly looking at the floor, clearly trying to decide if she should say anything else that would get her into more trouble.

"Please, lieutenant, don't be shy."

She finally looked at him.

"Go ahead; enlighten me."

"A misnomer is a meaning that is known to be wrong—as if maybe a thing was named before it was known what it was. And from what I've heard from the men and women around here," she said confidently, "you're nothing like your namesake, Romeo."

Romeo's eyebrows rose so high he thought they might leave his head. He didn't know if he should laugh or be completely pissed. He did admire her audacity even if he didn't want to.

"Take the rings out of your nose and lip." He motioned to her face with his hand.

"What?" She blinked at him.

"Take the rings out of your face, lieutenant."

"It's regulation," her hand went to the small ring in her lip.

"I said take it out."

When she hesitated, he pushed out a sigh.

"Have you ever been in a fight, lieutenant?"

She hesitated again, looking as though she felt inadequate or bothered by the question.

"No, sir."

"That nose ring will be the first thing to be ripped out. And the lip ring the second, so take them out."

Andru sighed but did what he told her to do.

Romeo heard another soft cuckoo sound. He looked at Galen.

"What the hell is that?"

"I have no idea," Galen frowned.

"It's um ..." Andru's voice shook just a little. "It's my phone."

"What?"

"My phone. It fell in the river, and now I can't change the settings. It's broken."

Romeo looked at the ceiling as if patience would fall from it. Again they heard the cuckoo.

"Jesus, who's pinging you?"

"How would I know?"

Romeo narrowed his eyes at her blatant lack of respect.

"Give it to me," he snapped. "Give me your phone!"

He walked to the lieutenant as she bent to the floor and searched her backpack. She pulled out a small shirt, a scarf, gloves, a toothbrush, a banana, soap, and a hairbrush and put them on the floor.

"Really?" remarked Romeo. "Did you seriously just get back?"

"Yes," she huffed. "I said that. And I couldn't change the setting so I tried to hide it under my stuff." She found the phone and stood. "Here."

She held it out for Romeo, but the thick scent of that forest blew over him, stunning him speechless. He couldn't believe it. It was coming from her! And she was suddenly all he could see. He wanted to be near her. He wanted to crawl inside that smell until it coated him. He wanted to put his fingers in her mouth to see if her spit smelled like river water or wet leaves. He wanted … he wanted to do things to her.

"Here," said Andru, waving her phone back and forth. "Do you want it?"

At that moment the cuckoo chimed again, bringing Romeo back to himself.

"Did you even shower before you got here? You smell like you slept under a pile of wet dirt. And you look exhausted."

Her expression of embarrassment nearly made him feel bad, and he hated feeling bad. He snatched the phone from her hand.

"It's big enough," he said, staring at the picture of the blond-haired, blue-eyed man that had popped up on the screen. "You'll need a hands free while on duty. Do you have one?"

"No, I don't."

He flipped angry eyes to her, but only for a moment. The color of her eyes seemed to have changed a little. They were more amber, as if a fire were inside of her, and he suddenly felt that he didn't want to give her too much attention or he might lose his train of thought again.

"Who's Ibex?" He turned the phone out so she could see the photo. "That's what you have for his name."

"That's Dacon, my boyfriend."

"Really?" Romeo turned the phone back to see the photo. "The way he's blowing up your phone, I thought he might be your drug dealer. He looks like a drug dealer."

"I don't do drugs."

Romeo frowned; everyone did drugs. He held the phone out for Galen to see the kind of delinquent his new partner wasted time with camping in the woods.

"What's an Ibex?"

"A particularly wild mountain goat from the European alps," answered Galen after a moment of thought. "The male has a long beard and quite large curved horns."

"He's got the beard." Romeo lifted his brows in question. "So your guy has really large horns, huh?"

Andru stared at him, not exactly sure what to say.

"This guy could be a leader in Hitler's utopia. You know who Hitler is, right?"

Andru nodded.

"Don't get any blonder and whiter than that." Romeo tapped the phone. "Looks like a Viking."

The phone cuckooed and Romeo heaved a sigh.

"Sorry," said Andru apologetically. "We usually meet up after roll call. He knows I'm in the building and is probably wondering why I'm not responding."

"Ibex is a soldier?" asked Romeo. "He works here?"

"Yes." Andru nodded again.

"Tell him it's broken."

"What?"

Romeo dropped the phone onto the tiled floor, covered it with his boot, and crushed it under his weight.

Galen frowned. Andru's mouth dropped open wide.

"Why would you do that?"

"So I don't have to listen to that cuckoo anymore!" Romeo kicked the broken pieces of phone across the floor. "Now you can get a hands free."

"I can't afford one of those," she nearly whined.

"He'll buy it for you." Romeo jerked his thumb in the general's direction.

Andru looked at Romeo and then at General Galen.

"Sir," said Andru confusedly. "I don't understand what's going on."

Galen looked up from what he was working on. "Understand what?"

"Why I'm here."

"You were not told why I wanted to see you?"

"No," she answered, clearly concerned.

"You are to be the first captain's new partner." Galen motioned to Romeo, who had sat back in the chair in front of the general's desk.

"Why?" Andru looked at Romeo, her distress rising exponentially. "Am I in trouble? Did I do something wrong?"

"No," said Galen, clearly wanting to calm her down. "Not at all. This is a promotion."

Andru looked at Romeo, unable to keep the panic off her face.

"Not really promoted," smiled Romeo. "More like a lateral move."

"She will be a first captain's partner," said Galen.

"Yeah, but just because she's with me doesn't give her any more authority than she has now."

"Granted," said Galen. "But she is still a head above the rest simply by being placed in your care."

Romeo thought the girl looked like she was going to be sick. The thought made him smile wider.

"Is this …" she said to General Galen. "I mean … can I …" Andru looked at Romeo. "Can I … decline?"

The happiness drained from Romeo's face. He couldn't believe this girl didn't want to work with him. The nerve. People were lined up to be his partner. It was he who didn't want to work with her, or anyone else. He certainly didn't need her. He especially didn't need her stinking up his truck with her dirty human body. He didn't need the distraction of thinking about how good she smelled. He always worked better alone, and Galen knew it.

"Well," said General Galen. "I—"

"No," said Romeo and stood. "You can't decline."

Andru looked at her general for some kind of support.

"Here," Galen put his signature on a small military form and handed it to Romeo to give to her. "Give this to Lieutenant Katie. She will see you get a new phone."

Andru took the paper and nodded glumly. She knelt to the floor, wiping at the tear sliding down her face as she put her things back in her pack.

Romeo walked past the girl toward the exit. He banged on the door and his new partner nearly fell on her ass. "Let's go, dirt bath. I'm late because of you."

Andru slung her pack on her shoulder and turned toward her new partner.

"Lieutenant," called General Galen.

She turned around, her expression hopeful that he was going to say this entire thing was a huge mistake and she could go back to her unit.

"Yes, Lord."

"I know that he can be a bully."

Romeo impatiently knocked his knuckles on the door, annoyed that Galen called him a bully. Clearly he was the inconvenienced party in all this.

"Yes, Lord." Andru sighed, her hope deflating like a popped balloon. She turned again to follow the first captain.

"Lieutenant, wait."

She looked back to see the general walking to the black board holding a handful of pens. His expression was concerned, maybe regretful.

"Try not to let him get you down."

"I won't." She took a deep breath. "I won't."

There are days that pass with ease, so fast you don't know what happened to them. Then there are days that dig in their heels and refuse to move on. As if the Universe takes hold with such a tight grip it would tear off your flesh before giving in to your wishes. I'm beginning to have too many of those days.

CHAPTER ONE

The year is 2065...

IF HE SAYS WE'RE going to war, I might have to shoot myself in the head.

"Everyone knows we're going to war, Dru. It's in the air."

My fingers brushed my holster. I was glad there was no gun to fill it. Weary, and more than somewhat bored, I pulled the gray beret from my head to wipe a line of sweat trickling down the side of my face. When you're this high up, conditioned air and window shades can't save you from the heat burning its way through the triple panes. I leaned a shoulder on the glass and traced the red thread that created the full moon emblem of the Philadelphia Territory on the front of the hat.

"Stop it. There won't be a war."

Lt. James Von Warner, Loki to his friends, tugged a twisted white cord and pulled the window blind up past his head. Small black goggles forced the light brown hair from his face, leaving his expression open and exposed.

"This is Philadelphia, Andru," he said, motioning with a nod to the tiny people on the city street below.

I nearly rolled my eyes and punched him for using my name in such a paternal manner.

"We're the flagship city."

"No we're not," I frowned.

"Yeah we are."

"New York is the—"

"How long do you think the vampire lords will put up with this level of violence? I think ... do you wanna know what I think?" He continued talking before I could answer, as usual. "I think the vampires are used to being the aggressive party. I don't think our king is happy about being on the other end of it."

"Maybe not, but King Jagen is old—"

"Ancient."

"Okay, but he's not crazy. He hasn't made it to where he is with impulsive thinking or action."

"The separation from the States of America was only sixty-four years ago."

"I know the history; you don't have to go over it with me. You sound like a newsagent. And it doesn't mean we're headed to war. What do you think? We're due?"

He shrugged. "There are always random attacks, but I think the last few incidents were antagonistic." Loki wagged a finger at the window. "If they don't stop killing us, King Jagen's gonna declare war, and we're gonna try to fight, but we're gonna lose, and we're gonna die."

My posture slumped. I think even my eyes slumped.

"By the gods, Loki, you're too young to be this ... I don't know, depressing. The States don't want to go to war. The territories may be small, but we're not completely incapable."

"They could nuke us."

"No they can't. We're on the same continent." I was sure my head was going to crack open. "Understand? The same bit of rock."

He looked skyward and sighed. I followed his attention and squinted at the bright yellow ball in a perfect August sky. Its white rays were far behind the tree-lined horizon, relentless, and still so beautiful. I slid a pair of goggles over my eyes, unable to fight the harshness of the sun god's intensity. Most of the soldiers stationed here for any length of time on the high turret of Galen Manor seemed to become immune to the sunlight. I don't think my eyes could ever adjust to such a degree of brightness. I swear Loki's irises have faded from a dark chocolate brown to the same honey color as his hair since he started this position two years ago.

My eyes fell to the street encircling the military mansion like a blacktopped moat. Then I looked beyond to the woods of Galen Park. Everything appeared peaceful, but I understood his fear. If the violence from the States continues, King Jagen will declare war, and we will probably lose. Jagen, though not one of my favorite undead, is not a particularly bad ruler. Nor can I completely disagree with a decision of war. You can't declare a section of the country separate, only to take it back half a century later or underhandedly try to destroy it. Maybe the vampire coerced the American government into handing him its northeastern states, creating our monarchical society as it stands today. However, that was a long time ago and long before a third of our population existed.

Besides, King Jagen never said he would set the vampire loose on society. He didn't even have that kind of power, then. I've heard more than once that the general public's distasteful reaction to the existence of vampires caught him completely off guard. Considering there were so many movies and books about them, Jagen assumed humans truly wanted vampires to be real. Unfortunately, people thought the Morning Star himself sent him and the other nine ancient vampires to begin the apocalypse. So to keep the peace, and save their asses, they coughed up the Eastern seaboard and a few surrounding territories. Then came the riots, and true mayhem broke out as the American government's decision shocked and appalled most of the world.

Loki snapped his fingers in front of my eyes. "Gimme my weed, sweetheart."

"Keep out of my face," I said, slapping at his hand. "And don't call me that again unless you want this to be the last time I make a run for you."

His mouth turned into the sweetest smile I've ever seen on a grown man. That's why I do these things for him. I also do it because, for most of the day, he's stuck up here like a rat in a cage. I dug into my pocket for a blue plastic bag half full of homegrown marijuana. More accurately, it was New York grown in Lord Orel's territory.

"I mean it. Those people are weird. Give me a reason not to go back, and I'll take it."

"Jacob's not that bad. Is the little military girl afraid of the big druggy man?"

"He's like five foot six, and how about if I let you drive down to that zoo to get your own pot?"

The green bud reeked in my pocket since I had picked it up, but he inhaled at the mouth of the bag anyway. "That Neanderthal's got the best stuff."

He sat on the edge of his desk and knocked over a full glass of tomato juice onto his materials and icona keyboard. He grabbed a wad of napkins from too much restaurant takeout off the corner of his desk and hurried to staunch the flow. Tomato juice is a real bitch to clean up. I know, I drink it all the time and have had my share of accidents. In fact, tomato juice is popular here in the Territories. It's the most abundant beverage we have. Since our beginning, we've held the favor of the farmers. The States have been screwing over the American planter for more years than I've been alive, so they decided to give Lord Multan, our domestic and foreign trade representative, firsthand buying privileges of their fruits, vegetables, and cotton. It was about 2040 when their government discovered what was going on. While legal, it was underhandedly sneaky. As you can imagine, the Americans were pissed. But If they didn't have their heads so far up their asses buying the same items from Canada, South America, and Puerto Rico, it wouldn't have happened.

The situation is unfortunate because by holding Pennsylvania, Connecticut, Maine, and New York, we have plenty of farmland. What we lack is the technological industry. Most of the business moved west when the vampire took over. The States forbade its scientists to share new developments in almost any area, or to fraternize with the scientists from Genesis. Consequently, we're a little slow. Don't get me wrong; we're not in the Dark Ages. Our people come up with amazing technology all the time, especially for military use.

At the inauguration of the vampire's reign, around the turn of the 21st century, the States kept a silent political distance, apart from the necessary trade and peace agreements formed at the onset. Eventually, global curiosity grew, holiday tourism spread to us, and we became quite the novelty. With affordable rates, families can lodge in The Vampire's Bedroom. It's much the same as any hotel chain except there's a vampire behind the desk at night, and the lobby décor looks like a horror film set from any generic goth movie. No mints on the pillows though. Hot Dots instead, which are a soft, round, red candy that gushes red cinnamon liquid when you chew it, turning your teeth and gums blood red for a short time.

There are too many vampire nightclubs and restaurants to count. They serve things like Bloody Mary Burgers and fries in the shape of small wooden stakes. Vampire clothing shops sell dark flowing capes, giant hats with feathers in the top, and poet shirts. No real vampire would wear these items, even if they were born in the era. Keeping the tourists happy with coffin key chains and black bat pencil tops is essential if we want the revenue. Each territory weaves vampire lore into its natural tourist destinations. For instance, the territory of Maine's history had Samuel Mayall's first water-powered woolen mill in the city of Gray. The British would've lost money if the colonies began making wool, so Samuel smuggled his plans for the mill in bails of cloth that he traded to Native Americans. When the British realized what he did, they tried to kill Mayall with poisoned hatpins and boxes filled with guns ready to fire. What the tour now reveals is that Mayall dodged those bullets and survived that poison because he was a vampire. He's dead now, killed in the civil war, but his mill lives on.

Lately, however, the president of the States has been up front about her distaste for us. She meddles in our business negotiations with other cooperative nations, chastising them, and making it increasingly difficult for their citizens to get a permit to vacation here. The fact is that the longer the Genesis Territories go on as a separate free country, the tighter it entrenches its fangs and weaves itself into societies everywhere with new allies. Only six months ago, King

Jagen persuaded the strict German government to house a Genesis embassy outside Hamburg to make contact with the undead there. They hope to come here where they won't be viciously hunted.

The problem is that weeding out the psychos is a long, tedious process that expends military personnel and money. Let's face it, they are vampires, and some of them could use a vicious hunting. And although we have steadfast rules governing this nation, it's not an absolute monarch. Proper channels take time. Bureaucracy isn't racist. In the beginning, King Jagen and the governing lords enacted a standard set of laws, with special, quite specific regulations for the undead population, who are more docile than literature portrayed. This may have to do with being able to get a meal without trickery.

Our King Jagen, along with the other vampire leaders, holds a position and a title. Lord Multan is our trade representative. Lord Brasov, our Lord of Justice, heads our judicial system. However, we do elect judges, mayors, governors, and the like to do most of the work. In the end, Brasov's word is law, but mostly he lets his employees do their job. We're more of a constitutional, or limited, monarchy. Each lord shows higher interest in the grander and more ceremonial aspects of the position, like being a noble figurehead allocating most responsibilities to those elected to work for them. Each of the territories is run in the same basic manner as before they separated—or converted—as the States are so fond of saying. The vampires have never wanted total transformation or to get rich. They've always seemed to have enough of that. They sought the land where they had a safe haven to roam.

Loki finished blotting up the juice and handed me the soaked napkins to throw away. "You know what? You're beginning to sound like my mom."

"I'm not being your mom," I smirked, pursing my lips in a motherly gesture. "I'm just saying, buy your drugs from someone less gross—and don't worry about war. We're not going to war."

"How do you know?"

"Lord Galen will figure it out."

"And if our spooky Lord of War can't? Will you stay?"

"Here?"

"Yes, here. If there's a war, will you fight for them?"

"Them who?" I knew whom he meant.

"The lords. The day-cold. The dusty old vampyre."

"Yeah, I will. It's our job to protect the people living here. Be that human, or the nocturnal minority. Just because they chose a way of life different from the people in the States doesn't mean that life is worthless."

I rubbed my hand over my face. Now I was up on my soapbox. I stopped before I said I'd fight to the death, because I wouldn't want to find out what the States would do to anyone, civilian or military, human or vampire, if that government caught them alive when that war was over.

"I wish I had your conviction."

"Look at it this way," I said, "if we go to war and die, we'll get to the afterlife sooner."

"I'm too young to die! Besides, Heaven isn't ready for me ... or I'm not ready for Heaven."

Heaven is not where I'm going, I wanted to say, but didn't want to start another debate over religious afterlife.

"I don't like fighting," he said. I wanted to make the obvious comment about him being a soldier, but he suddenly looked too young for this job. "Everyone on the outside is so angry at the vampire that they fight amongst themselves without realizing where the animosity comes from. My parents decided to move here because there were fewer restrictions than in the States." He smiled. "They're potheads. Back then, it was peaceful. They didn't care if there was a king representing the country. England still has the royal family, even if only in name. King Jagen doesn't do much to run this country either."

"He runs enough."

"Not really."

I didn't agree. Jagen micromanages. He has to. One thing he needs to be successful as a ruler is happy, healthy humans—not only for food, but to sustain his way of life politically and militarily.

There aren't enough vampires to put his territories in the running as a super power—not even close. King Jagen needs humans to want to live here.

Loki shrugged. "We've never been to war, and it seems the States are involved in a military dispute every few years. It's different now. There's too much tension. I knew someone who died in the attack at Penn University." He shuffled about uncomfortably. "War is remote, but still ..."

I put my arm around his shoulders to hug him sideways. He's about four inches taller than I am, maybe five foot eight, but his broad frame made him hard to hold.

"My grandmother always said not to waste time worrying about what might never happen. If Jagen declares war, then worry. Even if he does, we're not going to die."

The change in his eyes was subtle, but those sweet Bambi orbs turned dark. It wasn't the color, but the thoughts behind them. They fell to my muddy uniform. He picked a finger in the buttonhole at the top of my black shirt. Caked-on mud fell in a semi-dry plop to the floor and I pushed his hands away.

"Don't touch me. I'm dirty and I'm sore."

"What happened?"

"Some idiot tried to beat me up."

"Who won?"

"He's at the hospital. You wanna go ask him who won."

"Calm down." Loki plopped into his desk chair, gliding backwards as he leaned. He stretched his arms behind his head. "I'm sorry. I didn't mean to bruise your ego. Let me make it up to you with dinner and a little reefer."

"No." I waved my hand. "I'm fine. I'm going to Romeo's apartment to watch a movie."

A buzzer sounded. Loki rolled his chair to the view screen that monitored the outside hall. He rolled back and banged the door lock on his desk. His partner stepped inside with a red sack, a newspaper, a cup of something hot, and a donut stuffed in her mouth. She motioned hello with her elbow as she raced to her station. I yanked off the goggles on my way to the door.

"Oh hey," said Danielle, smiling. "Don't leave me alone with him."

"I was going to molest him, but now that you're here I feel a bit uncomfortable."

She laughed. I tossed the goggles. She dropped her pastry to catch the flimsy plastic. The door closed on my smile.

CHAPTER TWO

I WIPED THE SWEAT off my chin and refrained from overthinking that conversation. I was depressed enough. The latest attack Loki spoke of forced night-shift human soldiers like me to work days for the last three weeks. The vampires picked up the slack at night, but the streets needed a heavier presence during the day. I had been trapped in despair with the sticky, heat-crazed lunatics. I really didn't need to contemplate the long-term social and mental ramifications of terrorism on the community and state.

I dusted some of the mud off the front of my uniform. I clicked the button for the elevator and automatically reached around for my backpack — that I left in the Emergency Dispatch Office. I smacked the elevator button again, and chewed a layer of skin off the inside of my cheek. My body slumped against the wall, and I wondered who would clean up the mess if I ripped my head off my shoulders. I took a deep breath and closed my eyes. I smelled damp earth almost immediately. Darkness crept around me. Whispers filled the silence. I called for Romeo. A barely audible ping swam in the dank confusion. There was a sudden bright light.

"Lieutenant."

Romeo?

"Lieutenant."

My eyes flew open. I pushed away from the wall in a panic. It took a few seconds to gain perspective and to understand that I was still in Galen Manor, in the hall of the high turret. Not in a dream — I wasn't in that damn dream.

"Are you all right?" asked Lord Galen. I turned toward the end of the hall to confront the vampire. The owner of that deep voice had a sometimes odd, almost eclectic, European accent. He was looking at me from inside the elevator. "You called your partner."

He commanded the elevator to wait and he came to me. I was a bit dazed. Whether it was from him or the dream, I couldn't be sure. He looked perfect, as usual, almost like a statue. His hair, easily mistaken for black against his skin, is the darkest brown. Although he usually wore it bound and clubbed back, today it was loose and pulled to one side, ending about mid-hip. His dark brows framed the palest green eyes. And he was frowning, which forced the inner corner of his eyebrows close to his narrow nose.

"General," I said, straightening to a courteous military stance, with my head straight, eyes down, feet apart, and forearms flat against the small of my back.

Lord Galen, our Lord of War and Peace, is the only vampire leader that doesn't hide out or delegate anything. He takes his duties as general of the Genesis Militaries very seriously. Like the other generals, he has a proxy during the day, General Simon DeFarr. But like most of the vampires over eight hundred years old, he's awake much of the time, so DeFarr's job isn't so tough. However, I'll admit that in the past two years we've all had our hands full. The vampire lords are more vulnerable now than ever. Such is the price of fame, fortune, and land ownership. Giving up their anonymity has cost them the element of surprise, which is a predator's greatest asset. With so many vampires in one large area, a few well-placed missiles would make them history. Of course, the cities would fall into ruin, and many innocent humans die on the same continent.

"Are you all right?" he asked, waving for me to relax my stance.

"Uh ... yeah ... I'm fine. I was ... I think ... I mean I was having a nightmare."

He always makes me stammer. I truly hate that I sound like a moron — the way my brain shuts down when he's around. You'd think nine years of close connections would rid me of this childish infatuation, but at times like this, it seems to get worse.

"Sleeping while standing can do that," he said.

"Do what?" I said.

"Give you nightmares."

I frowned. "Huh?"

"Are you quite sure you feel all right?" he asked, waving his hand in front of my eyes.

"It's been a long, hot day," I said, pulling at my beret and running a tired hand over the top of my head.

"I would not know."

"No," I said. "I guess not."

He stepped closer. I moved until my back hit stone. He took another step forward, ignoring the thumping of my heart. He raised a hand, and the heat radiating off my body charged the space between us. His fingers skimmed the area around my right eye where I was hit, and he traced my eyebrow around the steel barbell pierced in my skin. I inhaled a deep breath from his closeness—and from pain.

"The skin has swelled around your jewelry," he noted.

I nodded because I find it difficult to speak or think clearly when he's near me.

"You should hold ice to it." He slowly wiped the corner of my mouth and then turned his pale finger out for me to see the smear of bright red across its tip.

"I bit my cheek," I said, my fingers blotting where he had just touched.

"While dreaming?"

"I guess."

"Do you have nightmares often?"

"Well," I smiled, "only if I fall asleep against the wall."

See, I do have a sense of humor. It just takes a bit of pain to bring me out of the lust-induced stupor I sink into when he's around.

His mouth turned up in a thin smile, and he didn't move, even though he was so close common etiquette would suggest he do so.

My nerves wouldn't allow me to look in his eyes, so I stared at his mouth. It had an intense redness to it, like a perfect apple, and his teeth were as white as freshly fallen snow. It's not an abnormal condition. The inner mouth of a vampire, especially the older ones, is almost always deep, rich red. Without any other fluids going into their system, all the naturally pink body parts deepen in color, especially the mouth and the rims of the eyes. It even affects their nail beds. King Jagen keeps his fingernails long. They look as if they've been painted crimson, and the extended length is cloudy white. It's creepy.

The awkward moment turned to panic as Lord Galen considered the blood on his finger. For my own personal reasons, I'd rather he not taste it, but Romeo tells me he doesn't drink the blood of humans anymore. He says that since they've been in public, Galen hasn't wanted to do anything to force the vampires back into hiding. Apparently, at one time his eating habits were vicious. I've heard exciting rumors that he hunts deer and other things in Galen Park, the wooded area around the manor. He stared at the blood on his finger.

"You don't have to …" What am I going to say? "lick that." Oh, that was perfect. "That is, I mean, I … I won't be offended if you don't." Fabulous recovery!

He wiped his finger on his palm and then smoothed his hands together until the blood was gone. I was irrationally insulted. I kind of wanted him to lick his fingers uncontrollably as people do after eating fried chicken. As if we were teenagers, and he couldn't get enough of me. The things I think at times are truly pathetic.

He brushed his hands down his pants, and I noticed his clothing. The long-sleeved shirt was emerald green and awakened the blanched green in his eyes. The shirt was snug, and the lines of his undernourished chest were visible. His black pants laced up his abdomen, and full-length military boots covered his calves. The clothes, though well-made and of good quality, made him look almost emaciated. I liked it, just as I like almost everything about him.

When I remembered that he could see me, I closed my mouth and forced myself to breathe. He stood still and let his eyes wander.

His gaze can be a real palpable thing. It makes me nervous. He does that type of subtle magik on me often. I find it confusing, because most of the vampire lords don't bother with the human class unless to feed. For that they have what the media has labeled "habits"—an elite group of humans passed around for bleeding and sometimes sex. None of them are as young as me. Younger people are naïve, in essence too easy to control. Apparently, that's a turnoff if you're looking for a challenge in your food.

I've asked Romeo why all humans aren't considered too young. He said that some vampire see us as pets, sort of. Consider the attention span of a puppy. Then think of the calm, almost sly machinations of an older dog or even a mature monkey. The adult animal understands and does things the younger have neither the patience nor experience for. I understood, and then I smacked him in the back of his head for comparing humans to dogs.

Older vampires stay away from military personnel because Lord Galen doesn't appreciate his soldiers treated that way in any of the territories, even if they're willing. For the most part, the lords don't want us anyway. They sum up military personnel in one phrase: definition-mindless. We hear it often.

Lord Galen finally stepped back. His eyes focused on my chest, or I should say my shirt.

"Dirty," I said. He raised his brows slightly, and my eyes went wide. "Not me, I mean the shirt. I'm not dirty." I looked at my sleeves, coated with a fine layer of mud dust. "Well, I am dirty, just not … I only meant I'm not a dirty girl." I opened my mouth, but nothing else came out. By all the gods, my stupidity amazes even me.

He moved to the elevator, motioning for me to follow. I did, and it wasn't only his stature that had me feeling like a lost animal trailing the wolf into his den. He seemed a tad predatory this evening. I moved to his right, twisted my beret in my hands, and placed my back against the wall. I needed the distance. I truly hate these feelings, because I'm not like this with the other vampires in our manor, Lord Cherkasy and Lord Pune. None of the others make me feel like an elevator is a sacred space where you can't talk. The general brought his brows into a frown, as if he were studying me. He clasped his hands behind his back.

"Up early again," I said.

"The sun is down."

I glanced at my watch: 19:15. I looked at the sunrise/sunset clock hanging high over the steel doors. Big green numbers read 19:57. "Not yet."

"One of the benefits for living so long, being so old," he smiled, white fangs barely visible. "Level five?"

"No, I uh, I have to stop by the E.D.O."

"Right," he said, "your belongings."

"Yes. Wait, how did you know?"

He grinned the way Romeo does when he knows a secret, but coming from Lord Galen it was freaky. "I know most of what goes on here, lieutenant."

I stared at him for a moment. I wasn't sure what he was implying, but I knew I didn't like it. "I'll be sure to keep my thoughts secure—around you." And I meant it.

His expression changed from slightly amused to, I don't know, agitated maybe. His head lowered a touch as his body shifted position. The whole movement was far too delicate for a human, and I would've missed it completely had I been able to blink. Unnerved, I pushed a little harder against the wall. My heart thumped again. I knew he could tell it wasn't from fear—not completely. It made the small elevator a little bit smaller, and much more uncomfortable.

"Lieutenant, your thoughts are more difficult to reach than anyone I have touched in a long time."

"Have you been touching where you're not allowed?" The words were sharp, accusatory. I shouldn't have said them. But my life depended on keeping the vampire out of my head, and I was curious why he would say such a thing.

He said nothing. He gave no acknowledgment of my tone, and no answer to my question. The next few moments passed slowly, unnaturally so. The soft hum of the elevator was the only sound. It was disturbing how he watched me, almost as if I wasn't there. Still … I didn't hate it.

"Always whin," he said softly to himself, "and broom." He moved, and my initial thought was that he meant to come closer, to touch me. I flinched, and he turned away. With a sudden rush, the elevator doors opened, siphoning the intimacy from our tiny cage. In poured the warmer and more public air, until I felt let down and cold. I acknowledged the figure standing in the doorway waiting to enter. Roeanne James, a doctor at Jefferson Hospital and a fellow movie nighter, stood waving at me, with her big, giant grin. Her long, naturally curly hair was pulled up high, and long dark ringlets fell over her little ears.

"Hey," she said. Her smile faded when she realized the general was with me.

I nodded, remaining quiet against the wall.

"Ms. James," said Lord Galen.

I have to admit I was curious how he knew who she was. I slid my beret down on my head and peeled myself from the wall. I motioned to the door with a firm hand. I wanted him to go first, and not out of respect, but because I truly didn't want him at my back. He nodded his head to Roe as a greeting and good-bye, nothing kooky. He stepped off and veered right towards his office in headquarters. He threw a sideways glance back to me. "Good night, lieutenant."

His voice danced inside the elevator. A rush of power around my feet spiraled up my body like a tingling ribbon until the current reached my head. I took a sharp breath, because I could almost see it. The whole thing took maybe three seconds, and still I was dazed. I shook a fierce tremor up my back to clear away the magik.

"What's wrong with you?" asked Roeanne.

I moved past her to the middle of the lobby to watch Galen open the doorway and walk into headquarters. "Could you feel that? Did you feel it?"

"What are you doing? Feel what?"

I'm not stupid. I know he can scent the changes in my body when he's near me, even if he's never acknowledged it. I've caught him watching me. There are even times he seems to want to tell me something, but he stops himself just as he did a few moments ago.

"Feel what?" asked Roeanne, waving a hand in front of my face. "I didn't feel anything."

"Never mind. I'll be back."

"You were supposed to be here twenty minutes ago." She groaned. "And I was ten minutes early."

"Sorry." I started for the dispatch doorway. "The elevator was slow."

I quickly made my way through rows of cubicles that made up the Emergency Dispatch Office and saw my bag in a corner near the desk of my friend, Relina. Without disrupting her, I snatched the pack up and then backtracked to the lobby, where a group of soldiers was making their way into headquarters from the main entrance. They walked closer to Roeanne than was necessary. They had big smiles, and one wished her a very good night, but only if he had anything to do with it. When she flipped him the finger, the laughter bounced around the generous lobby. Before anyone had the chance to say another word, I pulled Roe behind the information desk to stand by the elevators.

We settled by the shiny black doors, strangely modern in the middle of the dark stone. I had a strange thought of how many times I've stood on this very spot waiting for the elevator to take Romeo to his apartment. I know he's the big bad vampire, a first captain under the general, but sometimes I need to see him safely on the elevator before I go home. Crazy, but it's something I can't seem to help. Many days I sat on the steps of the main entrance watching the sunrise over the trees of Galen Park. Except today, like everyday for the past three weeks, the sun is on the other side of the building when my shift is over. The white marble steps outside are already covered in a dusty shade of gray, giving a soft, touchable appearance to the day. It's a pretense. All day I worked in that ninety-nine degree sauna, and unfortunately, when the sun left he forgot to take the heat and humidity with him.

The heat is only one of the reasons I enjoy night work. Even in the frigid days of winter, the nighttime is gentler and gives the meanest criminal a softer guise. For some, like my best friend, Alivia, night work makes her feel lonely and isolated. For me, I like to watch the sun through the front window of our home roll under the horizon. I wait for my day to begin as most others wait for theirs to end. Romeo thinks I'm obsessed, but really, I'm fascinated with how the world can shift from one type of socialization to another by the mere rising and falling of that one big star.

I heaved my bag over my shoulder and felt impatient, exhausted, and dirty. I brushed the crackled mud off the knees of my black and white fatigues and wondered who the hell has a pigpen in the middle of the city anyway? It can't be legal. I pounded the elevator button and dropped my bag onto the floor.

"Why can't this thing ever work the way it's supposed to?" I grumbled.

Roeanne shuffled in her white rubber doctor's shoes. The blue surgical scrubs made her average height seem short, and her slightly over average weight seem heavier. Her small blue eyes stood out against her naturally freckled nose and cheeks.

"You should look into anger management," she said. "I heard about your run-in with the car thief, or vandal, or whatever he was."

"Why me for anger management?" I frowned at my words.

"I was there when he came into the E.R.," she said. "From his state, I assumed his assailant would be right behind him. Then I heard the attacker was you, and I felt sorry for him."

"I didn't just attack the guy. If you can believe it, he was stuck, hanging out of a car window. He and his pals were trying to steal the damn thing, and he literally got caught by it. The others ran when they saw us. I felt bad for him—until we pried him out and he hit me."

"Is that why you broke his hand?"

"It was the first thing I did!"

"I feel so much safer when you're out there," she said, playfully patting my back.

"Nuh-uh. No more. Do you know how many weirdos I meet on a daily basis? I've had more incidents in my three weeks on days than some have in a year. The daytime squad is calling me Flypaper!"

"Flypaper?"

"For freaks." I threw her an irritated glance. "I'm getting very tired of it."

She covered her mouth to muffle her laughter.

"You're going to hurt yourself." I poked at the elevator button. "Anyway, I'm done. I asked to go back on nights. Maybe, finally, being the partner of a first captain will get me something other than ragged on."

"Even with all the grief, isn't it a nice change of pace to be in sync with the world? You know, out amongst the living? At night there's all those mean, nasty, stray vampires, and of course, your partner," she smiled.

"No. I can handle the strays and Romeo. It's humans that give my nerves a workout. Give me a nasty vampire any day, and I'm in ecstasy!"

The dark-haired lieutenant at the information desk laughed.

"Not me. Some of them are creepy, and that one scares the hell out of me."

"What one?"

She leaned in to whisper, "Lord Galen" and then moved closer. "I think he looks evil. Don't you?"

I couldn't disagree more. Galen's face might be severe, with the contrast of skin and hair, but I think he may be one of the most beautiful men I've ever seen. The elevator doors finally opened. Roeanne's arm jerked when she grabbed my bag. She had to drag it instead of carry it.

"What do you have in this thing?"

"Romeo's clean laundry."

She flashed me a look.

"Don't," I said. "Just don't say a word."

CHAPTER THREE

"FIVE," SAID ROE.

Her voice isn't on computer recognition, so the elevator didn't move. She raised her eyebrows, and I repeated the order. The steel box hummed to life. Relief was only five floors away. To shower, eat, and unwind with a movie would certainly make my day.

"What's the show, *Alice in Wonderland,* or something Disney?" Roeanne asked, leaning her body against the elevator wall. "I don't think you can trust a vampire who likes Disney movies. It's weird."

I couldn't argue. Romeo's fascination with all cartoons is a bit obsessive. Although I'm not sure if his interest in cartoons is worse than any man's interest in childhood things. Of course, the sadistically sexual aspects of the films that Romeo swears are deliberate elude me most of the time.

"It's Alice, but not Disney. We're watching a version from around the nineteen-nineties. It has real people in it."

"The nineteen-nineties? That's ancient."

"All the movies he picks are ancient, Roe. He's a hundred years old."

"He's a freak. There's always a princess and a nasty queen who wants someone's body part in a grinder. The young prince is trying too hard to get the princess to marry him before she's hacked to pieces. It's all psychotic symbolism."

"I think he has fantasies about the wicked stepmothers and their daughters."

"Stop," she groaned. "I don't want to hear about it."

"Have you ever seen Alice?"

"I'm not much into children's stories."

"This is a good one. It's my favorite of the Alices."

We stepped off the elevator into a long stone hallway. The passage was dim, not to say gloomy. The same electric torches from around the manor decorated the walls on the upper barrack floors. Only vampires use these levels, and they don't socialize too much, so the walkways are narrow. There's enough room to stand next to someone, with a little bit of space extra. Light gray doors lined each side. Identical keypads are at the left of each door, which remain unnamed and unnumbered for safety. If someone, somehow, broke in, and wanted to harm one vampire in particular, they'd have to take the time to go through each room. In this hall alone are over twenty rooms. There are five floors, three halls per floor, and each hall looks exactly the same. Romeo and I have been partners too long for me not to know his room.

Roe stayed close, as if our upper arms were glued together. I could feel her energy, which was anxious and vibrant, almost painful. I understood why she was afraid. I just didn't agree.

"Why is it so dank?" she asked. "It's like the basement at the hospital. I don't think I'll get used to it. Three months or thirty years, it'll still be scary."

I touched the stonewall with my fingertips. It wasn't cold to me. Roe touched my arm and it gave me a shock.

"Is anyone here? I mean besides a sleeping vampire."

"No." I rubbed my arm where it tingled from the jolt. "Alivia should be on her way. Dacon and Lucas aren't finished till twenty-thirty, and the rest aren't awake."

We stopped at the fifteenth door from the end. I scanned the bar code on my I.D. at the bottom of the keypad. I pushed my thumb on the screen and started the numeral code when the door swung open. I automatically shoved Roeanne to the side. I pulled my right arm back to punch whatever was in front of me. Livi's startled face was inches from my hand.

"Mother Moon," I said. "You scared the hell out of me."

Roeanne came to stand beside me, rubbing her arm where I had pushed her. Livi settled down and then smiled.

"I got here early," she said, stepping back so we could enter.

"Obviously."

The air conditioning unit was on, but the apartment was warm, with the smell of homemade tomato sauce and garlic. I hadn't eaten since this morning and wondered why I wasn't hungry.

Roeanne plopped herself on the black sofa against the wall. I kicked my bag to the corner before I made my way to the matching chair at the far end of the room.

"What's wrong with you?" asked Livi.

"I've had a really bad day," I replied, dropping my body onto the leather. I gave a halfhearted smile and was mildly surprised that my facial muscles would move into that particular position. What is it about a bad mood that when you're alone, it's not as bad as when you're around people — especially cheery people?

"Don't worry," she said, wrinkling her nose at my dirty clothes. "I have the best dinner planned."

Livi's eyes gleamed. She flashed her big smile, and it was almost enough to make me forget the events of the day. Her deep brown skin was nearly flawless, as always, and her lips were full, like her Jamaican grandmother's. Splatters of sauce and grease covered the old black shirt she wore shoved into an equally dirty pair of dungaree cutoffs. The tactical holster hung low and empty on her hip, the strap sliding just above her knee. She's taller than I am, about eight inches over five feet, and definitely much prettier.

"Salad. Pasta. You will be wined. You will be dined. What could be better?"

I rubbed my brow. Being left alone might be better. What I said was, "A shower would be good."

"I guess this would be a bad time to show you the windowsill," Livi said, her face changing into something of an anguished pucker.

I stared at her for a moment and then rushed down the short hall where double-lined darkening drapes were drawn over a small window. I pushed aside one of the panels and covered my eyes. A piece of the sun hung lazy and unforgiving just over the horizon. Even with my eyes half closed, I could see that the once exotic, brilliant, and fully flowered plants were brown, wilted, and dehydrated, like a desert of fallen warriors. They hadn't been cared for in weeks. I got very warm inside and cursed that damn vampire.

This whole scene was sadly reminiscent of a year ago when there was an herb garden here in the most beautiful terra cotta pot. It was the length of the sill, about two and a half feet long, and full of life when I gave it to him. Livi used the herbs for cooking, but Romeo swore he'd take care of them. When I found their carcasses burning in the sun, I threw the whole thing at him. I missed him by a hair. He begged me to give him the plants. He swore he wouldn't fail me again. He was so eager to show me that he could care for them. I told him that even though these particular plants thrive in sunlight, this window has the sun for most of its descent. By 18:00 the sill is on fire, so he had to water them frequently. He knew to check them and talk to them every day.

I stomped back down the hall to the kitchen, a small room about half the size of the living area. I filled a cup with tap water and glanced at the clock on the wall over the doorway. Big green numbers blinked 19:45. I had ten minutes, maybe.

With the girls at my heels, I grabbed my pack from the living room and rushed back down the hall. I tipped the water into each pot, for what good it would do them. I shoved the glass into Livi's hand, and I pushed past her and Roe to the only door on the left side of the hall.

"What are you going to do?" Livi rushed to stop me as I punched in the code to unlock the bedroom door. She extended her arm between the reinforced wood and me. "What are you going to do, Dru?"

"Nothing."

"You're such a liar. Don't do anything like last time."

"Last time?" asked Roe. "What did you do last time?"

I smiled. Livi's shoulders hunched in frustration.

"To make a very long story short, she chained that vampire to his bed while he slept. She hung a makeshift crucifix, mobile-thingy over his head. Then she bloodlet him with cuts on his arms and burned his hands with an ultraviolet flashlight."

"That's horrible!" Roeanne gasped, raising her hand to her mouth. "Oh, wait, I didn't know he was Catholic."

"His parents were from a village near Tuscany," I said. "They moved to New York in the early nineteen-thirties. He and his sisters were the first generation born in the States, when they were still united."

"Ultraviolet flashlight?" asked Roe. "I've heard of them but haven't seen the effects."

"It's like having Amun-Ra right in the palm of your hands," I said. "We use them to search for vampires who've been sentenced to death, or sometimes when we find a nest of fugitives. They're good for any situation where you need a vampire on his knees."

Roe's eyes widened.

"What did he do to you?" she asked, swallowing hard.

"You mean to deserve it or afterwards?"

"Both."

"To deserve it, he bit me without my permission." She squinched up her nose in an elfy little frown. She knows it's his legal right to take blood from me, his partner, if he needs to. And I'm more than obliging. I mean, hell, I have scars on my fingers from him sucking on them like a lollipop. At the time, however, we'd only been partners for maybe two years, and we didn't exactly get along. "I was asleep. He came into my apartment on my night off, and he bit me."

"He can be such an asshole," Livi said, shaking her head.

"I know," Roe said, "but crucifixes and ultraviolet light? He must've been badly burnt. That seems a little harsh."

"He bit me on three different parts of my body."

"Why would he do such a thing?" she exclaimed. "He's not usually like that, is he?"

Romeo isn't usually like that? Which Romeo was she referring to? Livi and I stared at each other, dumbfounded by her poor judge of character.

"He said he hadn't fed in a week, which was true, and that he couldn't control himself. He said he came to talk, but I was lying there so naked and enticing."

"And quiet," Livi added. "Naked isn't anything compared to quiet. Romeo's most turned on by Dru when she's not yelling at him."

"He bit my wrist and said he got carried away because I tasted so good." He also said he couldn't control himself because my blood has a real kick to it, which is when I found out the differences in me went further than I'd ever considered. Still, it doesn't matter what my blood tastes like. He shouldn't have touched me without consent.

"Well, maybe he couldn't control himself," Roe said.

We stared at her. She shrank from our gazes as if we had pushed her.

"To answer the rest of your question, he apologized to me."

"Yeah, but only after he broke his restraints and chased her out the door, down the emergency steps, and twice around the court-yard," Livi laughed outright. "His hands dripped blood like melted wax. He finally collapsed in the horse stables. This guy Gabriel, a friend of mine, fed him so he would heal quicker. Well, Dru paid him. She didn't want Romeo to bleed to death. That is to say she didn't want to go to prison."

Liv and I smiled. It was a long time ago, but that recollection always affects me in a good way.

"What did Dacon say about the whole thing?" Roe asked, looking at us as if we were ghouls wading in the River Styx. "I'm sure he wasn't too happy."

"We were together at the time so, no, he wasn't happy."

"He didn't condone what you did though?"

"Actually, Roe, I had to physically stop Dacon from doing permanent damage. Ultraviolet light was a compromise."

"If you're going to do something cruel just because he didn't water your plants, I don't want any part of it." She huffed her way into the living room.

I thought about running after her and arguing that she didn't understand. How dare she try to make me feel guilty for something she knew virtually nothing about? I think smacking her around was somewhere in that thought as well. Not that I had to burn Romeo, but he had no right to terrorize me, and I had every right to retaliate. He violated me. I didn't feel safe in my own home for months. He's just lucky I kept my mouth shut and Lord Galen never found out, or he would've paid with more than scalded hands.

I started when Livi touched my shoulder.

"She doesn't understand vampire dynamics. She hasn't worked with them the way we have to know he was trying to dominate you. Dru, crosses and all that crazy shit aren't necessary. I mean, really, they were only plants."

My body practically lit on fire. Never, ever, say anything against nature to a practitioner of witchcraft.

"He killed them. They are living beings, and he killed them."

She cringed, and her grip tightened on my arm. Then she leaned into me.

"I know how you feel about that stuff, but burning him or lining his bed with rosaries is fighting dirty. You have to be above it. Be a good person," she spoke out of the corner of her mouth to conceal her words. "You are more than that. Literally."

"I won't hurt him." I smiled and turned the knob. "I'll play with him a little, that's all."

Livi threw her hands up and I crept into the dark room. I whispered his name as I closed the door. Nothing. I had about five minutes before the sun set completely, but it never hurts to be sure. Romeo is one hundred years undead. He was twenty-five when he was converted, but the living age doesn't count. One hundred is young as far as certain powers are concerned. He doesn't have the strength to rise while the sun is descending, like Lords Galen and Jagen, so I still had time.

※ ※ ※

THE LAYOUT OF HIS room is more than familiar, so I managed in the darkness without stubbing a toe. I shoved my muddy clothes in the left corner by the closet, along with my holster. I patted my chest and inner thigh to make certain the patches still covered my cross tattoos. Like a cross, a tattoo of a religious symbol can repel a vampire if the undead were a Christian. Unlike ultraviolet light, a symbol won't do much to physically stop a threatening vampire, but it's nauseating. It mentally weakens them, so you have the opportunity to strike. Most Christian vampires can't help but feel ashamed of their decision to become the undead. They're so hungry to have a new start, an immortal life, that they convince themselves their god will understand, until they're converted. This is why there's a legal age limit and two years' worth of steps to go through before turning to the unlife. The churches haven't softened on the subject of vampirism as the undead hoped. Not even close.

Romeo was a devout Catholic before he changed. He's vomited at the slightest touch of a cross, or even if one was in the vicinity. It's something I don't want to see twice and why I will never hang a religious artifact over his head again. Holy water should not hurt anyone, but Romeo, like so many other vampires, is plagued with the guilt of the ages and held hostage by those ancient superstitions. The truth is that the water and the crosses wouldn't hurt or debilitate vampires if they weren't so ashamed of what they are. With that in mind, I've wondered what fueled Romeo's unlife decision when he was so devoted to his faith.

I crawled into bed wearing only my underwear and bandages. I was dirty, but he wouldn't care. I felt around, traced the outline of Romeo's body, and found his arms up with his hands behind his head. He sleeps that way because he says it makes him feel less dead when he wakes up. I lay on the soft cotton sheets beside him and snuggled under his arm, with my head in the crook of his shoulder. I wrapped my arm around his waist. There was no point in keeping my eyes open. I couldn't see anything in the blackness of his room.

I settled in, breathed deeply, and caught only the lightest scent of detergent from his sheets. Romeo doesn't have a smell, good or bad, and I'm not sure why, but it bothers me. I rubbed my fingers over the top of his bare chest, looking for his aura. One of my strong suits as a practicing witch is compassion. I can feel the emotions, or even the personalities, of others. When a human sleeps, the aura relaxes. It doesn't get weaker, but softer. That's not how it works with the sleeping undead. When awake, their essence—who they are—isn't easily felt, but I can feel it. When they go day-cold, all emotion seems to go away. I can't sense their intent or energy, and reading a vampire should be no harder when day-cold. I do feel something, but I've never been able to name it. It's a strange void. No, it isn't a void. I feel a fog, a kind of naked fullness. I've wondered, does the soul flee or become trapped in the human shell, pushing to get out? Romeo either doesn't know or won't tell me. He says that in the minutes before he falls asleep and wakes up he feels tense, a panic.

"Like you're being trapped?" I asked.

"Not really," he said. "Sort of. Maybe."

I molded myself around his body. He's told me that for all the people he'll share his bed with when he's awake, and there are many, none will lie with him once the day-cold hits. Not that he'd allow that kind of intimacy. That would be asking for death. Still, it must be sad to know the truth. I myself have never had an aversion to his stillness. Perhaps that's because there's enough about me that isn't quite normal, not quite human.

I dug my nails into his chest and thought how firm, yet pleasant, his body is when he's asleep. Of course, he's not speaking, so that could be the pleasing part. But truthfully, I like the feel of him. The sensation isn't human at all. Well, his skin is like human skin, only softer, without bumps or scrapes or anything to mar the sleekness. No matter how much blood a vampire has consumed, making their appearance seem human, you'll always know the truth by the feel of the body. It's strong like a machine. To this day, there's an unknown quality in vampire blood. It's called DNA-V, magik, a disease, and even demonic. It morphs both the internal and external fabric of the host. It transforms each organ into a nearly imperishable structure, working in unison to break down and utilize its only food: blood. The veins, arteries, and tendons become as tough as steel rope. Up to forty-three percent of fat cells are absorbed, and the elastin in the body shrinks, pulling the skin taut over stronger, firmer muscles. This is the source of the stereotypical emaciated vampire, though if you're a bigger person at conversion you won't become petite just because you died.

You can feel the raw power just beneath the skin's surface. If you trust your partner, it can be intoxicating, even frightening, if you're into that sort of thing. Of course, the one true drawback to being a vampire is that they're not alive. Their strong bodies degenerate quickly, which is why they need blood frequently. Because they hold no true moisture or water inside their systems, they burn like tissue paper. Some scientists believe the reason they fall into the day-cold sleep is to prevent accidents of the sun.

I lay against Romeo and thought about what kind of revenge I'd like to use on him. I can't do serious damage without being a devious bitch; frankly, I didn't have the energy. My body and blood are two of the best tools I could use against him. We share a mutual lust. Over the years, he's made it clear what he'd to do me if I'd let him. He told me how many times and in what positions. As long as I keep myself under control, I should be able to make the bastard suffer sufficiently. Most men hate a tease. Vampires hate to be teased like no one else. It isn't in their nature to ask. They're taught civility, but what they really want to do is to pick and take.

❁ ❁ ❁

I RELAXED MY BODY with deep cleansing breaths for concentration and for centering the mind. I envisioned the air I was breathing had substance and weight. I visualized the bulkier mass surrounding me, then passing through each chakra and going around each limb until I was covered in my own breath. Using cerebral strength, I focused my thoughts to realign my belief of reality. As I drifted, I concentrated on the deep waters and the luminous flowers blooming along the lush green countryside of my ancestors. My soul, my spiritual body of energy, lightened and lifted. I detached, moving over to roam a familiar dimension — a wicked, enchanted world intricately woven and ingeniously concealed on a plane parallel to the one in which my physical being resided. I flowed as though a phantasm. When my consciousness reassembled, I was safely on this new plane. I walked naked, the dewy grass cool under my feet. Before me, the ancient tangled trees of the forest stood.

My task is to find the hidden entrance to my home away from home. It always takes a few moments for my mind and eyes to adjust so that I can see the opening that is obviously there when you find it, and still nowhere to be found. I followed the green path leading to the realm of the Faerie Kingdoms. Yes, there are people who call it Fairyland, but it's so much more than the silly mythical place where Tinker Bell came from. It's a vast, complicated world of indescribable beauty. Here, the rainbow overhead has twice the brilliance that it does in the human realm. The air is clean and tastes sweet on my tongue. The smallest daisy flowers at my feet make the most exotic flowers of the earthen plane look and smell dull.

I plunged a hand into a puddle. The water is cold to drink, yet warm to bathe in. The sky here is always at a twixt or tween time, such as dawn, civil dusk, midday, or astronomical twilight. It changes from dusty, subdued blues to the clear brilliance of noon, to the rich textured blacks of midnight, and the awakening fiery hues of the morning hours. Flowers and herbs long extinct in the human realm prosper here. The woodlands are dense, with tall standing trees filled with diverse winged creatures bathing in the light, or mating in the rolled oak leaves.

I walked quickly, combing my fingers through the tight bushes of peppermint. Long stems of burgundy hollyhocks tapped against my thighs as I passed. The thick scent of heather clung to the air. I spied a black raspberry patch, and concentrating very hard, I picked one. I tasted the sweetness without truly eating it. The thick juice, oddly enough, sometimes stains the skin on my corporeal fingers on the physical plane. Further along the path, the powerful trees of apple, oak, and the faerie favorite, willow, widened on either side of me. Their overhanging branches create a thick green canopy that provides shelter and a cool breeze from the warm rays of our sun. The truly mystifying beauty, however, is the nebulous nature of the crepuscular rays forcing their way through the dark woven shelter. It illuminates the many shades of green, red, blue, and yellow from the flowers and the iridescent wings of the smaller faeries fluttering all around.

Two tall, thin elves made their way to my side. They're a strong, pleasant breed of fey, but not my kind. Both have long, golden hair, and large woodland brown eyes that change in shade with each species of tree they touch. They have no wings, but their untiring speed and aberrant grace make it seem so. We made eye contact, exchanging greetings in a way that isn't physically speaking, but not specifically telepathic. They settled their hands on my ghostly shoulders in a familiar familial greeting. For all practical reasoning, I'm a human being. Though I've been touched by fey magik, I can't tear a hole in space to enter or leave the realm as most others can. I must rely on my mind to take me there, which is why I'll never be a solid entity.

The native beings of this plane touch the flowing, thrumming energy that creates my presence. However, I'm also not as ethereal as a ghost, but something between the two. Solid enough to touch others, only not corporeal enough to firmly grab hold of them. I'm literally a tween faerie. I was born to human parents, but no human had to tell me I was different. At birth, my human soul was bound with the essence of a faerie creature, giving me the inner knowledge of life and magik that only the faeries possess. Shifting planes came naturally at an early age. To the best of my knowledge, I'm one of a kind. I've shared this secret with precious few. Early on, the fey elders schooled me in the animosity that the vampire has for other magikal creatures, but especially the earthen people. They taught me stories and riddles that will dictate my behavior around the vampire forever.

A few small River fey passed me. Their sparkled wings held their golden jelly-like bodies off the ground. Deep in their oval faces were large, round, mirrored eyes that glitter the same as their wings. A human will see his or her most desired wish in those eyes. I see only the faerie-human blend I become when I'm in this world. It's a bit smaller than my human height of five foot four, though the shape of my body is human. The color of my skin is black, just like that of the Fear faerie with whom I'm connected. My hair is dark forest green and a mess of short shaggy locks. My teeth are sharp and my ears are pointed. My eyes aren't their normal hazel. They are the color of chrome, shining like the bumper of an antique car. My wings are dark as onyx, and attached to my spine, shoulders, elbows, and wrists. When I extend my arms, the wings resemble those of a bat. I have control over them as an animal has of its tail. I'm, obviously, of the dark breed of fey.

The River faerie collected speed, and in turn, the elves made haste. I picked up my speed to a half run, heading up the steep green hill to see the Kingdoms that lay beyond. Catching a glimpse of the tips of the castles, I broke into a full run and raced the creatures around me. As I neared the top of the hill, I ran even faster until I reached the hill's edge. I flung myself into the air. I spread my arms and my wings wide. I glided smoothly, changing my body's position to alter direction toward the valley where the castles stand. Where they have stood for many millennia. They're majestic in their glimmering splendor, yet inviting to even the most impoverished passerby. No matter how many times I come to this realm, the sight of the enormous and secretive world of Faery nearly paralyzes me.

To the east is the gold and silver castle of the light fey — to Scotland the Seelie Court and to Ireland the Daoine Sidhe. Some refer to them as the Trooping faeries, a term coined by humans that were lucky enough to see the trooping of their horses through the hills called a faerie rade. They're most aristocratic and simply amazing in their white, valiant splendor. A wide variety of species belong to this class of fey, including water and flower faeries, sprites, and golden elves.

To my right in the west is the Onyx Castle of the dark fey. The Unseelie Court. My clan. Our family is also ancient and imperial. Since Romeo had me watch *Snow White*, I've always felt our oldest matriarch, the faerie Sage, rivals Snow White's stepmother in elegance, stature, and sagacious nature. No other matches her consort, Alder, in darkness, cunning, or sheer beauty. We're dark, ranging from the slightly mischievous to the possibly deadly. But we've suffered a cruel injustice in the minds of humans. They deem us wicked and thoughtless. Okay, we can be, but no more than a hurricane or volcano eruption. We're a part of society, because there can be no light without dark. We're a necessary function. The dark and the light make each other possible in every way. However, dark doesn't mean we're rogue. All families hold explicitly to the laws. There are no excuses for heterodoxy in the clan. Those who can't abide by the laws of land and nature are banished, or worse.

I flew swiftly through the air over the rich heartland separating the castles, in which was upwards of two hundred miles apart. A brilliant rainbow arced, cascading down beyond the kingdoms to another land altogether. I brought myself to the dark tower, searching for members of the Fear faerie. A deceiving name, for we aren't fearful. We provoke it. We're not deadly, not usually. Fear is something we ingest, gaining sustenance and satisfaction from all the negative emotions any human or being is capable of feeling.

My life has always been much more than the physical boundaries into which I was born. I've learned that not only are most of us not free, but we're also not what we seem. Most of the wonderful qualities in any species can't be seen. The extraordinary is something to be confided, shared, and brought to the surface through trust or love.

I stiffened my wings for my descent into the courtyard. I had intended to land near the king's butterfly stables. As I was some fifty feet above the ground, an unnatural feeling seized me. It ripped through my body. It shook me so that I was unable to stay in flight. I curled into myself, pulling my arms around my body to create a protective shell from my hardened wings. I crashed into the smooth, black stone wall of the courtyard, and lay dazed, though not seriously hurt. I managed to push up on my elbows to look at my body. I was in one piece. I can't die here, but so much blood was on the ground, it made me wonder if I could. A Razain butterfly, as big as a pony on Earth, poked a tentacle near my face. It lifted its dark head as if to show me the small, curly haired girl skulking across the yard with pieces of my wings. She entered a doorway set into the black stone that wasn't there a moment before.

"Not my wings!" Dread broke my concentration. My mind pulled back to my material self. I screamed as the Realm thrust me out, and I jumped in the dark.

"It's me." Romeo stopped my hands from hitting him. He pulled me close so my cheek rested against his cool chest. "You're fine."

A knock at the door startled me again.

"We're fine," Romeo said.

"I fell," I whispered, trying to catch my breath.

"You were there? On the other side?"

Romeo is one of a few that know I'm different, though, to my credit, he doesn't know the extent of it. He thinks I'm a practicing Wiccan with faerie tendencies and a little magik. That's what I told him. The magikal power I possess is unheard of in a human, and he knows better than I do what a very bad thing that is if you're surrounded by vampires. Ancient faerie lore says few, if any, friendly encounters have occurred between the fey and the undead. They are notorious throughout the supernatural community for usurping the power of other beings. To some magikal species like shamans, they're known as siphons. They're paranoid as well. Always looking for threats, waiting for someone to try to take them over. Vampires see pressures that may not even be there. They would consider me a true danger — a danger big enough to kill for, if only for the magikal power I may be able to give them.

I twisted around to get space, but Romeo snuggled against my back.

"You have that smell I like," he said, pulling my arm to his face so he could run his lips against my skin. "The woods ... freshly cut grass."

"Something happened. There was someone, but she was ... a shadow."

"A shadow?"

"Yes and no. She took my wings. Only ..." I was having the hardest time explaining, because I didn't truly understand it. "It wasn't real. She felt like intuition or forewarning. Not so much genuine."

"You can't get hurt there, can you?" He buried his nose in the back of my hair.

"I can, but not like this. Not usually."

I took a few deep breaths and cleared my throat. I felt Romeo's worry. I felt his questioning mind, but I had questions too. My inability to be a complete entity on the faerie plane renders me unable to experience certain things. I can smell food and taste it slightly, but I can't gain sustenance from it. I can feel pleasure and pain, but not in the physical sense. Only in the positive or negative energy directed at me. I fidgeted in Romeo's arms. His concern made me uncomfortable. He pulled me around so we were face-to-face in the dark.

"Your eyes are dull," he observed. "They're gold and green, and ... what are you afraid of?"

"I don't know." I tried to push away, but he wouldn't let me go. "Nothing. I'm okay."

The coolness of his skin was refreshing. I felt his lips against my shoulder a moment before he kissed me there. He pulled my hand to his face and bit softly near my wrist. He spoke in dulcet tones against my palm.

"I can hardly think over the pounding of your heart. Your rushing blood has a cloying scent, like overripe fruit."

"That sounds disgusting," I said, making a nauseated sound.

"No," he said, "I like it. You know how much I like it."

Now my feeble game of "bleed me if you can" begins. I made the barest of moans when he licked my wrist, a small gentle sigh.

"Not yet. I need to get a shower before you suck me dry."

"Why?" He pulled back and I could feel him thinking. "What's going on? Why are you naked in my bed?"

"I had a really bad day."

"Uh-huh." He knows me well to sound so wary.

"I'm not naked," I said, letting my body wilt against him. "I need a shower, but I wanted to see you."

"You could have showered and saw me after. I'm not going anywhere."

"I came in here to change, and the bed was inviting. It felt good to lie down."

I moved myself to all fours above him. My hands were over his shoulders, but my legs brushed the sides of his body. I could feel his hunger and knew blood wasn't all he wanted. That wasn't unusual.

"Listen, I know you don't like it, but can we watch a vampire movie next week? You know, like *Blade*," I asked. "The old version."

"No."

"Why not?"

"No."

"Don't be an asshole."

"What?" I knew he was abstracted. "I'm an asshole?"

I felt the electric energy from his long fingers hovering near the silver rings in my belly button. The air hummed with his excitement to touch me. He didn't. He was trying hard not to attack me, if only because his predatory instinct tells him that if he runs too fast, the little bird will fly, fly away. The problem is that he's ravenous and truly starving.

"Please. It's one of my favorite movies, and I'm tired of fairy tales."

"I don't care," he sighed.

I smiled. He was making it easy for me to enjoy yanking his chain.

"Cover your eyes. I'm going to put the light on," I said, sitting up on my knees.

With a hand on his wooden headboard for support, I reached up and clicked on the brass lamp that rested on his chest of drawers. The dusty yellow light settled softly on his naturally tan skin, ashen from lack of blood, yet dark against my coloring. When I met Romeo, his hair was a messy halo of tight brown curls. He wears it short now, but it still twists and separates into shaggy waves, giving him a bed-head look. Medium thick brows framed dark brown bedroom eyes, also dulled from lack of food. The line of his nose isn't quite aquiline, but unmistakably Italian. He stared at me with drowsy, half-closed lids. He isn't sleepy. Vampires are never sleepy. They're awake or they're not. There's no in-between, unless they're severely blood depleted or mentally drained, which Romeo tells me I do to him often.

"I like your outfit," he said. "I should say I like the body in your outfit, and the blood in that body."

He rolled his tongue over his bottom lip. He tapped the patch I used to cover the cross tattoo on my chest, near my heart. Then he reached up, unhooked the barrette to free the long hair from the top of my head, and roughly sifted through the short hair on the back and sides. He threaded strong fingers down the length of it, while little pieces of mud fell onto his chest.

"Tell me again why you're half naked?"

"I was—"

"Don't get me wrong. I like it. I'll take it. It's much more pleasing than the covered you." He was about to grab my ass and pull me down, but he stopped suddenly, as if a light dawned and he knew better.

"What the hell is going on? Why are you being a cock tease?"

"I'm not. I missed you, that's all."

His expression softened, and he pulled me to lie on him. I stretched and laid my head in the middle of his chest. My body covered his, and I could feel his firmness through our underwear and thin cotton sheet, though not excessively so. Being deprived of blood doesn't allow his body to show me how very happy he is that I'm on top of him. Not that he'd be embarrassed if he could show it. Confidence has never been his problem.

He pushed his pelvis ever so slightly, and I continued to do things I knew he'd enjoy, like gently moving my hips. I traced lines on his arm as I told him about my fight. I rubbed my feet over his, and when he sighed, I pretended not to notice. He loved the attention, the touching and squirming—even if he thinks I'm up to no good. He won't touch me overtly or say a word for fear that these are truly innocent gestures, and if he calls me on it, I'll stop. The mere fact that he can't acknowledge any of it puts him in a bit of misery.

His phone beeped. He quickly reached a hand over to the small night table, trying to get out from under me.

"I'll get it," I said. I shimmied up, allowing my lower stomach to hover near his face. Forcing him to be so close to the pulse in my belly has somewhat the effect of shoving breasts in the face of a human man. He dropped his hand, defeated, as I had to straddle his stomach while I leaned over. In my awkward position, I managed to find his vid-phone unit under the papers crowding his night table. We use portable phones at work to keep our hands free. I have to use it here, because Romeo doesn't own a computer or a standard phone. The blue light on the side of the unit wasn't flashing, telling me the caller wasn't on video, so I secured the small speaker cuff over my ear.

"First Captain Romeo Fortunato's phone. How can he help you today? Oh, hi." I glanced down. "It's Dacon."

As I spoke, I kept my attention on the vampire. He moved closer, tracing his fingertips over the pentacle tattoo on my left hip. His eyes closed as his hands caressed my bare legs.

"Okay, I'll see you soon." I tossed the headset where I'd found it and squirmed my way back down Romeo's body. "Dacon's going to be late. He said we could start without him. Romeo?"

He opened his eyes, and they were burning red in his head. The whites were veined and bloodshot. He pulled me down, licking my neck and collarbone. His tongue was cool, deliberate. I gave a double meaning groan. Maybe it felt good. Maybe I was irritated.

"Romeo," I said, my voice huskier than I wanted it to be. "Let me shower. I'm not clean."

"I like the way you smell." He licked me again, a slow rough wash of the tongue.

"Let me get a shower, and I'll feed you later."

"No." A command. Inhuman. He held me tightly. "Kiss me," he demanded, his lips barely touching my ear.

"No," my voice shook, as if I was afraid, but it wasn't that.

"Let me."

My thoughts muddled as his eager mind corrupted his voice, turning its natural melody into a seductive weapon. He chipped at the barrier of protection I held in front of my mind. His cold words sounded warm and inviting, so much so that I could've listened forever and done willingly what, otherwise, I would not. How eloquent and persuasive he could be when the animal is hungry.

It was also very illegal.

He rolled us until he was on top, rocking his pelvis between my legs. When he's like this, his fangs seem longer to me. They're not; they don't grow. I think I'm overly sensitive when he's ready to strike.

"Let me," he whispered, poking his tongue in and out of the silver coil earring winding its way through the holes in the edge of my ear.

I nodded and then quickly pushed at him.

"Stop it," I said, shaking my head to clear my thoughts of his magik. "No."

His hand moved to my neck. His fingers tensed. It was a violent gesture even for him. Though I can admit he was famished, and I was playing with fire.

"Why are you doing this?"

Love and War — and Eternally Damning Prophecies ∞ 39

"Doing what?" I swallowed.

"Andru, I'm so hungry. I need to suck faerie."

I pulled him close for a small kiss. I traced my finger along the soft line of hair traveling from his hairline down to the front of his ear.

"Wait a little longer. Let me shower. Then you can have whatever you want."

"But you promised."

I sighed. That was true. I called him last night to find out if he was going to stay for movie night, or go to the local nightclubs and hunt for food. By hunt, I'm not suggesting he'd take without consent. We have clubs, bars, cafes, and the like for a vampire to feed on the conferrer. He had intended to go out, so I promised him my blood if he stayed. He agreed because he loves my blood. Almost any vampire would rather have blood from someone they know than a stranger. I wouldn't have been so quick to offer if I'd seen him in the three weeks I've been on day work, but I missed him. It's a miserable truth, and, goddess, it's one I can't seem to help. Only now, the ruined figures on the windowsill are a testament to my hatred, and I'll let him shrivel up and die like my plants before I feed him.

"I know; just a little while longer."

"You're up to something," he whispered.

"You're hungry and paranoid. What am I doing that's so abnormal?"

"You're being nice to me."

"I'm always nice to you, you big jerk."

He dropped his head on my chest, staying like that for a long time to control his hunger. His heat or power pulled back and drained away; when he looked up, his eyes were brown and shine free. I pulled myself out of the twisted sheet so I could settle on my side away from him. He snatched away the paper I had grabbed from his nightstand before I could read the first scribbled line of the poem he had written. He shoved it under his pillow.

"Romeo, I wanna see. Let me see it."

"No."

"Are they about me? Do I inspire you?"

"No. You irritate me. Ow! Fine, I suppose irritation is a type of inspiration, but not for poetry," he said, tracing patterns on my dirty skin with his tongue.

"I have something for you," I said.

"Chocolate chip cookies?" he asked, tightening his grip.

I wondered where he had gotten that idea and frowned.

"It's been so long since you gave me chocolate chips cookies."

"I told you I wouldn't do that again. You get carried away."

"I can't help it," he said, his weight pinning my body to the bed. "Between the taste of chocolate, and the taste of your mouth, I get delirious."

"And that's why I'm not going to do it. You nearly ripped me apart last time."

"Come on, I'll be good. I'll drive the truck for an entire month."

"You always drive. And no, I won't do it. Don't think I didn't notice that you mentioned the taste of chocolate before me."

"Not consciously, I'm sure."

"Even worse, I'm sure."

I pushed him to get off and he fell flat on the bed. His long legs and arms extended outward like a dark star in a sea of pale blue sheets. That man wants me, and all I can think of is my wonderful plants. My babies. My wonderful, dead plant babies. He's such an ass.

"You owe me one, Dru," he scowled at me. "Big time." He sat up, bending at the waist—an odd move that humans just don't do. "I want you, and I want it all."

"Later. Find me something in your closet I can wear. I didn't bring any clothes. Nothing else fit in my bag but your uniforms."

"Hey, if you're gonna bet with the best—"

"Yeah, yeah, you're an idiot."

"Is that the 'something' you have for me?" he asked, squinting his eyes. "Uniforms?"

I nodded.

"Don't do that again," he said. "I thought it was something good."

I sighed. One minute, he's sexy. The next, I hate the very ground he walks on. At this very moment, holy objects seem a better option than sexual torture, or any other kind of torture. He bounced out of bed, went to his dresser, and pulled out a pair of men's black boxers along with a black tank top. He gave me a nasty smile.

"That's not the best you can do."

"Until you tell me what you're up to, it's the best I can do."

I grabbed the underwear and went to my backpack for the medicinal balm I use when my muscles are sore. I left the room with him following behind. I could feel him looking at my ass. I didn't care. Romeo's leering eyes and constant sexual innuendo are about the only action I've been getting. It's been years since I split with Dacon, but it's just too difficult to start a relationship. Honestly, the thought of having to answer to someone gives me man-cooties. Still, it was good to have someone to hold on cold nights, and hot nights too.

Romeo passed me. His shadow drifted around my legs, a small, satisfying vampire prank. Similar in concept, not scale, to what his father did earlier in the elevator. I wondered if they conspire about how to harass me, or if they're just so much alike they find the same things amusing.

I locked the bathroom door and flipped the light. It annoys me how clean Romeo's bathroom is. I know he only uses the shower, but he's still a human male ... or half of him is. There should be clothes lying around. Even the floor is clean. Apart from the endless pieces of notepaper from his poetic scribbling, and the dirty kitchen from his less nocturnal friends, the rest of the apartment is immaculate. A picture never moved. Granted, there are only four, all of which I gave him, but nothing is ever out of place. It's never dusty—not ever. It just annoys me.

The mirrored cabinet over the sink contained three items, all mine. I took out a brush and dragged it through the length of hair on the top of my head. The dirt hit the sink like fresh sawdust. I touched the skin over my eye where Galen had touched earlier. It was sore, a little bruised, but not too swollen. The left side of my lip was a bit puffy; I saw actual clean streaks on my lower neck where Romeo licked the dirt off. When my daytime partner swung at the guy we pulled from the car, he hit me in the kidney. It hurt, but I couldn't see any evidence of it now. My back reminded me of the weird little girl taking my wings. It disturbed me more than I could admit.

The gray under my eyes was becoming my prominent feature. I rubbed my face trying to wipe away the circles. One day of decent sleep would help, but I didn't get that if I wasn't sleeping in Romeo's bed. I still can't fully understand why he relaxes me the way he does. I wish I knew why he gives me the best sleep I've ever had. If he knew the answer, he'd never let me forget it.

I peeled off my dirty underwear, tossed the silk onto the floor, and flipped the thingamajig to start the shower. After I rinsed the caked mud from the piercings in my ears, the small barbell in my brow, and the two-inch barbell on the back of my neck, I washed it all with soap—twice. When all the mud was gone, when all the jewelry moved freely, and when my nails were clean, I stood with my eyes closed, allowing the misery to slide down my skin, circle the drain, and trail the pipes.

I dressed in the underwear Romeo gave me. The boxers were fine, a bit slim because Romeo has no hips, but they would do. The tank top was tight and revealing—I supposed that was better than loose and revealing. In the Realm, I would be overdressed, or at least considered modest. That difference in culture got me into trouble when I was a young girl. I had a hard time understanding that what was acceptable behavior in Faery wasn't acceptable here. Dacon helped me with my clothing choices when we started dating. He stopped me from walking around the house in my bathing suit. He said it made him, and all my brother's friends, a little nuts. He also made sure my party skirts didn't show less than what was respectable.

I emptied Romeo's clean uniforms from my backpack so I could make room for my dirty clothes. I would look later for something in Romeo's closet to wear home. The front door opened and closed. I listened for the usual greetings and recognized the voices of Lieutenants Lucas and Sara Jackson. They're brother and sister. She's the vampire. Sara's tall, about the same height as Luc, and I think he's somewhere around five ten or eleven. She's an incredible soldier. Years ago when I was in training, she was my designated sparring partner. She taught me a bunch of tricks on how to kick vicious vampire butt. We get to work together every once in a while, and I always enjoy it. Her brother Luc is just about her twin, only with short blond hair and darker blue eyes. He's pleasant as well, and much more jovial. He's the light to her dark. When Luc graduated the program two years after me, Sara transferred from instructor to active duty to be his partner. They've been together ever since. Honestly, I think they're sleeping together. They're too cuddly. Not hanging all over each other. More like always holding hands and always touching in some intimate way. It's strange.

Romeo thinks I'm perverted. He's the only vampire I know that gets freaked out from incest. In fact, most of them are fine with it. Once someone becomes a vampire, it's as if they don't feel the ties that bind, or the restrictions that we do. Maybe they do and like it. Anyway, Romeo says he and I hold hands and touch, and we're not fucking. Still, if I find out Luc and Sara are sharing a bed, even platonically, I'm going to heave.

THE SWEET AROMA OF pasta sauce crept into the bedroom. I wasn't hungry, but I wanted to eat. I finished my hair, which means I combed it off my face only to have it fall back down. Luc waved when he saw me coming down the hall. The action caught his sister's attention, and she did the same. And ick, they're holding hands again!

CHAPTER FOUR

THE SMALL KITCHEN WAS full. Livi stood at the stove, stirring a few pots with sauces bubbling over. Hard to believe, but Romeo taught her most everything she knows about cooking. When we first started movie night, she became the designated chef because she enjoys it. Romeo was disgusted. He said he couldn't stand to watch us eat the crap she was serving. He said the smell alone was enough to make a human drink blood. Because he came from a family where food was as important as the air we breathe, Livi figured he knew what he was talking about.

I peeked in the pots. One was full of red sauce, while another held white. One was smaller than the other two and filled with homemade potato gnocchi, my favorite. To my surprise, Dacon was here. He and Romeo were by the sink in the corner. With an arm outstretched, Dacon was leaning on the little counter. The half wall overlooking the living room was at his back. His words sounded fevered, and his brows furrowed.

Dacon is ruggedly handsome, like a prison inmate. Ironically enough, before he joined the military he'd gotten into his share of military trouble. Three years ago, he let Livi put small braids in his dirty blond hair. Some of them fell out and others didn't. Now it's messy, with a few thin dreadlocks scattered throughout. The elastic band that usually ties it back was stretched around his fingers. Tatters of hair covered his dark blue eyes.

Romeo was in front of the sink, still wearing only the dark blue boxers from earlier. He had his arms crossed high, almost as if he were cold. He nodded while Dacon spoke, wearing his ranking officer's disposition. He moved only his eyes to look at me, as if he felt my stare. Maybe he had. If you look at the two men, Romeo seems much thinner, but they have similar builds. The difference is that Dacon is thirty-four years old. His body is manlier, bulkier in the chest and thighs. Romeo was only twenty-five at conversion, so his frame is leaner.

Livi kept busy with her pots, trying not to laugh and keeping my game a secret. I pinched her arm as I passed.

"I'll get that spoon for you, Liv."

The dish drainer was behind Romeo, so I leaned between the two men, putting a strategic hand on Romeo's bare belly as I reached behind him. I took care not to be unnecessarily invasive, but I touched everywhere I could. He lifted his head slightly to look at me again.

I waggled the spoon at him and he nodded. I skimmed my body against his as I turned, partly out of a desire to fuck with him, and partly out of a desire to …

I faced Dacon and smiled. I grabbed the two long braids of hair on his chin, noting the touch of blue wax on each end. I loved it. I tend to love everything Dacon does.

"It's been a while," I said.

"Three weeks," he said, holding up his thumb, index, and middle fingers.

"You look good." I reached up to kiss his cheek.

"I know," he said.

Romeo made a noise between a laugh and a grunt to show what he thought of Dacon's conceited nature. Dacon snuck his hand under the hair resting on his forehead. He shoved it back, only for it to fall on his face again. The gesture was so familiar; it made me remember us as teenagers in the summertime when he would let his hair grow, and how he would fool with it until his mom made him get it cut for school. He wrapped a hand around my neck and pressed the metal bar against his palm.

"When I got here and the movie hadn't started, I knew it was your fault."

"Bite me."

The way he grinned made me step back. He seemed to be in a mood, and I should definitely stay away from that. Dacon and I have a long, sometimes confusing, history. He's four years older and was my brother's friend. Not his best friend, but the friend you aren't sure you need, and the one you definitely don't want your sister to go near. On my seventeenth birthday, he stopped by my house after getting out of jail for aggravated assault. He'd started a fight in a bar the night before. He came to my bedroom and wished me a happy birthday—so I seduced him. Well, I suppose we seduced each other. I had ignored his not-so-subtle hints for a couple of years until that afternoon. It wasn't because I didn't appreciate what he thought of me, but my mind was perpetually on supernatural things. I had no time for anything but witchcraft and faeries until a few months after my sixteenth birthday. I suppose my hormones finally kicked into overdrive. I flat out asked if he wanted to teach me to kiss. He said "yes" before I had finished my question. It was a very good kiss. We got carried away, so it was the first time I had sex too. It really was an amazing kiss.

Later, my brothers Vincent and Max beat the crap out of him. He still has a small scar on his left cheek from Max's school ring. We hadn't told them we were together, but there's a look you have after sex that you can't hide. Dacon's parents were never around, so I took him home to tend his wounds. After a few hours of sleep, we had sex again. He said it kept his mind off the pain. So Dacon was my first kiss, my first boyfriend, and my first everything. We were inseparable for nine years before he broke up with me. He wanted to take our relationship to the next level. He wanted to marry me, but I kept stalling until he had enough. It took a long while, but we don't hate each other. In fact, we're so very close that if I lost him, I'd be ruined.

"I've missed you," I said. "I don't get to see you nearly as much when we're on days."

He's easier to hug than Romeo, because at five foot ten, he's two inches shorter. He hugged me tightly and lifted me off my feet.

I was high enough that I could see Roeanne staring at us from the living room through the half wall. I wondered if she was still angry. He set me down and his eyes fell to my chest. I caught his eyes with mine.

"Is everything okay? You're so serious?"

"Just frustrated," he sighed. "I had one of those days where everything that could go wrong did. This daytime shit sucks. My partner is a weirdo. I can't stand her."

"Mine too! It must be daytime people."

"Yeah right," said Livi.

"Day lover," I said the word the way it's meant to be said, like a curse.

"I never thought I'd miss Precious."

I cringed. Precious is Dacon's newly converted partner. She's twelve years undead and being reborn didn't improve her personality. She came from a wealthy family with Argentinean roots living in Nebraska. She converted to piss off her parents, practically starting a war with the States over age of consent, citizenship, and a host of political issues. If Precious was my partner, one of us would be dead.

"If you'd rather be with her, then I feel for you, Dacon."

"Thanks, but people in very thin glass houses ..." He looked at Romeo, said "Fuck it" and drained half of his beer. "I'm a lucky one, right?"

"You know it," I said and pushed him into the half wall.

His blue eyes glimmered, and he tugged one of my tank top straps off my shoulder. "I like this whatever you call it."

This is the hard part with Dacon. Our relationship was very sexual, and even though we aren't seeing each other, it's difficult at times to push those feelings aside. I was about to hike up the strap when Romeo did it for me. He finds my relationship with Dacon annoying. He says I screw around too much and that our relationship is enmeshed and peculiar. He also thinks Dacon and I can't get on with our lives because we never really broke the bond. I say we're best friends, so why do we have to "break the bond?" He says it's because that's how it's done. I tell him he's jealous. He tells me I'm dreaming.

"Oh yeah," I batted my eyes. "You like this? It's a Romeo original. He swears there's not a thing in his nightwear collection more suitable for this time of year."

I nonchalantly touched Romeo with my body as I talked. I leaned on him with my bare foot topping his and rubbed my arm against his. It was easy to flirt with the two of us half dressed. He was ignoring it really well, much better than I expected, but when I moved away, he grabbed my hand and held on tight. I pulled, stretching our arms out.

"What's up with you two?" Dacon said.

"Nothing. He's hungry."

Romeo has a reputation for being a pig. He can't just eat. He has to make a huge sexual production out of it. They all do it, but Romeo doesn't only take the cake, he rolls in it, and makes you lick it off him. Of course, I couldn't really blame this particular cake on him, considering I was mixing the ingredients. This is what happens when you're always trying to bite your friends — no one trusts you.

"I'll let you finish your conversation," I said. "We'll catch up later."

I tried to pull my hand out of Romeo's, but he tightened his fingers until it hurt. I used my free hand to pry at his grip.

"What are you doing?" Romeo asked, his brows pulling tight.

"Me? You're hurting me."

I noticed then that he was breathing. I could suddenly feel his pulse through his hand as if it were beating in his palm. I stopped fighting then. The beating heart of an unfed vampire isn't a good sign for the conferrer.

"You two need some alone time?" Dacon asked, banging his empty beer bottle on the counter.

"Dru, I need that spoon," said Livi.

Romeo stared at me a few seconds longer. He was in less of a good mood than earlier.

"Let me go."

When he did, I quickly turned away and handed Livi the spoon she didn't need. She flashed me a quick smile.

"No meat?"

"Would I put meat in any food you're eating? No. I wouldn't do that. I didn't cook your sauce with sausage. I'm not stupid."

Oh, kay. I plucked a fork from the drawer and made my way to the living room.

"Heads-up," Dacon called.

I ducked an incoming beer bottle tossed from the kitchen. Luc caught it, popped the top, and covered the neck with his mouth before the foam oozed down the sides. I leaned down and kissed his cheek. Sara sat curled up, looking girlie at his feet. She pushed up on her knees to kiss me on the cheek.

"You smell sweet," she said. "Like tobacco. Like Romeo." She settled back into her spot at Luc's feet, her arm stretched over his knees.

Roeanne sat on the side of the couch closest to Luc, so I settled down on the far end, leaving a space big enough for two people between us. I doubted she wanted to talk to me anyway, and from where I sat, I had a view of Dacon's back and the side of Romeo at the sink. I felt better with him in my sight.

"What does that mean?" I said to Sara.

"Only that I can smell him on you. Romeo's scent doesn't bother me too much."

"Romeo smells like pipe tobacco?"

"Kind of like cherry tobacco," she said, "but not."

"Not at all," said Luc.

"I took a shower, but I didn't bring anything to change into, so I'm wearing what he gave me."

"That's why you're dressed like that?" smiled Luc. "I thought maybe you spent the day here." He made a sexual reference with his hand while he drank his beer to the bottom of the label.

"No, I didn't spend the day here, you dumb dope."

"Dumb?" He was buzzing, so his voice was loud and cheerful. "Dope?"

Livi brought dinner bowls for Luc and Roeanne, and for a few moments the only noises were silverware tapping stoneware and bottles hitting the small table.

"Roeanne told us about your mishap this afternoon," Lucas said while shoveling food into his mouth. He always eats that way, and I absolutely hate it. "She said you put some guy in the hospital."

I looked at Roeanne. She took her eyes off her bowl long enough to smile. I smiled back and was glad she wasn't angry with me. It escaped me why I was relieved, but I felt better knowing she wasn't.

"It was a long day."

"So, how'd you get all covered in mud?" Sara stifled a grin. "I mean … was it mud?"

I sighed and she lost it, laughing like a loon. You'd think for someone her size the laugh would be deep and impressive, but it isn't. She filled the room with the laughter of a ten-year-old girl. It's the silliest sound, and it doesn't suit her.

"It's all over headquarters," she said, "but I wanted to hear you describe it."

"Scab picker," Dacon said, trailing Romeo into the room.

She completely doubled over, which made us all look twice. She never acts that way. She's never that happy.

"It's not that funny," I said.

"There's nothing like someone else's misery to make a vampire's day," said Romeo. He smiled at Roeanne as he passed her to take the seat next to me. I could feel his thoughts in my head. He was trying to "guide" me. If he managed to get me under his control, he'd ask why I was acting strangely. If I weren't careful, he'd turn this whole thing around. Fuck!

"Don't start without me," Roeanne said as she headed toward the kitchen with our bowls.

Dacon shoved his way between Romeo and me.

"You sit over there, Liv," I pointed to the end seat on the other side of Romeo.

She shook her head. She wasn't sitting next to Romeo, and she waited for me to move. I sighed. Okay, all I have to do is focus and keep things physical. All touching, no talking. Most vampires can't resist that. Hell, most men can't resist that.

"This is Roe's seat," I said as I sat down, relieved that I'd thought of it. Romeo held my arm to keep me next to him.

"I'll sit on the floor," said Roe as she trotted in from the kitchen. She handed Dacon and Luc another beer and then passed me to sit on the floor between Alivia and Dacon's feet.

I gave Romeo a dirty look. I wasn't convinced that he hadn't put that idea in her head. He put his feet on the small ottoman, pulling me to lie next to him. His head fell against the back of the couch, and he grinned like a well-fed cannibal. His attention was attracted to Dacon unbuttoning and pulling off his shirt, leaving his suntanned neck exposed. Dacon must have felt his stare, because he didn't even turn his head to threaten the vampire.

"If I feel the slightest touch of pointy tooth enamel, I'm gonna fuck you up."

Romeo glared at me.

"Soon," I whispered.

He glared harder.

Colorful shapes rose on the big screen. Previews for other classic movies splashed a harsh glow into the dark room. I squinted my eyes at the information assault coming from the eager pitch of Territory Platinum credit cards, Vampiria life insurance for the cautious vampire, and a chain of vampire strip clubs. You could go there if you were interested in watching a "drain-train" in complete live action right before your very eyes! I hadn't even heard of a drain-train until I became a military officer. It's as gruesome as it sounds. I decided to close my eyes until the movie started.

Just until the movie started …

CHAPTER FIVE

I STOOD IN MY kitchen. The walls, decorated with a hand-painted mural of spring leaves climbing a white trellis, was a project Livi toiled over years ago. The vines tangled and passed the top of the doorway to disappear into the living room. I wanted to follow it, but the table was missing. There was a large pentacle on the floor. Romeo stood with his back to the window over the sink. Bright sunlight poured through the stained glass, surrounding his body. The white beams speared him. They flowed through his eyes and mouth, creating three small pools of light on the slate floor in front of me. It resembled the triple moon, a symbol all witches live by.

Lord Galen was in front of the cupboards, to the left of Romeo. He opened the refrigerator and cold air swept through the room. He picked a large butcher's knife from a cauldron on the top shelf and handed it to Romeo.

"Trust us," Galen said.

Neither of them moved, but my wrist was slashed lengthwise down into my hand. Blood ran into my palm, dripped off my fingertips and turned black as it hit the slate tiles. I held my hand out to show them the cut had grown, continuing in a straight line up my arm to the shoulder.

"Help me."

A genderless child came to stand between us. It had long, curly brown hair that Romeo twined around his fingers. He pulled the child close to his chest. Blood welled in a thick line where Romeo sliced its throat. He quickly tore the head away from the body. Bone, muscles, and flesh separated — snapped like dry-rotted rubber bands. Viscous black liquid oozed down the headless torso and pooled around my feet. Romeo tossed the head in the sink and let the body ease itself into the bloody puddle threatening to saturate my knees.

"Ignore it," Romeo waved his hand. "You have to help me."

He turned his attention to Galen. As if they were taking turns, Galen walked to me, black boots sloshing through the thick red lake.

"Heal yourself!" he yelled, his eyes running the length of my body.

I started and slipped into the doorframe. He grabbed my arm, saving me from falling completely under.

"I can make it better," he said.

Crimson drops splashed when Galen plunked to his knees in the blood. His hair rested on the surface of red only seconds before it was sucked under. He stuck his fist into my belly, creating a gaping hole. His face became slick and red as he licked at the wound that seemed to grow larger on its own.

There was no pain, but I was frantic with fear.

"I am helping," he said.

"You don't drink blood."

"Only yours," he said. "My sweet, sweet Anastasia."

My breathing hitched. It was unsettling to hear him speak my given name. Though not a secret, I've done my best to keep its use to a minimum.

He licked slowly, slithering an unnaturally long tongue inside the blackened mess of flesh and veins. I watched, mesmerized. It should've hurt, and it made me sick to see it, but it felt better than anything that had ever touched my body. I lost myself. I fell back. The floor was clean now, and I hit the tiles shivering. Romeo blessed himself, and Galen walked into my view.

I raised a weak hand to them.

"Die later," said Galen. "Right now you need the fear."

He lay on top of me. His long hair fell around my face, creating black isolation, as if I were trapped alone inside his head. He pulled the strap of Romeo's shirt off my shoulder, below the cross tattoo over my heart. He licked the skin there, a wet, bloody caress of his tongue. It felt good. I was weak in the knees, and my body shivered.

Galen hissed a freakish sound but moved as if nothing had ever felt as good as my injured body. My back bowed off the floor. My bloody stomach pressed against his.

"Dru?"

Romeo's voice came from somewhere in the kitchen. Galen leaned closer, as if to get my attention. He put his lips against mine.

"I will not let you stay here," he said. "My head is not your concern, and you will kill me."

I reached to hold him as he fell upward into a black hole.

"Don't go!"

"Dru?"

Romeo's voice again. A touch louder, and it was getting closer.

❀ ❀ ❀

My eyes snapped open. My head was on Romeo's chest. I jerked back to see him, but he was as normal as ever. My eyes darted around the room. I saw no knives, no blood, and no Galen. I looked at the vid-screen. The Mad Hatter was yelling at a rabbit and a little girl. Romeo put his hand against my head.

That was quite a dream, I heard his voice in my head.

I pulled away, angry he was listening to me dream.

I wasn't in your mind. I swear it. I can tell from the beating of your heart, your breathing, your body heat.

He held up three fingers in some kind of salute.

"Peace?" I said, my voice hoarse and dry. "What the hell is that supposed to mean?"

"Shh," Sara said.

"Not peace," Romeo said. He pulled me close, his cool lips touching my ear. "It means I'm being honest. Honest."

I studied his face. He was just Romeo. He snuggled into me, buried his nose in my hair, and took a deep breath. I curled myself around him, feeling a desperate need to be comforted. I'm familiar with portents. I know oracular dreams, but I didn't understand the basic notion that played out in that nightmare. It isn't the first of its kind, although no others have been that graphic — or just wrong.

The blood speeding through your body is making me feel demented, Romeo continued.

I lifted my face to his. With a hand on his cheek, I led him to my lips. When we parted, his expression was close to terrified.

"I want to be held," I whispered. "I want you to do it."

He watched me with caution, his expression uncertain. Maybe he was uncertain of his own feelings. I don't know. Or afraid that he's in way over his head, at least where I'm concerned. At times, he looks at me as if his world would crumble if I were gone. Then there are times he talks to me with such disdain that I think I must have seen ghosts that just aren't there.

"It's unnerving to have you want me like this," he said. "You're up to something; I know it."

I couldn't tell him that my behavior earlier had nothing to do with my feelings now. What Galen had done to me in the dream, though gory, was erotic and left me empty.

Relax. You're buggin' me out.

I took a deep shaking breath and nodded. I rested my head on his shoulder, but he pushed at me. He pointed discreetly to Dacon, sitting next to him. Dacon's thick brows hung heavy over his eyes in a kind of painful frown. It wasn't pain though, but fatigue. He held his braids between his fingers and ran them down to the end, over and over. Besides being tired, he looked normal to me. I shrugged.

Romeo pointed a finger towards the floor where Roeanne sat between Dacon's legs, her arms wrapped around his calves and her cheek resting on the inside of his knee. Romeo pushed me again, raising his eyebrows. I didn't know; no one told me about a new romance. Now I understood why she was so pissy with me when our conversation turned to Dacon. Romeo tightened his arm around my back. He pulled me to him, so I was more than leaning on the right half of his body.

I barely have control of myself. You have to feed me. You promised.

Screw it. Screw the plants. Screw revenge. I ran my hand over his chest. No! I can't go there. I will not touch him at all. I will end this now, and he can go out to eat. I should say I've changed my mind. I pulled away from him, but he quickly grabbed hold of my wrist.

"After the movie," I sighed.

He gave a nasty snap of his teeth. I knew it was too much to ask that he'd be satisfied with a finger, but I offered it anyway. He took it, shaking his head no. He put my finger in his mouth and slid it quickly over one of his canines. It didn't hurt—not really. His mouth worked on me like it had extra muscles and a mind of its own. A rumbling sound came from low in his throat before he rolled on top of me, crushing me under his weight. He grabbed a handful of my hair and pulled my head back. His tongue traced a line along my skin. He didn't care if we did this in public. I did. Romeo can get carried away, and I didn't want my lust overflowing to the masses. I snapped my fingers.

"Movie stop," I said, and the figures on the screen froze. "We need a food break over here."

"Thank god," said Livi. "I have to pee so bad."

She shuffled past all our legs in a mad dash for the bathroom. Romeo's mouth lingered over the area of wet skin on my neck. Dacon cleared his throat.

"Are we interrupting?"

"You should see his face," Lucas smiled, leaning back in his chair for a better angle. "He doesn't even know we're here."

I pushed Romeo back as much as he'd allow. His eyes were bleeding red and demonic. He stared at me for a long moment, his eyes falling and then rising in a very slow motion. He was almost beyond hearing me. I slid out from under him, but he held onto my hand as if we were forged together. His urgency surrounded me, pushing me faster down the short hallway toward his room.

Livi opened the door to the bathroom, caught Romeo's eyes, and backed away. "Someone's in trouble."

He smiled as we passed. Wide. Fanged. Evil.

"You need help," she offered.

"No. I think he'll be okay." I pulled him into the bedroom, and I fell against the door. The room was like a tomb, only the soft glow of the single yellow light coming from the back corner. He buried his face in my neck, licking and sucking my skin. I heard the door lock and felt his hands under my tank top. He gave a very male, very frustrated growl when I pushed them out and away from me.

"You promised," he said. "Anything I want."

He backed up. The motion was liquid and elegant, so not human. He was a gliding angel when he wanted to be. A fallen angel maybe, but just as beautiful. He held my fingertips to guide me to the bed. While pressing our palms together, he slipped his fingers through mine. His ashen skin made dark lines against my light hands, and it was very sexy. He took the straps of my shirt between his fingers and pulled it off my shoulders, only to have me put it back.

The entire scene was turning into something from a vampire movie—and not a good one. I tried to stop my body from reaching out to his, as much as his lust and thirst assaulted mine, but it was hard to concentrate or breathe. It was at this moment that I knew I was no longer the seducer. I screwed up. I truly screwed up. I smacked his hands away when he tried to inch my shirt up. He yanked me forward. The air moved swiftly around us until I was lying on his bed with the hard weight of him pressed between my legs. I closed my eyes tightly, gripping the sheets underneath me, because if I didn't touch him, I wouldn't want him. Right? He kissed my collarbone and licked a path along my chest. My hands tightened on the sheets until my fingers ached.

I have to stop this. I'm going to stop this.

"Let me do things to your body no one ever has," he said. He drew back to look at me. I grabbed his face in my hands, and he was so real, so strong. What a mistake this whole thing was.

If I say the words aloud, it will be a reality. Truth. My final word.

"No. I will not have sex with you."

"You want me. I can hear it in your voice. I taste it in your sweat."

I hate it when he says those kinds of things to me. To clarify, I love it when he says those things, so I hate it when he says them. It's hard for me to make sense when he's like this.

"Stop it," I said, in the lowest, most non-convincing way.

His stare pushed against me like suffocating summer air. The lust in his eyes is obvious, no matter the color.

"I'm as close to animal as a human can get, Dru." He put my wrists above my head, and I wasn't happy about that. "I can smell how much you want me."

"I'm not denying that I want you."

"Tell me how much you want me."

"I am not going to do you … it," I said, squeezing my eyes shut.

He laughed. Yeah, well, the words didn't convince me either. He pressed me again until I pushed up to meet him. He licked the underside of my arm, and a small shiver went up my back.

"You are damn sexy," he said.

See, now that gave me some sense. It truly irritates me when he talks that way. As if he is amazed that I could possibly make him feel good. Each time he says something off the cuff, something he is really feeling, it comes out shocked. He doesn't understand the offense he pays me with his own astonishment.

I moved when he tried to kiss me. His brows furrowed, and he was thinking those thoughts of his. I lay my palm flat against his cheek, feeling the softness of his skin against my own. I think he knew he could have me. All he needed to do was keep playing the game. Keep touching me until I couldn't take it any longer. What he didn't know is why. Why was this time different than all the others? I'm usually in control. I don't let him feed if I'm feeling particularly vulnerable. I was fine before I started this — before that dream.

For the record, there are valid reasons why I've never slept with Romeo. It's not because he isn't sexy. He truly is. Between his looks, and the way he looks at you when he wants you, he is irresistible. The problem is, he is my partner, and when we met, I was with Dacon, so I was off-limits. It's hard to overcome that friendship wall. Besides that, he's human horny. He sleeps with anything that floats his boat. Anyone. Anywhere. Anytime. To Romeo, sex is conquest, and that makes sex with him not so special. Not to mention we're very connected, as partners tend to be. Strengthening my bond to him with that kind of intimacy is a no-no. It's a big no-no with razor-sharp teeth. Still, it's been a long time since I've let anyone touch me.

His forearms trembled. His hunger, so fevered from deprivation, made it impossible for him to draw it out any longer. He held me to the bed with a strong hand on my chest.

"May I?" That's how Romeo has asked me to be his dinner since we met.

"No," I said, barely audible.

His anger pushed at me. The vice grip he used to imprison my wrist told me to rethink my answer. This was the big moment, if I wanted it. It was my chance to avenge my plant babies. If I say "no" again, he won't drink. He can't. It's the rule. Impatience tensed through his body. I couldn't speak. This is what I wanted, right? The angrier he is, the better. Right? Because he killed my plants. Right?

"Please." Even his eyes pleaded with me. He was too hungry for this game. His voice held more than a hint of desperation. That one word was laced with so much need I couldn't truly understand. I nodded my answer before I finished my thoughts or made a real decision. I don't know why I play. I always get burned when we play. He relaxed his body a little, but waited for me to say it aloud. Miscommunication has been a problem of ours in the past.

"Okay," I said.

"Look at me."

It's not necessary for me to "look into his eyes" for him to take control or embrace my mind. Romeo is too strong to need eye contact, so this is just another way for him to seduce me.

"Look at me."

My eyes rolled up to meet his, and in the three, maybe four seconds before he thrust his power into me, I felt nervous, small, and afraid. Then he swept over me, around, and inside me. It was as if his soul leapt from his eyes into mine to burrow into my brain. Both my mind and body bathed in a thick, hot liquid. My body heat intensified, and his teeth pierced my skin like a toothpick in mercury. He gripped me tighter. His mouth became a vice around the wound, and I cried out. His body moved on mine, in time with the motions of his mouth. I held the back of his head to keep him at my throat. I wanted him inside of me, but he wouldn't stop for that. He couldn't stop for that.

Vampires thoroughly enjoy intercourse. They will even ejaculate if their body is full of blood. However, after conversion the hard climax is from the blood. Putting intercourse with a feeding is like asking to have your body ripped to pieces. In the throes of that type of passion, a vampire can't decipher between your moaning in pleasure or moaning in terror. It's all so closely related—for them.

He reached for my tailbone and pulled me against him. Pushing harder, and getting faster. A warm glow of energy welled inside my chest. He stroked each organ, ingesting the life that rode with my blood. His heart pounded against my chest, and his body jerked against mine. He was now panting out air while he sucked down my blood. My own senses were ready to erupt when he tightened his arms and rolled us. His legs locked around mine to keep me still, and he rolled further until together we hit the floor. He released his hold only to bite me again. He shook his head like a dog tearing at raw meat. His jaw clamped and he pulled blood from the wound so fast my heart stretched wide, the beat lingering. He slammed into my mind, and I gasped aloud.

❀ ❀ ❀

THE SUN APPEARED SUDDENLY, and my eyes narrowed at the brightness. I heard the song of midsummer birds as I walked outside to find my mom, dad, and brothers. We were in the backyard of the home where I grew up. I could smell the sweet honeysuckle bushes mixed with the lingering summertime fragrances of charred wood, pool water, and sweat. My brothers, Dacon, and his friend Kenny were in the back of the yard near a small fence they were supposed to be fixing, tossing a football. My parents were on the patio bickering over who was the better driver. It was the fifth of August, my brother Max's birthday.

My head was dizzy. I was aware it was a memory, but it was so real and inviting that I had to doubt which reality was which. I happily walked to my parents. I put a hand on my father's shoulder like I had all those years ago. He felt solid under my skin, and he turned a warm smile to me. I saw him up close for the first time in nine years.

"My Nastya is here," he said.

I had forgotten how deep his voice was. I felt myself smile, and then I slipped back a step. I tried to hang on, but my thoughts, my muscles, everything relaxed into oblivion—a sweet, lazy euphoria. I wanted time to cease and allow me to live in that moment for eternity.

❀ ❀ ❀

WHEN MY SIGHT RETURNED, it came to focus on the black ceiling of a small room. Romeo's face came into view, while his hand seized my jaw. I watched him rise above me. A thick string of blood hung from his open mouth. He pushed his flattened hands against my chest. I watched his panic, his horror. I watched it all, and didn't care. I felt so good. Too good to let it go.

"Dru, please don't do this. Please don't do this to me." He took a deliberate breath of air. His face came down on mine. He blew into my mouth, and only then did I understand what he was doing. He yanked me up onto the bed. "Dru, answer me!"

I don't know how much time passed before I saw Dacon and then Roeanne. She pushed both men away from me to put her fingers against my neck. She cringed at the blood on her fingertips.

"Oh wow," she said, moving my head to the side. "Look at that bite. She has a pulse. It's low, but it's there. Her eyes are open." She shouted into my face, "Andru, can you hear me?" She tapped my cheeks lightly.

When our eyes connected, there was a pop of bright gold. Roeanne drew back, and I inhaled a deep breath of air into my lungs; it was a course, heavy sound. I let it out for another. I'd like to say the movement felt good, but it took too much effort to feel anything less than laborious.

"I can hear you," I said, exhaling the clinging remnants of Romeo's magik.

"I'm going to call an ambulance," Roeanne said as she rose from the bed.

"No. Wait." I struggled to speak. "I don't want that. I'll be okay."

She came back and sat on the edge of the bed. She picked up my tingling hand in a gentle, reassuring gesture. Her eyes bounced from my chest to the bite on my neck.

"Do you understand that your heart stopped? You seemed to be in a catatonic state. A doctor needs to look at you. You could have a serious problem."

"She does," said Dacon. "I'm staring at him."

"That's not fair," Roeanne said, looking at Romeo.

"Fair? Is a selfish vampire who doesn't give a shit about anything but his own satisfaction fair?"

"Dacon, it's a nasty bite, but he didn't drain her. Biting shouldn't make her heart stop, unless something is already wrong with it."

"Biting her neck isn't all he did to her, is it?"

"What?" asked Roeanne.

"Vampires can do more than drink blood, Roe."

She was still puzzled, and a bit naïve.

"The embrace," Dacon said, his voice louder, angrier. "It feels better if they pry into your mind."

"I've heard it talked about, but I don't really know what that means," she said.

"Their emptiness leeches off every part of you, not just your blood," Dacon said, glaring at Romeo. "The older ones can open your mind to enhance the high on both ends. They can force you to relive your dreams, nightmares, and sexual experiences. Whatever emotion gives the vampire his or her biggest kick. If they drink too long, taste the life of their victim so close, they want it all. Once they have something sweet and forbidden, they get greedy. They're vicious that way. They'll drain a person's existence to make themselves feel whole."

"You're describing something cruel," Roeanne said, looking at Romeo and then back to Dacon. "He was only taking blood."

"You don't need a locked room to take blood," said Sara.

"Our blood is like candy," said Lucas. He was trying to be helpful, I think.

"Like a liquid chocolate bar," Livi said, nodding in agreement, "with blueberry undertones and orgasmic overtones."

Dacon made a face at her attempt to lighten the mood. I pushed up on my elbows. Romeo stood by the doorway, his arms wrapped around his chest and his eyes fixed on the floor.

"My heart never stopped. It only slowed down. Romeo was in too much of a state to realize that. And he's not entirely to blame. I pushed him. I've been pushing all night."

Romeo looked up. My blood covered the bottom part of his face, and it looked sickening. He sat with me, pushing the hair away from my cheek. Shallow tears trembled in his eyes like the surface of some dark lake. He'd done a bad, uncontrollable thing that was very unlike him. He had gone deep, to a sacred place in my mind that's off-limits.

"I'm so sorry," he said with emotion more honest than I'm used to getting from him.

His tears didn't slide, but mine did. Without thinking, I wiped his face. Feeling his warm skin brought the memory back in a rush of shared vibrations. He had experienced what I had. He felt my memory through me. He knew how it touched me and how I suppressed the hard tears. I smiled a sad-happy smile. For as much as it hurt, he showed me my dead parents. He gave me something priceless, even if it was accidental.

"I didn't pick that memory," he said. "It just popped up."

I was fairly sure that was true, because I didn't think he would've willingly showed me a family moment when he was in such a sexual state.

"I've never done that unintentionally. I've always had … I almost ripped your mind apart. I don't know what happened."

"Yes, you do."

"Forgive me," he whispered, hugging me and lifting my upper body off the bed.

I really did. If I hadn't teased him all night, he would never have been so out of control. He never would've done such a thing, even if I'd asked. Romeo knows where that kind of embrace can lead. Tapping into memories is an art that will come easier with age if you possess that skill. Under fifty years, a vampire hasn't learned how to access power of that magnitude. That's good, because deep mental embracing is addicting for both vampire and conferrer, and possibly fatal for the latter. However, if you're a vampire that has survived fifty years, hopefully, you've learned about the sanctity of life. Most importantly, you've learned how to control your impulses. Though, as I said, I helped push Romeo out of control, so it was partly my own fault.

"I'm not angry with you," I said.

"I don't know why," said Dacon.

"I was teasing him. He hadn't fed in two weeks, and I've been goading him all night. I wanted to turn him on, so I could turn him down."

"Damn," laughed Lucas. "She was trying to kick your ass."

"Why would you do that?" Dacon asked, his features twisting into irate confusion.

"Because I killed her plants," said Romeo.

Alivia, who was still standing by the door with Luc and Sara, let out a loud bark of laughter before slapping her hand over her mouth. After a second I laughed, and then Sara, the girlie giggler.

Roeanne followed quietly behind. The three guys looked at each other. Dacon's eyes said everything to Romeo I wouldn't allow him to say aloud, and though Luc was having a good time, I knew he backed Dacon completely.

"I'm fine," I said, patting Romeo's face.

"You're lucky," said Roeanne.

"Absolutely," I smiled.

I pushed Romeo away and swung my legs around so they hung off the bed. Lucas knelt in front of me.

"Locking the bedroom door to feed your vampire," he said. "What a sleaze."

"A girl has to do something with her free time."

He sobered a bit. "You're okay?" he asked as he patted my hand.

"I'm fine." I lightly smacked his cheek. "Get the hell away from me."

When I stood, I swayed. My head felt light as air. Before I caught my balance, Dacon scooped me off my feet.

"Don't go near her," he barked at Romeo.

Honestly, the people in my life are so dramatic.

❀ ❀ ❀

DACON WALKED OUT OF the bedroom with me in his arms. He sat me in one of the small kitchen chairs next to the table.

"Water?" he asked.

"How about juice?"

"I don't get it, Dru," he said, pulling a glass out of the cabinet. "Why do you put up with him?"

"I can't *not* put up with him. He's my partner. He's a fixture. Anyway, he's not that bad."

Dacon snatched my hand from the table. He shoved the soft pink scars in my face.

"He gnaws on you all the time. He treats you like an object." He leaned close. "How many of these little 'bites' have you healed with your own magik so there'd be no scar at all?"

"He doesn't treat me like an object," I said, yanking my hand free. "I let him do it because he's my friend. He doesn't force himself on me."

"Doesn't he? If he asks for something, can you say no?"

"He doesn't control my mind, Dacon. I was playing with him tonight. We got carried away. Let's not make this an excuse to rip into our friendship."

"Friendship?" he said, with wide, angry eyes. "Is that what you call what the two of you have been doing the last few months?"

"Let it go."

"You know they are enticing by nature. Plus, Romeo is feral. He's Lord Galen's son. That should tell you something about the workings of his mind. Jesus, Dru, he's a hundred years old. If he gets too worked up, he could tear you apart. Why would you play with him like that? Especially knowing he hadn't fed in two weeks."

Saying I wanted to seduce him and then shoot him down was not only redundant, but when said aloud, it also sounded plain stupid. At the risk of looking like a four-year-old child, I shrugged my shoulders.

"A long time ago, they had to be persuasive to stay alive, but there are many ways to feed now," Dacon said as he filled my glass with a pitcher from the refrigerator. "Romeo has a long list of conferrers. He doesn't need to use you."

"He doesn't use me," I said. "I'm easy, that's all."

He flashed me a look.

"I meant more convenient. Look, he's always there for me. He'll do anything I ask."

His eyes widened.

"Feed him, fear him, fuck him, and what? He'll be your lap vamp?"

"No, Dacon, it's not like that. Why are you so hardheaded?"

"He's a dog, Dru," he said, stamping his left foot on the floor — a habit he grew into while dating me. "He'll let you down. What kind of relationship can you have with someone like that?"

"We're not in a relationship. At least not the kind you're insinuating. We were fooling around. Why do you refuse to allow yourself to understand?"

"Say something that helps me to."

"When my parents died and my brothers moved, I had you and Alivia to count on. For a while now, I've also had Romeo. None of you have ever let me down."

"Really?"

"Maybe Romeo and I didn't hit it off at first, but we've worked past that. You know we have. You three are my family. I'll do whatever you want, whenever you need me to do it."

"That doesn't mean you have to be his personal dinner table."

"I'll do anything for you too, Dacon."

"It's not the same."

"Isn't it? I'll wash your car, or take care of you when you're sick. I cleaned that disgusting wound you had that made me physically ill to look at." He frowned. "I'd even tell your mom you were in a coma for a year, and that's why you haven't called her."

"Of course, but—"

"Romeo doesn't need me for those things. He needs me to be a great partner and cover his ass with my life. He needs me to feed him when he doesn't have the time or energy to go find someone."

"Does he need to lock you in a bedroom when you feed him?"

"He likes drama," I smiled. "I'll do what he asks, because whatever the three of you want, you get."

He dropped against the refrigerator, looking at the glass of tomato juice as if it was going to do tricks.

"I guess you're right in that we are a family. I suppose if Romeo asked me to feed, I'd let him." He smirked again, but less angry this time. "I've let him do more to me than that."

"It was just a kiss, and you were drunk … and it only happened three times," I grinned.

He frowned.

"Look, Dae, he likes it when we play sexual games."

"I remember being in that circle. I know you like it as much as he does. I guess it stings a tiny bit seeing you like that with someone else, especially him! He's such a … Mr.-Beautiful- twenty-five-year-old-body-forever-writhing-all-over-my-ex-girlfriend-jerkoff." He shook his head, averting a fight. "I know I have no right, but nine years die hard. No twelve, if you count the years my feelings went unrequited."

I went to him.

"I wasn't going to argue. It's flattering."

He rolled his eyes.

"Is that why you didn't tell me about you and Roe?"

"How do you know about that?" he whispered.

"Is that why? Because you didn't want to hurt me?"

"I guess," he sighed and spoke even lower. "I didn't think you were seeing anyone, and I didn't want to throw it in your face."

"Always thinking of me," I said, wrapping my arms around his waist and hugging him. I grinned up at him, and he tightened his arms around me.

"For sure," he said, twisting Romeo's shirt in his fingers.

I looked around and saw we were alone.

"Now I know why she doesn't like me."

"Roe likes you. She doesn't understand you at all. You're harsh, and she's not used to someone with your attitude."

"Harsh? Please, Dacon, don't get me started."

He pulled me back when I tried to move away.

"What does that even mean," I snapped. "She's not used to a woman with attitude? You make it sound as if she's from the nineteenth century."

He shushed me.

"I'm serious. I met her mom. She waits on Roe hand and foot, almost as if she's a slave. It was kind of sickening. Creepy."

He met her mom? I pulled away, but Dacon tightened his grip on my upper arm. The glass of tomato juice suddenly became the focal point between us.

"Are you going to let me drink that?" I asked, very cautious of my words.

"Doubtful."

I hadn't noticed how glassy his eyes were. He was still a little angry and having way too much fun. I went for the glass as he lifted it high over my head.

"Don't you dare!"

"You said whatever I want, I can have."

"Why would you want to douse me with juice?"

"Because."

My eyes fixed on the glass. Talk about flashing back to childhood memories. I jerked my arm free, but I was too slow. He turned the glass over. My hand covered my head, as if that would protect me. The cold juice trailed down my neck and in long cold lines down my back.

"Dacon, it's freezing! You're such an asshole."

He waited with cautious eyes for my reaction. It took me a moment to decide which emotion I was feeling more. Anger. Joy. Aggravation. But when Dacon's deep laugh filled the room, I was in love. Sometimes he reminded me of the best parts of him. He pulled me close with both arms and licked sticky red juice off the side of my face. His tongue felt as good as I remembered. His embrace was familiar and not as platonic as it should've been. When his hand slid to my ass, I should have stopped him but I laughed, settling into him further.

"I truly can't believe you just did that."

"Neither can I."

We turned to the doorway, where Roeanne stood in front of Sara, Livi, and Luc. She didn't have the amused smile on her face that they had on theirs. Definitely not. She looked hurt. I felt immediate guilt as she walked calmly, yet precisely, into the living room. I tried to relay with my eyes that Dacon should go tell her it didn't mean what she thought it did. Sometimes the personal space we'd normally have is gone, even though we aren't a couple anymore.

He stared back at me, a complete blank, and then he shrugged. His mouth curled into a smile, and his eyes sparkled with laughter.

"Let's take a shower together," he whispered. He put a hand over his mouth to stifle the noise you make when you're suppressing laughter. This must be fatigue combined with alcohol—he didn't have that much to drink.

"Don't be a dick," I said. "Go to her."

He kissed my head, hard and quick. Laughing, he grabbed a few paper towels and then made his way into the living room. Livi tiptoed a circle around me to avoid the mess. She tossed some kitchen towels she got from under the sink, but they flew past me into Sara's waiting hands.

"Go in there and talk to Romeo," said Sara. "He's being a priss about this entire thing."

She had on her serious, disapproving captain's voice. Sulking wasn't an option in Sara's world. Romeo could bat her around like a mouse, but because he can be depressive and regretful, she thought he was weak. She was right about me talking to him, though, and I was feeling sorry for myself for having to do it. Romeo is moody. That makes him difficult to comfort. He never wants to leave his foul mood until he's reveled in it for a good long while. I took a towel from Sara and swabbed it over the trailing red lines down my arms and legs. I was in the hall when Lucas jumped in front of me. He danced around like a boxer, lightly tapping my face to spur me on. I slapped his hands away before I continued on my way to Romeo's dark bedroom of horrors.

CHAPTER SIX

THIN DROPS OF JUICE formed a line on the hallway floor. A circle of dots collected where I stood in the darkened doorway of Romeo's room. He sat very still on the edge of the bed, facing the opposite wall. He held his head in his hands. I stared at his bare back before I closed the door and went to him. After a moment of him trying to ignore me, I pushed his elbows off his knees and crawled onto his lap. I wanted eye contact, but he wouldn't allow it. He finally grabbed my jaw, yanking it to the side so he could see the damage he'd inflicted.

"I hurt you," he softly said. "If you were human, you'd have—"

"Hey," I said, hating it when he said things like that. "I am human." I wanted to smack the side of his face, but I didn't. He was upset. I can deal with the rude comments. I smiled. "Wanna lick me?"

He huffed before falling backwards onto the bed.

"Romeo, look at me." I crawled up to his head. "I'm trying to be sweet."

"Your sweetness is what started this horrible ball rolling."

"I love it when you use nineteenth century sayings."

"That's twentieth, and you're not helping." Romeo can be quite sensitive about his age. I forget, because it's a dumb thing for a vampire to be sensitive about.

"I'm trying to make you feel better," I said.

"Don't."

"Besides, I wasn't trying to be sweet earlier. I was going for manipulative and cunning."

"The sweetness I was referring to wasn't your actions," he said, raising his brows.

Oh.

He tossed his arms over his face so his elbows were pointing up at me. We sat in this ridiculous position for another minute before a high-pitched beeping sounded from somewhere in the room. Romeo stretched over to the nightstand and picked his phone off the top. He looked at the small display and then threw it. It twirled across the room, where it smashed to pieces against the wall.

"Galen wants to see me," he said, wiping at the area around his mouth where my blood was beginning to peel away in dry flakes.

"Does he know? How would he know?"

"He made me. He feels what I feel. Knows what I know. I didn't have the sense to block him out of my mind before I nearly ripped out your throat. Not that I could concentrate on anything else while you were clutching onto me in that fucking way you do."

"Well, it's not his business."

"I almost killed you tonight, Anastasia! That's exactly his business."

His use of my name quieted me. He hardly ever calls me Anastasia, and I don't like it when he does. Most times, I feel as though Romeo and I are on the same level and we're equals. I know he's nearly one hundred, but in so many aspects, he's young and normal. Except the times when he uses my name. It's as if he's showing me just how much older he is, how much wiser. It makes me feel like his misbehaving daughter.

"You didn't almost kill me." I said it, but I wasn't sure if I completely believed it. Without my magik, he might have turned my mind to toast. "I'm harder to kill than that. I'll go and explain how it's not his business."

Romeo lifted my hand to show my fingertips. He gripped my jaw and tilted my head to the left and then to the right. "You have marks all over your body from me."

"No, I don't." I knew that was true, because I heal those marks that I think will leave a scar.

"I don't think your being there will help," he said. "What would you say? That you're a witchy little faerie? And Romeo getting carried away and draining your body won't hurt you?"

"No. I can say that it's my choice and none of his business."

"Oh sure." Romeo pushed at me to get off him. "That'll go over like a lead balloon. Dacon's right."

"Don't start feeling sorry for yourself. You didn't force me."

"Coerce."

"Fuck you."

"I rely on you too much. Your complaisance makes me lazy."

"I am not complaisant," I said, balling my hands into fists.

"Dru, please."

"Regardless," I shook my head, "it's none of his business. Or Dacon's."

"Yes, it is Galen's business. I'm his first captain. I can't go around hurting or killing humans in the heat of passion. Cause you know what? It looks really bad!"

"Oh, everyone knows you're all dangerous."

"Not for taking blood. They think we have better control than that. But if Galen's first officer can't control himself with his own partner, who he ..." I lifted my brows and turned my ear to hear him clearly. "... cares about. It makes everyone wonder if we can control ourselves with a stranger." He patted my leg for me to move. "I gotta go. I don't want to be late for my tongue-lashing. If I keep him waiting, he'll think of a few more ways to hurt me."

"Tongue-lashing? You're funny today."

"You're not making me feel any freakin' better. Now move."

"Not until you kiss me."

"No." His look was fierce, and then he closed his eyes. "Why do you torture me?"

"Because you like it. And you can handle it."

"Like I handled it tonight? Get off me. I don't even want to be this close. You might as well have FAILURE stamped in big red letters on your forehead."

"Why do I get the letters? I didn't fail anything. It was your lack of discipline and lust for my very soul that sent you over the edge to almost kill me. So why do I have to wear the letters? Anyway, I don't look good in red. Not especially."

"Stop, please!" He was completely exasperated. "If I give you a kiss, will you shut up?"

I smiled.

"Do you trust me?" he asked seriously.

"You're such a freak. You're troubled in the head."

"I'm a vampire," he said simply.

"Do you get that from Galen? Because he's your daddy and the ultimate control fanatic?"

He laughed, but not happily.

"I've never met a person or vampire with less self-control than Galen."

"You said he hasn't fed off a human in eons or slept with someone in about fifty years. He's the epitome of self-control, isn't he?"

"He's fucked a vampire more recently than that, but he doesn't trust himself around humans. He doesn't want to rip them to shreds." He gnashed his teeth at me. "Especially little ones like you. You could never handle him."

"Who did he sleep with? Who? What vampire?" I really wanted to know what kind of person Galen would take to bed. What did "recently" mean?

Romeo put his fingers to his chest and opened his eyes wide.

"You? That was like twelve years ago, and you don't count. He loves you. He hadn't done it for a gazillion years before that, and he hasn't done it since. I think that's control."

"It wasn't twelve years ago, and he's not in control. He's emotional and controlled by his fear. Fear that if he hurts someone he'll be forced to go back underground, but he won't do that. He'd rather die. And you know there's no easier way for a vampire to lose control than by bleeding and fucking—so he doesn't do either."

I sighed.

"I'm wondering if it's possible for you as a somewhat sentient being to delve deep into that murky mass of gray matter you call a brain and find another word for it besides fucking?"

"It could be possible, but at the moment I don't see any other word," he said, rolling his eyes upward as if to look inside his head. "You listen to me. My father, your general, is on the brink of insanity. Everyone's afraid of him for a reason."

"You're worse than Dacon with all the drama. Kiss me so you can go get hollered at."

He put both hands on either side of my face. When he started to say he was sorry, I kissed him. It was a sweet kiss, light on the passion, heavy on the safe and comforting. He set little kisses on my chin and nose.

"You're a mess," he said, trying to put his fingers in my hair.

"It's Dacon! He's drunk and doesn't even know it. He acts like he can handle his liquor, but it's not true. Just so you know, you're on his shit list. You ARE his shit list. One day, he's gonna stake you while you sleep. You're going to say something stupid, and all his built-up resentment and rage is going to …"

I stopped because Romeo wasn't listening. He was staring at my neck. It pissed me off, while at the same time making me happy. I knew I shouldn't do it, but I turned my head so he could see the bite more clearly.

"It's bad," he said. "I'm really sorry. Does it hurt?"

I nodded. "Maybe you could—"

"I could heal it for you. If you want." His eyes stayed focused on the wound. He raised his head, his nose searching for my blood scent.

"I do want you to heal it." Truth is, the fey magik heals me quicker than most, with less scarring. But this bite is in an obvious place, and I'd rather not have a scar at all. Besides, there's no fun in healing myself.

We both shivered when his tongue connected with my skin. He licked a few times, his mouth warm after ingesting my blood. The sharp sting of his blood came after he tore the skin of his top lip with his teeth and kissed the wound. He slid his lips back and forth against my skin. When his tongue gently traced the lines of the wound, I trembled with pleasure and felt a spark between my legs. He wrapped his arms around me. His strong hands caressed my back, slid over my ass. Then suddenly, I was in the air and on my back staring at the ceiling. He was standing next to the bed pointing his finger at me.

"Would you stop already?"

"You're still hungry."

"Stop it!"

I kept my smile and stuck a finger in my mouth.

"I'm surrounded by children." He took the corner of the flat sheet and wiped the red wetness from his body. "You're all slobs. Damn it, all this is your fault! The whole night became a game of who could hold out longer, and I was the one who was starving. You should have let me go to the club."

"How did you figure it out?" I asked, stretching out on my side and resting my head on my palm. "You know, about the plants."

"You were definitely up to something so I …" He laid his fingers to his temples and squeezed his eyes shut.

I sat up.

"Whose? Mine? Whose?"

"Livi was practically throwing her thoughts at me, she was so nervous about what you were going to do. Roe was preoccupied and a little more difficult," he smiled and raised his brows. "She thinks you can be a bitch. She thinks you treat me unfairly." I threw my hand over a fake yawn. "That was a real great plan you had there. Push my buttons until I kill someone. A couple of masterminds you and Livi are."

"She didn't have anything to do with it. You're pissed, so I'd say it worked. In addition, you're in trouble with the boss. I figure I'm two up in the win column."

"You're hilarious,' he said, yanking a pair of pants from the pile I put on his dresser and not caring that the rest of the clothes fell onto the floor. "What I like most is that there's real genius to your humor."

"Romeo, did you completely lose control and try to kill me so I wouldn't yell at you for destroying my plants? Or do you secretly want to convert me so I'll be at your side for eternity?"

"I didn't try to kill you," he said, his shoulders tensing. "I would appreciate it if you didn't talk about it that way."

"I'm sorry. I really am. It's all my fault," The words I choked out were so dry that I nearly coughed. I scrambled off the bed and onto my knees in front of him. I wrung my hands, blubbering loudly at his feet, "Oh please, please forgive me. What will I do without you, Romeo? I'm a complaisant shell of a human being when you're not here to feed from me. Your leaving makes me wonder, what will I do?" I threw my arm up to my forehead. "By Jupiter, what will I do?"

"You know what?" he said, sidestepping away from me to get to his closet, where he grabbed a uniform shirt from a hanger. "Because you're such a cold blooded ... witch, I'm not going to tell you what else I found out."

That got my attention. One of the best parts of Romeo is that he loves to gossip. No other vampire does it. They don't usually sit around and chat with one another. Romeo and Sara barely speak unless it's work related. If two or three are in the hallway together, none will say a word. They're like shadows moving about, but never really connecting. The leaders, the older ones, are the only vampires that tend to hang in a pack, but they're always swimming with humans. It's odd to me that after all this time in the open, they're still as solitary as they are. They never want to draw too much attention to themselves, and they try to pass for human when they can. Vampire soldiers will befriend the family of their human partner, becoming loyal and protective. In turn, they feed from the members of the family, thus assuring a balance of sustenance and safety.

Romeo did the same to me. He's close with my brothers, Max and Vincent, and Max's family. They liked him long before I did, and Max's kids adore him. When I visit them in the States, he meets me there. Since he's unable to set foot on our neighbor's land without a pass, which are only allotted to dignitaries, he takes an underground route. I won't ask what that really means, so I won't have to lie if we're ever caught.

Normally, I would be pissed that he listened to Livi and Roe's minds. It's against the law and a rule that you don't invade your friends without their knowledge. It was over and done with, so I didn't care to argue.

"Please tell me," I said, scooting on my knees to his feet and folding my hands together. "You have to tell me. Please, please tell me. What did you find out?"

He sidestepped me again, ignoring me while he finished getting ready. He leaned over a small round mirror planted on his chest of drawers and raked his fingers down his short waves, not making much of a difference. He ran a hand over his mouth to remove the last bits of my blood, and then he sat on the bed to lace his boots.

"Tell me," I begged, walking on my knees toward him. "Tell me. Tell me. Tell me."

I finished lacing his boots. When I was done, he stood with his arms out wide.

"How do I look?" he asked.

"Beautiful. Like Marcus Aurelius going into battle." Ass-kissing goes a long way with Romeo. I sat on the bed, my ears, mind, and eyes open and eager for this new information.

He stuck his tongue at me — and then he was gone.

CHAPTER SEVEN

IT TOOK MY BRAIN a moment to realize he wasn't there. Fuck. I hate when he does that. I hate it! Sometimes, in the middle of an argument, he will just disappear. I truly friggin hate it. I smoothed my hand over his bite. His blood hastened the healing, but it still ached.

Livi poked her head in the door.

"I felt the coolness of death rush by. Did he leave?"

"Yeah." I reached in the corner for my backpack. "I'm going too."

"It's only quarter after twenty-three hundred," she said. "If you go, that leaves only Luc, Sara, and Dacon."

"Where's Roe?"

"She moved out. Said she was paged and had to go to the hospital."

"Why can't you stay?"

"Because it'll be a couple's thing."

I shrugged and almost said the obvious about Luc and Sara, but I knew what she meant. She came into the bedroom and closed the door.

"Do you know what's going on with Dacon and Roe?"

"Do you?"

"Maybe. They're almost as creepy as the other two." She looked at me sideways. "Jealous?"

"It's been four years, Liv. It's not like we haven't dated other people."

"Not a fellow movie nighter."

"It's okay." I sat next to her on the bed. I used Romeo's sheet to wipe the sticky juice off my arms. "It's a little weird, but only because I have to learn to stifle myself. I don't want to start trouble.

What happened in there was because my hormones are out of control because I haven't been touched in about a hundred years."

"Maybe you want him back."

"Please. No. You know how much we fought. At least the way we fought at the end anyway. He could never let anything go. He's still like that."

"Well, I don't think he liked that you were in lo— had feelings for Lord Galen."

"Our fights weren't about my infatuation with Lord Galen. He didn't even know about it until Romeo took it from my head and teased me. Asshole. Those fights came after everything else failed to push me down the aisle. My commitment without marriage wasn't enough."

"He wanted to be the one you loved most."

"I loved him with everything I had, Liv. But he needed me to qualify or classify my relationships, and I can't do that." I blew a sigh. "You staying or what?"

"I'm going. Let me get my stuff."

"Take your time. I have to get a shower."

❀ ❀ ❀

AFTER MY THIRD SHOWER of the day I rummaged through my bag, confirming what I already knew. My uniform and underwear were too disgusting to wear even if it was a short trip. I searched Romeo's drawers and found no other casual clothes besides underwear like he gave me earlier. I decided to take a pair of his new fatigues and a newer short-sleeved black work shirt. The pants were way too long. I cuffed the bottoms so I wouldn't trip over them. My own belt wouldn't hold the extra material around my waist, so I used one of his. My holster belt fit fairly well, but it was a little bunched. The thigh strap was a bit too high and didn't fit as comfortably as it should, but it would do. Overall, I felt like a kid wearing her dad's clothes.

I threw the much lighter backpack over my shoulder, took my beret, and headed to the living room as if I had a purpose. The lights were low. Dacon sat in the middle of the couch, while Luc was back in the chair with Sara at his feet. They were touching more than necessary. One day they would kiss in front of me and I would be sick right there on the spot. I just knew it.

Livi motioned me into the kitchen. She was leaning on the sink where Romeo was earlier, watching the movie through the half wall. It seemed she didn't want to be too close to anyone, and I thought I might know why.

"Thanks for cleaning up," I said as I glanced around.

She smiled. Dacon snuck through the darkness when he heard my voice.

"I've got to be in by six," I said, tapping my wrist where a watch should've been. "I'm still not used to getting up so early."

"Same here," he nodded.

"Stop griping," Livi said as she slung her bag over her shoulder. "Day work is much nicer than your spooky ol' nights."

"You're a freak," said Dacon, grabbing her for a hug. She tried to pull away from him, but he wouldn't let her. She smiled awkwardly, shoving at him until he acquiesced and let her leave the kitchen.

"Look," I said. "Don't fight with Roeanne because of me."

"Nastya, please." Dacon took my beret from my hand and slid it on my head.

I softened at his use of my family nickname.

"No one could mean enough for me to hamper my feelings toward you. I don't even think I could. Like you said, we're a family." His damp hair skimmed my cheeks when he kissed me on the forehead. "Wet, tiled kitchen floor? Bring back memories?"

"Stop it." I pushed him away, but he caught my hand and held it as we walked to the door.

"You could have driven her to work," said Sara.

"I offered," Dacon said, widening his eyes.

Luc looked up. He and Sara stared at our folded hands and then at Dacon.

"You heard me offer! What was I supposed to do? She's angry with me."

"For practically having sex in the kitchen with your ex," said Sara.

"We weren't having sex," Dacon exclaimed, his mouth dropping open. "Just … groping a little."

Dacon and Luc gave small identical laughs. Sara huffed a deliberate sigh and went back to watching the movie.

CHAPTER EIGHT

I JOINED LIVI IN the hall. Before the apartment door closed, she took my hand and practically dragged me down the hall. We got to the elevator where she smacked the button about six times. She stood quietly and stared at the doors. I wondered if she was thinking of her reflection like I had earlier, or if she'd even noticed it. She kept a tight grip on my hand, and there are only two reasons Alivia holds hands.

The first is fear. Anytime she's afraid, she holds the first hand she comes across—like during a scary movie, or when she's around Lord Brasov, since he petrifies her. The other reason is that whenever Livi has something she needs to discuss, she gets clingy and odd. Her grip was so tight that my hand started to ache. I was about to pull away when the elevator doors opened. She pulled me in and said "ground" to the elevator.

I was feeling grumpy again. My exhaustion from the workday and Romeo's transgression was catching up. I didn't feel like playing games with Livi's sensibilities. I figured I knew what was going on anyway, and I wasn't quite sure I knew what to say about it. The elevator became deathly quiet, barely humming like when I was with Lord Galen. I wished I hadn't thought of him.

"You have your keys?" Livi searched her bag. "I can't find mine."

"Yeah. You drive here?" She shook her head and I sighed. Livi's jeep isn't my favorite ride. It's loud and bumpy, but I was tired enough to fall in the dirt. She'd have to drag me by my collar. Of course, I was wearing Romeo's clothes, so if I had to be dragged … Livi got quiet again. I was too strung out to let the silence continue.

"I know how you feel about Dacon," I said. "I've known for a while."

"I don't—what do you mean? That would be weird."

"It's not weird," I said. "We're together enough, aren't we? And he's a great person."

I'd noticed an attraction between them last summer. I searched my feelings then and threw the idea of them as a couple around in my head. After crying like a moron in isolation, I concluded that if they made each other happy, I'd have to learn to live with it. I can't deny Livi much. She's a good friend to both of us. She's my best friend in the world, which isn't an easy job. He'll treat her well, and I'll be glad to know he's with someone who adores him.

I glanced at the floor. For a moment, I thought I might cry. Somewhere inside I felt that if Dacon had a successful relationship, it would show that I was the one who failed— that my way of loving was wrong, like so many things about me.

"If this hurts too much, I won't do a thing," Livi said as she turned to face me.

"No, it's fine."

"You two are so close."

"I'll be fine." I gave a smile that I didn't feel. At that moment, Livi seemed so tall, or maybe it was that I felt really small.

"I wouldn't ask either of you to change," she said. That was another reason the idea of them together didn't make me totally ill. Livi would never ask me to stay away from him. She's secure enough to know that if Dacon says he's yours, he means it. Fidelity was never his issue. "And if—"

"We won't get back together."

"Don't do that," she said. "It's like you're mind reading because you hang out with that vampire so much."

"We don't spend that much time together."

"Dru, since you've been on double day shifts, I hardly see you," she said, pursing her lips. "Before that I hadn't seen you in weeks, because you slept with Romeo every day after work."

"You make it sound like we're doing stuff."

"I don't know what you're doing."

"You know I'd tell you if we were having sex."

"I don't know any such thing. You don't tell me anything anymore. You're never around."

Livi was hurt. I could see that, but I wasn't sure why. She and I usually spend some part of our days off together. Although it's true that I hadn't been around the house lately.

"I'm sorry. My car is so temperamental that it's easier to go to his apartment after work than walk home."

"I get it," she said. "Kind of. Seriously, he's a bit of an asshole. If you're not having sex, then what do you get from him?"

"What do I get?"

"Sex I understand. It feels good. It's gratifying, and he's good at it. What I'm saying is, if you two aren't together, it's like you're having a relationship with a guy that you're not really having a relationship with. You need to get away from him. You need to find someone else."

I didn't know what to say. Truthfully, I was a little blindsided. If anyone understood my relationship with Romeo, I thought it was Livi. But, if I couldn't define it, how could she?

The elevator dumped us into the main hall. There was a profound contrast to the peace of the upper barracks. The ground floor was alive with the midnight shift. The stone amplified the laughter and made the room an echo chamber. People flowed back and forth, and there seemed to be a buzz in the air.

We stopped at the front desk and waited longer than normal for our weapons because of the crowd. When the desk lieutenant put our guns on the table, I immediately signed for mine under her strangely watchful eye. I had apparently become quite interesting. Livi checked her gun over as if it could possibly not be hers. She does it every time. Finally penning her name, she slid the molded metal into her holster.

I glared at the staring lieutenant before I left. Then I peered into headquarters, hoping to catch sight of Lord Galen. If you look through the doorway at the correct angle, and he has his office door open, which he usually does, you can see inside. Too many people were walking around for me to get a good look. I wondered if he was still chastising Romeo.

"If you'd told me we were going to stand in this hallway all night, I would've brought my sleeping bag."

"Hmm? What?"

"Jesus, are you ever going to get over him?"

"Get over Jesus?"

"You may not have talked about him for the past few months, but I know you're still into him," she huffed.

"Jesus?"

"Dru!" She stamped her foot, pushed me aside to clear her view into headquarters, and then wrapped her arm around my shoulders. "I don't see him." She led me through the large doorway to the outside.

"I was looking for Romeo."

"Sure. That's who I meant." She gave me a motherly look. It was her "you're so pathetic" look. "It's not safe for you to be near Lord Galen."

"You know I know that. But do you know how truly un-fun it is to be in — to really like someone who doesn't know you exist?"

"Uh, yeah. We just talked about how I like your ex, and he barely notices me."

"And if the guy did know, he probably wouldn't care. It doesn't help that I have to see him with Lord Cherkasy coiled around him like the rotten snake she is."

"He did change her. She's drawn to him as any vampire child."

I scowled at her. Livi hugged me tighter as we moved down the stone steps. We maneuvered through the crowd and weaved back and forth until we hit pavement. Our journey home isn't long by car — a short ten minutes. Walking is twenty-five. Of course, the shortest walk would be too long for my tired legs.

"I think he's totally unaware she's there most of the time," said Livi.

"Yeah, okay, because she's not beautiful at all."

Livi waved to a young female vampire with short hair riding a white horse with brown spots on its butt. She had an innocent smile and at conversion couldn't have been more than twenty-five—the legal age of consent. Her horse trotted the circle of street around the manor heading for the south entrance to Galen Park. Her male partner caught up to her. They picked up the pace and clopped away in the same direction we were going.

"Let's not talk about the lords—let's talk about him," said Livi, widening her eyes.

"Him?"

"The ass. The vampire. You seemed to be enjoying Romeo a little too much tonight."

"Oh, him. That's a polite way of saying it."

"Tell me what happened in his room when you passed out—or before you passed out."

"I was enjoying Romeo a little too much." We laughed. "I don't even really know. I'm only sure that he reeled me into the zone, and the great seduction became my own."

"Oh yeah, the zone. He thrives in the zone. What happened at the exact moment you tranced out? Were you having sex?"

"No. I told you we haven't done that. I kind of wish we were. Well, I think I wish we were."

"Too bad. Romeo's a bit of all right."

"You just told me he was an ass."

"He is, but he's got this quality—a certain something that makes you want to molest him, and then let him molest you right back."

"That certain something is the face of a dark angel and the mouth of a con man. And you should know."

It was interesting to see such dark skin turn red. Livi gave into Romeo a few years back. If I recall correctly, she gave in for a few nights for a few weeks in a row. When she came down from the vampiric cloud, she described being with Romeo as the most trans-euphoric experience of her life. That's how we now describe something we really enjoy, even if we're not sure what she meant by it.

"He's definitely the forbidden fruit," she said, exhaling as if she was smoking the after-sex cigarette.

"I don't understand how he can be smooth and charismatic, but only half of the time."

"He's smooth when he's hungry. He's charismatic when he's horny. Take it from a fairly seasoned player, Romeo is a cad."

"Yeah, but underneath that idiot shell there's this … I don't know. Sometimes he just looks at me, and I'm lost. My heart starts pounding, and I think I want—"

"Oh my god, I was right. He's in your blood. He's gotten to you."

"No, he hasn't."

"Has too." She pulled at my shoulder to stop me from walking. "Romeo is a big, ugly, stupid guy who doesn't know the first thing about honoring a woman. Now you say it."

She's right. He's a big, dumb guy. But …

"Say it!"

"I know he can be a moron, but—"

"Oh my god! You want Romeo." She threw her arms in the air. "You want Romeo as your guy. As a boyfriend? Don't you?"

"What about me says that I'm stupid? What I want is to be close to someone, and he keeps pulling my strings. He's the only person near my strings, and I know how sad that is. I'm surrounded by all these men I'm not allowed to do anything with. Dacon's off-limits, 'cause he's the ex. Romeo's off-limits, 'cause he's the jerk. Luc's off-limits, 'cause he's doing his sister."

"Loki likes you."

"Loki likes everybody."

"You really are having a crisis."

"I'm so screwed." My shoulders slumped. "Now, Dacon, he was good at it. I'm talking good at it. I think he was born knowing. It has to be a gift from the gods."

"Or the goddesses," Livi smiled and then stopped.

"You're not going to get all wigged out if I talk about how Dacon is in bed," I said.

"Not at all. I was fantasizing. Tell me more. Exactly how was he so good?"

"Can't it wait?" I said, pulling her along. "At least until I'm getting it on a semi-regular basis, before you force me to talk about the best sex of my life?"

"Okay. But I want you to show me the details with pictures, graphs, and even pie charts."

"Fine."

"Maybe use different colored pencils for emphasis on major greatness."

"Yes, fine."

We walked on, Livi lost somewhere in sweet dreams of Dacon, and me in my own sick thoughts of how completely Renfield I had become. Wanting Romeo, blah! Scrounging around for any little piece of attention—how pathetic! I did not want Romeo as a boyfriend. I didn't think I was that far gone. Sex would be good, though. For Romeo, sex comes second only to drinking blood, and that can be a lot like sex. The near ten-year buildup alone would make it worth it.

A black news van sped past with the full moon symbol of our territory emblazoned in crimson underneath the larger network logo. It reminded me of Galen.

"Have I told you I've been in the clouds with Galen again?"

"Really? Since when? Are they prophetic?"

"How would I know? My dreams rarely come true, and these only started a couple of weeks ago. They don't seem particularly oracular," I lied. "Lots of gore usually. I dreamed of him earlier during the movie when I was lying on top of Romeo."

"No wonder you attacked him."

"I didn't attack."

She smiled.

"I encouraged."

She laughed outright.

"Anyway, tonight's dream was so real I could smell the blood. I could feel his hands on me."

"Ew, that is so—ew. Jesus, Dru, he's old and—old. He looks like death's brother."

"You don't think he's attractive at all?"

"I don't know," she sighed. "Yes, he is. Nevertheless, when he's emaciated, like he's been, he's gross. Why does he do that to himself? Why doesn't he eat?"

I shrugged.

"His face is handsome—I guess. But he's—ew. Just pick another vampire." She narrowed her eyes at me. "I got a voice mail from Malena. This was earlier, while you were in the shower."

"About what?"

She paused.

"She said Romeo and Lord Galen were fighting."

"Why didn't you tell me?" I asked, looking back at the manor.

"Because I didn't want you to get upset. And I really didn't want to go with you to look for him."

"But I should go."

"No. This is why I didn't tell you. It's his fault, Dru. He tried to rip your throat out. Lord Galen *should* beat the shit out of him."

"He beat the shit out of him?"

"Ugh, Dru! Even if Lord Galen threw him across the room without touching him, he would've deserved it."

"Did he use that kind of power on him?"

Livi crossed her arms over her stomach. She was very angry.

"Liv, I yanked his crank until I broke the machine."

"If he was that hungry, he shouldn't have let you near his machine."

"Now I know why that lieutenant was staring at me. I look like a bitch not helping him."

"You know I care about Romeo, but he doesn't always think clearly when he's around you. He has major brain block where you're concerned. Have sex with him already, so he stops wondering what he's missing." She picked up the pace, and I followed. "Malena also said he tried to bite Lord Galen after raving that he was a cold and lifeless junkie."

My mouth dropped open. Romeo called his father a blood junkie? He tried to bite his dad? Forcing a bite on a human is punishable by death. Forcing yourself on another vampire is also a definite bad. It's rape, and the victim has the legal right to destroy the aggressor if he can. Romeo can get nasty if he's losing a battle, but he's never stupid. Although I knew what he did was wrong, I couldn't help but smile with pride. It takes a tremendous amount of nerve to do something like that to a vampire as old as Lord Galen. My smile turned into laughter, and Livi and I nearly fell into the street from the hysterics.

CHAPTER NINE

WE WALKED UNDER AN arched metal sign that read "Galen Park." The name gleamed like polished silver by the street lamp. Dumb name. It was a tribute from Lord Luise Cherkasy, from a daughter to her father. After the Territories were won in 2002, construction began immediately on Galen Manor at the site of old Philadelphia's City Hall. It's the second largest of the five state manors, with approximately two hundred soldier barracks, four silos, a private courtyard, a conference hall, and a restaurant-nightclub called Pune Hall named after our own Lord Pune. And because he likes to hang out and bullshit with the soldiers, we call the place "Court," as in his royal court. The manor was fully completed in 2024. The land stretching an eighth of a mile around the structure was used to create the park. It is, in actuality, the border between the manor and the rest of the city—the moat around the castle, if you will.

"Park" is a loose term, though. It's more like woods with a path at the north and south sides. The foliage is dense. The south end permeates with the strong, sweet scent of Nicotiana, Lord Pune's favorite flower, especially at night. Each entrance has its own fragrance in honor of one of the lords of this manor. Lavender was planted at the west gate for Lord Galen and peony for Lord Luise. Gardenia is there for Romeo in the north, though he's only a lord's son.

You can get turned around if you enter the wooded area unattended. I think spells were used, vampire magiks, to disorient. Romeo tells me that isn't true and I can't sense any magik other than the natural, but I still think he's lying. There are two guarded streets at the east and west ends. The east gate, in front of the manor, is for incoming vehicles only. The west gate directly behind is for departures. Both are heavily armed and difficult to pass on foot. For that, you use the north or south walkway.

The paths are set with cobblestone and wide enough for a military truck to pass freely. Lamps light the trail. For security purposes, it's illegal for any civilian to use either trail after ten in the evening unless escorted by an officer. A specific military division patrols the park—not like Livi's friends on horseback who stick to the outside perimeter. This particular group hides out all night, every night, and in all weather, waiting for odd things to happen. The department is D-squad or Death Squad as they are nicknamed, because most of them are vampires.

If a civilian saw one of these guys in the bushes late at night, I guarantee he would run screaming in the opposite direction. This group takes solitary and squares it. I've heard they feed on the bigger deer in the park. I've also heard they sometimes join Lord Galen. Creepy vampires aside, the park is gorgeous. It's home to a diverse group of trees and flowers—simple and exotic—and inhabited by skunks, deer, owls, and bats. Part of the horseback officer's job is to keep the outside safe from strays. Attacks are infrequent, but male deer get ornery at certain times of the year. Our trek in the park is usually pleasant. About a third of our walk time home is nice in spring and summer, even if a bit cold in the winter.

"Let's get back to sex," Livi said, linking her arm through mine.

"Please stop," I said. "Let's talk about anything else."

"Okay, fine," she said, sliding her boots along the path, kicking small stones on the bricks. "How are your brothers doing?"

"Good. I got a letter from Max. Willow and the kids are doing well. Vince is fine. Now that the business is making money, Max wants to adopt a baby this time. Willow always wanted a bunch of kids."

"Three kids is a lot."

"What about you? Have your thoughts changed since —" I shrugged "the last time we talked about having kids? Because Dacon wants babies."

"I haven't really thought much about it. Right now, I'm not interested."

"I never think about it. I love my niece and nephew, but I don't want a baby. What would I do with it?"

"Too much work," Livi nodded.

We meandered along the path — because I honestly couldn't move any faster than a meander. Approaching the trail's halfway clearing, we saw the brown-haired male soldier who was on horseback. He was kneeling on the ground in the middle of the rest area. He held what looked like his partner in his lap. It was hard to tell from my angle.

"That's your friend," I motioned to Livi with my head.

"Jefrey and Teena," she confirmed.

I stopped with no urge to continue. When I saw the two on the ground underneath the dirty lamplight, all kinds of alarms went off in my head. I crouched and hugged the side of the path. Livi moved on for a few more steps to get a closer look. Then she too backed away from the middle of the trail. She swiped twice for her weapon that hung lower than normal because of the short pants. I yanked mine and we eased forward.

Jefrey sobbed. He rocked the girl in a simple motion.

My skin trembled even as the entire area felt calm, eerily desolate, as if we were in a tunnel or a cave — someplace closed off. There were no footsteps or voices, only so much nothingness. We looked around, examining the woods that loomed over us in quiet blackness. I reached into my bag for a flashlight. The narrow beam gleamed brightly in the dark. I studied the clearing where Jef and Teena lay on the ground. Livi stooped by the female, checking for a sign of life, but the girl was motionless. I could see what made Livi draw her gun. Teena had an arrow through her chest.

"Help me move her away from this light," Livi said softly, leaning close to the distraught man.

"Don't touch her," he snapped.

"She needs a doctor."

He stared at the blood covering his hand and shrugged Livi's hand off his shoulder.

"She was ahead. She flew off the horse. I came right away, but there was nothing I could do. I was afraid if I pulled at the arrow it would do more damage."

As Livi tried to persuade him to move, I made my way to the bench along the perimeter of the circle, tucked away in the edge of bushes. I went to my knees behind it, hidden by the greenery that's so dense this time of year. Again, I listened—not just for people, but for the normal sounds of the night. Crickets. Animals. Wind. Something. I snuck my hand in my bag and reached for my headset. I pressed the small button linking me to the Emergency Dispatch. A soft chirp sounded, letting me know the phone was trying to connect to a secure line. A second chirp, and then the indicator light turned red.

I peered up the empty path and then moved farther into the bushes. I shined the flashlight, squinting as if it would let me see more in such darkness. There was nothing around and I wondered with curiosity, and a ton of anger, where the fucking Death Squad was. This was *their* job, damn it. I made my way back to the path but stayed near the border for cover.

"There's nothing here," Livi said, stepping from the bushes on the other side of the clearing and shaking her head.

I glanced into the trees, cursing the fact that I wasn't carrying night vision binoculars or any other useful toys, since I was officially on day work. If I assumed Teena was the target, which seemed likely, the shooter would be gone and there probably was nothing to find. Of course, maybe the man was the target. He sat in plain sight in the middle of the clearing, so it was doubtful. I couldn't shake the feeling that this entire scene was too damn odd. I could hear Jefrey crying, and the agitated horses, but beyond that, it was a total dead zone. I still didn't feel comfortable on the path. I motioned for Livi to come to me just as a breeze flowed through the air, forcing the hair on my arms to stand on end. The horses started up the path as if pushed.

"Did you call E.D.O?"

"I couldn't get through," she said. "Where's D-squad? I'm going to get the horses."

I turned to Livi's friends. The man rocked the girl's lifeless body as he whispered in her ear. I moved closer to them with a new thought. I took a better look at the arrow sticking from her chest. The end of it slanted toward her head, suggesting the shooter was higher than she was, and she was on horseback. My stomach did a little flip. I looked into the trees hanging overhead like dark, thick fingers. Then I noticed that I could hear things. All the small night-time noises were back as crickets clicked and branches swayed.

Livi emerged and tied one of the horses to a narrow tree just beyond the clearing. I shook my head and started toward her.

"No! Get off the path," I hissed.

"What?"

"Move," I motioned for her to go into the bushes. Then I heard a clicking or creaking sound. "Shh." We froze and listened. The clearing was at my back, and I could hear Liv's friend talking softly, but there was something else—a sudden, quick "thwip."

Livi must have heard it too, because she dropped as quickly as I did. The sound of metal skittered along the cobblestones beside us. I pushed her to run up the path. I started off, only to feel a sharp and sudden pain that forced me into a sideways stumble. My body hit the ground, and fire shot up my leg. My flashlight banged the stones, and I screamed, clutching my gun so tightly my fingers ached. I rolled onto my back and shot two rounds into the trees, more from pain and the uncontrollable tightening of my fingers than from a conscious thought of hitting a target.

My shaking hand grabbed at the arrow that had speared the soft meat on the back of my right calf. It was clean through and I couldn't pull it out. I was sitting in the middle of the path, exposed. I dragged myself from the line of fire. Livi was suddenly over me, pulling me quicker than I could go on my own. She propped me up against a tree, closer to the clearing than I liked.

"What the hell," she said, trying to help, but not wanting to touch me.

"Gods, it stings!"

"Hold on. I'll—"

The bushes on the other side of us moved. Liv turned and fired into the greenery. Out popped a scrambling figure. The person regained balance and ran up the pathway.

"Go," I said. "Just go!"

She jumped up and ran. The tied horse became frantic, and I wasn't sure if it was spooked from what had happened or if something was nearby. I situated myself in a better position. It was too dark, even with the light from the clearing, but I put my gun up in front of me. After a moment of silence, I felt around the area where the arrow entered my calf. I smelled the blood on my fingers. My tongue numbed when I touched my finger to it.

Something rustled above me. I used the tree for support and struggled to my feet. I was halfway standing when a figure eased gracefully from a high tree branch about thirty feet away. It dropped quietly to stand on the ground. I pressed my back to the tree and put my gun up.

It was a female vampire with black hair. The dingy yellow light softened her hard features. She was slight in build and I would've thought I could kick her scrawny ass, even with the arrow in my leg, but she looked so damn confident. Something about the way she faced me said she was too familiar with this type of confrontation. She stared at me as if carved from stone. I held my gun tightly, aware of Jefrey weeping behind me. I was willing to bet she wouldn't let me go get him.

"You have to give me what I need. And then I will go."

She wasn't smug. She wasn't demanding. She was most definitely not from around here. Her words held a light Spanish inflection, but that in itself was not so unusual. It was the way she held herself. She would be easy to find, because she would be hard to forget. That is, of course, if she didn't kill me.

"You killed someone. I can't let you go."

She spared a quick glance in Jefrey's direction and narrowed her brows, her expression was almost regretful. She looked back to me then to the bushes where her friend crawled out. I took that moment to let her know where I was with our situation—I shot her in the left shoulder. She acknowledged the hit, but barely, and then she started for me. I moved from the tree, fired twice, and missed. She slammed me back into the tree. I fired again, hitting her in the same shoulder. She cried out, and I banged my gun against her chest. When she fell back, she kept hold of my shirt, tossing me onto the hard stones. My knees hit the bricks and I cried out in agony, using a hand to brace myself so I didn't end up with my face in the dirt.

A gunshot sounded, and then another right behind it—an explosive echo like a deep-toned firecracker. Jefrey had fired his gun. He'd found his target, because I felt the spray of blood hit the side of my clothes. Still on my knees, I turned as quickly as I could and pointed my gun at the vampire's back. She was in front of him, in shock, groping at a bloody hole on her left side. She moved, and another shot sounded, again followed by the echo. Her hand splattered all over my face. By the gods, was he insane?

"Hold your fire!"

I grappled my way to my feet as quickly as I could, so Jefrey could see I was there. I didn't want him to shoot me with a bullet from his gun. He's a night soldier with night ammunition; his bullets are for vampire, so they detonate after hitting a target. The bullets are powerful enough to blow my heart out of my chest, if they manage to pass the vampire.

"Shit, Jefrey, hold your fire."

Rage filled him, flowing through his face and down each shaking limb. When I regained my balance, I shot the vampire in her left thigh with my gun, a 9mm Glock. It wouldn't do much besides make her sore, but I wanted her in as much pain as possible. The new pulse-gun we were experimenting with would've put a real hurting on her. The small light burst was quick and deadly. It would've been perfect for this situation.

I hobbled to the vampire and pushed her to the ground, with a foot against her back. My heel crushed into the back of her neck. She squirmed, trying to swipe my foot out from under me, so I shot her right hand. I really wanted to shoot her foot just for the fuck of it, but I was afraid she'd bleed out before we could question her. She was obviously without the bow and arrows, but I looked for other weapons. Jefrey stalked towards us and walked into my outstretched hand.

"Get back. Help is on the way." Of course, I had no idea if that were true, but I had to say something. He was red with anger and practically jumping in place.

"Why? Why would you do it?"

The girl's head pressed sideways into the brick, but you could see she was trying to answer. She had already started to heal. She was way over fifty years old.

"Accident," the vampire mumbled. "Getting ready for—"

"Shut up," I said.

She pulled her hand to my right foot and rubbed the bloody mess over my boot. She mumbled some incoherent babble, and I kicked her hand off my shoe. The hurt in Jefrey's eyes made me want to blow her head off. I lifted my injured leg and bounced my full weight on her neck. Her garbled cries of pain from crushing her windpipe would have to do.

Livi came trudging down the path with a young girl slumped over her shoulder. She tossed her motionless body on the ground next to the vampire. The girl's face looked bruised, and her eye was red and swollen. She had a gnarly branch sticking out from the spot between her shoulder and collarbone. Blood soaked the shirt around the wound.

"She's a she," I said, "and human."

Livi nodded and held up a crudely made bow.

"No arrows, but I'm guessing she's the one that got you." She saw the gaping wound on the vampire. "I heard the shots. His first?"

"Yeah. Is yours dead?"

"Nah." Livi held out her arms to show me the small thorns stuck in her dark skin. "The little twerp kicked me into the huge thorn bush near the gate. I tuned her up a little is all." She laughed. "With her own weapon."

The vampire began to struggle under me. She couldn't see the young girl from her position and was making frantic grunting noises. Either her throat healed quickly, or I didn't do as good of a job smashing it as I should have.

"What ... did you ..." she choked and gurgled and then said something like, "I kill—"

Livi rolled her eyes.

"Like I killed her," the vampire gasped and gagged blood onto the ground in front of her mouth.

A loud shot rang out and then another discharge. Bright sparks flew from my boot. I jumped back, throwing my hands up to shield my face. A spray of blood and brains splattered all the way to my waist. I fell into Livi, unable to put weight on my wounded leg. "What the fuck!"

I practically leapt over to Jefrey. Gripping my gun tightly, I clocked him across the side of his head. He fell to the ground as blood sprayed from his mouth. I snatched the weapon from his hand, braced myself on my bad leg, and kicked him in the side to keep him down. Again, much hurt for me, but mission accomplished. He crawled to the clearing and slumped himself over Teena's frozen body. I was disgusted. I put my gun away and limped to Livi. She held her hand out to me for support.

"Four showers," I said. "Four showers in one damn day."

"Dru, he's gonna get in trouble for that," Livi said, gaping at the headless vampire.

"No kidding."

"She was probably a terrorist, and he killed her. And I mean killed her for good."

We stared at the decapitated body, brains, and heavy chunks of skull mingled with dark blood oozing from the neck. Our attention caught a bit of something that fell off my pants into the pile. I had to admit it was very unlikely she'd be coming back from that one. I've seen a vampire beheaded cleanly and live, but I'd bet not even superhero blood could fix this mess.

"I don't know. She might not be a terrorist. Maybe she's just a kook."

"Where's the second squad?" Livi asked as she looked around. "They should've caught her out there. Kooks don't get this far into Galen Park, and you know it. Look, he's a friend. He's upset. You would've done the same if it were Romeo."

"Yeah, so?"

"So," she paused for a moment, "say you did it."

"What?"

"Say you did it."

I wasn't angry with her for asking me to lie. Only a bit surprised.

"They'll know. He won't be able to lie, and he has residue on his hands."

"You fired your weapon, so you'll have it too."

"My night gun's at home." I held up the weapon I'd been using for three weeks. "I used this day gun, Liv. The burn is different." I motioned to the dead vampire. "The damage is different."

"No one's going to notice that," she frowned.

"He's too fucked up to lie."

"Exactly. They'll never get a straight answer out of him. He's a wreck." She moved closer to me. "Once you've given your statement, they won't need to ask him. Tell them you took his gun because he was distraught, and then the vampire tried to get away. I'll say the damage was done by the time I returned with the girl."

I sighed.

"You've lied to them before and gotten away with it. You're a first captain's partner. They'll take your account of the situation as genuine." She put her hand on my arm. "He'll be punished for that. They won't do to you what they'll do to him."

I stared at both bodies lying on the path. It's true that I've lied to superior vampires without them finding out. Because if you believe it, I mean truly believe it, so will they. The difference is that the lie was mine alone, from my state of mind, of which I have complete control. Still, Livi was right. I would most definitely have killed her, and her friend, and probably her family, if she had killed Romeo.

"Fine. I'll say I did it." I waved a tired hand. "Go tell him to keep his mouth shut."

CHAPTER TEN

I DIDN'T HAVE MUCH time to think about the decision I'd made before Livi rushed back to warn me. I sensed Romeo before I saw him. It gets like that when you've been close with a vampire for any decent length of time. Their magik seems to glide in before they do, searching for you, especially if you're angry or upset. I knew Lord Galen was with him. I could feel it in Romeo's energy. I watched the path on the other side of the clearing. I could see them in my mind's eye the way I had dozens of times before: two moving phantoms, shoulders back, an effortless, almost gliding stride. Then abruptly, they walked out of the darkness, out of the recesses of my mind to appear in the lamplight. The power they radiated forced you to understand that they're not at all human. Romeo told me that most humans don't sense that influence the way I do. He said I feel it because I'm a witch, and if people knew how truly magikal they are, they wouldn't trust the vampire at all.

Romeo was shirtless. Dark marks mottled his face. He had bloody cuts on his chest, neck, and arms. Lord Galen wore the same emerald silk he was wearing on the turret, but it was dirty. Still, they were an amazing presence. I've never wondered why he chose to take Romeo. It's always been obvious. I leaned on Livi. I closed my eyes and readied my mind for what I was about to do.

"Would you look at them," she whispered. "Holy shit, you don't stand a chance."

About twenty soldiers had stopped inside the clearing, and emergency medical personnel poured from behind them. The medics headed straight for Teena, and our two presents on the ground. They carted the young human girl away on a stretcher. Someone grabbed

Livi. Day shift Captain Gloader, General DeFarr's first, came straight to me. Without caring that I was injured, he pulled me aside, took Jefrey's gun from my hands, and started with the questions. I limped down the path, explaining how Alivia and I had problems with our headsets when we called for emergency assistance. He told me four cadets on their way from training came across Jefrey and me with guns up, talking to a living female vampire. He raised his brows when he said "living vampire."

I told him what happened—my version. I recounted with a straightforward, and somewhat detached posture, how the disturbed vampire killed Teena and injured me, and how her accomplice ran and then attacked Livi. I told how I brought the vampire down, but even with her injuries, she struggled stubbornly and fiercely when she thought her human associate was hurt. With my tone of voice, and my overall sincerity, I believed he realized shooting her in the head was a last resort to ensure all of our safety.

At the conclusion of my almost meticulous account a hand tightened on my shoulder and jerked me off balance. It was Romeo, and he caught me before I fell. I was irritated until I saw his face. Dried blood covered it, and I could tell his nose had been broken. I saw bruises, cuts, and what looked like claw marks on his chest. I couldn't believe his father would beat him so badly for what happened between us.

"You look horrible," I said.

I turned to Lord Galen, who was with a medical officer inside the clearing. I took an angry step towards him, but Romeo grabbed my shoulders. He shook me, a near violent snap.

"Pay attention," he demanded and extended his arm and finger over my shoulder. "North," he said and then half turned and pointed behind himself. "South." He pointed to our right. "East." Then he pointed down the path, but more toward the bushes. "West." He grabbed my shoulders again. "Do you have it now? One day it will save your life. I swear I could spin you around the barracks' hallway and you wouldn't know how to get back to my apartment."

"What are you talking about?"

"In there," he knocked his first two fingers against my temple. "You have no idea where you are in there. I can't enter your mind and find you when your brain is so crowded with misdirection."

I was so angry I chomped down on the inside of my cheek.

"I don't want you in my mind. My brain is not crowded, and I'm not misdirected."

"No? Then why is there always this …" he held his hands wide, looking for the right word "thing keeping your mind in such fucking chaos?"

I knew what he meant. It's magik—only that word suggests it's simple. I also use meditation and discipline to keep my head unreachable to vampires like Lord Galen, and his daughter, Lord Cherkasy. It's a bonus, and a pitfall, that Romeo has trouble getting in.

"Maybe you're just not strong enough to tap into my head. Did you ever think of that?"

He took a deliberate breath and set his hands on his hips. Like so many of Romeo's gestures, it was feminine, only he never looks feminine when he does them. The way his back curves when he rests his weight on one leg is quite sexy. I didn't know I was staring at him until he cleared his throat, and I looked up into angry eyes.

"I was strong enough to dig into your head earlier tonight in my bedroom."

I glanced at Captain Gloader, who was hovering nearby.

"Because I wanted it," I said as nastily as I could. "I let you."

He glared at me, and I knew in his silence that he wondered if that were true. He can, and has, pushed hard enough to get through my mental barricade, usually when I'm feeling under the weather. Because we're so close, some thoughts even transfer without him trying. However, I let Romeo think that everything that happens between us is something I allow. He can't ever believe he's stronger than I am. That's part of the magik. Knowing I have certain mental talent makes him edgy, and I admit I nurture that fear. He's suspicious by nature, and there are times he doesn't trust me at all. He probably shouldn't trust me. The same way I don't completely trust him—a vampire, a mind reader, a man.

"We're partners," he said, "so you'd better hope I'm strong enough. Fortunately, for you, your panic hit me like a spray of bullets to the chest. I felt your pain and fear. I could smell it." His tone was miserable. "I knew where you were. Almost." He rubbed the back of his hand over his brow. "We gotta stop spending so much time together."

"Fuck you," I said.

Because of my conversation with Livi, I was feeling hostile about that subject. My attitude surprised him, and he scowled at me. I didn't know what to say; I was in pain and had already forgotten most of the conversation. I didn't understand why we were arguing.

"Screw you, and I don't fuckin' panic." Obscenities, yeah, that'll do. "And if you felt my pain, what took you so long to get here?"

"I wasn't in the command center. I ran into these people outside of the park." He looked around at the other soldiers as if he couldn't stand any of them. As if they were lesser beings he was forced to exist with. He gets arrogant when he's truly miserable. "Galen and I were twenty minutes away when I realized something was wrong."

Oh. That's impressive, and kinda weird that he felt my emotion. I see what he means by us spending too much time together. I would've liked to watch him run though. I don't get to see him use the great speeds some vampires are capable of, except the disappearing act when he ditches an argument. It's one of those things that make the vampire seem as foreign as they truly are.

"I used a car, nitwit," he said, glaring at me as if I were a complete ignoramus. "I drove here."

I let the misery go. I didn't think he read my mind intentionally. He probably just picked the thoughts off the tip of my brain. I wasn't trying to hide them. I let the insult go too. He was pissed, and he needed to take it out on someone. That was fine. I could take it.

"Well, it took you long enough," I said. So maybe I couldn't take it.

"I'm in pain, Dru. It's hard to move."

I stepped back before we started hitting each other. I moved toward the others in the clearing. He pulled me back, and I groaned. I wanted him to leave me alone. He washed a hand over his face, and it looked strange. I touched him gently on the cheek, close to his nose.

"Are you okay?" I asked and he swatted me away. "He hurt you good, huh?"

His expression turned angry, but his eyes searched the ground, avoiding me.

"Telling him that you're a grown woman, and what we do together isn't his business didn't help."

I cringed. I felt awful, like it was my fault. Oh right, it was my fault.

"Why aren't you healing?" I asked him.

"I'm being punished."

I cringed again. For Lord Galen to force Romeo's body to stop healing so soon after Romeo fed is no small feat.

"Does it hurt badly?"

"My ribs are cracked, and two are broken. My thigh is ..." he moved a hand over his lower hip. "it's ..." he let out a painful breath. "My shoulder was dislocated, and four fingers are broken."

"All of your ribs?"

"Enough."

"Does it hurt to breathe?" He frowned at me. "Well, not breathe, but move."

"Yes."

"And your nose?"

He wiped at the blood slowly running down to meet his upper lip.

"Yeah," he said in a softer tone, "he broke my nose."

"I'm so sorry. Truly, Romeo, I'm sorry." If there was anything else to say, I didn't know it, and he wouldn't let me help, so screw it. "I need to get to the medics. I have to get this arrow out of my leg. I'm feeling dizzy and a little weak."

He looked puzzled. He hadn't noticed.

"Help me."

"You walked over here, didn't you?"

I rolled my lips against themselves and closed my eyes. I knew he was in pain and I was trying to be sensitive. Maybe it was the fact that someone tried to kill me, because all I wanted to do was beat the crap out of him. I limped to the other soldiers, chewing the sore spot on the inside of my cheek.

As Livi predicted, Jefrey and Teena were gone, whisked away to be seen by the vampire that made Teena. I heard someone say it was a descendant of Lord Pune's. Ninety-eight percent of converts don't share royal blood, so I'd say that Teena's family is fairly connected. Livi was sitting on the bench, shirtless and wearing a black bra. One of those thin ambulance sheets was lying unused in her lap. A medic held a small, bright lamp over her while another gently pulled thorn needles out of her upper chest and shoulder with long doctor's tweezers. She was quiet, yet every now and then, she'd swipe at a single tear rolling down her cheek.

Livi can be a total badass. She can do serious damage, but she has a low tolerance for pain. It makes her angry, which helps in a fight, but after the adrenaline rush, she's usually a disaster. This moderate display of distress is a treat for the rest of us. Lord Galen sat next to her. He slowly, absentmindedly rubbed her hand between his as if it were cold, while Captain Gloader talked close to his ear.

I grunted at Livi. She half smiled and swiped another tear. I turned my back on them, knowing Lord Galen was watching. He could feel I was pissed at what he did to Romeo. I'm not sure why he cares, but I think he does. I sat on the bench across the clearing, shivering in the heat. I stretched my leg, and a few minutes later a medic was crouched in front of me. She pulled off my boot to show the bloody sock. She took a pair of scissors from her bag and cut the unusually long pant leg all the way to my knee, without asking why my clothes weren't the right size. I supposed she'd seen stranger things.

"Are you numb? In pain? Sick?"

I stared at her for a moment. "Not numb, but numb, yeah. And dazed, I think. It doesn't sting, but it stings a little. A little."

"Did you hit your head?" she asked, shining a light in my eye.

"No. I don't know."

"I think you're feeling the effects of blood loss," she said as she felt around my head. "You're in a bit of shock." She cut the bloody sock and examined the skin around the arrow. "I'm going to stop this from bleeding, and we'll lay you down."

I nodded. Suddenly all I wanted to do was lie down.

"I'll also check to see if this arrow is dirty. But I think if it had poison on it, you'd be dead already."

She was wrong about that. I felt the sting of toxin when the initial pain ebbed, like ants marching under my skin. The taste of it coated my mouth. It was a natural poison from a plant called aconite or wolfsbane, or even monkshood. I use it regularly for medicinal purposes, which is why I recognized it in my system. A normal human would be dead by now. But not only is my body acclimated to the drug, my faerie bond cancels out most natural toxins. Faeries couldn't survive in nature if it could kill them so readily. They're susceptible to poisons, but the dose would have to be very, very high. It's not too big a deal. A doctor may wonder why I didn't get sick from it, but average MDs study natural poisons very little. They'd figure I was lucky that not enough poison entered my system to do real harm.

Romeo made his way to me. He looked down almost sweetly and then abruptly turned irritated when the medic tossed the large piece of pants material on the ground with the sock.

"Those are my pants," his words were an indignant accusation. "They're new."

"You didn't mind it when I wore your boxers and tank top," I said, stamping my left foot into the dirt. "If you'd clean out a drawer for me, I'd leave clothes at your apartment so I wouldn't have to steal from your closet."

"I don't want your girl shit in my apartment."

"You are twelve years old!" I nearly jumped in place. "You have arrested development at twelve fucking years old."

"Lieutenant," hollered the woman at my feet. I stared down at her. When she didn't say anything, I raised my eyebrows. "I need you to be seated. I need to stop the blood."

I didn't even know I was standing. This is what he does to me. Lord Galen was listening along with everyone else, and I felt absolutely stupid. I flopped down on the metal bench, wishing Romeo would leave.

"Just because your daddy kicked your ass tonight doesn't mean you can be a nasty prick to me."

There were a few murmured "uh-ohs" from the close crowd of soldiers. The muscle in Romeo's jaw ticked. He started for the pathway where the vampire was still dead on the ground. He turned to Livi, who watched him with the full weight of her large eyes. He dropped his angry gaze to the ground and walked away.

I slumped against the back of the bench. I wasn't in the mood for his shit. I felt vulnerable. The fearful feelings you get when you realize you did escape death, but only by the grace of the gods, or because the bad guy wanted you alive. Either way, it was unnerving how out of control it all was. I ran my fingers through my hair and wanted to throw up. Okay, I didn't want to, but I was completely nauseous. My heart rate was up. I was sweating. My body was about to get rid of the wolfsbane, and not in a pretty way.

The medic looked at me.

"You're too pale. I want to take you to the ambulance so you can lie down. Get blood to the heart. I'll finish this in there."

"What's your name?" I asked.

"Shannon."

"I feel sick, Shannon." My chest trembled when I let out my breath.

"It's the blood loss. It happens. If we go to the ambulance, you'll begin to feel better."

"No, I mean sick, sick."

I turned my head to the side and vomited on the empty half of the bench. My stomach heaved three times before I could take a breath. I gripped my fingers around the seat while my stomach convulsed, pushing out what was once my dinner and the poison that had settled with it. I spit the bitterness in a harsh burst through the connected leaves of the metal bench. When I was completely through, I wiped my mouth on the shoulder of Romeo's shirt. I took entirely too much pleasure from that petty act.

"Get me a blanket and some water over here," Shannon called out. "You're definitely in shock. We need to get you to a hospital."

The thought of water made my stomach flop around. A man with two short pink ponytails trotted up with a bottle of water and a blue blanket that he wrapped around my shoulders.

"Thank you, Dustin," Shannon said without looking up from her work. "You need to go to the hospital."

"I'm not going," I shook my head.

"You're going into shock. We need to monitor you. You need to have intravenous fluids."

"I'll be fine."

Shannon sighed. She looked at Dustin, who shrugged.

"I'm nearly positive this arrow didn't hit anything vital, simply because there's not that much blood."

I looked at the red sock on the ground. It looked like a lot of blood to me.

"You can move your foot, your toes, and your ankle without pain. It seems to have just speared the meat. You can even stand without a problem, but it should be x-rayed before we do anything else. You need a few shots to stop infection and —"

"Just cut it," I said. I didn't want to deal with the effects of the poison any longer. If she removed it, it would bleed more, and some of the aconite would go with it.

"I can't. If you bleed anymore we risk you passing out. You need better medical attention than I can provide here."

"You don't need a hospital to cut an arrow in half," I said, knowing that if the arrow were tested while I was in the hospital and they found the toxin, they wouldn't let me leave before subjecting me to tests. "I'm fine. Just do it here."

She frowned and then, strangely, looked back to Lord Galen, who was listening. He nodded to go ahead. She looked back at me, slightly confused.

"Before I continue, do you want something for the pain?"

"No."

"Oh, kay."

She dug in her bag for the instruments she'd need. She put on a fresh pair of gloves before she snipped the back end of the slim arrow with a pair of silver metal cutter type scissors. With long tweezers, she placed it in a small container, sealed, and labeled it. I could feel someone hovering nearby, so I kept my head down. I didn't want to talk. It was probably Romeo, and I definitely didn't want to talk to him. I held the bottle of water with both hands as Shannon pulled the rest of the arrow out of my leg. Blood glugged from the hole without much pain.

"You okay?"

"Fine," I said and stopped her when she tried to put a bandage against my leg to quell the bleeding. She looked at me as if I were mad, before she dropped the rest of the arrow into another container. She pushed my hand away and sprayed my leg with something that burned like hell. I jerked back in reflex and nearly punched her in the head.

"You have to go to the hospital and get stitches. It's only a few minutes away."

"I'm not going."

She sighed and finished wrapping my leg with a long white bandage.

"Let me get a few things to show you how to care for it." Gathering her materials and the containers with the arrow, she walked up the pathway.

Waves of that awful sickness washed over me again. I had a sudden thought that there was too much poison on that arrow for my body to handle. I sure hoped that wasn't true. I was about to lie down on the bench when someone walked up to me. I wasn't in the mood for conversation, so I looked at the shoes to see who it was. The boots weren't military issue. They were dark blue velvet, embroidered with a gold paisley pattern. They were pointy—very pointy. Romeo would die before he wore boots like that. My eyes drifted up. The rest of the presentation was no less impressive. Dark blue pants fit snug over slender legs. Matching blue coattails fell to the bend of the knee. Wide gold French cuffs matched the coat's round buttons. He had the shirt's high-standing collar turned down under the chin, and golden tassels adorned strong shoulders.

Through this pomp was King Jagen. Head vampire. The oldest. The leader of the Genesis Territories. The one with the most power. The one that scares the living shit out of me. I had no idea he was here in Philadelphia. It wasn't a pleasant surprise. It never is. His narrow face was looking down at me. He waited patiently, smiling pleasantly. His doll-like stare weighed heavy upon my head. With a start, I realized I'd never been this close to him. I hated it. I jumped up and the blanket fell off my shoulders. I positioned my arms behind my back.

"My King Jagen, I apologize. I didn't see you there."

"Obviously." His smile widened, purposefully flashing sharp white teeth. When I said the Territorian military is a lax bunch, I didn't mean Jagen or anyone around him. No one says anything stupid or nasty within a one-mile radius of his ears. No one says anything if they can help it. "You are Lieutenant Andru Weber?"

"Yes, my Lord."

He shot a glance up the path to the vampire.

"There is a discrepancy in the story I have been told. Will you help me to understand?"

"Yes."

"I am told you shot that vampire to death."

"Yes."

I was trying for professional, but I was lightheaded and struggled to stay on my feet. I couldn't control how hard my body was shaking. Jagen's voice is heavy, but not course. A raspy whisper, pleasant to the ears, meant to entice and at the same time threaten. He revels in his supreme title, relishing every perk that comes with being the ultimate vampire leader—having others grovel is one of his favorites. Most people think he's charming. I've yet to realize that side of him. Maybe I don't want to. I see a power-lusting, self-centered dictator that elicits pleasureless chills along my spine. I liken him to a hungry wraith waiting for you to weaken so he can devour your essence whole. Of course, I have no reasons for those feelings. Everyone in the world has their own theory about the life he and the other lords have led, but never have our leaders done such things in my presence.

"I am wondering why you would kill our only probable association to terrorists," he said. "Our policy is to take criminals alive. Have we changed that?"

He looked at me. An arm bent over his stomach, while the other held his pointed chin. His white hair clung to the near end of his velvet coat. He narrowed his white eyebrows over the most frigid blue eyes.

"Well?"

I kept my mind empty, which was the easy part, but I couldn't meet his eyes. It wasn't because of the lying, but because of a deep-rooted instinct for survival.

"No, King, that hasn't changed. She … she was gaining strength. She threatened to overpower me. I had no cuffs to bind her, and she—"

"You are telling me you were afraid of a vampire with gaping, bleeding holes all over her body?"

"Yes."

He stepped close enough to knock me back onto the bench. I was truly relieved I had a second off my feet. Before I could regain any sense of calm, he lowered himself in front of me. The coat's stiff velvet creaked in protest. He inhaled and then let out a long breath in my face. I caught the scent of flowers—carnations, my favorite. I've been told saints smell like flowers after death.

He cocked his head to the side. His black pupils expanded like a camera lens engulfing the entire glacier-like iris. All that was left were two black holes in a sea of glowing white marble.

"You are lying to me, lieutenant."

"Search my mind. You'll see it's the truth."

"I have." He brushed cold fingers across my forehead. "The front of your mind believes this lie. However, there is more. Something in your eyes and heart allows me to see this story is untrue. You tell me lies. So I ask again, why did you kill that girl?"

"She killed a soldier. When she tried to resist, I didn't think twice about using force to contain her."

I wasn't lying about that, but I wasn't calm. He made me feel like he knew the secrets of my soul, and by the gods, I had plenty.

"Must I pry open your mind?" he asked, gripping my jaw tightly with his bony fingers.

I tried to say no, but there were sudden, painful stabs inside my head, as if a pencil dug into a raw wound. The hurt ran down my spine and then splintered out along my nerves. My ears ached. Tears dripped quickly down my face from the building pressure, but I couldn't scream. I was paralyzed.

Lord Galen stepped beside him.

"She has answered your questions, Father. Stop terrorizing her," Galen spoke softly. His voice flowed over me. The energy was smooth and strong enough to push aside the magik surrounding me. When Jagen's hold popped, I cried out in agony and relief.

"Am I a terror?" asked Jagen. "I am protecting myself and all my subjects from a potential criminal within the system."

"You asked," Galen said. "She answered. Let it be."

"Apologize," said Jagen, and I wasn't exactly sure who he was talking to.

"My King?"

"Apologize for what you did, lieutenant."

I almost let out a cry of relief. If apologizing would end this nightmare and he would leave me alone, I would gladly say it. I took a breath and opened my mouth, but nothing came out. My torso tightened. It compressed against itself. I couldn't say a word. I couldn't draw in air. My chest was so very heavy, as though a ton of bricks was suddenly inside me. Spasms of pain surrounded my heart. A simmering pressure burned inside my body. Small piteous noises came from my throat and I grabbed at my chest, trying to suck in just an ounce of air. Jagen stayed close, staring into my face.

My body shook. Whatever bravado I had possessed crumbled like dried, burnt leaves. With bulging eyes, I pleaded with him. I clutched the long lapels on his wonderful coat, twisting the soft material in my fists.

"This is not your place!" Lord Galen said as he crouched beside him. His protest drifted to a clipped guttural language I didn't understand, though I understood the pleading tone well enough.

"Would she have apologized if she had not lied?" Jagen jerked up and away from me. I fell. My knees banged hard against the brick when his coat ripped from my clenched fingers.

"Would she argue with you?" asked Galen, and I could hear the panic in his voice. "Who in their right mind would argue with you?"

My eyes pleaded with Lord Jagen's unforgiving stare, that nasty piece of carved marble, so like life only dead behind the eyes. Galen stood. I felt his strength pushing around me with no more effect than hot air. Livi and Romeo were suddenly at my sides, holding me upright. Not a muscle in my chest would work. My lungs, everything in my body was as solid as concrete. My chest was so rigid I thought it was going to crack in on itself. I felt the blood collecting around my eyes.

Romeo grabbed my shoulders. I opened my mouth wide, more desperate than I was the moment before, and the moment before that. My life was hopelessly slipping away, and I couldn't do anything to stop it. Thick white fuzz clouded my vision. I was suffocating, truly suffocating.

CHAPTER ELEVEN

ROMEO'S VOICE ECHOED AS if he were talking in a tunnel. I cringed. Did Jagen kill him too? Would I have to put up with him in the afterlife as well? I reached a sore hand up to touch my face and hit something hard. I pulled at the oxygen mask so I could breath — well no, because I was frustrated and wanted the thing off my face. I heard a noise like someone hissing as the automatic blood pressure cuff tightened around my arm. Small white shelves let me know I was in an ambulance. They have ambulances in the afterlife?

Something warm touched my leg. I jumped and immediately groaned in pain. I slowly propped my aching body on my elbows to see Shannon putting yellow tape around a new bandage on my calf.

"I fixed you up while you were unconscious." She pointed to an x-ray hanging on a light board on the side of the van. "Your partner called for the x-ray ambulance. It showed up fifteen minutes ago. You have no splintered bones or anything more gory than a couple of holes in your leg. There wasn't any toxin on the arrow, but I still put a decontaminating spray on the wound. It has to set for twenty-four hours, so don't get it wet."

Nothing on the arrow? I didn't have the energy to care about that now.

"I mean it," Shannon wagged a finger at me. "Don't get it wet."

I nodded.

"Don't be alarmed at the dried blood around your ears."

I hadn't been alarmed. I hadn't even known. My hand flew to my ears. The skin on my jaw and neck felt dirty, tacky. My fingers were tinged red.

"The pressure of whatever King Jagen did to you burst your eardrums. Lord Galen healed you. Somehow." She shrugged. "I'm going to get instructions on how you can take care of this wound and when you should go to the hospital for a check-up."

She walked around the open ambulance door and out of sight. Romeo came from where Shannon left and jumped in the van. He patted my side for me to move and then sat on the small space of stretcher.

"How do you feel?" he asked, taking my hand so he could bite the ends of my fingers.

Like shit, I answered silently. *Is he still here?*

"No." He shook his head. "What were you thinking?"

I didn't lie.

"Dru ..." He pushed out an angry sigh. "You're such a punk." He played with my hand, rubbing the backs of my fingers against his lips. He shook his head. "You scare me sometimes. You think you're a badass, and you're just not."

I turned my hand in his and gently touched his healed nose. I moved my fingers to the wounds on his chest that now looked like healing pink scratches.

"Daddy's not mad anymore?"

"He had more important things to worry about than making me suffer."

With that, I slapped my left hand around his wrist for support, and with all my might, I punched him in his side. I let go of his wrist as he slid into some air canisters against the side of the vehicle. I cried out from the intense pain all over my body. I grabbed at everything and comforted nothing.

"What the hell was that for?" Romeo asked, clutching his side.

"For earlier," I said and started to cry. "For you being you." He had the decency to look ashamed while I massaged my burning throat. "And for not helping me out there."

"I did! I did what I could." He scrubbed at his head. "I tried to make you pass out."

"Why the hell would you do that?"

"I didn't want you to suffer."

"You mean you couldn't watch me suffer."

"What's the difference?"

"The difference is, you fu—"

"Stop fighting." Lord Galen walked to the open ambulance doors. "Give us all some peace." He smacked my booted foot off the stretcher, hurting my muscles everywhere. "I have told you before to keep your hands and your feet to yourself, lieutenant. Am I clear?"

I felt like a total moron. It didn't help that I had to untangle myself from the oxygen mask. Livi staggered to us and bumped into Lord Galen. She gave him a quick glance before she took a small piece of his shirt between her thumb and index finger.

"Nice material," she said.

She gave him a big smile, and he gave her one right back. I think he was so taken by her attitude that he didn't realize how amused he truly was. Livi stumbled to the first step on the back of the vehicle. She sat on her knees and leaned her arms on the bottom of the stretcher near my feet. Her eyes were glazed over, lids half closed. "How are ya?"

"Fine." I looked at Romeo and nodded my head in her direction. "What's her deal?"

"She complained about the pain, so they gave her some drugs. I think they gave her more than they should have."

"I took an extra pill when the nurse wasn't looking," Livi smiled. She turned abruptly, almost falling off the step. "Romeo, Romeo, love of my life. My sweetheart, I'm so tired."

I've never seen Lord Galen look so happy. A sweet smile curved his lips, and Romeo's too, as they watched her sway back and forth. Why do guys like to see women drugged and vulnerable? I guess that's a stupid question.

"Hey, Dru, remember that time when you dared Romeo to cross state lines?"

"No!" Romeo barked.

"You remember, Dru," she said, looking at him as if he were insane. "You wanted those candies and told him you'd show him your—"

"No, Alivia," said Romeo. "No one remembers that, because it didn't happen."

I looked at Galen slyly. He leaned his shoulder against the ambulance door, ready to be irritatingly entertained by the drug-induced confessions of a woman who knew too much.

"Oh, oh, or the time—"

"I don't remember, Livi," I practically jumped down her throat.

"You know I love you a lot," she said after turning to Romeo. "You're gorgeous and you're … Italian. Do you know why Italians are dark?" She winked, or tried to, and rubbed the skin of her arm. Romeo opened his mouth, but she cut him off. "Do you think you could take me home and put me to bed?"

Lord Galen made a small sound that I think was actual laughter.

"You wonder why I hang around with these people?" Romeo said to Galen as he left the ambulance. He smiled at Livi. "So you love me, huh?"

She swayed and then slammed her hands into Romeo's chest. Taken off guard, he stumbled back against Galen, who caught his balance. She punched Romeo, and he growled in her direction.

"That's for being such an asshole and for trying to kill her!" Then she burst into tears.

Romeo sighed and rubbed his jaw. I didn't think she hurt him physically—maybe just his pride.

"I am thinking that you keep their company because you like to be hit," Galen said.

"You wonder why he's friends with us?" I asked, a tiny bit annoyed and hurt.

"That is … out of context," Galen said, looking startled and a little embarrassed. "I—"

"Let's go home," Romeo said, moving toward Alivia. He looked at me. "I'll come back for you?"

"No," said Galen.

I immediately began to fidget. I should've known this wasn't over. Romeo stared at me. He made it clear that he'd ignore Galen and would do whatever I wanted. This sentiment wasn't lost on Galen, if his expression was any indication. However, after what happened, I wasn't going to argue even if Romeo was on my side. It did take me a moment to make up my mind though, because for maybe the first time in my life, I was going to be alone with Galen for more than an elevator ride—and for the first time in my life, I didn't want to be.

"I'm fine. Be good, and don't take advantage."

"Moi?" He was laughing as they shuffled down the path. They didn't go far before Livi threw her arms around his neck and let him scoop her up in his.

"Does he wonder why you hang with us?" I heard Livi ask. She said something else, but they were too far for me to hear.

I timidly glanced at Lord Galen before I lay back on the stretcher. I tried to lie somehow in a position that cradled my aching everything. I had that vulnerable feeling again. I wondered why Jagen hadn't killed me. I could ask, but I was fairly sure I didn't want to go down that path just yet. The thought of it made my stomach sick. I turned my face to the side of the ambulance, toward the shelves and drawers with their clear plastic windows. I stared at gauze bandages as the heavy tears dripped sideways onto the small, square pillow under my head. I put a hand over my mouth to stop the noise, even though it didn't really work.

Lord Galen took Romeo's seat on the stretcher. He smoothed my hair, which is to say he touched the stubble at the back of my head. His touch was soft and warm like the breeze outside. That small acknowledgment made the tears flow faster. I didn't try to contain myself; it hurt to use those muscles. I curled my body away from him.

"He is a scary man," said Galen. "I believe he would have seriously hurt you had Luise and I not argued on your behalf."

I turned to face him. By his expression, I could tell he was unaware that knowing Jagen was going to kill me was information I didn't need to have confirmed. "Lord Cherkasy is here?"

"Was. She came after the vampire Teena's official death at the manor. She argued what difference it made who killed a killer. By then the reporters had arrived. She made the point that by torturing you outside in a park, he was creating a very public, very sadistic reputation for himself." He senselessly brushed his hand up my cheek to catch the tears on the side of his finger. He rubbed his fingers together, staring at the wetness with interest.

"What did you argue?"

"That you are my soldier and my cross to bear," he said, lowering his hand into his lap. "I will judge the deed, and I will decide the punishment."

I thought of Romeo when he said punishment and was instantly angry. It didn't help that he had just called me his cross to bear.

"Like you decided Romeo's?"

"You are angry with how I handled that situation?"

"You beat him," I said and pushed up on my elbows. "You broke his bones, for goddesses' sake. You had no right to do that."

"I have every right. And I will have you know he did a little beating of his own."

"He was defending himself."

"Defending inappropriate actions."

"You shouldn't have touched him until you heard the entire story."

"How do you know I did not?"

"Did you?"

"I did not need to," he practically yelled. "I still do not!"

"Of course—"

"No! He is mine, lieutenant. I felt what he did to you." His voice was changing. It wasn't so much a British accent, as is his normal, but a burr. That's what Romeo said it's called when you're from Scotland. I'd heard him talk that way before, usually when he's yelling at Romeo. Galen flattened a hand on his chest and leaned closer to me. "I felt it in my throat and in my head. I knew what he was feelin' while his mouth was on your skin. I ken what he wanted to do to ye."

His speech was as disconcerting as his tone, and I moved back, away from him.

"But you weren't there!"

His eyes widened.

"Oh, was I no'?"

"What?" I scowled at him. "What does that mean?"

He started to speak, but stopped. He frowned, then swallowed, and stared at me. I used that moment to continue my course.

"You only felt the deep-down, innate emotion."

"That is correct," he said, unnecessarily enunciating, as if he had to think on each word to get it right.

"But you're not considering who we're talking about—how much control he has and what could've happened for him to lose it. You treat him like a loose cannon, but you don't know what led to that moment. You can't punish him for doing something wrong until you know how it happened. He didn't plan to hurt me."

He made a very ungracious sound. "He never plans to, but he does it all the same."

"I pushed until he lost himself. He's usually in perfect control. You know he's a freak about it."

"You are a military officer and his partner, not a dinner table. He should not have been doing anything with you to get carried away with."

"That's not fair. We can do whatever we want. It's our business."

He snapped at me like an angry dog, and I jerked back. I'd never seen him do anything like it, and to say it was weird was an understatement.

"He knows better," he said. "I have taught him not to starve himself. Plain and simple, he is not to use you or your body in any way."

"You think Romeo uses me?"

Of all he said, those words stuck with me. It was a trick question. No answer was going to satisfy me, and he probably knew it. His eyes flicked to the faded scars on my fingers and to the fresh puncture wound on my neck. "I think he is persuasive."

"You think he uses me."

"Perhaps use is insensitive. Let us say take advantage of."

"Do I look helpless?" I asked, thinking he was trying not to upset me.

"I do not think you are helpless. A vampire can be a strong, sometimes overbearing force."

"Is Romeo the only person who doesn't think I'm a no-brainer who stumbles blindly into less than honorable situations?"

"I do not think that."

"The big bad vampire overpowers poor little Andru. He persuades the frightened female to do nasty things behind closed doors."

"I do not—"

"Because if you do, you're very wrong."

"Andru, I do not believe you stumble anywhere."

"Yes, you do. You just said so. Maybe not in so many words, but still." I struggled to sit up, bending my good leg and keeping the injured one straight. He put up his hand to help, but being the non-stumbler that I am, I ignored it. "Let me tell you what happened. I wanted him to touch me, and I wanted him to bite me. I wanted it so badly —"

"That he abused your need."

"No. He didn't question me. He gave me what I wanted."

"If I had not ..." he began then restarted. "If he had hurt you, if your sadistic game turned unpleasant—more unpleasant—and he hurt you so badly you died, or worse, he converted you without your consent, would you be so righteous?"

"I wouldn't blame him for an accident that happened while doing something with my complete consent. I know the hazards of a vampire going down on me. I'm not a child."

He quickly looked away from me as if he were embarrassed to hear me say such a thing. Maybe he was angry to hear me say it. He ran his hand over his mouth and chin, and then through his hair. He was like a ball of energy with no place to fall.

"You are impulsive, lieutenant. I do not like it."

"I'm not as impulsive as you think. I make my decisions, even quick ones, in direct contact with my brain waves. I wouldn't have let him touch me if I didn't want him to."

He sat quietly. He opened his mouth, but the air was left empty, and I had a sudden thought.

"I'm not using Romeo, if that's what you think. I'm not trying to push him to convert me and then claim it was an accident, or that he did it on purpose, and then try to get benefits from Crime and Retribution. I don't want to be a vampire."

He looked as if I'd hurt, or offended him. He shook his head to stop my apology. He seemed distant now, almost miserable.

"You tease him."

"We play."

"Your psychological games will ruin you both."

I stared at him. I wanted to understand the man as well as the general. Only, it would never happen — because he's also a vampire, and being a vampire means he's complicated to the tenth degree.

"You and he are together then, yes? In love?"

His tone was very matter of fact. Of all the things I imagined he was thinking, whether Romeo and I were a couple wasn't one of them. The fact that recently I've wondered the same thing made the question all the more uneasy.

"Yes. No. I mean, yes, I care for him. Must I be in love with him to seduce him? Would it have made a difference? Would his punishment have been less severe if we were a couple or it wasn't about blind lust?"

He smiled, but it wasn't happy.

"With a vampire, lieutenant, it is always about lust, in one form or another."

"All I'm saying is what you did to him was cruel and humiliating."

"I got carried away," he finally said. "Romeo has a way of pushing me to lunacy's doorstep."

"Like I push him?"

"By the end, we were not even fighting about this particular incident."

"Oh." I carefully maneuvered myself to a sitting position with my feet on the floor. "I wasn't prepared for you to agree with me. I have plenty of argument left."

"Not you."

I frowned and smiled nearly at the same time.

"I used to believe it was Romeo who provoked your arguments and kept them going. I think I was wrong. I am thinking I was wrong about many things concerning the two of you."

Those bleached eyes were less than two feet away and had me wondering if he'd done something horrible to someone he cared about. Was he trying to stop Romeo from doing the same? The silence grew. The night's warm air suddenly felt awkward. I became aware that he was staring, and that I must look terrible. With the tears and dirty hair, and my face smeared with blood, I couldn't be a pretty picture.

"Oh, umm, thanks for the ear thing. That's a neat trick."

"One I trust you will not need again."

I washed my hands roughly over my face, wiping the red grit onto my pants. I found it difficult to think of any words to continue our conversation. Vanity will do that.

"You look fine," he said. His fingers lightly touched underneath my chin. "Sincerely."

I concentrated on anything but the fact that we were so close that I could reach out and touch him without fully extending my arm. He smoothed my cheek, speaking low in the cramped vehicle. "It upset me that he hurt you."

When he says stuff like that, my insides get all discombobulated. My brain doesn't work when he stares with such intensity. "He who? He Jagen?"

"No. I did not want him to hurt you either, but I meant Romeo."

"Oh. I'm fine. We sort of do that to each other."

"You hurt each other?"

"No," I laughed. "I meant we get under each other's skin, and it probably looks worse to other people than it truly is."

He nodded.

"You scared me tonight. The arrow, shock sickness, and Jagen … I was afraid for you."

"Oh well …" I was uncomfortable with this level of intimacy from him. It was nauseating. I pulled back a little, looking anywhere but at his face. "I'm okay."

"Yes. I see that." He pinched the loose pants material at my knee. He pulled it gently to get my attention. "Will you tell me why you lied tonight?"

My eyes snapped wide. If I'd had a mouthful of drink, I'd have spit it out. I was unusually shaken. Probably from being awake for nearly twenty-two hours, recovering from attempted murder — twice — and maybe because I wasn't used to being this close to the object of my desire.

"I didn't," I said so low the words got lost in the air.

He forced me to look at him by holding my jaw, the way Jagen had earlier, but unlike Jagen, he was gentle. His hand was warm. His touch made my heart beat faster.

"You are lying, and I think I know why, but I want you to say it."

"Are you going to pull apart my mind?" The tears caught in my throat.

"I asked. It is your decision to answer."

"He's a soldier — a nobody to Jagen. He would've killed Jefrey because he was grief-stricken and lost control. It's not fair."

"Is what is 'fair' for you to decide?"

"No, but she killed his partner. I would've done the same. I wouldn't have cared about the rules."

Galen nodded and let go of my face.

"What will you do to Jefrey?"

"I will talk to him."

I let that go. I had already done all the saving I was willing to do for a long time.

"What will you do to me?"

"I will take you home," he said, cocking his head.

"And beat me up there?" I couldn't keep the panic out of my voice.

He laughed, not loud, but abruptly.

"I have no intentions of touching you in a hurtful way."

"I heard you didn't touch Romeo, so is that a clever play on words?"

"Perhaps ... but not for punishment. Near suffocation is reprimand enough."

Before his words had a chance to soak into my brain, Shannon tossed a box filled with my boot and medication onto the end of the stretcher. She had an e-clipboard under her arm. I could see the red glow of the screen I was to sign. She handed me a clear vial of pink pills from the box and told me to take one every twelve hours — or twelve every hour. I nodded. She gave me another pill container with big white pills and said something about infection. I nodded again.

"Are you going to take those pills?"

"No," I answered, looking at her and then Galen.

"Were you even listening to me?" she frowned and huffed at once.

"I don't take medication," I shrugged.

"Oh," she said. "Not even recreational?"

While it is true marijuana has been legal in the States since 2021, legal here since 2016, not everyone smokes or uses. "I do. I have. But not normally."

There was no way to tell her that I can't do those things because I can never let my inhibitions get too low for fear I may start blabbing about my other self.

"The pain may well outweigh the medication not being your thing. If you don't need it, don't use it. Take it home in case the pain gets bad. There shouldn't be infection, but it's an open wound. You may need something strong for the aching and itching as the healing progresses. The arrow was very narrow. I don't think you'll need stitches, but you may want to get a second opinion. Sign here to acknowledge that you were treated and released."

Shannon tapped the face of the clipboard with a stylus she pulled from the side of the unit. I signed next to her signature. She tapped it again, and a small disc ejected from the side of the clipboard. In red marker, she wrote the date and her name across the side.

"There's a phone number for questions on the disc, along with instructions on how to care for the wound."

Reaching into her jacket, she pulled out a thick, square bandage and some extra gauze. She threw them both into the box.

"I'm good. You can save that for someone else."

"Are you trying to make this difficult for me?"

"Not at all," I said, surprised.

"She can try nerves of steel," said Galen.

"I can't," I said.

"Just take the patch. It's not a big deal. I have hundreds."

I gave in, truly not wanting to be a pain in the ass.

"Do you have a way to get home?" she asked. "Because you can't walk on that leg."

"I will take her," said Galen.

"Good. I hope I don't see you in the E.R. in the next few weeks with some senseless infection. Take the medicine."

I smiled, but not fully. I appreciated her help — sort of. Shannon patted my leg one last time and looked at General Galen reverently before giving a small bow. She walked to an area along the path where her equipment made a pile and started to pack it away.

I turned to him. "My Lord—"

"Do not call me that," he said, waving a hand.

"What should I call you?"

"My name."

"I should call you my name?" I joked.

"Your name?" He frowned. "What?"

"Never mind. I can't say your name. It sounds odd to me."

"You think my name is odd?"

"No," I smiled. "Calling you your name is odd. You're my general."

"Galen is a name like any other."

"Not like mine."

"Are you not fond of your name?"

"It's not that. Whenever I meet someone, they say, 'Andru, that's a boy's name.' As if I had no idea. It's annoying."

He nodded. "Then why not introduce yourself as Anastasia?"

"Because my first name isn't Anastasia. It's Anastasia Druc—"

I stopped myself. I couldn't believe I was about to tell a vampire my full given name. I could never give someone that kind of power over me. My parents gave me three names, Anastasia Drucilla Ekaterina, and yet no middle name. My mother didn't believe in them. She said your name should be long and then abbreviated, or you're given a nickname so no one knows the truth of it. She was born on the West Coast in the States to parents who had immigrated to North America three years before she was born. They instilled rich Russian, highly pagan folklore into my mother's upbringing, and she was a good witch, if a little paranoid. Galen waited patiently for me to finish.

"Well, it's uh … I mean, it's a bit formal. My brothers gave me the nickname Andru."

"Names have changed so much. I doubt I consider anything too odd. Besides, I like Andru. I like the sobriquet."

"The what?"

"I enjoy its history."

"What do you know about my history?"

He climbed out of the ambulance, peering thoughtfully around the park. He pushed his sleeves up a bit higher and then nonchalantly shoved a few strands of hair behind his ear.

"How should we get you home then?"

Avoidance is an art.

"I haven't a clue. You can't carry me the entire way."

"I can." His eyebrows rose high over his eyes. He smiled as if to say what a great idea.

"No. I'm telling you that you can't. That's ridiculous. I'd rather walk."

He let out a long intentional breath to say I make his life so very difficult.

"I will take you by car. Would that be satisfying?"

"Yes, it would."

❀ ❀ ❀

WITH NOTHING TO FOCUS on, my mind began to collapse. My body ached as if I had been clubbed. My stomach was sick. Everything had happened in such a whirlwind that I couldn't quite comprehend how I had gotten to this moment. The entire day had been shit. The fight at work. Romeo's bite. The fanatical vampire. The lying. Fighting with Romeo in front of people, and then the altercation with King Jagen. Suddenly, my life felt very out of control. I knew I could never let myself be that close to Jagen again. He would kill me out of spite, even if I'm not a full faerie. Romeo told me this on many occasions. I rubbed my tired eyes. I took a few deep breaths to calm myself, and I could feel the tears close again.

"Lieutenant Weber."

I jumped and nearly wobbled off the stretcher. A tall man with cropped dirty blond hair was standing at the back entrance of the ambulance. His brown eyes were wide. His uniform was pressed and tidy.

"Jesus, I'm sorry. I didn't mean to scare you. Lord Galen wanted me to tell you that there's a situation. He's needed and will be a few minutes; you should wait for him."

"Fine," my voice was hoarse. It seemed foreign to me. I was so damn tired.

The man smiled before turning toward the horses on the path. He untied the reigns from the trees that they were secured to. Teena's horse leaned into his chest when he stroked its head. He whispered things to the animal and then guided the pair up the path.

It took me all of two minutes to realize I wasn't going to wait for Galen. I was over-tired and antsy. I took my boot from the box Shannon gave me and gently put it on. It wasn't high enough to touch the wound, and the leather kept my ankle secure, which made it feel better as I started up the pathway. I didn't look back to see if Galen was close, nor did I want any of the medical staff to notice I was leaving. I figured if I didn't see them, then they wouldn't see me. I walked normally, as normally as I could with a hole in my leg and my pant leg ripped to the knee. I kept a quiet, even pace until I was out of sight. On the outside of the park at the street intersection, I leaned against the light post. My leg was throbbing. The warm air made my stomach feel as if it were full of curdled milk. I questioned my judgment in not waiting for Lord Galen, but only slightly. When the light turned green, I crossed the street. I walked with more of a limp and favored my right leg as I made my way farther from the others, confident no one had seen me.

I had six long blocks to walk before I was home. The pulsing in my leg had me seriously doubting that I was going to make it. The second time I stopped was on the front steps of a doctor's office. Resting my forearms on my thighs, I stared at the ground. I let my head hang as if I'd be sick at any moment. It was truer than I wanted it to be. I felt a tug on my hair and waved a tired hand over my head. The tug came again. I swore softly, but deliberately and harshly. When a small faerie replaced my view of concrete steps, I swore again.

"Go home, Tweek," I said. "It's not safe."

She hovered near my hands, staring at me in disapproval. The diminutive, bright faerie hardly looked like Tinker Bell. If she paused long enough for a human to see her properly, they would run away. Though Tweek is of the light class of fey, she doesn't look like what most humans perceive a faerie to be. She's more a dragonfly with an elongated neck. She can use her arms a bit more dexterously, but her legs hang strangely off the sides of her body. She can look very human if she chooses, but she would still only be four inches tall.

"Go away. You shouldn't be here."

Tweek and her mate Pip visit me often, usually in the relative safety of my home. She doesn't give off enough paranormal power for any vampire to feel. At least Romeo never seems to notice her, but I still don't like it when they follow me away from home.

She flew close to my face, and because I was in a bad mood, I snatched her up like catching a fly in the air. She bit my palm, and I threw open my hand as if I were tossing dice. She tumbled around the air before catching her balance. Buzzing quickly to my ear, she bit me again. I was too tired to care about any of it. I closed my eyes, and a few tears dripped onto the steps. I felt small feet settle on my hands as they dangled between my legs. When I opened my eyes I saw that Tweek's upper wing on the left side was bent at the top. One of the problems with being of the dark breed of faerie is that I can lose my temper far too quickly. I sometimes use aggression when gentility would serve me better.

In my remorse, I remembered that Tweek's venom is a bit euphoric. Biting was her way of helping; my pain was an undesired byproduct of the biting. I couldn't be angry when she was only trying to make me feel better.

"Sorry," I muttered.

I stood and stretched, forcing the faerie back into the air. The ache in my leg was slightly more numb than painful. I was glad for it, and walked on without another stop to Old Clementine Lane. I turned down the wide, tree-lined street. Four overhead lamps hollowed out the darkness from one end to the other. At 1005, I turned onto the curved stone trail cutting its way through our front lawn. Tweek zipped down the sides of the path. She hovered in the lilac bushes straddling the front steps. Most flower faeries don't give off enough energy to attract attention, and I do enjoy the aroma of flowers, but Livi thinks both the front and back gardens are unruly. She doesn't like it because the fey play tricks on her when she goes out to cut the flowers back. Last summer while she tidied up, they kept replacing the weeds she had pulled. You couldn't see the faeries; one minute she would pull a weed and the next it was back. Dacon and I thought it was very funny. Livi had another word to describe it.

Besides Tweek flitting around, the garden was asleep. Except at the corner of the house near the pink lilacs, I noticed a flattened circle of grass with a surrounding ring of uneven mushrooms. It was a faerie ring. Normally, they're no big deal, but I can't have one on my front lawn, at least not in plain sight. I held the wrought iron railing while I scraped my boot through the charming oddity. I looked into the tree hovering over my front lawn.

"Don't do rings," I whispered. "I told you before. No rings."

It dawned on me that there might be someone watching this freakish display. I stopped and headed up the steps to the front door.

CHAPTER TWELVE

THE WIDE DOOR WAS slightly ajar, so I had only to push it the rest of the way. The familiar yet slightly unmixed scents of basil, sweet thyme, and heather filled my senses. I entered the living room and tried to swing my backpack off my shoulder and onto the floor underneath the bow window as I do every day. I couldn't do it. I'd left the damn thing in the park. I wasn't worried, just pissed because it'd be taken to headquarters, and I wouldn't have my keys or vid-set until I got back to work.

The fireplace crackled. The dark gray stone was aglow, casting eerily dancing shadows on the mottled green carpet. It was pleasant, considering it was about eighty-five degrees outside and the room conditioning unit was on. Nevertheless, Alivia loves a roaring fire. I'm very sure she sweet-talked Romeo into making it, because fire isn't something any vampires want to play with on their own.

The cauldron that normally hung inside the fireplace was off to the side. Cold red alder ash from the ritual house cleansing I'd performed a few weeks ago filled it. Burning herbs to cleanse my aura seemed like a good idea until I looked at the mantle. Dried herbs and half-burned candles cluttered it from one end to the other. Some had so much wax covering the holder that I couldn't move them. I sighed at the muddle of lighting sticks, small stones, and unpolished crystals that Livi keeps asking me to neaten up. I knew my athame was somewhere up there, but the mere thought of sifting through the mess for a knife and a handful of herbs irritated me.

Romeo was on the couch against the stairway wall. He was on the far end near the kitchen reading his palm computer in the dark. Livi was asleep, sprawled the length of the sofa with her head resting on his lap. I limped to the kitchen and using a chair for support, I searched the cabinet next to the refrigerator for a bag of cayenne pepper for the bleeding wound and a small bottle of comfrey leaf tincture for tissue damage. The taste of aconite had turned my stomach again, and my own retching disgusted me. I rinsed my mouth thoroughly before I headed back to the living room. Romeo looked up.

"How is she?" I asked.

"Out to lunch. You?"

"I've been so much better." I leaned against the doorframe. "And I have to make honey bandages."

"Honey bandages?"

"Sterile bandages dipped in honey to put over the wound after I clean it."

"I know what it is," he rolled his eyes. "I've seen you do it a bunch of times. And you want to do that now?"

"I have to make it fresh."

He raised his brows as if to further question my motives.

"My leg is sore. It's an anti-inflammatory. Will you help me?"

"No," he said as he looked at my leg, "it looks fine." Then he looked at my face. "You, however, look like you need to lie down."

"I really do."

"I called Dacon. He was going to come over and tend to his precious Nastya, but I told him I'd stay with you girls."

I frowned at that. I would've rather had Dacon take care of me. He'd probably stay the night, and we wouldn't fight, which is more than likely with the vampire. Romeo smiled. I was too tired to care if he purposely read my thoughts or that I was too mentally depleted to keep him out.

"How was your time with Galen?"

"What?"

"About forty minutes ago, the hair on my arms stood at attention. I felt the familiar brand of anger he serves only to you. I guessed you opened your mouth and pissed him off."

I didn't hear what he'd said—not really. He reached over and took my hand. He tried to guide me to sit on the floor in front of him. His presence was thought-provoking, and I hated that. I pulled my hand out of his, knowing it wasn't a good thing to let Romeo comfort me. He kept a small smile but stayed very still, with the calm and patience only the vampire possess. My hand tingled. I liked it. My body was demanding some kind of closeness. The fact that he's handsome made my knees weak. The fact that he's a vampire made me want to go crazy—show him the wildness of the faerie. The pang of blood seeped over my tongue from the small hole I had reopened on the inside of my cheek. I wondered if he could smell it.

"Tried to bite your dad, huh? Got a face full of fist, did you?"

His smile faded. Agitation poured into him, and I was happy about it. The farther from me he was, the better we'd both be.

"I'm going to clean up and go to bed. Would you put her in her room?"

"She can stay here," he said, still staring at me without blinking, an edge in his voice that was not there a moment ago.

"Take her up, please. She doesn't like to wake up on the sofa."

He passed me to climb the steps with Alivia gathered in his arms. I limped behind. The graceful Romeo and his pathetic, yet oh so faithful partner Anastasia. He tapped the first door he came to with his foot and then disappeared into the blackness with Livi's limp body. I leaned a hand on the wall for support. I passed the guest room and bathroom for the last door on the right. I stumbled to my bed in darkness. I switched on the small lamp resting on my night table and pulled a cloth from the top drawer to clean the blood and dirt off my gun and holster. The gun needed a thorough cleaning before debris collected and caused problems, but it would have to wait.

I took off my boots and hurt my leg twice taking off Romeo's pants. In frustration, I threw them and his underwear in the trash can by the door. The underwear wasn't ripped, but it smelled like panic and desperation. Maybe the odor was ordinary dirt and sweat, and the desperation was my own unobjective interpretation. I was too exhausted to think clearly, and they were Romeo's, so I didn't care.

I shuffled across the floor to an altar standing in the east corner—a three-quarter inch round table of ash wood with solid oak legs. Dacon handmade it for me about ten years ago when we moved back to the Territories after my brother's twins were born—after I gave birth to them. Willow, my brother Max's wife, needed to have a hysterectomy, through medical necessity, at a very young age. After months of counseling, they asked if I'd be a surrogate. Dacon and I moved to Colorado, in the States, where Willow's doctor had relocated his practice. Twelve months later, they were parents of twins. Easy peasy. Actually not so easy, and it was far from peasy. I wear the scar from the emergency caesarian. However, the check they gave me nearly paid for my half of this house, so I'm not complaining.

I knelt in front of the altar and lit a white candle for protection. After a moment's debate, I decided against the red. Red is for courage, which I needed. It also enhances sexuality, and I really didn't need any more of that. Not with Romeo down the hall. I set the white candle in the middle of the altar on a round piece of glass marked with a pentacle, the sacred representation of the elements and spirit. I squeezed my fingers around an oblong chunk of fire agate I picked from a box underneath the table. I needed its powers of protection and calming. I needed it to ground me. Probably another witch in my position would use iron, but iron and faeries don't mix. Iron can be fatal to a true faerie, so I stay away from it when I can.

I bowed my head and thanked the ancient god, Jupiter, for his protection, and for helping me keep my wits about me when faced with the female vampire. Of course, I didn't think Jupiter would be happy that I lied to the leader of my country, so I thanked the Celtic goddess Mene for my life. I figured she would understand.

I limped to the bathroom, where I lit a myrrh candle perched on a small shelf next to the mirror. That along with a ladybug night light in the wall outlet gave enough brightness for me to see my way. I brushed through the longer hair on the top of my head, brushed my teeth, and then washed my face and neck in the sink. I glanced in the mirror. I wasn't too gross. Well … I wasn't disgusting. I relaxed on the toilet lid to relieve the pain in my leg that had started again. I was exhausted. That made it easy to ignore the fact that I hadn't gone to the bathroom in almost twenty-four hours. I didn't have to go now. I didn't want to think about my body changing. It's happened before. Small adjustments in my magik, and sometimes my appearance, like, say, eyes or hair color turning a little darker or lighter. It isn't a problem, but I didn't want to deal with it tonight.

I poked at the bandages over my cross tattoos. The stress of two showers and a dousing of tomato juice had taken its toll. I stared at my leg. I knew I should undress the wound and put on the herbs, but I didn't think I had enough bandages to redress it. I turned attention to the tub and wondered how the hell I was going to get a shower without getting my calf wet. I wiped at a small tear. I was happy to be alive, obviously, but I was embarrassed about an arrow striking me. As a military soldier, getting hit with unfriendly fire is almost as humiliating as being tortured in front of a bunch of people. True, I couldn't speak while Jagen was in my head, but the look in my eyes told everyone I was begging for my life. Desperation is an emotion no one wants to share with a crowd.

I closed my eyes and breathed deeply to stop the tears. The flat darkness under my eyelids was serene, like still waters in the storm around me, until a burst of light snapped inside my head, leaving a blanket of fear-filled shadows. A musty odor overwhelmed me. I knelt on a bed of black dirt. Frantically, I dug my hands into the earth. Screams filled the silence.

My head jerked up. I blinked at the sink in front of me. I relaxed my fingernails from doing any further damage to my thighs and brushed away the small amount of blood that welled from the crescent slits. I had no time to consider what I'd seen because Romeo passed the bathroom door. He backed up, looked at me, and blinked twice to make sure what he was seeing was accurate. I crossed my legs to cover the marks I'd made on my thigh.

"Why are you sitting in the dark—naked?"

"How am I going to get a shower and not get my leg wet?"

"You can't. You'll have to take a bath."

"I hate baths."

He smiled.

"Let your leg hang over the tub, and I'll help you." I stared up at him. "Don't get too excited," he said. "You might hurt yourself."

I crumbled then. My breathing shook and tears pricked my eyes. I couldn't help it. Romeo knelt in front of me and slid his hands up my thighs to my hips. It wasn't an excessively sexual gesture. It was Romeo being Romeo.

"Please don't cry," he said as he pulled my hands from my face. "That's all the comforting I've got for tonight, so did it work?"

I laughed through the tears. He always makes me laugh. Even in my hollow state, I was fairly intrigued at the thought of him washing my back. He affects me more every day—something I'm sure that I kind of hate.

"I mean, hell," he winked, "how lucky can you get to have escaped death twice in one night."

I held up three fingers.

"Yeah," he nodded slowly, "three times."

He rested on his knees to better sit and stare at me. His eyes were clear, bright, and focused. I liked that my blood did that to him.

"I'm sorry about earlier in the park." He caught my eyes with his. The look was deep, and it made me uncomfortable. "I don't like anyone to see me like that. Especially you."

"Why especially me? We're partners. You should come to me for help."

"It's hard to explain," he said, resting his cheek on my thigh. "I just don't like it."

"Is it a guy thing?" I smoothed my hand over his soft brown waves. "You don't want me to see you weak and powerless?"

"Something like that." He tensed, suddenly disturbed. "I wasn't weak or powerless. I was overpowered."

"Like there's a difference," I smiled.

He shoved his nose in the line of my crossed legs, inhaled, and then moved his hands around my back to pull me closer. His lips touched my breast. This was Romeo being Romeo, and it was also an overtly sexual gesture.

"You realize this is only the fourth time I've seen you completely naked?"

"I'm not counting," I said.

"I am." His muscles tensed. His skin felt warmer than a moment ago. I was now hyper-aware of how my body affected him.

"Like it?" I asked.

"You know how you make me feel."

"Insecure," I smiled. "And you hate it."

"God damn," he inhaled again. "I love the way you smell." He pulled back to look at me. "What are you ... are you teasing me again?"

"No." This was a big moment for us. Despite petting and playing, what we did earlier was only the second time we had taken things so far. "If I give you a second chance, will you go all lethal on me?"

"I can handle it," he said and pulled me into his lap.

He latched his mouth over the bite he made in his bedroom. It hurt, but it healed to a cleaner wound that wasn't as bad. Then out of the blue, or inside the pain, I thought of Galen. For a brief moment, I wondered if it was right to make love to one man while thinking of another. Then Romeo's tongue touched the inside of my mouth, and almost every thought was lost. I couldn't keep track of any one thing except that his mouth was warm and soft, and that he wanted me. I kissed him with an aggression built over four years of being alone. There have been a couple of people since Dacon, including Dacon every now and again, but we keep that to ourselves. I hadn't found anyone I wanted to be in a relationship with. To be fair, no joking at all, I didn't think it could get much better. Livi was right. I was so fucked.

Romeo's breath was hard against my face. His heart began to beat in time with mine. He grabbed the back of my head with one hand and squeezed my rear end with the other.

"Wait," I said. He didn't. He pinned me against the bathroom wall. He kissed me until I squirmed in his arms and pushed at his shoulders. "Romeo, I have to shower," I said when his mouth let me have enough air to speak. "I have someone else's blood and guts all over me."

"We've played this scene before," he said as he pulled back. "I don't think I care."

"Listen, we can take a shower together. It will only take a few minutes for me to rinse the gore out of my hair. Romeo, please."

"Fine," he hissed through gritted teeth and set me down. "But we can't get a shower together. You're not allowed to get your leg wet."

"Oh. Yeah. Okay. Go in my room and wait for me. I'll be ten minutes." He leaned his weight on one leg, like an irritated teenager. I stroked his healed chest down to his stomach. My hands settled lazily on his waist, and I dusted my fingertips across his warm skin. "Give me five minutes."

He leaned into me, took a deep breath, and then scrubbed his hands on the top of his head. "Fine."

I WAS SHOCKED THAT I wanted to have sex, but I really did. Maybe it was almost dying, or maybe it was the fact I hadn't had it in about a year. I finished cleaning up in record time. I threw my head under the spigot in the tub and quickly washed my hair. I washed the rest of me without getting into the tub and brushed my teeth again. I put fresh bandages on my crosses and then wrapped myself in a towel. I was freezing. The fire had kicked the conditioning unit into overdrive.

MY ROOM WAS ALIVE with flickering candlelight. Anywhere there's a flat surface, I grace with a candle. Romeo had lit about eight of them. All white. Most of the white are gardenia, his favorite. Golden points jumped against the heather gray walls. Shadows danced on Romeo's bare back, where he lay across my bed. He slid around until he was sitting on the edge and motioned with his fingers for me to leave the doorway. I was already shivering, and now I was shaking. This was a step I wasn't sure we should be taking. I moved between his legs, and his hands trailed up from the bottom of my towel. His fingertips slid over the scar on my lower stomach on his way to touch the rings in my belly button.

"It's ridiculous that babies came out of you."

I let the wet towel fall to my feet. Romeo's head fell against my chest. His fingers dug into my backside. He breathed deeply and kissed my skin.

"Stand up," I said. "I want to undress you."

He moved slowly. I wasn't sure if he wanted to savor the moment, or if he was afraid of it. His boots were already off, so I unbuckled his belt, unzipped his pants, and lowered them to the floor. I wrapped my arms around his bare thighs to feel the strength in his long legs, and I tossed the wet hair from my face to see his expression. He was mesmerized at the sight of me on my knees in front of him.

"This is turning out to be the strangest night," he whispered.

"I thought that too," I smiled. "Stranger than usual?"

"For sure."

He wrapped his hand under my chin and pulled me to stand. Immediately, he lifted me off my feet by the backs of my thighs. He walked out of his pants, across the room, and shoved me onto the edge of my dresser. He pushed his body against mine, pressing me so hard I had to rest my hand on the top of the dresser for leverage. His tongue was inside my mouth, as eager and ready as the rest of him. I snuck a hand between us, reached inside his boxers, and wrapped my fingers around him. I had never touched him like this. I had seen him naked, and I felt him through clothes, but never like this. His skin was soft, and he was so hard that I couldn't help but tighten my grip. His fingers tangled in my hair as he forced my head where he wanted it. He breathed heavily and my own blood scent hit me from when he drank hours ago.

He suddenly pulled back, looking at me suspiciously. It was as if he didn't know me, or was seeing me for the first time. He gets like that when he's about to lose control. The thoughts in his head are unfocused as he struggles to keep himself in this reality.

"What are you trying to do to me?" he asked as if he were just now joining our activities.

"I want to make you feel good."

He took me to the bed. His eyes were slack and excited at once. It was a very male expression, and his age and knowledge showed through. His maturity disconcerted me, took me off guard, and I felt young, almost shy. Was he thinking that this would be our first time? In nine and half years, it was our very first time. He touched between my legs. His fingertips traced the scar again.

"Why do you shave?"

"I don't—much," I said.

"Why don't I remember that?" His eyes glinted like red jewels from the candlelight. He flattened his fingers and palm against me. "I should remember that."

When he brushed his fingers across my chest, I pulled him to me. He kissed me as if he were still starving. We rolled over, and I licked my way to his waist. I bit him through the soft cotton material.

"Wait." His shaking hands gripped my arms. "Dru, wait."

I stuck my hands under the boxers.

He sighed deeply, but pushed my hands out. "W ... w ... wait. You've been through a lot today." I bit his chest until he moaned. "Oh Dru, please ... oh, hell ... I don't want you to freak." I bit the skin near his nipple until his back bowed off the bed. He wrapped his hands around my thighs, so I had to straddle him, and he pulled me closer.

"Freak?" I said against his chest.

"Oh," he pushed himself between my legs. "That feels good. No, I mean, because you made a … made a mistake. You might think I'm … um …"

"Mistake?"

I closed my mouth around his chin and gently sucked. It's an odd erogenous zone, but for Romeo, it's mind-numbingly erotic. It's so sensitive that he can't stand it. His hand gripped the back of my head—to stop me, or keep me there, I wasn't sure.

"I don't want," he slurred, eyes closed, heart pounding. "I don't want you to …"

I winced as my calf throbbed under the strain of my bent leg.

"You don't want me to what?" I slid his finger into my mouth.

"Uh … I don't know. To um, freak out. To think … to think …"

I ran my tongue up and down his finger.

"Wake up thinking … I can't … shit, will you … no, I mean … I can't concentrate."

"I don't want you to concentrate."

"And I don't want you to freak out."

I dropped his hand, beginning to understand.

"You don't want me to freak, or is it you don't want me to think you're going to sweep me off my combat boots so we can be the new super couple of Galen Manor?"

He stayed quiet.

"What's going on?"

"Nothing," he said as cautiously as if he were dealing with a rabid vampire.

"Do I look like a moron?"

"What?" His nerves caught in his throat. "Of course not. What?"

"You haven't vampired me. Is it so hard to believe that I want this? Maybe I need to have … sex." I was going to say uncomplicated sex, but Romeo is anything but that.

His eyes were wide, their natural color rushed back.

"Not now, it isn't."

My eyes narrowed, and he put his hands up to defend himself.

"I've had this discussion two other times tonight. I was sure you knew me better. I would never be stupid enough to ask you for a c-c-commitment. I don't even want one—not from you, anyway. Gimme your hand."

I gripped his wrist for support and climbed off the bed, because in that position, I just couldn't do it myself. I limped to my dresser and pulled an old red terry-cloth two-piece bathing suit from my pajama drawer.

"I'm not brainless," I said as I put on the suit. "No one uses me. Not even you."

I dropped down onto my pillow. Truth was, I didn't know if he stopped us because he thought he was overpowering me, or he just didn't want to be with me. When you've flirted with someone for so many years without anything substantial happening, you begin to wonder if it's real or habit.

"You should go," I said.

"Why do you wear these to bed?" he asked, tugging at the knotted strings at my back.

"You've asked me a hundred times." I jerked away from him.

"I don't remember."

"You don't listen to me. That's why you don't remember."

"I do listen … most of the time … sometimes. Your mom made you wear them, or something like that."

"She grew up in Arizona," I said mechanically, "and wore bathing suits as underwear all her life. She did the same for me and my brothers, but I like them better as pajamas—because there's nothing restrictive while I sleep."

"I remember now." He cuddled me from behind. "It's sexy."

"Just go," I sighed.

"I don't want to go."

"I'll bet. But seducing you is one thing. Convincing is another."

"C'mon. You hardly had to convince me."

"Did you really think you were taking advantage of me?"

"A little. You were upset, and I push. You know I do. It wouldn't be right if we were together because I took advantage."

"I don't believe you," I said, only slightly sullen.

"What? Why?"

"You know I want you." I could say that easily because we were in the dark, and not face to face. "And you know I know better than to ask you for what you are incapable of giving. It's a shame you didn't understand what kind of relationship you could have had with me."

"Dru." He tried to make me face him. "I only wanted to protect you. I didn't want you to be mad at me tomorrow for taking advantage of your state of mind."

"Bullshit."

"It's not bull," he insisted, forcing me onto my back so he could see me. "Why else would I stop?"

You just do not want me, that's why, is what I wanted to say it, but I couldn't handle it if he agreed. I shrugged my shoulders as well as I could on the bed.

"I was trying to be nice," he said.

"It's not as if I want to keep you," I said with more anger than intended. "You're not worth that kind of effort."

"That's nice," he scowled. "Good to know you wouldn't even consider me for anything more than getting laid."

"Don't act wounded. The only person you wanted to protect tonight was you. As far as feeling bad about not being boyfriend material, all I can say is that you created your reputation, so live with it."

He paused and then laughed quietly.

"Okay, I submit. A part of me wanted to make sure you didn't expect anything from me."

"Dacon and Galen think you use me, Romeo. I didn't for a minute think you did."

"I don't. I don't usually."

"My mind isn't weak. Stop acting like it is."

"I don't. Ugh, I really blew it, didn't I?"

"You can't even imagine how much. You think the last ten years went by slowly. We'll see if you can survive the sexual tension of the next ten."

He sighed, snuggled behind me, and snuck his tongue under the end of the metal in my neck. He tugged at the ball until it hurt, and I groaned in pain.

"Let me make it up to you."

"No." I pushed his hands away. "It's time for you to leave."

"C'mon, I'm begging. If I were standing, I would go on bended knee. I really want to see everything you've got. All that faerie power that only a vampire can appreciate."

I turned and punched him in the chest.

"Stop! Reading! My! Mind!"

"I can't help it," he laughed, throwing his hands up to guard against the assault. "You think so loud I can hear it." Trapping my arms between us, he kissed me on the lips. "You're never going to let me see it again, are you?"

"No."

"I'm pathetic."

"Yes, you are."

I kissed him though. I made the gesture passionate, inviting, and so hot I knew he couldn't help but try for more. He took my hand and bit my fingers. "C'mon. Show me what you want to do to me."

"I won't," I said. "But know this, I'm creative. And you know what else? I'm really good at it."

He tried for another kiss, and I shoved him away.

"I'm so frustrated I could kill someone," he said as he scratched his head.

"You're in good company." I put my back to him. "Now get out."

He was suddenly on his knees beside the bed.

"I've been an ass," he said as he bit the tips of my fingers again. "Not just now—the whole night."

"I know."

"I've been so busy, Dru. I'm sorry about your plants, and nearly ripping your throat out."

I stared at him.

"And I do … care … about you."

I looked in his eyes and thought that somewhere inside he probably cared—maybe. I didn't know where that might be, or how much space that caring took up. I wasn't so sure it mattered. After these last few months of constant attention, it was clear that dating Romeo was the wrong thing to do. He put up his hand in the salute that he had made at his apartment, but I cut him off.

"Would you just leave already?"

Gods, I wished he had let Dacon come over. At least I would have someone to hold. No, I would definitely be having sex. Dacon's a great "holder," but no reason to waste talent. I was sure I had thought that loud enough for him to hear. Suddenly he was shoving his legs into his uniform pants. Not exactly pissed, but not too happy either. He blew out the candles and didn't waste time getting into his boots. He didn't even lace them. Yep, he heard me.

"Your name's been taken off tomorrow's duty roster—both of you," he nodded toward Livi's room.

"How do you know?"

"Can't you trust me?"

I sighed. If he didn't want to be with me, he should've let Dacon come. I think I finally understood that he truly doesn't want Dacon near me, but he doesn't really want me either. He was so miserable that he didn't kiss me good-bye. He drifted like a shadow from my sight. I didn't hear him in the hall or when he closed the front door, but I knew when he was gone. I was all alone, again. He would go to a bar for vamps, and the people who cater to them. The Range is his favorite. It's close and expensive. I hated him.

The clock read zero three-twenty.

CHAPTER THIRTEEN

I WAS ASLEEP BEFORE I could think anymore about my partner or my love life. I drifted easily into fitfully fatigued oblivion, until a line of feathery softness trailed the side of my face. I brushed at it. It came again, only slower, tickling more than the first. I scratched at my cheek. Again it came, and I swatted the air before turning on my side.

"Stop it," I demanded. Goose bumps rose along my right arm. I swatted again. "Pip, stop it."

"Pip?"

The voice was deep, masculine, and somewhat angry — and not faerie at all.

Startled, I reached out for my gun. When my hand careened into the nightstand, I cursed aloud. "Who's there?"

"Galen."

I heard him move around the room. I blinked until he came into focus at the foot of my bed. The outside street lamp fell harsh across his chest. His emerald shirt appeared as slick as the jewel, almost as if it were wet. I glanced at the open curtains and window shade.

"I closed that shade."

"Did you?"

"I never open it, so it's the same as closing it." I dropped back onto the bed. "You scared me. You should knock, even if you use the window."

"I apologize. The house was asleep. I did not use the window."

"I didn't hear anyone at the door."

"I hardly wanted you to limp all the way down the steps." There was laughter underneath his words.

I sat up on my elbows, eyes half open. I tried to scowl but my face hurt. In fact, my whole body hurt worse than it had an hour ago.

"Romeo locked the front door. He always does."

"I did not use the front door."

"Is something wrong?" I asked. "I mean, is that why you're here, because something's wrong."

"I brought your things," he said, motioning to the floor where my backpack and box of medicine were now sitting. "You refused to wait, so they were all I needed to see to your home."

"It's four hundred," I said, looking at the clock. "Did you just finish up?"

"We found the bodies of four second squad soldiers in the park," he said, leaning against the window frame and staring out into the night.

"I'm sorry."

He watched the sky a moment before turning to me.

"Who is Pip?"

"Who?"

"When I touched you … your face, you said Pip."

I stared, panicked a little, and then thought about him touching me. How odd and intimate. Is that how he wakes his soldiers, or his friends?

"It seemed like a name," he said.

"What? Oh, I don't know. I was dreaming."

"Dreaming again? Not like last time."

"No, not a nightmare."

"May I ask what you were dreaming about?"

"No."

Yes, my attitude needs adjusting at four in the morning when I'm nervous and working on half an hour of sleep in a twenty-four hour period.

"You are in a poor mood," he blandly said, giving me that vampire stare.

"I'm sorry," I said as I pulled the cooling cotton sheet to my neck. "Romeo and I ..." That's it, tell him that story. "I had a bad day, and then a bad night, and it got worse and worse."

"Worse than Jagen?"

"Well, not better."

"I will admit it has been a long, unpleasant evening." He came to stand by the side of the bed. He raised his brows at me, waiting for an answer—as if I should know something. When I didn't say anything, he said, "You are oddly at ease for my first visit to your home and your bedroom."

Honestly, I was having a hard time keeping my eyes open. I cared that it was my general's first visit, but it didn't seem a worthy reason to force myself awake.

"Do you mean me harm? Are you gonna hit me, knock me around? Throw me into a wall, or put a neat little hole in my body and drink from the fount that is me?"

"What? Of course not. What do you mean to be saying something like that?"

My sleepy eyes snapped open at his appalled tone.

"I was kidding," I said as hastily as I could manage. "Sorry, I didn't mean to be insulting."

He waved a dismissive hand, quickly calming.

"I meant only that my presence tends to ... at times I make people uncomfortable. And if you want me to go, I will."

"I'm sorry," I sighed. "You don't have to go. I'm not anxious. I don't have the energy for it."

"I bet you would find the energy if Jagen walked in," he said, giving me a small smile.

"Or maybe I'd just pass out," I smiled back.

He turned back to the window and was quiet for some time. It made me nervous, as if he were listening to me breathe, and I had the distinct impression that he wanted something. He pulled the leather strap holding his hair back, wrapped it around his wrist, and then tucked the end under itself. With graceful motions, he ran both hands through the long, dark strands as if relaxing in the freedom. He pulled most if it over his shoulder. The ends snapped against his pants, and it took real effort not to twist my fingers through all that wonderful hair. I sighed for what would never be mine.

"Is there anything you need before I go? A glass of water or a pat on the head?"

"You're funny."

"You are all right then?" he smiled.

"I'm perfectly not needy at the moment." I half smiled as my eyes slid shut. "Want," I whispered and tried to joke. "There are many things I want."

I felt the bed dip as Galen sat next to me. I tensed as much as my aching body allowed. I cracked my eyes open. His body blocked most of the street lamp's glow, so his face was in shadow.

"What do you want?" he asked.

He touched the large vein in the bend of my arm — the same one Romeo ran his tongue over earlier in the evening. He traced it down into my hand and then swept his fingertips up my curled fingers. The explicit gesture confused me. It made my head feel dizzy.

"Your mind is locked, Andru."

"Stay out of it," I whispered.

"I do not pry. I am speaking of earlier. Jagen's anger had much to do with his difficulty reading your thoughts. If he cannot see inside a mind, he believes it to be hiding something. Your protective nature is hard to understand."

I couldn't stop my eyes from closing. The exhaustion was like a drug I couldn't handle.

"Who do you protect yourself from?"

"Everyone."

"From your partner?"

I nodded.

"From me?"

"Especially." I wasn't sure I said that aloud.

Galen's cold hand closed over mine. He moved toward me, and I felt his cool cheek against mine. His lips touched the edge of my jaw. Lethargy enveloped me as his fingertips trailed down the other side of my face. For a brief, cloudy moment, I pondered the strangeness of what was happening.

"Oidhche mhath, Poppy."

My mind roused a fraction at hearing a very old nickname. Then I tumbled numbly into sleep, forgetting nicknames, sex, vampires, poisoned arrows, and the feeling of Galen's body so close to mine.

CHAPTER FOURTEEN

"DAMN IT, DRU!"

I jumped to a sitting position.

"What! What?" I reached out and my hand knocked the lamp on my nightstand onto the floor. It broke, from the fall or my hand smacking into it, I couldn't be sure. I groped around the bed blinking rapidly, waiting for my sight to clear. The brightness around the edge of the window shade gave a gray shadow to my room and made everything a little fuzzy.

"What the hell happened?" Livi stood in the doorway to my room holding a vial of pills in her hand. "I half remember falling all over Romeo. Please tell me I didn't have sex with him."

"You didn't." I slumped down onto the bed. "You did fall, but he was being good last night."

"Oh, thank god. These are the pills they gave me, right?"

I threw my hand over a yawn and nodded.

"The medics gave you a bunch to stop your whining, and then you took more."

"Oh, okay then. Did you have sex with Romeo?"

"I tried."

"Did you let him see you like that?" She pointed accusingly, or even disgustedly, at me.

"What?" I looked down at myself. "Naked? It's easier to have sex that way."

"Not naked. Your magik is coming out."

I glanced at myself again. I was fully awake now. I did not need to blink to see that my skin from head to toe was as black as tar. Shit.

"You look as if someone colored you in with charcoals."

A romantic notion from the sketch artist, but there was nothing romantic about my body at the moment. I was perfectly disturbed that this wasn't a conscious act, nor did I feel the slightest hint of the change.

"You didn't do it on purpose, did you?" Livi asked as if she had read my thoughts. "I don't like this, Dru."

She doesn't like it? Well, it doesn't please me either. I mean, hell, this has never happened before. I haven't shifted shape without conscious effort since the early days. I'm a strong Wicca, and ever since I learned how to switch forms I've been careful who I transpose in front of. Partially out of preservation—no one needs to know I can do it, but also because I don't like to see the fear and loathing in their eyes when they see what I can do and what I truly am.

I sighed, and, that quick, my magik let down and invited the intermingling fey to metamorphose. The power rushed through me. As in the Realm, my appearance is close to my namesake, but still a blend of human and fey. My eyes mutated to a glossy, chrome color. My fingers grew small talons. Black, oblong-shaped crystals formed a line down the sides of my legs. Stubby, gray bones sprouted along my brow line, and slowly my teeth sharpened.

Fortunately, I was able to tense the energy enough to catch the full burst of magik before the entire transition—long before my wings formed. That part is nearly impossible to stop once started. Unfortunately, the magik released was enough to heal the wound on my leg. My muscles jumped, quivering as the hole healed to its normal condition. Such an alteration is the way of my other self. As the fey magik emerges, it repairs all weakened structures in my body that would cripple my defenses. Which is why, normally, I'm careful not to allow the transformation when anyone beyond my circle of friends has seen me injured.

"What the hell is going on?"

Livi's voice startled my concentration. She had watched me trance out, and from the look on her face, she wasn't happy. I took a huge breath, knowing that while I suppressed the complete conversion, I didn't have the strength to pull back the changes that had already occurred. Not yet.

"I won't bite you," I said, waving Livi into the room. "Besides, you've seen this before."

"Oh my god," she whispered. She stood stunned, shivering from the sound of my raspy voice. Unlike the full Fear faerie, one of my changes, or I should say defenses, is that my voice is deeper, maybe course. It invokes fear magikally, purposefully. "I've never seen you change in your sleep."

I used the top sheet to cover the bottom half of my body. There wasn't anything I could do about the voice.

"It's a little unnerving, I know, but, it's not like I ever sleep with anyone."

"Crap." She shivered again. "What's wrong with you?"

"I'm not sure." I scowled at her. "Nothing is wrong with me."

"Well, something's wrong."

"I'm fine. I can control my magik."

I said it, knowing it was only part true. Something was definitely happening, and I was damned if I knew what. There's no handbook for this sort of thing— "Humans with Faerie Magik, Know Your Glamour, Know Yourself." It's not like that. I figure things out as I go.

"You better do something before this happens around the wrong person."

"Jupiter, Livi, you worry too much. Come sit down."

She did, but nervously. She sat on the edge of the bed, and I stayed where I was. I watched the vast array of emotions glide across her face. Normally Livi trusts me explicitly, but when I'm changed, I'm a bit too fierce, too savage for her to understand. She trembled and the fear seeped from her pores, rising like mist on the air. The scent hit me, and I shivered with absolute pleasure.

"Are you okay?" she asked.

I nodded. I didn't want to remind her how negative emotions satisfy me. How her fright strengthens me, charges me with a pleasing rush of heat, much like the effects of a glass of wine.

"You're beautiful, Alivia."

She pulled back, her aura turning color from its normal greenish creativity to a darker shade of panic and dislike.

"Your eyes ..." her voice was soft and afraid. "It's weird how I can see myself in them. Your voice is so ... it's so awful. Now you're looking at me as if I'd taste great with a sweet sauce."

"We would never harm you."

That was only partially true, because I'd do almost anything to keep her emotions negative. Even though her feelings are hurtful, they aren't so much harmful. I realized that was splitting hairs, but what could I do? Her anxiety fed me. It nourished me. I needed to have it or it would be difficult to return to human. I leaned towards her, wanting more of the pungent odor she so willingly gave. I forced the mistrustful emotions that my close proximity coaxed. It filled me, and I shuddered with pleasure.

Her rear end edged the bed until she nearly fell off.

"Don't sound so hungry when you talk, and I just might believe you. Why are you like this when you're ... like that?" She pointed at my body. "Everything seems pleasurable, especially my terror."

"You know I'm a faerie that's stimulated by distress," I said, moving on my knees toward her. "Your fear is satisfying, and somewhat sensual. We can't control that."

"What's with all the 'we' stuff?"

That stopped me. I had no answer for it. It was different. It did seem unnatural, yet I couldn't seem *not* to do it. "We ... I don't know. We're changing and we ... I ..."

"That's perfect," she said. "You're sure no one can feel this power you're using? Cause that's all we need."

I glared at her, because I can completely control some things.

"The containment magik around this bed is always secure. We're fine. I mean ... I'm fine."

She went to lean against the far wall. The knuckles on her fingers were white around the vial of pills.

"Stop talking like that. Stop talking period. It's scaring me. Change back, Dru. You have to change back."

I moved against the headboard, because admittedly this whole thing was unnerving. The fact that I can ingest negativity and enjoy it so much upsets me sometimes. Besides, Livi's reaction bothers me. My brothers did the same—still do—which is why no one sees me in this state very often. Except Dacon, who has never had "the face." He loved everything about me. He's the only person who's seen me when the fey magik completely merges with my human body—when I get the wings. I don't know what Romeo would think. It isn't on my list to find out.

I closed my eyes and crossed my legs, hoping that I'd be able to do this. Normally, I needed more time to gain the strength to shift back. Disturbingly enough, drinking Livi's forced negative emotion made me feel quite strong. I centered my power. Collecting the magik to a point in my chest, I pulled the fey back inside. My physical human body devoured the fey. It swallowed my twin. The black, chrome, and crystals all absorbed inward to let my human self emerge. I shook it out. When I opened my eyes, Livi was straightening my room, putting dirty clothes in the hamper.

"Better?" I asked.

"Yes, thank you."

I flung the bed's top sheet outward. Romeo's socks flew onto the floor in front of Livi.

"So tell me, why did you try to seduce Romeo again?" Livi questioned.

"You know why."

"Tell me anyway," she smiled as she picked up the socks.

"He was looking all strong and sexy. He apologized, so I decided to give him another chance. It was outstanding. You know that first-time exploration?"

"Hardly the first time," she grinned.

"Completely naked first time."

"Oooh, what else happened for the first time naked in almost ten years?"

"I was on top, doing all kinds of things to him, and he was all red-eyed and shaking."

She cuffed the socks together before she threw them into the pile. "Aaaand …"

"I'll give you one guess."

She sighed. "He opened his mouth and his personality came flying out."

"You can't even imagine how bad it was."

"He's an idiot. You do know that?"

"I guess."

"You'll find someone besides a royal or his egocentric son."

"Livi, do you think I'm gullible? Do people use me?"

"What? No, you're not gullible. Who said that? He said that?" Livi's light Jamaican accent flared as it does when she's very angry. She sat on the bed and hugged me tightly. "I told you, he's an asshole. Don't you think on what he said, because he's stupid and you're going to find someone." She laughed. "He'll probably have a psychotic ex-lover who's a vampire, and he'll hate nature, but at your age, you take what you can get."

"A hopeless romantic and a cynic—a girl after my own heart. Maybe my dreams should be about you."

I shoved her off the bed and onto the floor. She fluttered her eyelashes as she pulled her way back up the mattress.

"Listen, I'm only going to say this once. I don't believe it, and you shouldn't do it. But I want you to feel better."

"Oh, this sounds fantastic."

"Well, this is a supportive talk, right?"

"Oh boy."

"Why don't you tell Galen how you feel? Maybe he's hard up too," she giggled helplessly. "Maybe he's lonely and wants to be held by someone. Seeing how you're the only one who has those kinds of thoughts about him, you're the likely candidate to do the job."

"Despite what you think, I'm very sure many people have those thoughts of him."

"Sycophants, terror mongers, and psychopaths don't count."

"Well, thanks, but I'll just bet Lord Cherkasy has those thoughts about him."

"That confirms my description of his flock. Speaking of her, she tried to help you last night."

I shrugged. Livi sat down on my bed and pulled me to lay my head on her lap.

"Thank you for what you did, or what you tried to do for Jefrey," she said, sifting fingers through my hair. "I never expected any of that to happen. I didn't know King Jagen was here."

"It's not your fault."

"I wanted to spill it long before he tried to hurt you, but Lord Galen pushed me back. Literally. He hurt my chest when he shoved me onto the bench. I know he knew you were lying."

"He knew. He held you back because if Jagen knew you lied too, he'd have tried to kill us both."

She sprawled next to me on the bed.

"What was it like to be suffocated without a hand on you? Did you think you were going to die?"

"I think so. It happened so fast, but kind of in slow motion too. Does that make sense? But, no worries. It was my fault. I agreed to lie."

"How could you take that from him? Not use your magik to stop him from hurting you?"

"If I use magik, I'm dead. I may be strong, but I can't overpower Lord Jagen, Galen, and the rest. Not together. Even if I did manage to somehow escape, I'd be a fugitive. They'd find me."

"Those vampires are nuts to discover true magiks."

I nodded. "They'd never let me slip through their fingers."

"They might have killed you on the spot if they thought you were the faerie from King Jagen's stories," she said, hugging me sideways.

"They won't find out, because I don't think about any of that when I'm near them. I have amazing strength of mind."

"All our lives depend on it," she said and gave a small laugh. She poked her foot into my bandaged calf and then ran her fingers over my neck where Romeo had bitten me.

"Your bite is completely healed. Is your leg healed too?" I nodded. "How are you going to explain that little trick, Miss Amazing Strength of Mind?"

"Romeo used his blood to heal my neck, so that's not a big deal." I looked at my foot, flexing. "I guess I'll have to pretend."

"Oh jeez!" Livi jumped up. "I forgot to tell you Roeanne called earlier."

"Do I have to care?"

"Shut up. It was actually Dacon calling from her phone. He wanted to see if you were okay, and he wanted to tell us that he's been at the hospital since his shift started this morning."

"What's wrong with him?"

"Not at the hospital like that. That guy you sent to Jefferson with the broken hand — he's dead."

"Dead?" My eyes widened. "I didn't do it. All I did was break his hand."

"Not you. Dacon said he wasn't in his bed for early morning rounds. A search found him in a morgue drawer, and in the trash can, and under the coroner's desk."

"Eww. What does that mean? Why was he still there?"

"Dacon said his hand needed surgery." She smiled. "Nice job. He said the hand surgeon on call wasn't available until sometime tomorrow."

"Okay, fine. What does it have to do with me?"

"Nothing, just listen. He said at the nurse's last check in, at twenty-three hundred hours, he was in bed asleep."

"Any visitors?"

"None that anyone knows of. He wants you to call him or Captain Patrice if you think of anything."

"What could I think of? I didn't know the guy. I hurt him before he hurt me. That's about the extent of it."

"Dacon wants you to try to remember anything unusual."

"Well, it's not unusual, but I forgot to hand in his effects. I was so pissed after that fight I went to talk to Relina in the E.D.O, then went to give Loki his pot, and forgot all about it."

"His what?"

"His pot."

"Not Loki. You said you didn't hand in his what?"

"His belongings. The stuff he had on him when I arrested him."

"Oh. Why did you have his stuff?"

"Because we took him to the hospital first, and I didn't want him dumping anything useful."

"That's illegal," she said, giving me an odd face.

"Romeo and I have done it before." I shrugged to make light of it. "And If I'd handed it in when I got back to HQ, his stuff would've been waiting at the detention center, and no one would've known."

"That's so illegal."

I shrugged again. She was closer to my bag on the floor, so she grabbed it and fished inside.

"Dacon also said Roe offered to come and check on us if we needed her."

"They're talking?"

"Apparently."

"What did you say?"

"I told him it was a sweet offer, but we're fine."

I didn't feel like putting on a happy face for Roeanne—not that I would have to. I'm sure she'd understand if I was a bit miserable, but she'd want to look at the wound, and I don't have one anymore.

"I didn't sleep well," Livi said as she pulled the plastic bag from my backpack. "I guess because of the drugs I was on. I kept waking up, thinking about that vampire and the girl. I think they purpose-fully separated us. They shot you so you couldn't run, and then that human took off so I'd follow. Don't you think they wanted us apart?"

"I kinda thought they were trying to kill us."

She took a moment to frown at me as she dumped the plastic bag with the contents of the deceased man's belongings onto the floor. There were only a few things. Keys. Wallet. Some folded papers.

"Maybe you're right," I said. "The vampire said she let the girl shoot Teena for practice. I think she insinuated I was the target."

"You? That doesn't make any sense."

"I don't know. She was under my boot and majorly pissed off. Maybe she was talking out her ass."

"The human girl would have to be controlled by the vampire, right?"

"I guess."

"They hurt you, and then the human ran so the vampire could get you alone? They were waiting for you?"

"Waiting for me why? Why do target practice? Why not kill me? She'd have to know Jefrey would call for help."

"But he didn't," said Livi. "He was too upset."

"Maybe he couldn't call out like we couldn't."

We stared at each other. We both knew that coincidences are usually anything but.

"Well, that human couldn't conquer anything on her own," said Livi. "She was weak. She'd be a bigger pain to have with you unless you had a specific use for her. Did the vampire say anything else to you?"

"Everything happened so quickly. Jefrey was freaking out. He shot her. He asked her why she killed Teena. I don't remember what she said then, but when she came from the tree she said … give me what I want and I'll go, or something like that."

"So she wanted something?"

"I guess."

"What could she want?"

I shrugged.

"Maybe it's something you don't realize you have, or something you know. Something you were told."

"My first thought was that she wanted my gun. It can't be something I know, because no one tells me anything. I'm a foot soldier."

"Okay, so you have something she wanted. What do you have?"

"I'm poor too. That's another perk of the foot soldier."

"Dru, be serious."

"Livi, I don't know. I haven't bought or been given anything. I have nothing worth killing over."

"Not worth it to you, but maybe it's something you've had for a long time, unaware of its worth."

"It wouldn't be a personal item, Liv. She wouldn't seek me out for my old belly button jewelry. It would have to be work related, espionage stuff, and I don't have anything a terrorist would want. I haven't been given anything important. Ever."

"Fine."

She turned her attention back to the belongings of the dead man I put in the hospital only yesterday.

"So who do you think would want ..." she squinted at my handwriting on the side of the plastic bag "... Brian McKenney dead?"

"How on this earth would I even know? I hadn't seen him before yesterday."

She opened his wallet.

"Should we be doing this?" I asked. "The guy's dead. And it's illegal."

"You're going to talk illegal after you took his stuff before he was booked?"

I sighed. She gave me a serious scowl.

"He was a criminal," she said as she flipped through his pictures.

"He still has rights. I mean, the dead have rights. Captain Gloader will want this stuff. Not to mention his family."

"We'll give it to them when we're done." She pulled out two small blue rectangle pieces of paper. "License. Automobile and citizen."

"Permanent resident?"

"Yeah." She studied his picture on both cards. "He was born here. Let's see, Mr. McKenney was twenty-seven years old and lives ... lived on Wishart Street in the Kensington area."

She opened some papers folded in an untidy square.

"Look at this."

She handed me a letter from Life Changes, a government organization that conducts all legal human-vampire conversions. Lord Orel heads the institute in New York, but there are subsidiary branches in each territory. It seemed Mr. McKenney was in conversion counseling for the past nineteen months. He was scheduled to change over at the beginning of next year. Along with the letter was a change of license form not yet complete. He needed to send it by October 20 in order for his conversion to go through.

If a vampire is picked up without a new citizen license to go with his after conversion identity, it's the law for him to be put to sleep—that is death. Underground conversions aren't tolerated. They happen, but not too often, because the penalty is so stiff. Romeo says if death weren't the price for illegal conversions, vampires would try to convert every person they ever loved, liked, hated, or owed a favor to. Humans would be dying all over the place. I say too many vampires equals revolution for the king.

"Here," said Livi, "look at this."

She handed me another paper with the word "lundi" printed in pencil at the top left corner.

"What's lundi?"

"I don't know," she shrugged.

A five-inch photocopied color picture of trees was in the middle of the page. It wasn't a good one. It almost seemed abstract, but it was fuzzy and pale because the printer that produced it was almost out of ink. I suspected it was somewhere north of Philadelphia—not because I'm so intuitive, but because a small "n" was printed at the bottom corner of the page. There was also an LT written in ink on the right side of the paper next to the picture.

Another paper was a list of things he was supposed to buy at the store, and the last was an address at Tenth and Spring Gardens streets.

"That's about where he was trying to steal the car," I said.

"Here, look at this."

Livi handed me a three-by-five note card with the number P235 in small red print. The back of the card was torn, as if something were taped to it.

"That looks like a car license or a partial," said Livi. "Maybe."

"Find out the license of the car he was trying to steal."

Livi shuffled through my bag and handed me my small log and ticket computer. I went to the last form, because although the incident happened at thirteen hundred hours, the E.D.O didn't dare give me another call. "Look at this."

Livi took the palm computer.

"Psycho-235980."

"It's the same plate." She leaned against my dresser. "Maybe he wasn't stealing it. Maybe there was a key on this card."

"If he had the key, he wouldn't have been hanging out the window."

"True," she shrugged. "Maybe he lost it."

"Far-fetched, but you never know, I suppose." I went back to the paper with the picture. "So, this is a location? But where? What if it were—"

"A drop-off location!" Livi snatched the paper from my hand.

"Jupiter, Liv!" I grabbed it back. "I was going to say a destination. I mean, really, he could've been on his way to his grandma's."

"He wouldn't need a secret map to get to his grandma's."

"It's not that secret." I flipped the paper upside down and back. "It's a park or something in the north—in a place called Lundi."

"We have a lot of parks in Philly, but I've never heard of one called Lundi. If a key was on that card, then it's reasonable to say he would drop off the car at a location or give it to someone to drop off."

"Maybe LT is the location," I mused. "Maybe there are many locations, and this paper specified which one—LT or lundi." I again flipped the paper upside down and back. "Well, maybe. This picture could be anywhere though. And why that car?"

We looked at each other at the same time.

"For whatever's in the car," Livi said softly.

Over the last few years, the popular method of terrorism has been car bombs. The attack, and subsequent fire at Pennsylvania University that Loki spoke of, began as a car bomb.

Livi rushed to the phone.

"Did you find the owner of the car? Was it impounded?"

"Nothing came up on the initial search, so we called it in and tagged it for tow."

While she connected with the Emergency Dispatch, I fingered through the small compartments in McKenney's empty wallet.

"Oh," she said. "The car's still there."

"Look at this." I pulled a pale yellow card from a small slit cut into the back lining of the wallet. "He's registered to vote in the States."

"No," said Livi. "You can't vote in the States if you're a citizen here."

"Well, it's his picture, but a different name. Seems he's also Bob Thorgood. I think someone should talk to his family."

"I think we should," she smiled. "You think he's involved in the bombings? Maybe that's why he was killed." I smiled at her enthusiasm. She stood on my bed. "We could crack this case wide open!"

"You're so dumb," I said and pulled her ankle until she fell onto her back.

CHAPTER FIFTEEN

LATER IN THE DAY, a friend of Livi's called to tell her about the second squad soldiers that were found a hundred yards or so from where we were attacked—each with an arrow in their heart. They died—and stayed dead. The organ had too much damage for extraordinary measures to work. The young human girl that Livi captured was in lockdown to find out what she knew. Early gossip said she didn't know anything.

I put in a call to Captain Patrice. I told her I had McKenney's belongings and my suspicions about the car he was breaking into. She said she'd send someone over there to take a look around.

I asked for permission to stop by McKenney's home and ask a few questions. She checked with General DeFarr, who said to bring the man's belongings into headquarters and stay away from the McKenney house. He said a formal investigation was under-way. Until I was officially asked to be a part of it, I had to stand clear. I expected as much. General DeFarr and Romeo don't get along, and most days DeFarr treats me as if I'm the vampire. I spent a half hour asking—no begging—to at least be allowed to go to the house to see if I recognized any of McKenney's family or friends from the group that left him stranded in the car. DeFarr finally agreed, but I wasn't permitted to talk to anyone. He didn't want me harassing the family or making the situation worse.

"The guy's dead. How could I make it worse?"

"McKenney was ripped to pieces," said DeFarr. "Have a little compassion, even if he was into illegal activities."

In the middle of my tirade to Livi about being labeled with Romeo's callous attitude, she reminded me of last night when we nearly laughed ourselves blind after she told me about him trying to eat Lord Galen. I guess I sometimes deserve a warning.

I showered again to wash the dried blood from my leg where the wound used to be. I wrapped my calf with the extra bandage Shannon the medic left in the brown medicine box. I thought about wearing long pants, but it was hot outside so I settled for a t-shirt, shorts, and work boots. I practiced hobbling around the house until Livi said I looked convincing. She bet me a dollar I would never pull it off. I didn't take the bet.

Before we left, Livi got lost in the living room closet looking for two black arm bands for us to wear out of respect for the dead soldiers. I tried to get out of it. At work, I would have to, but now, and in the heat? Livi said it was important for us to show support whether we were on duty or off. She's right, and it isn't that I don't care, but she's wearing three-quarter sleeves. My arms are bare, and the elastic will be tight and hot on my skin. I griped a lot on our way to Livi's jeep until she told me, "Shut up, show a little respect, and put the damn thing on your arm or I'll break it." Put like that, spandex was the perfect thing to wear in the hot August heat.

THE HOMES IN THE old Kensington area were constructed about a hundred and thirty years ago for the people who worked in the nearby factories of Harrowgate, which are now the renovated apartments and art studios of Harrowgate. At that time, it was a poor, blue-collar neighborhood. After Galen Manor and the park were built, the businesses had no choice but to move outward, making downtown family housing scarce. Those with high-paying jobs moved to Port Richmond, Kensington, and other neighborhoods skirting the center of the city. Two or three homes were bought and refurbished into one big townhome. The streets are tree lined, but they don't have lawns or big yards.

They have a high-end look, yet stark. I guess for some that's a favorable feature when owning a home. Scarce greenery means less work.

It was a mistake to drive down McKenney's small street. Too many people were there to pay respects. It took a good fifteen minutes to ride the block. I had to limp from two streets away where Livi finally found parking—a little too close to a hydrant. Even though she has military stickers on her car, you never know when someone's in the mood to bust balls.

We put the black arm bands in our pockets, because drawing attention to ourselves isn't what we wanted. Outside the house, I took careful notice of the people standing around, without seeing anyone familiar. I was too preoccupied with McKenney hanging from the car window to remember the others that had abandoned him so quickly. I truly didn't know if they were male or female.

With so many mourners, we didn't think we'd be noticed, so we casually entered the house. Garlic and cinnamon wafted around the room, probably from the myriad of covered baking dishes on the living room table. Livi spoke briefly with his grandmother and told the overwrought older woman we were old friends of Brian's. A military team was talking with the father in the kitchen. I didn't see his mother. I did notice quite a few vacation pictures of him and his family in the States. Since I couldn't talk to anyone officially, twenty minutes was all I could take of the crying. Even with the air-conditioned cold, the room felt claustrophobic. Outside, I listened to McKenney's friends tell stories. They seemed like good people. Do criminals stand out in a crowd? Well, yes, actually, they do.

Fifteen minutes later, Livi came from the house and we huffed our way to the car. She was out of patience too. The heat was getting to both of us.

"All that grief seemed put on to me," she said.

"Everything seems put on when you're suspicious," I shrugged.

"Why don't you try limping on that very hurt leg of yours?" she asked, pushing me in the back on the way to the driver's side of the car.

I cursed and slowed my pace. I needed to get home before I bumped into someone important. I stood at the passenger side door. It was too hot to willingly enter a jeep without a cooling unit.

"I'm fairly certain his grandma was sincere. I think they'd all be genuinely hurt even if they knew he was a criminal, or if they were all criminals."

Livi froze at her opened door. She moved back, looking at the canvas top of the jeep. "My door was unlocked. I know I locked it."

"My side's locked. I don't see anything out of place."

"I never forget to lock my door," she said as she ducked inside. "Nothing's missing. You have your pack, right?"

"Yep. I think you probably forgot."

She checked the back of the jeep and under the hood. It's never a bad thing to be careful, but I was hot as hell. I opened my door and got in.

"Come on," I said. "Let's go see what's at the Psycho."

"McKenney's gram mentioned that he was in the clink a few years back. She said his vampire lawyer got him off."

"In jail for what?"

"Something about suspicion of DUI, and a gun in the backseat."

"He was falsely accused."

"They always are," she smirked. "She said one gun, but I heard friends upstairs say a trunkful. Maybe there are guns in the Psycho. Well shit," Livi said as she turned the engine over and pulled onto the street, heading toward the highway. "I don't want to force entry into a car that might be loaded with handguns or worse."

"Who said anything about breaking into the car?"

She smiled.

"Patrice said she'd have someone there to look it over, or have someone watch it until the explosives people could get out there."

"Dru, they're called the EOD, or just the Disposal unit. I know a few soldiers down there. They're painfully serious, and can get a real hard-on when it comes to stuff like that, so don't go calling them anything stupid to their faces."

"Damn, Liv, you know someone in every squad. Exactly how many people have you had sex with?"

"I didn't say I got it on with these people. I just said I knew a few of them."

"Did you sleep with any of them?" I asked, watching her face as she eased the jeep into Allegheny Avenue traffic.

"I wouldn't say we slept."

I laughed and thought she was seriously kidding herself if she thought Dacon would even remotely go for that.

CHAPTER SIXTEEN

I CALLED CAPTAIN PATRICE on the way to Spring Garden Street. She told me she had someone drive by earlier, but no one was available to watch the car. She didn't think she'd have someone free until sundown when the vamps came on shift. That told me how much she agreed with my thoughts on McKenney's death, and possible occupation. Then she hit me with the kicker. She asked Livi and I to watch the car but not go near it. She was sure she'd have someone out there soon.

There was an accident on the highway, and naturally, we got stuck in traffic. We sat on I-95 with gas fumes from a thousand cars permeating my head for almost forty-five minutes. It was just another Monday afternoon. I had a thought that I'd rather be on duty.

SPRING GARDEN IS A two-way, four-lane street with a wide median. Livi parked on the north side, far from the Psycho, but kept it in sight. We stared at it before Livi slumped her head against the wheel.

"I need to eat."

"In this heat?"

"I'm starving."

"Well, the experts won't be here for a while so we have time." I pointed across the street. "Go get something at that diner down there."

"You want?"

"I'm not hungry."

"You're always hungry."

I shrugged.

Livi eyed the Psycho as she passed it. It was a nice car, considering it was about thirty years old. The paint was excellent, and I knew from yesterday the upholstery was decent. Livi looked back and gave me a shrug. I guess there were no bombs lying on the front seat or a note on the dash saying the bad guys were held up at the old factory.

I left the jeep in hopes I would stop sweating, wondering about my lack of appetite. Normally on a hot day and sweating as I was, I'd be famished. It would seem the profound grief at the McKenney household filled me up. I noticed after I was there about fifteen minutes that I couldn't concentrate. My body absorbed the family's anguish the same way it does when the fey feeds on negativity. It's happened before, but not to that degree. If I'm around high-energy people when they're miserable, I become slightly energized, but nothing like today. Although I'm serenely satisfied, I feel sure that when the euphoria wears off I'll be very upset about this new development. Probably I'll be more disgusted than anything else.

I'll admit, if only to myself, that my body's changes are beginning to unnerve me. I haven't gone to the bathroom in almost two days. That's certainly not normal. It feels like a pressure is building, as if I'm a pot whose lid might suddenly fly off. It's not a happy thought. With my issues, I need to stay focused and in control. I crossed the street to meet Livi as she came from the diner carrying a big brown bag.

"Is that all for you?"

"No. Where are we going to eat? I can't sit in my car. It's too hot."

"There aren't any benches," I said, looking up and down the street at the old houses converted to stores.

We looked at the Psycho next to us and then at the building it was parked in front of. It was a church and rectory—the Biblical Nautical Pentecostal Lady of Towers. I'm not joking. We looked at one another and again at the Psycho. Livi shrugged.

"It's probably fine. I doubt we're right about it being filled with anything other than gasoline."

I agreed silently, and we climbed onto the engine hood of the car. We settled our backs against the windshield. I figured that if McKenney could drive it, we could sit on it. Livi handed me a veggie burger and a tomato fruit juice.

"Listen, Dru, when the troops arrive, try to stay in the background," she said, pulling a Waldorf salad and a beer from the bag for herself.

"That'll be hard considering it was my arrest that put us here."

"What I meant, Miss Priss, is the more engrossed you get, the easier it is to forget about the leg," she said as she stared at me.

"Oh," I sighed. "Sorry. I don't know where that came from. I don't mean to be a bitch."

"Lately," she said, giving me a sly look.

I flipped her the middle finger.

"Dru, three weeks ago you were reprimanded for jamming a pen in some strange vampire cadet's hand for whistling the cat call to another cadet."

"He should know better than to do stuff like that—especially around an officer."

"Granted, but the other cadet was his girlfriend." I opened my mouth, only she kept going. "Last week you were reprimanded again for calling Gloader an annoying dickwad. Yesterday you thought it a good idea to get Romeo so worked up he nearly ripped your throat out. *And* you did it on purpose. Early this morning you snuck away from our boss, the general of our militaries, when he told you to wait for him."

"How did you know about that?"

"I have a friend in Advanced Training Class. She was there."

"I didn't sneak," I said, rolling my eyes at another one of her friends.

"Dru, the girl said you literally snuck out of the ambulance and skulked up the walkway."

"Galen didn't order me to stay."

"It's Galen now, is it?"

"You know what I mean." I bit into the burger I wasn't hungry for and spoke over the food in my mouth. "He didn't order me to stay or wait—just told the officer to tell me he'd be busy for a while."

"You knew what he meant. He'll probably talk to you about it when you go back to work."

"I'm sure he doesn't care that I didn't let him take me home."

"That's not the point. He told you to wait—take you home?" She was frowning so hard I thought her eyebrows would meet. "He wanted you to wait for him so he could take you home? What does that even mean?"

I sighed again. "Look, lately my confidence is low, and I'm easily distracted. It puts me in a bad mood. That's all it is."

"Oh, you have low confidence. That explains it. Oh wait, it doesn't. When most people have low confidence they get more introverted, not less. They don't go looking for fights."

"Okay, okay. I'm not sure, but I think I feel this way because of —you know."

"I knew you were going to say that," she said, dropping her fork into the salad.

"Yeah, well, something's going on—inside. I feel like I might lose control."

"Oh my god!"

"Not completely!" I looked around to see if anyone was nearby. "Don't get all nutsy about it. I'm not a loose cannon or anything."

"You said you'd never lose control of IT."

"Sshh! I only meant that I feel odd. Sometimes I feel like my body is trying to tell me something. It's as if I'm supposed to know something."

"Know something? Know what? What does that mean?"

"If I knew ..." I said, and then stopped before I said something really mean.

"Maybe the prophecy," she said.

"Stop it. Like I'm supposed to know anything about an old, made-up vampire prophecy?"

"You don't know it's made up."

"The fey don't know anything about it. Druid-Pagan ritual books and codices from hundreds of years ago don't mention anything like it."

"Romeo said a lot of those books were transcribed from Latin and Greek and Sumerian," she said, "then rewritten into English, so you don't know what was originally foretold."

"Foretold?" I smiled wryly. "There's certainly nothing in them like what Jagen told Romeo about—all faeries coming to crush the vampires or whatever he said. He's a paranoid fanger with a mad-on for power. He can't be trusted."

"Wow, tell me what you really think about our king." I tried to speak, and again she cut me off. "Even if it's not very often, your old books always have something to say about the vampire and the fey. There's always a connection."

"Because they hate each other," I said.

"One point of the king's prophecy is the half faerie-half human is the harbinger of death. The holder of secrets to the vampire race."

"How do I fit that description? My parents were human. I'm not a half and half. I don't have a faerie soul. I have my soul. I don't have faerie blood. All I might have is a … a piggy-back soul, like an ethereal hitchhiker." Livi smiled, and I frowned. "Don't you think I'd know if I were born to bring down the entire vampire horde?"

"Maybe that's what your body is trying to tell you."

"No. Besides, I don't want to do that."

I looked around. It was still technically day so we should be safe from vampiric ears, but I wasn't comfortable with this topic of conversation in such a public space.

"That's irrelevant," she said. "If you're the main ingredient in the vampire Armageddon, there isn't anything you can do about it."

"There is no half human-half faerie! Something magikal attached itself to me, but you act as if I had no choice in the matter. That the magikal thing clinging to me can make me do stuff. That it's my doom whether I want it or not."

"Maybe it is."

"Fate is not set to that degree. There isn't one particular outcome no matter what path we choose to follow."

"How do you know?" she said. "You only live the path you choose. You haven't a clue where other roads would leave you off. One thing is for sure; Jagen believes the human with the faerie soul will destroy him. And sweetie, you're the only one I know that has anything faerie attached to their body."

I fell quiet. I was eating food that I wasn't hungry for, and now I had a headache.

"All right. Fine. Don't remind me." I took another bite of my sandwich and pointed. "Is that Dacon?" Livi glanced up to see her new love. I said a quick spell: *Leave right now, this thinking brow, just as the breeze, these words will leave.*

Silly spell, but it's simple and it works well with the handful of faerie dust I blew into the back of her head. The spell would push our conversation to the recesses of her mind; the dust gives extra magikal kick. It helps clear her brain of any wandering thoughts of me. The spell is easy, almost like hypnosis. I've been doing it to her and Dacon for so long that it's a piece of cake. The dust doesn't use any significant amount of power. It just comes when I need it. It's natural, like dandruff or flying. The immediate transformation of my other self gives off a lot of power, but once that's over, I could spread my wings and fly, and the vampire wouldn't feel the magik. Of course, they would see me flying, so I don't do it.

Livi assured me it wasn't Dacon and we ate our lunch with a new conversation—another topic that I didn't really want to talk about.

"You should've seen how irate Lord Cherkasy was last night. She was freaking out."

"I'm sure she figures that if she's good to Lord Galen's soldiers, he'll be good to her."

"I don't know." Livi shrugged. "I think she meant what she said. She didn't care if you killed a person who killed one of her vampires. You're suspicious of her because she gets to do things with Lord Galen you never will."

I threw a miserable look at her as I chewed the food I didn't want as if I were feeding on nails.

"Never mind. Sheesh." She pointed to an old man sitting on the ground near the corner. "I should bring my easel down here. I'd use up my charcoals in minutes."

"You could have a show and call it 'Philadelphia is Phugly.'"

"I don't know. How about, 'Pestilence is Pure?'"

"I don't think pestilence is pure," I said.

"That's irony."

"Oh."

❁ ❁ ❁

I GATHERED UP THE trash for Livi to take to the can outside of the diner. About twenty minutes after sunset, Romeo pulled up in our truck. He came strolling across the street with the EOD in toe. His strides were long. He held his shirt in his hand. He doesn't sweat, so I can only assume he's attempting to impress the eight-person bomb crew with his body. Funny, because I wouldn't describe Romeo's body as impressive. There's definition and strength to it, but I think I'd describe it as lithe before impressive. No one seemed to be looking, so maybe everyone agreed with me. Two female soldiers rushed ahead of the rest.

"Could you get down," demanded a blonde woman holding a huge duffle bag of equipment. "It may not be safe."

I guessed she didn't see the sense in sitting while you ate. Livi moved from leaning on the car as I began to shimmy off.

"Don't you need some help with your hurt leg?" Livi asked.

Romeo came to stand next to Livi.

"What up, brown shuga?" he asked, nudging her with his elbow.

"Fuck off, blood junkie." She made a face as if she were bored with him already. "Why don't you make yourself useful and help her down?"

He looked at me. He was still angry from last night. I could practically smell it. Gods, how disgusting is that?

"She got up there on her own, didn't she?" He gave Livi his full attention. "Besides, I was hoping we could—"

"Does being a half-breed leave you with half a brain?" she asked, shoving at him. "A half set of morals? A half code of ethics? Half the amount of sympathy a human has?"

He grinned at her.

"Put this on," she said, yanking the shirt from his hand. "What are you—a stripper?"

"I was late." He took the shirt back and buttoned up.

"Are you okay?" the woman with the duffle bag asked me. "I can help."

"Thanks, I ... um ... hurt my leg last night. Well, today actually. This morning. Really, really early. It's not bad, but okay, bad enough." I truly needed to shut up.

Romeo wrapped his arms around Livi's waist

"Listen to me, worm food," she said, pushing him away. "You will never, ever be confused with Prince Charming."

"That's not what you said earlier."

"Leave her alone," I said, pretending to gain my balance on the pavement as the girl helped me.

He waved me off with a backhanded gesture.

"On the street, my dark queen, you proclaimed your love for me," he said, taking Livi's head in his hands. "When I took you home, you tried to persuade me to make love. You said, and I quote, 'Romeo, if I don't remember this, we'll do it again tomorrow when I'm so ... so... *sobler*.'"

Livi couldn't keep from laughing a little bit. She shoved at his shoulders when he kissed her cheek. A few of the people from the bomb squad were laughing, because Romeo is a laugh riot if you hardly know him, or he hasn't tried to rip your throat out. The blonde set down her bag to help me walk halfway down the street. This was ridiculous. I had to leave.

Four soldiers blocked off a portion of the main road, redirecting traffic onto a side street further up the block. Livi moved away from Romeo to help two others section off a very wide, near circular perimeter around the car. I moved out of the way, past the rectory of the church. Romeo followed.

"That's a cute shuffle you got there. I like the way you bounce. You look like you belong in porn."

He acknowledged me. I supposed that meant he forgave me. I ignored him.

"Tight shirt, blue jean cutoffs, boots—if that doesn't say porn, I don't know what does."

"My shirt is not tight, it's normal. And what was I supposed to wear in this heat?" I pushed him away.

"I'm trying to say you look sexy," he said, giving me the smile—the boyish one that says he wants to play.

"Oh, sexy. When you said porn, I assumed you meant the cheap and slutty kind of porn."

I put a hand on his chest to keep him at a distance as he leaned into me. Only distance wasn't what I was thinking when my fingers were against him. The muscles in my hands twitched. Gods, my body was constantly overreacting. I couldn't remember ever feeling this undisciplined.

"C'mon. You're off tonight. Let's go do it. I'll make it worth your time."

I stared at him. By the gods, I was truly thinking about it. I shook my head.

"You just woke up, and already you're this focused."

"Hunny, I'm horny when I'm asleep."

I thought about hollering at him for the "Hunny" comment, but an icky feeling went through me. I wondered if he thought I found his sleeping body pleasing. He knows I don't mind it, or I wouldn't sleep with him. But does he think I want him sexually when he's day-cold? Does he think I do things to him? I was suddenly so freaked out that I limped away from him.

"I thought for sure when you left me you would've found someone to satisfy the urge."

"I did. I mean, I was on my way to do that, but I needed to talk to Galen. I couldn't find him. Then someone said he took you home, which I knew he didn't do, because I was there. When I searched for him up here," he pointed to his head, "he cut me off."

"I don't understand."

"I couldn't communicate with him. He can lock me out if he wants."

"I know that, idiot. I don't understand why you didn't eat?"

"He rarely does that," he said, looking at me, "unless he's doing something really private. And even then, not so much."

"Be a little more obscure, because I don't understand what you're getting at."

"Maybe he stopped by your house after I left?"

"What are you accusing me of?"

He realized I was getting angry, so he leaned into me as if he were going to kiss me.

"I'm sorry," he said, inhaling a long breath next to my cheek. "I can smell him all over you."

I pushed him, even though he barely moved.

"Fine, he was there. Now get away from me."

"I was kidding," he said, amusement fading, and I watched emotions flash across his face. Annoyance. Jealousy. Anger. "What? Who? Galen?"

"Yes, and what difference does it make?"

"A big difference."

"To who?"

"To me."

"Let it go."

"Why lie?" he asked, with hands on hips to show his disapproval.

"I didn't. He dropped off my stuff and asked if I needed anything."

"I know what you needed, so exactly what did you tell him?" he asked, his eyes widening. "And then what did he do?"

"What is wrong with you?" He scowled at me, so I did his idiotic three-finger salute. "I'm telling the truth. Nothing happened."

"Oh." He sounded relieved, and satisfied, like that finger gesture was the almighty high of my honesty. "Why didn't you say so?"

"I did say so. You're the one who's making a big deal out of it." Though, I did remember that he had called me by my childhood nickname. That was kind of a big deal, because I couldn't figure out how he knew it.

Romeo shrugged and then looked at the people working on the car. They were finished underneath and now trying the doors. "Still, I couldn't find him last night. I looked everywhere."

Maybe he's as sick of you as I am, I thought really loud. I limped a few feet away and swore under my breath. It was too difficult to pretend. I didn't want to bump into Lord Galen and make a fool of myself, or worse.

"I'm going home. I've been in the heat all day, and I feel like hell. Call me if you need anything. It's all here though, I guess. You know this guy's dead, right?"

He nodded, still watching the squad deftly picking their way into the Psycho.

I limped further down the street toward Livi's car. I would have to get the keys unless she wanted to leave too, but I didn't think she would.

"Something did happen!"

Romeo's voice burst the silence around me. I kept my pace around the red tape and fluorescent cones. I limped half a block out of my way to get to the car, but he was next to me, as if dropped from the sky. I yanked the door open only to have him push it shut.

"I told you everything. Besides, he's more than an adult." I paused, because that made absolutely no sense. "Anyway, he can do what he wants, or who he wants. Are you really this jealous?"

He smirked. "I'm your number one, and everyone knows it."

"First off, no, you're not. Second, not of him. Of me."

"Good question," he said thoughtfully, "but no."

"Then what's the problem?"

"I worry."

"About him?"

He sighed. "He's an unpredictable man and a hazard to your health. Will you stop fucking around with nasty vampires and find a normal, human guy to torture."

I pulled back my fist and he jerked his hands up in protection.

"Sometimes I hate you. You say the most mean, sexist things. The lords are ancient, but none say the abominable things you say. Let me clarify something. I don't need you to worry about me. I'm an ace at taking care of myself." He opened his mouth as if he wanted to protest but said nothing. "Do you remember the last normal, human man I spent time with?"

"That was bad." A slow grin crept over his face. "But they're not all going to date you to get to me."

He was smug, and I wanted to hit him, but the truth was just that.

"Uh-huh. Whatever. Just leave me the hell alone. You're the one who never misses an opportunity to tell me how the old, influential vampires don't want anyone like me. How a vampire like Lord Galen would never be interested. So I, or you, should have nothing to worry about."

Livi trotted up behind Romeo. She handed me a chocolate soft serve ice cream cone with rainbow jimmies. I bit the point and hurried to lick the trails running down the sides of the cone. Livi bumped Romeo's body with her backside. When he pulled her close, he nuzzled his face in her neck and they fell against the side of her car. He whispered in her ear.

"Never gonna happen," she said and then frowned at me. "What's up? Why do you have that face?"

"She's hiding what happened between her and Galen when he stopped by your house last night."

Livi's glassy gaze settled on me. "He was at our house?"

"Only for a couple of minutes."

"In her room," said Romeo.

"Ooh, the vampire of her dreams in our house," Alivia said as she snuggled into Romeo. "How exciting is that?"

"Please don't say that around people," I said as I looked around.

"Sorry, Dru, I can't keep it a secret any longer. I'll admit that what I heard was through the wall, but it was disturbing all the same."

"Do tell." Romeo grinned.

"She said, 'Please Galen, I need to feel your strong, unholy body between my soft female legs. Let me have all you have all night long, my sweet vampire man.'"

I grew defeated as my ice cream grew smaller. "I did not say that."

"But it resembled that?" asked Romeo.

"No!" I tried to push them away from the car door. "You're both acting like idiots."

Livi was absolutely giddy. She stood there, wrapped in vampire, flicking small peanuts from her ice cream to the ground. That's when I realized she must've taken more of those pain pills. She was way too comfortable with Romeo. "Then Dru said, 'I'm gonna ride you till dawn, my black-maned god.'" She turned her head to look sideways at Romeo. "Is maned a word?"

I laughed as I gagged ice cream into my hand. Romeo was trying to be serious, but I saw his body shake with laughter, and the smile on his face, even though he buried it in Livi's hair.

"Wait. Wait," she said. "That's not all. They were in such a sexual frenzy he tore her clothes off her body. I heard it!"

"Really?" said Romeo.

"I can't believe she didn't tell you. Oh, and he healed her leg too. Said it was so she could get into better positions. Take a look."

I don't think my mouth could've opened any wider. I know I couldn't keep the surprise off my face, even if what she said was supposed to be a joke. I glared at her, but her slow understanding of what she'd done told me how high she really was.

Great, everything is fun and games until someone kills a faerie.

Absorbing my near hostile reaction, Romeo glanced at my covered leg. My heart began to pound. I wasn't sure what to do. So I got angry. I would fight my way out of this, kicking and screaming.

"Are you two finished?" I tossed my ice cream on the ground and wiped my hands on my pants. "Are you through making fun of me, because I've had enough of it. Give me the keys and get away from the car so I can get the hell out of here."

Livi knew she had messed up, but I don't think she was sure if I was angry with her or if I was playing the part to get out of the trouble she'd put me in. I didn't know either. It seemed she'd pulled the lid off a large container of outrage. Livi pulled Romeo from the car, but I took a step toward them before I got inside. Sensing my anger, Romeo put his hand up to stop my tirade.

"You saw what he did to me last night," he said. "Your body can't handle what mine can. He'll hurt you if you give him the chance."

I was so angry and so tired of him interfering that my whole body trembled.

"Fuck. You. You annoying jackass."

"Dru," said Livi, sensing I was becoming unhinged.

"If you make him angry enough, he will hurt you," Romeo said as he took my arm.

I jerked out of his grip. Last night's frustration had returned. I was on a roll and the hill was steep.

"Just stop it. You overreact every time I'm near him. You never miss an opportunity to throw the fact that he doesn't want me in my face, yet you won't allow me to be alone with him for more than a minute and a half. You say you don't want me, but every time—"

"Dru," Livi interrupted. "Don't," she said, not wanting me to turn this into something it wasn't. She was trying to stop me from making a fool of myself or getting into trouble. It didn't matter and I didn't care.

"Every time I'm near another man, you practically piss on me. Yet, when we're alone you can't say enough things to turn me off, or get me angry, or put me down. What do you want from me, Romeo? Seriously. What do you really want from me?"

His eyes widened. Unconsciously, he pulled his lip into his mouth as if trying to figure out the question. It may have been the first time he was speechless. It was definitely the first time I'd ever asked a blatant question about his feelings for me. When he didn't speak, I drew my own conclusion.

"So, if you want nothing from me, how is any of what I do your business?"

"Please," said Livi. "Calm down."

"Tell me, how does your father coming to my house affect you at all?" I asked.

Silence.

"Maybe we talked until the sun came up. Maybe he told me he could smell how much I wanted him, and then offered to make me feel better than any man ever has? What if he really meant it?" Romeo's words used against him were cruel, but I wasn't feeling anything better than that.

His brown eyes slipped away. Angry red dots popped around the irises, and I honestly had no idea why. Did he really not want me to be with anyone else? Could he be that selfish?

"Don't pretend to be upset," I said. "You've made your feelings clear, on more than one occasion. It shouldn't bother you if I said he was the best sex I'd ever had, or if I tell you how well he handled me." I stepped closer to him and lowered my voice, as if I were divulging classified information. "The things he did to my body made me feel like I'd only ever been touched by boys."

Livi's expression fell. She was confused. She wasn't sure if I was making it up or retelling the event. Romeo's hands fisted. He looked at me with bloodshot, unblinking eyes. He knew I was lying. He also knew it was what I wished for, and he didn't seem to like hearing about it.

"Good part is, now I can go to your father when I want to get off. No more barking up the wrong undead tree."

"Oh, Dru," whispered Livi. "No."

Okay, I'll admit that I'd overdone it. I couldn't seem to stop myself. It took a few seconds for the light to dawn, but after a moment I realized they both were staring over my shoulder. I turned around—slowly. Galen was next to me. So close, I couldn't understand how I didn't feel his presence. I looked up at his face.

"Glad to know that I please you," he said with only a very small smile.

My mouth dropped open so wide that the gray bird perched on his raised hand could've flown inside and nested. I'd lost my anger, and every coherent thought I'd had.

Livi covered her mouth with her hand so the laughter wouldn't break through. Romeo smiled like a creepy, fanged Cheshire cat. I hated him.

"I ... I am ... they ... so ... I was trying to ... make a point."

"I may be interested in a point that has you coming to me 'to get off.'"

"Really?" I dumbly said.

"Of course," he said. "I aim to please all my employees." The bird flew to Romeo. It bobbed up and down on his arm. "He has missed you," Galen said to Romeo.

Romeo made kissy noises. "Who's my favorite bird," he said, and the small parrot went wild. It squawked loud enough that people on the block turned to see.

"Have you named him?" asked Livi, holding Romeo's shoulder for support as she stroked her hand down the bird's tail feathers.

"Nope, it's still just Bird." Romeo's anger toward Galen was clear. From yesterday, I supposed, but I didn't know and honestly didn't care. I was feeling agitated again and wasn't in a mood to decipher their problems. I had more than enough of my own.

"I have to go," I said.

I opened the car door and pushed everyone back a step. Galen gave me a cross look before heading toward the bomb people. I took Livi's keys and got in the car, taking care to play the invalid bit.

Romeo shoved Bird up onto his shoulder while Livi tightened her arms around him. She bit teasingly down his neck and jaw. Before she could wrap her mouth on his chin, he connected their mouths in a kiss. Livi … monogamy … doubtful.

I turned the jeep's engine over as I watched the trunk of the Psycho pop open from a relatively safe distance. I knew that if they were opening it on the street, it was probably clean. Livi moved with Romeo to get a better look. I was about to pull away when I saw Galen on his way to me. My stomach felt weird when he rested a hand on the door.

"Cheers," he said. "We can link this to terroristic activity."

"Guns? Really?"

He nodded.

"Well, no biggy. He was probably a flunky."

"It is one more piece, and there were others. Perhaps you could identify them. You could come to headquarters to check the computer photo files."

"Those guys were on their way out the instant I pulled up," I said, shaking my head. "I was at his house today and didn't recognize anyone. I didn't hand in the guy's personal belongings though. I could go through them. See if I come up with anything."

"I would rather you bring them to me." I guess my pause was a fraction of a second too long. "Have you already looked through them?"

I smiled.

"Once you found out his death was under suspicion, did you not think the material in the wallet may have important information?"

"I did think it might have information; that's why I looked through it."

He gave me a look of annoyed disapproval.

"There were conversion papers," I said nicely. "And I think one paper is a map. Maybe. I'm not sure."

"I will send Romeo to pick it up at your home. You will be there, yes?"

I nodded, even though I didn't think Romeo would want to see me for a while. I know I didn't want to see him. The truth is, I had the papers on me, but I wanted to go through them again, and Galen didn't exactly ask me, so I didn't offer them up. It isn't lying. Not really.

"Earlier," he said, and jerked his head toward Romeo and Livi standing with the other soldiers. "What was that about?"

"Romeo was just being an idiot," I said, feeling my face turn hot. "It, uh … he was looking for you last night and couldn't find you."

"Oh?" He looked back to see Romeo. "And that bothers him?"

"He says he's afraid you're going to hurt me," I rubbed my forehead and signed.

"Hurt you?" He cocked his head. "In what way?"

My mouth hung open for a second. How do you tell someone that he has a reputation for being sadistic and cruel? He must know it, but I didn't want to say it.

"You know … if I make you angry."

"I see." He nodded then, catching on. "Are you afraid of me?"

My heart jumped into my throat.

"I … um … no. I don't think so."

"I could think of better things to do with you than throwing you from a rooftop," he said, one side of his mouth turning up in a lopsided half smile, "or breaking a few ribs."

My first reaction was, damn, he does throw Romeo off buildings. My second was relief that he didn't want to break my bones, mingled with confusion at what he meant by thinking of better things to do with me.

"Better, how?" I blurted and instantly regretted it.

"Oh well," he mildly said. "Depends on your transgression, I suppose." He frowned. "I still cannot see how your argument with Romeo led you to say—"

I shook my head back and forth to dismiss his question. I had something else on my mind.

"Did you kiss me last night?" I asked, only slightly sorry I had.

"Are you accusing me of sexual harassment, lieutenant?" he asked, his brows rising high.

"What? Oh, no." I wondered if I looked stupid, because I was almost too embarrassed to speak. "I ... no ... I'm sorry. It's only that ... I thought I did. I mean, I thought you did. Never mind."

"Are you dreaming about me now?" There was laughter in his voice and a small sarcastic smile on his face. It didn't make me embarrassed this time. It made me angry. He and his son had a way of getting under my skin until I was too incensed to think clearly, or at all.

"I guess," I said with an edge in my voice that I couldn't seem to control. "No, actually, it was before I fell asleep, when you were asking me about—" I stopped. I was unable to talk about my strength of mind with him, and that agitated me further.

He smiled, looking down at me as he straightened his position. "No. I did not."

"Oh." The tension drained from me, and I felt silly. Unconsciously, I touched my mouth with my fingertips.

"Before I forget, you may return to night duty."

Now that was what I wanted to hear. "Really!"

"Yes, really." He glanced into the car at my leg. "You should take a few nights off."

"I'm okay."

"It was not a suggestion. I will not see you until Friday evening at the conference."

"Conference?"

"Jagen is making a statement about last night's situation and doing some political maneuvering."

I sighed heavily. Every time Jagen addresses the media, he does it here in Philly because we have the largest military base. If ever Jagen has to be in public and somewhat vulnerable, he wants to be near his general of militaries.

"He is not coming to get you," said Galen.

"I know." I fidgeted in my seat. "It's that conferences are a nightmare with the press from the States. It seems like we just did this a week ago."

"Fear does make time fly."

His smart mouth reminded me of Romeo. A more subtle Romeo, but it's all the same in the end.

"I'm not afraid of King Jagen."

His eyebrows rose high.

"I'll admit he ranks high on my freak-o-meter. But I'm not afraid of anyone."

He smiled. "You should report to the Conference Hall at eighteen hundred." He walked halfway across the street before he came back. He handed me a beret that he had unhooked from his belt. It took me a moment to realize it was mine. I hadn't thought of it or even known I had lost it. He bent down again to get a closer look. "Lieutenant Jefrey Lantz told me the female vampire had words with you."

"A few."

"She said?" he raised his brows again.

"Oh, uh, I was thinking on that earlier. She said, 'Give me what I want and I'll go,' or you can go. Something like that."

"You can go where?"

"I don't know. Just leave, I think she meant. As in she wouldn't kill me if I gave her what she wanted."

He tilted his head in thought for more than a few moments. I was beginning to feel stupid. He glanced back at the Psycho surrounded by military people.

"Could they not be separate?"

He wasn't really talking to me, and I didn't know where his idea was going, so I stayed quiet. Unfortunately, that seemed to irritate him.

"The female in the park, she asked you for what you have. It seems that what you have is this one's personal items."

"You think they're related? I honestly hadn't put one with the other."

"It is possible. Knowing what we know now about the vehicle."

"You think she'd kill for what I took from McKenney? Sounds like——." I didn't want to say, because he was the general, but, "It sounds like you're reaching."

"Apparently this Brian McKenney was flagged after you and your partner entered him into the system. Teena Hagan and Mr. Lantz's first detail last evening was to question him about an armed robbery a few months ago. Lantz was late for duty, so Teena went alone. Her notes said he was heavily sedated and rambled about his mother and the trees in the country."

"That's weird." I thought of the paper with the picture of the trees on it.

"Was Ms. Hagan killed," he thought aloud, "because she spoke to Mr. McKenney?"

Again, he wasn't really talking to me, but I had to speak up.

"Still sounds far-fetched. If he'd said anything helpful, Teena would've gone to Romeo straightaway."

"Unless she was under the impression that everything he said was worthless—the way you think his possessions are worthless."

I frowned.

"I am right," he said, looking at me, but not.

He sure was certain in his convictions. Does it take a criminal to know one?

"Be aware. I will have your home watched as a precaution and send Romeo with you now to get the decedent's belongings."

I didn't have a chance to protest because he was walking away as he was talking to me.

CHAPTER SEVENTEEN

WEDNESDAY CAME AND I limped through a memorial service for the soldiers who were killed in the park—three men and one woman. We didn't know them personally but felt it was important to go. Not only am I a night worker and have regular dealings with the D-squad, but Livi and I were involved in the crime scene, so it felt right to attend. It was depressing. They all had a ton of family.

I spent the rest of the week at home by myself. It was hard not to sleep the time away. Livi was working so I had nothing to do but clean my weapon, which took about two hours. Intense boredom set in and time passed unbelievably slowly. I started having dreams of people coming into the house while we slept. Livi feels it's because I'm not used to sleeping at night, and because I obviously have boogeyman issues. I think the fact that I was almost killed over a dead man's wallet warrants a bit of paranoia. Maybe if I truly had an injury to take care of, it would have been easier to deal with all the free time. However, I was perfectly healthy and out of my mind with scenarios involving McKenney's friends coming to find me.

Romeo had taken the man's things, only to bring them back on Thursday. He said Galen thought I might have insight as to what was there, so he wanted me to look over the pages and come up with some theories. It was difficult, but if I wanted to go back to Galen with something useful, I had to make up my mind about the validity of a map. I had to seriously look at the paper as if it were a destination.

Romeo told me "lundi" wasn't a park. It means Monday in French, so that was helpful, and we still assumed "n" was for north.

The only thing we had trouble with was LT; none of us had a clue what that meant. After searching the map north of Philly, Dacon came up with the Pocono Mountains. He thought maybe LT meant Lehigh Tunnel. The surroundings are suitable, mountainous, and heavily wooded. It's easy to pass into New York for discreet crossing of territory lines.

Vampires like to hide in mountains. They go underground for shelter during the day and take their captured food to the tunnels to feed without consequences at night. However, tunneling is a dirty, dangerous job, even if it's effective. Years ago, they used old mine shafts. We got smart to that and devastated and sealed the mines we knew of. A few were so old that they collapsed with undead inside. In one instance, six vampire lords voted against going in for the rescue. The shafts were too dangerous, and the vampires were buried alive. To this day, the thought makes my skin crawl.

I didn't know what tunneling into the Pocono Mountains would be good for, or where it would lead. The mountains aren't close enough to the States for illegal trespassing, but Romeo said he and I would check out the theory on Friday after the conference. If it were a dead end, and we drove two hours to nowhere, my aggravation would be nothing compared to Romeo's.

CHAPTER EIGHTEEN

By 17:00 on Friday, the heat was high, and I was dressed in a black, short-sleeved dress shirt, urban fatigues, and spit-shined boots. I armed myself with a clean weapon, my badge, and my attitude. Livi kept an eye on Channel 4's coverage of the local and foreign media ushered through the east gate of Galen Manor. She turned off the vid-screen after becoming annoyed at my annoyance.

It bugs me when reporters from the States battle with our soldiers about carrying weapons into the manor. They say it's their right—"It's for protection" and that "the element here is brutal." They say things like, "How are we supposed to come to this place unarmed?" As if the Territorians go around shooting each other dead in the streets. As if we're the Old West, terrorizing ourselves and killing hundreds of our own people in the last three and a half years. Our crime rate is comparable to the States of America and to most major countries. The attitude gets me so angry that I holler obscenities at the screen. I do it often. I did it today.

I decided to wait outside for Livi to finish getting ready. I hung my shades on my face, keeping my beret on my belt and my cloak draped over my arm. Both were standard for official military business, no matter what the temperature. We decided to hike it through the park. It was much too hot to ride in Livi's jeep or my clunky car, and with the extra traffic, it would take twice as long. I didn't hobble in public the way I had during the week. It was five days since the incident, and I figured I didn't have to play up on the wounded leg crap. I would walk slowly and sit more, but I wouldn't get excessively weird about it.

❀ ❀ ❀

DOZENS OF SOLDIERS CROWDED the grounds of the manor, so we headed to the south entrance of the Conference Hall. It was near 17:30. The day was waning, so I snapped on my cloak and beret before heading into the building. Con Hall is a large stately room used for press conferences involving old vampires, i.e., heads of state. The flag of each territory decorates the upper perimeter. Philadelphia's flag is spread wide on the back wall of the stage, which is situated about three feet above a large standing-room-only area. For this occasion, a few chairs were set up for the media's equipment.

Livi and I pushed through the room to the exit leading into headquarters. We picked up our assignments from the duty captain before we made our way to our lockers. I passed Romeo's workspace, a claustrophobic corner close to Galen's command center office. The oak desk and comfy chair are at least fifteen years old, yet look brand new. They are both piled with papers, digital files, and the like. A vid-phone on the desk rings constantly, with no one there to answer it. The duty captain frequently gives Romeo folders that he adds to the peacefully preexisting mountain.

Technically all of these things should be in an office somewhere, but Romeo doesn't want one. To my knowledge, he's never had one. He should have a secretary as well, but no one can work with him long enough for the position to remain filled. Galen has appointed him assistants in the past, but they never last. If it's a man, they fight instantly. If it's a woman, she holds her tongue, seduced by his looks and humor, until his true colors shine and the frustration becomes too great. In his defense, whenever he's asked for something, no matter how obscure, he produces it. It must be the superhero memory.

I caught myself getting excited to see him, and it disgusted me. He came to visit me only once during the week, for maybe five hours, and he spent most of the time studying the map. It didn't bother me at all. I spent some of the evening watching him have a serious conversation about terrorism with Dacon and an even more serious debate about the comic book hero, the vampire Nos, pitted in hand-to-hand combat against the twentieth century superhero, Superman. Dacon favors Nos because of his ability to think clearly while in battle. Apparently having a level head will win over brute strength any day. Whereas Romeo feels Superman is superior in all supernatural aspects, and he has the neat laser-beam eye thing. Of course, there's the deadly kryptonite. But then, Nos has a curfew.

Romeo did do something odd before he left that day. I hate that I've been thinking about it. He caught me in the upstairs hall and knelt in front of me. He smoothed his fingers over the area of my calf that should be scarred but isn't.

"It's healed nicely," he said. I nodded, uncomfortable with his proximity. When he stood, he rested an arm above my head and remained so close that I had to stay glued to the wall. "I never pretend to be upset."

"Huh?"

"It bothers me," he said and punched the wall next to my shoulder. "More than I can talk about. More than I can admit."

His fist made a deep hole in the wall. Dust and debris fell to the floor and all over my shirtsleeve when he yanked his hand out. He shook away the pain and left. It took me until yesterday afternoon in the shower to understand that he was answering my outburst from Spring Garden Street.

I WONDERED AS I rummaged through my locker if I'd get to see him before the conference started—not that I really wanted to. The sun hadn't set, and the conference would be over before it did. Jagen and the others wake early for these things. They always finish their portion of the meeting before most other vampires stir to life. This is done for two reasons I know of. The lords want to freak out other countries by showing they can be awake during the day. It works, even if everyone knows they can't go outside. The second reason is that Jagen would rather not have so many undead walking about while our house is so full of guests. The chance of a "misunderstanding" is greater when our nocturnal population is forced to mingle with the paranoid and frightened guests from the States.

Most of the reporters will broadcast live, stay for Q&A, and be on a plane by zero hundred. A few will stay overnight. We are another country, and some enjoy visiting the natives. They want to drink and be merry with us. Some even have mates here. Most Territorians find States men and women interesting as well. States women are said to be the most outspoken sexual partners, and many of the female reporters have vampire lovers here. They're usually married, living in "proper society," but have a flame on this side of the territory dividing mark. The human is embarrassed of what her family or god will think of her for loving the "damned," so the vamp is kept secret. I feel sorry for the vampire. I have known a few who were involved this way. They wait years for the bedroom promises to come true. It is sad when it doesn't happen—sometimes a lot more brutal than sad.

Years ago, a male vampire had waited sixteen years for his girl-friend to leave her husband. He wanted her to raise her children here. One weekend they had a fight. He lost control and killed her. He was executed, of course, but in truth, she's as much to blame as he. You can't play with people like that, let alone an undead.

"Helloooo." Livi waved her hand in front of my face. "We don't have to be at our posts until seventeen fifty-five, so I'm going to see Dacon in dispatch."

I nodded. I wouldn't follow that story too closely. I could only be so happy about my ex and my best friend. Feeling lazy and a bit tense, I decided to move the stack of digital files from Romeo's comfy chair to the floor next to the desk. When I sat down, my foot hit the pile and they slipped, washing the floor in green discs, like a strange-shingled roof on the floor. I closed my eyes and counted to ten. Sometimes, I can't seem to catch a break. I shuffled on hands and knees and gathered the plastic circles. It took about ten minutes of trying to put them into some type of order before I settled for a neatish pile. I felt guilty that I'd messed up Romeo's workstation, but not guilty enough that I'd try harder to fix it or tell him about it.

Headquarters had thinned and the Conference Hall was full. I saw Livi in the far corner by the steps leading to the stage. No more dallying—it was time to guard the king. At nearly eighteen hundred exactly, a heavy black door at the back of the stage opened. King Jagen came out, followed by Galen's daughter Lord Luise Cherkasy, Lord Orel from the New York Territory, Lord Multan from Maine, and our own Lord Pune. Romeo rounded off the group, closed the door, and walked to my side of the stage to stand by Lord Luise. Each leader was dressed in full military uniform, with weapon and cloak. It was impressive, if not a little over the top. They looked like a gang.

I was surprised to see Romeo. He isn't old enough to be up this early. Clearly, his animation had something to do with Galen, but I didn't know why this conference was important enough to wake him. Was it a show of solidarity? Most times, I try not to think too hard about what our leaders are up to. It hurts my head.

Romeo caught my eye and winked. He looked a tad out of it. If he were human, you'd think he hadn't slept in a while. There were darkish smudges around his eyes, and his posture was a little slumped. Still, it was quite a show for a simple conference. I supposed with the latest happenings that our heads of state wanted to put up a strong front, a show of force. Centuries old vampires gathered in a row equals a whole lotta frightening. You get the feeling that not only would they win a war, but they'd make the terrorists pay with their lives two times over, which is possible.

The reporters, camera agents, and the American Police Escorts—the only group permitted to carry standard guns—stopped their idle chitchat. A stillness quickly fell over the entire room as Jagen casually traversed the stage with the others fanned out in back of him, like an offensive line, but not too offensive. It gave the impression that all vampire leaders are unanimous in whatever Jagen had to say. The only sound was the soft buzzing of cameras linking the sight to the international network. What wasn't seen were the odd, almost greedy, expressions on the faces of the correspondents.

I liken it to an amusement ride. They're scared to be so close to the danger, yet excited and thrilled for the opportunity. That's because people everywhere are enthralled by vampires. They may hate them in public, but they'll watch them on computers and vid-screens in private. When in a vampire's presence, they show no contempt. The undead commands respect even from an enemy. It's an uncontrollable impulse. Something about standing in the room with ancient beings that bite makes people nervous, yet completely enthralled. Even I find it difficult to speak when so many are together, and I've lived here all my life. Of course, I have my own reasons for that fear, but Livi gets freaked out too. She's especially wary of Lord Brasov. He's a strange mix of Romanian and Jamaican. Livi says he looks at her as if she's the last Jamaican female on the planet. I've never noticed, but I trust her intuition.

Jagen stood on stage with the grace and nonchalance of a welcomed family friend. His long white hair rested perfectly on his ceremonial coat. As our king, he's a celebrity exceeding the expectations of the belittling rumors of other countries. In his defense, if he needs a defender, the decisions he's made concerning the Territories always seem to be for the benefit of our society. He's a strong power with an untouchable quality, and still most find his overall demeanor as someone not to be feared, but trusted and revered. Women and men both swoon at his unconventional beauty, holding fast to the idea that good things do come in pretty packages. I've never seen this in him. When he's near me, I'm not sure if I want to scream or hide. Possibly do one and then the other.

Jagen allowed a thin, closed smile to the audience. He then hesitated as a string of murmurs rose above the silence. Galen walked swiftly from the headquarters' entrance through the crowded room toward the stage. He looked tired, somewhat weak. He wore a plain white dress shirt with a small standing collar. His messy hair was pulled carelessly over one shoulder. His cloak billowed slightly as he walked. He looked like a gladiator entering the coliseum, ready to fight or do whatever is necessary to win. It was kind of dramatic. To his credit, he never had to pause. Everyone moved quickly—part respect and part horror. Some nearly jumped to allow him room to pass. His presence is threatening. I've seen people drop to their knees simply because he reprimanded them. Maybe if you're treated that way, you can't help but be dramatic.

He brushed past Livi on his way up the side stairs. On stage, he glanced at the quiet crowd. His dark, thin brows narrowed sharply. He placed his hand over the microphone, bending his six-two frame to meet Jagen's ear. When he'd finished, he turned and his boots sounded loudly as he walked to join the others at the back of the stage. Lord Cherkasy greeted him, connecting her hand with his. He didn't look at her, and I wondered how he could ignore her. The hair, dark as pitch, pulled high in a long, swaying ponytail. Her dark-rimmed blue eyes and radiant, pale face. Embracing is her specialty. There isn't anyone who can't look at her face, and then not get caught in her mind. She believes she's a queen, reveling in her title as much as Jagen. Most times, she dons outfits that rival his. Tonight, in her military uniform, she looked chic. So, of course, I can't stand her.

Jagen began to speak. He talked for twenty long minutes about the terrorist situation, the recent capture and subsequent death of Mr. McKenney, and the findings in the vehicle. He spoke of how he's interpreting these events, and how our patience as a country is wearing thin. Everything he said was significant, but my mind drifted as I watched Lord Luise insinuate herself into the middle of General Galen and Romeo. My teeth sank into the healed skin of my cheek, even knowing how she hates Romeo. I couldn't help but wonder if at some point he'd lean in and take her hand as well. Here were two royal children with their father, the happy family of vampire lovers.

Well, okay, Romeo and Luise were never lovers, so he says, but Galen and Luise used to be, just as Galen used to sleep with King

Jagen, his sire. Romeo says they haven't done anything like that in a ton of years. Livi, however, is right. The reason I hate Lord Luise is because she gets to do things with Galen I can't. Standing with her, his equal in so many ways, I saw that they suited each other. They made an outstanding couple. If the lords could truly hear my random thoughts, like Romeo says, she must have been amused.

"Wake up," said Livi.

I blinked at her dumbly. She was next to me, and I hadn't seen her move.

"You have that stupid look on your face." She stared straight ahead and let her mouth fall open.

"Go back to your post," I whispered.

"Are you concentrating on business?"

"Of course I am."

"I don't mean his business. I mean the business."

I dropped my chin to my chest so my laugh would go unnoticed. She never misses an opportunity to harass me about this situation.

"When you dream about him, are you two having molten sex, or are there lots of kids, with you pregnant again and him bursting through your thatched hut door with a few human sacrifices to feed the family?"

That was it. I turned and put my hands over my mouth to stop the sounds from breaking through. Thank the moon everyone was too busy scribbling on notepads, getting their questions ready for when Lord Pune came up front to speak. The guests would get an hour with our self-appointed Secretary of Territories and Lord of Congeniality. The vampiric host, if you will.

"Hey, look," said Livi. "They're leaving. Wait. Did you see that? I'm sure Lord Galen mouthed, 'I love you, Andru' before he left the stage."

Thankfully, the room was getting louder, because so was our laughter.

"You set yourself up for that," she said.

"How?"

"Must I do the stare again?"

"Please don't."

"You're lucky everyone's attention is on the king, because if they looked at you looking at the general, they wouldn't need telepathy to know what you're thinking. The Lord of War could file a sexual harassment suit against your eyes."

"I wasn't thinking about that. Not completely, and I try to appear interested in what's going on. You know, like I give a crap."

"The dreamy expression that lightens your face doesn't say I'm here for business. It says—"

"Stop it!"

An American Police Escort standing close to one of the more well-known reporters from Texas laughed. Livi smiled at him. For the most part, the A.P.E.s are kool. Sometimes after a conference, we'll hang out for a while. We compare stories on what group of politicians is more annoying to work for. Most agree humans are the worst.

I glanced at the podium. Pune was fielding questions like a pro. He has a great sense of humor that puts everyone at ease after dealing with the larger than life, spooky undead. Pune loves to socialize. He loves to be involved with the everyday. At around twenty-thirty when he finished questions, the Con Hall doors opened to begin another long hour of ushering people back to their vehicles, or directing others to Pune Hall, the nightclub on the ground floor of the northeast tower of the manor, where they were promised free drinks to help unwind.

When most reporters had gone from the manor, Livi and I made our way to the other side of the room while a few stragglers spent time talking live to all the good folks in the States. We stood near a large map of the Territories decorated with red pushpins to show where terroristic attacks had occurred in the past four years. We folded and stacked chairs as a way of appearing busy while bullshitting away the last few minutes of our detail.

"Look, Dru, the only thing you appear to be thinking is who's going to stitch up the lobotomy incision on your forehead. All you need are little cartoon birds tweeting around your beret. And one day, he's going to say something."

I trailed my hand through the sweaty hair on top of my head and then slid my beret back in place.

"I'm not that bad. You know how I feel, so you know what I'm thinking. But if it were that obvious, he'd have said something already."

"Honestly, I don't know what you see in him."

Here we go.

"He looks evil. When he passed me earlier, he felt like ice, or hell, or cold hell. I think it's better that he doesn't notice you. I think if he should ever decide to notice, you should haul ass in the opposite direction. I don't understand why we have to keep talking about him."

I banged the last chair against the rest.

"I'm not talking about him," I hissed, trying to be quiet. "You are. The rest of you always are."

"Because you're always thinking it."

"I'm not." I thought about that. "Am I? It's just hard for me to believe you don't find him the least bit sexy."

"I didn't say he wasn't sexy. I said he was evil. Evil overrides sexy — usually."

"I get what you're saying, but it's hard to stop an infatuation. That's why they call it infatuation."

"No, it isn't," she said, giving me a cross look.

"Well, you know what I mean," I shrugged.

"Remember who he is," she said, rubbing her hands over her face as if she was tired of this. "I'm not saying the old ones are void of emotion, but I don't know of one who fell in love with a human. Unless of course you count Lord Pune, who's fallen in love with every man, woman, and transgender human in our territory. I mean, damn, why him? Why did you have to fall for the only leader who's shown the least amount of emotion for more decades than we've been alive? Don't you get it?" She came closer to me, whispering even lower. "Everyone is afraid of him for a reason. And you have more reasons than any of us."

"I'm afraid too," I said. Then I did something Livi hates. I paused.

"Oh, god, there is a 'but' on your face!"

"There is not!"

"There is. You were thinking something but didn't want to say it."

"Can we change the subject?" I practically begged. I scratched my face with my middle finger, giving her a clear view of it. "I'll try harder. I won't think about him. I didn't mean to be so obvious."

"Obvious about what?" asked Lord Galen.

I gasped. I turned so quickly that I nearly fell. I stood wide-eyed and open-mouthed. He was maybe twenty feet from us. I glanced around the room, now empty of life besides us.

"Just the two of you," he said with a small smile. "Heads together, gossiping quietly."

"We weren't gossiping," said Livi.

"Why do you keep sneaking up on me?" I said, rather irritated and, obviously, without thinking.

"Sorry, my Lord," Livi said as she gave me an elbow in my side.

"Are you doing it on purpose?" I frowned.

She hit me again, which brought me to myself. Without the anger, I was left with a sudden case of paranoid paralyses wondering how much of our conversation he'd overheard. He clasped his hands behind his back and shifted his weight, but he didn't scold me. In fact, he seemed in a better mood. He appeared less drained.

"I suppose it really is none of my business," he said.

Livi was motionless. The panic in her eyes told me she couldn't have spoken if she wanted to. So much for acting normal.

"It's not that," I said. "You startled me, and I've lost my train of thought, my Lord."

"I asked you not to call me that." He motioned to my leg. "You look well."

"I am," I said, smiling stupidly.

There was an awkward pause, which is fine with anyone else, but this was more intense, considering he might have heard what we were talking about.

"Um, sir. I haven't had the chance to say that I'm sorry about the other night with Jefrey. When I ... kind of didn't ... I didn't mean to ... I don't know why I thought ... It was stupid, and I apologize."

"Running to the rescue of your friends will not become a habit?"

"Not at all. I wasn't—"

"Thinking. Not even a little bit."

"No." I glanced at the floor. "I guess not."

I looked up, surprised, when his bark of laughter broke the silence. "Was that a demonstration of abashed, ashamed, or embarrassed?"

"Embarrassed," said Livi.

"It needs work," he said, keeping a small smile.

I was suddenly very angry. Here I was trying to apologize, and he was being critical. I wanted to yell at him. I opened my mouth, and two things happened at once. Livi elbowed me in the side and Galen spoke.

"I am learning that harassing you has a pleasant side, captain. I was not aware of it until recently."

"Captain? Was that a joke?" I rubbed my aching side. "I took the promotional exam months ago, but I haven't heard a thing about it."

"You have heard something now."

It took a moment for his words to sink in. I had only put in for promotion because Dacon was doing it, aside from it being rather expected when you're enlisted for ten years. I was about ten months early, and I hadn't even studied. A thought made me suspicious.

"Are you playing with me? Are you going to deny it because of my—something stupid?"

He looked young when he shook his head. He smiled, and for a moment, I thought he was flirting with me.

"I have always been aware of your potential for juvenile behavior."

"That's a diplomatic way of putting it," said Livi.

I felt myself scowl. Seriously, my face crumpled without any knowledge or assistance from my brain. I think I'm getting tired of being the butt of the joke.

"Let us say your leadership capabilities, and your quick mind, outweighs you saying something stupid—most of the time."

"Thanks. I think."

"But I am warning you," he said. "Do not push me. I have less patience for commanding officers."

"Commanding officer?" Livi hit me hard on the back, sending me toward Galen. "Very nice!"

"Damn right," I said and pushed her back.

Galen turned and walked to the small desk in front of the stage. He was suddenly so deep in thought that he seemed miles away from where he was a moment ago.

"I'm a captain," I said, jumping into Livi's arms. She spun me so quickly my boots flew outward.

"I'm going to combine this and your thirtieth," she said.

"You're planning a birthday party for me?"

"It's going to be huge," she smiled and hugged my neck.

"I can't wait to tell Dacon," I said.

"He'll be so angry," she laughed. "He hasn't heard anything. Let me tell Romeo. And Sara, she'll be excited too."

"Don't make too big a deal out of this, Liv."

"Don't ruin this for me." She ignored my crass response. "Where should I have it? I could hold it at Valentina's restaurant, up around Old Byberry Road, because they have your favorite Russian food, or here at Court? If it's here, most of the soldiers will stop by."

"I don't know. I can't have an opinion. It's my party."

"I find it hard to believe that you have no opinion," chimed Lord Galen.

"She didn't say she didn't have an opinion," said Livi, laughing. "Just that she couldn't have one because she's the guest of honor."

Galen nodded his understanding and I frowned at the continued harassment.

"Nastya, would you join me in my chambers? I would like to discuss your previous tunneling experiences."

Livi's eyes widened until they nearly fell out of her head. Her mouth dropped open, and I did a superb job ignoring her.

"Now?" I glanced at the clock on the wall. "I have to be on duty at twenty-two hundred, and I wanted to get something to eat. But if it's important—"

"It is important." He looked at the clock on the wall. "This is your regular night off, yes?"

"It should be, but you know Romeo. Work, work, work."

"Who is this work, work, work Romeo?" he asked, giving me a strange look.

"He scheduled me tonight so we could drive to the location on the map that we found in the dead guy's wallet," I said, sort of whining, because I really wanted to eat.

"It is nearly twenty-two hundred now," he sighed. "You might as well eat. Can you meet with me on Sunday, around nineteen-hundred? Will that be satisfactory?"

"I think so."

"Let me know so I can keep the time open. And these," he picked a bundle of white material off his desk and threw it at me, "would be for you."

I caught two new captain's dress shirts. Four white crescent moon pins, each outlined in black, which was the official captain's insignia, were clipped down the front of one shirt.

"The tacks will be expected after Sunday and, of course, a white shirt for dress from now on."

"Thanks."

"Thank me by not allowing me to regret it."

CHAPTER NINETEEN

WHEN LIVI AND I were at headquarters, a good safe distance away from Con Hall, she jumped in front of me. "I can't believe he talked to you that way."

"What way?"

"He called you Nastya. No one does that but Dacon and your brothers." Her voice was filled with revulsion. "The way he looked at you."

"What way did he look at me?"

"He gave you clothes." She grabbed the shirts and shook them around. "No one gets clothes from him. Then he asked if Sunday was okay for you."

"He was being polite."

"He's the general, doofus. He's not polite. He doesn't give gifts to his employees, nor does he ask if they can stop by. He tells you what day is good for him, and you go."

I thought about what it meant that she saw what I've seen in the past. She gaped at me for a few more moments before a giant grin spread on her face.

"He has a major jones for you." I knew she meant it because she whispered the words as if it were the biggest secret. "If he'd had any blood in his body, it would've all been below the waist."

"Stop it. He's a guy, and he finds me attractive." I didn't think we could read any more into a few uncomfortable moments.

"I'm serious," she said.

"I see that." I walked around her and then stopped. "Even if. So what? What can I do about it? And weren't you just telling me that if he looks my way, I should run?"

"Maybe I was wrong. A vampire lord having the warm fuzzies for you can't be all bad. Why do you think he wants you to go to his chambers?"

"Ahh, gee, let me think—to discuss my tunneling experiences."

"You barely have 'tunneling experiences,'" she sputtered a laugh while air quoting.

"More than you." I made my way to my locker and tossed my new beautiful dress shirts inside.

"It's his chambers, Dru. There's a bed there." She linked her left thumb and forefinger in the shape of an "o" and then stabbed her right finger through it. I slapped her hands down.

"There's an office there too. It's a big one with cabinets and desks and phones and computers."

"Maybe you should ask him to the party."

"Yeah, sure. Excuse me, Lord Galen, boss, general, ancient vampire. I know this is outrageously uncomfortable, but would you like to be my date at a party where I might get drunk, and you might—"

"Get laid. I think he'll say yes to that, judging by the way he was looking at you."

"I was going to say, you might get puked on. Besides, I really don't think he goes to birthday parties or has dates. It's all too, I don't know—human."

"You mean normal."

She came close to me, pulling our heads to my open locker for privacy. "Think of it. Romeo says he hasn't had sex with a human since before the manors were built. You'd be the first warm woman he's been with in about one hundred years. You can keep your mind locked for a couple of hours. Be with him once. Enjoy the memory forever."

I pictured him the way I saw him one time after a staff meeting in his chambers. I had to go back to get my backpack, and he had already taken off his shirt and shoes to get ready for another meeting. I remembered how his bare chest and feet seemed to glow against the dark pants he wore. I wanted to touch the tattoos on his skin. Knowing that they've been there for so many years makes the ink more interesting. I tried not to stare, but it was difficult. I wondered how his body would feel against mine and thought that even if he only lay there, he would be good. I shook my head and noticed Livi do the same.

"You know what?" she said slowly, almost cringing as she spoke. "Never mind. You should stay away from him. I really mean it."

So maybe she wasn't thinking what I was.

"But you just said—"

"What I said was very wrong. Stay away from him. Especially now that you know he likes you."

"I don't know that he likes me. He was nice to me. Not a whole lot more." She tried to speak, but I closed my locker and threw my hands up. "Go. Go wherever you have to be as long as it's not near me."

"Congrats again," she pouted but kissed my cheek. "I'm going to go sit with Dacon while he waits for Precious."

"Why is he waiting for her?"

"He's working a double, and she's always late," she smiled. "I'll fill in the time."

CHAPTER TWENTY

I WAS TOLD ROMEO was in a meeting and wouldn't be ready until twenty-two thirty at the earliest. I looked for Lord Galen, but he was gone, so I made my way to the small lounge across from the duty desk. It used to be an office, but years ago we converted it to a break room. There's nothing to it: a counter, a few cabinets, a convection oven, and a fridge. There's an old video screen where some watch reruns of soap operas that Romeo calls "stories" from the turn of the century, and a few new shows of the same type featuring vampires in lead rolls.

A cat was in here at one time, but I don't know what happened to it. Dacon said he heard one of the vampires needed a snack. Livi said that should bother me, because I'm a witch. It doesn't. She said witches love cats. Maybe, but I'm also part of the Earth people, and cats aren't so faerie friendly. Many animals can see between the planes, and cats can't help themselves when they see something small and quick. I saw a tiny flower faerie mauled by an alley cat when I was a kid, and it traumatized me.

The room was empty and smelled of bleach, as if it had just been cleaned. I decided to eat toast with honey butter, my favorite, even though I wasn't very hungry. I also had a piece of cold pizza left on the table from the afternoon shift. No one should waste pizza. Unfortunately, the downtime allowed my mind to wander to some of the things I had been trying not to think about, like the dreams, the blood, and the death that occurs in each of those sleeping visions. It isn't always a curly headed androgyne, as in the dream at Romeo's apartment, but there's always the death of someone I barely know.

I'm not afraid of death, but the dreams are macabre. In the past, I've dreamed things that came true, but they were simple, like my brother calling, or waking up drenched in sweat from a cataclysmic wedding nightmare the morning before Dacon asked me to marry him. These new dreams are different. They're tales I'm meant to decipher, and that's irksome. I'm not good at cryptic. I'm good at secrets. I'm good at lying. My other life is completely hidden, but it's not oblique or puzzling. It's classified.

I washed my dishes and practically clunked my head on the cabinet to stop thinking. I didn't like topics that left me with more questions than answers. It's not in my nature to have to think too hard. I'm more reactive than analytical. Romeo assures me it's a fault. All right side brain usage leaves me too creative to see logical reasoning. I say that he should hope I never get too analytical, or our relationship is over. It's my flare for creativity that keeps me from under thinking his abominable behavior.

I picked up my cloak from the folding chair and headed to my locker to get my backpack. It was early for the midnight shift, so the area was fairly empty. Halfway down the aisle, I felt something cold dance up my back. No one was behind me, but I knew it was Romeo. He was playing games. I moved quickly up and down the hall, chasing goose bumps on my skin. I crept around the last row of lockers and spied him at the end of the hall, near the conference room. He was standing in the corner by a small desk. He had his face buried in his hands, hiding as much as any six-foot vampire can.

"Romeo, where for art thou?" I called as I ran down the hall. "Deny thy father and refuse thy name."

He peeked from behind his hands, saw me coming at him, and opened his arms. I threw my arms around his neck and he hiked me up.

"That's it," he said. "No more Shakespeare on movie night."

Sometimes there's a moment between two people. It can be subtle as this was, but there's still a vast amount of emotion behind the exchange. Romeo's smile, his happiness at me in his arms, was genuine. I knew it. He knew it. That he felt that way — the way I was feeling — meant more to me than I cared to admit.

"Put me down," I demanded, without losing my smile but not wanting to deal with whatever seemed to be happening.

"What is it about an armed female that gets me so hot?" he asked, tightening his fingers and playfully squeezing the back of my thighs.

"Girls with guns," said Doug, a friend of Romeo's in seventh squad. He was rummaging through his nearby locker. "It's sexy."

"But why?" I asked, looking over my shoulder.

"It's phallic symbolism," said Romeo. "Feminine and masculine. A girl with a gun is a girl with a cock."

"I don't know about that," Doug frowned.

Romeo laughed, a deep sound that made my knees weak. It was a good thing that I wasn't standing.

"Put me down," I again demanded. He pinned me with a bang against a metal locker. He was armed, and the butt of his gun jabbed the underside of my leg. "Stop it! This is seriously inappropriate."

"No one's here," he said as he looked around.

"Doug's right there!"

"I'm not here," said Doug, situating his holster and belt.

"See, he's not here."

"Your gun is hurting me." The second the words left my lips, I knew my brain had taken a vacation.

"What can I do? I got a big gun, and it hurts little girls."

Invisible Doug laughed.

"That's enough. Let me down."

I pushed his shoulders. It was like trying to move a concrete wall. Being a vampire has definite advantages. Romeo grinned widely. He pushed against me, harder and faster, until my back banged against the lockers, making a loud commotion. I punched him, but I was laughing too hard to make a statement with my fists. After a melodramatic moan, he jerked his body in mock orgasm. His head dropped onto my shoulder in fake exhaustion.

"Jupiter lives, Romeo, let me down!"

A familiar coolness circled the room. It raised the hair on my arms. Romeo's body swayed. He coughed as if something went down the wrong way. I think he was fighting the pressure of that cool force. I was fairly certain the feeling was Galen. He rarely shows displays of energy like that, but I supposed we were a bit ridiculous. Damn it!

"I would deny all and refuse anything for you, Baby," Romeo said, stroking his fingers down my cheek.

"Get off me, you idiot. He's coming!"

Romeo looked at me strangely. I think he was surprised that I knew Galen was on his way, even though he knows I sense things other humans do not. He's the one that told me. I had no idea no one felt the energies around them the way I did. I figured if you worked with vampires, eventually you learned to feel their intentions.

I threw my hands at his chest, and this time he fell back. His laughter faded to a knowing smile, and his shining eyes stared me down. He made me feel like a little girl and a beautiful woman at the same time. It's a Casanova move that he never pulls on me. I wondered why he thought I deserved the treatment. I forced myself toward my locker, hoping to remain buried while Galen passed through. Romeo, however, grabbed my arm. Using a loud, overdone English accent, he said, "You are mine now, milady. I will war with anyone to defend your honor." He gave a sweeping bow, one arm tucked underneath against his stomach, and the other stretched out completely. All he needed was a giant hat with a feather in it.

"Oh, please," I whispered and smacked the top of his head. "A woman's honor?"

"Wars have begun over less reputable causes," Lord Galen's voice preceded him from two locker aisles over.

Damn it. Damn it!

I snatched my cloak off the floor, but it was too late. He headed straight for us. My heart jumped into my throat. He had changed from the white shirt at the conference, and I wondered how much clothing he had stashed here at work. His pants weren't the usual black, but dark wine, like cherries. His shirt was deep burgundy silk with no buttons. One side of the material wrapped tightly over the other, creating a V neckline, no collar. The fabric twisted around his slim waist, and then disappeared into his pants. The sleeves were tight, pushed to the elbow, exposing a black tattoo around his forearm.

I forced myself to swallow, or at least blink, so I didn't look foolish, even though I thought it was too late. He stopped in front of Romeo—what a surprise—who was standing next to me. He lifted his right arm, giving a clear view of the tattoo there. You'd think for the ink being over nine hundred years old that it would look distorted, but no. It winds around his forearm just beneath his elbow, and it's as crisp as if it were done yesterday. Romeo told me it was a war symbol, but he lies. He always tells me miserable tales where Galen is concerned. I'm sure it's Celtic, and I'm almost sure it's a symbol of endurance or longevity.

Galen pointed a pale finger at Romeo. He didn't holler. He rarely does, but his brows pulled together tightly.

"Contain yourself," he said in a low voice that was close to harsh. "If you are going to act like a pubescent, I will be all too happy to treat you as such."

Romeo smacked his heals together with a loud click.

"I will control my wolfish ways, my Lord!" he said throwing his hand up in a traditional States Army salute.

"Do not taunt me," snapped Galen.

Romeo bowed and spun on his heel. When he passed behind me, he pushed a finger into my back before escaping into Con Hall, leaving me to fend for myself. Dick.

If Romeo's continuing antics bothered Lord Galen, he didn't show it. He made it look easy to dismiss Romeo, when I know it's anything but.

"Can you talk with me now? You seem to be free, at the moment."

I heard him, sort of, but a large leather book tucked under his left arm provoked my curiosity. I almost missed it, because his long hair was in the way. The book was old, with a rusted metal lock, and I recognized the symbols on the spine as Enochian. I'd seen a copy of it years ago, and I was sure it was a book of astronomy detailing lunar and solar cycles and powerful magiks. I couldn't imagine why he would have it. While it's true that here in the Territories you're free to practice whatever religion you wish, witchcraft isn't thought highly of even after the revival at the turn of the twenty-first century, and then again around 2035. You'd think a society filled with vampires would be more tolerant, but rituals and spell craft seem to be too mystical for the general population. I think if the public believed Galen was into witchcraft, they'd revolt. When I roused myself from that thought, I saw that Galen was looking at me looking at the book.

"Water damage," he said.

"Huh?"

"There was a leak in my chambers some weeks back. A few of my older books were damaged. This one had to be fixed." He showed me that the upper corner brass plate was newer than the others were. He smiled. "Aside from sentiment, it has no real value."

Older was an understatement. I wanted to ask who gave him the book—Copernicus? Galileo? Descendants of Turon and Pundacciu faeries respectively, or so I've been told. But I didn't necessarily want him to know I knew what kind of book it was. I don't know why exactly, but it seemed like the kind of information I should keep to myself. I nodded and I moved to my locker. I fixed my beret that had gotten askew from Romeo's shoving and put my cloak into the metal cabinet. If I stayed turned away from him, maybe he'd vanish without a word.

"And you," he said, stalling my motion. "Stop. Instigating."

Damn it.

"Yes, sir," I said and faced him. I truly didn't believe I'd insti-gated anything, but I was too embarrassed to argue about it. It isn't my fault Romeo does such stupid things.

"You have this way of — well, instigating," he said, narrowing his eyes at me. "Even if you do not do it on purpose. Do you realize the effect you have on him, at all?"

I was immediately irritated and shocked. "Did you just read my mind? Were you in my head?"

"You understand that even though I am a vampire, I am not ignorant, yes?" Galen said, his brows furrowed. "You realize there are ways of determining what someone is thinking without reading thoughts? Not every vampire is invasive and rude. Just as every human is not hotheaded, short-tempered, accusatory, and an instigator. Perhaps I knew what you were thinking because I have been reading your expressions for the last nine, almost ten, years. Your eyes enlarge until you resemble a doe, trying to relay innocence or irreproachability. I have been seeing that look since you became my son's partner. Difference is, now I do not always believe it."

My eyes widened further. Galen has never reprimanded me. Never. Even when I've done truly stupid things like call Captain Gloader an asshole, or lie to the king of our nation. He's suspended me, but he's never hollered at me. I suppose I deserved it considering I accused him, in a very public way, of doing something dishonest and illegal.

I was quiet for a few moments before I managed a soft—not to be confused with garbled—apology. We stared at one another, unsure of how to restart the conversation. Truthfully, I was agitated that he called me hotheaded, but how to argue that and not look like a hothead!

"Go ahead," said Galen. "You have something to say?"

I chewed the inside of my cheek, wondering if I truly wanted to evaluate my personality defects in the middle of headquarters. He raised his brows very high, as if telling me again to go on and ask.

"I forget," I said.

His smile broke into a full grin, pointy teeth and all. It made me smile, but I wished it didn't.

"I would like you to know that I am personally aware of disputes—wars, if you will—originating over deeds less honorable than the fight for a woman."

If I hadn't been standing still that would have stopped me.

"Way to make a woman sound like property."

"Not my intention at all," he said, his eyes widening.

"Defending a woman's honor by war is fiction created by writers and thespians to add drama to life, to stroke the female ego. No history book tells the story of a war starting specifically over a woman."

"Not true," he said and then paused. "I do not think."

"You're not talking about the big book that likes to blame women when all the bad stuff happens?"

"No." A deep frown set between his brows. "But—"

"War is ugly. Fabricating a story about how it started over the face of a woman is to romanticize or even trivialize something that should be taken seriously. But for some reason, it's assumed the average person will understand—condone even—a man getting so upset over the loss of a woman that he would start a war."

"If someone is angry with a lover it is difficult to make competent choices," said Galen. "Perhaps that is why people understand. It is nearly a rite of passage for a man to brawl over a lost love."

"That's not war," I said. "That's Saturday night at the Range."

"Still," he said, "I believe there are men who would fight for the woman they love."

I dumped out a huge grumpy breath. "I don't want a man fighting for me, let alone over me. Besides, if a person drops a lover for another, then they weren't that in love to begin with."

"You are young," he said with a small smile. "Are you suggesting anyone who has fallen out of love was not in love to begin with?"

"Well, maybe," I frowned. "Love isn't a choice. You don't choose who opens your heart. If someone gets inside of you to the point where you call it love, then it never leaves, even if you change or they change. You may not want to be with that person, but they're still rooted in your heart." He was about to speak, but I cut him off. "A lot of people call infatuation love, but it isn't. I think you can fall out of that."

"So you are saying there is room in everyone's heart to love ten people at once?"

"Putting aside the love of friends and family, because I don't think that's what we're talking about. Yeah, you could have sex with ten people and love them all."

"Equally?"

"How can you equate love?" I shrugged. "You feel it or you don't. You love people for different reasons, but not more or less. Can you say you love Lord Cherkasy less than Romeo?"

His brows rose high at the question.

"No, I suppose not. People stray for many reasons. Not necessarily because they fall out of love. With the threat of loss," he said and smiled, "I may start a war."

"No one would leave you." I stopped myself from smiling like an idiot.

"A testament to my temper," he laughed.

"Not at all. I only meant …" My feelings were banging on my chest, pushing at my mouth. "I only meant that you're … too nice of a guy."

He laughed again and moved toward me. He was so close. He seemed to be everywhere, and I was spinning, but relaxed, secure, and warm in his sterile eyes. I swayed and his fingers tightened around my upper arm. His earthy scent clung to me like heavy steam from a shower. Only this vapor had a scent like benzoin. The richness of him flavored my mouth—disturbing and arousing at the same time. He stood directly in front of me, yet I felt his lips against my cheek. His hair slid along my bare arms. I was distantly aware that there were people around us, walking by as if we weren't there. My nervous stomach felt hollow. Galen put a hand on my cheek, and I was warm again. The need for him nearly overwhelmed me, and still I couldn't move.

A cool tremor began to inch its way up my back. I felt slightly more solid, more real. The desire—or was it his desire—for us to touch eased. I was whole again, focused. Normal feelings of doubt, insecurity, pain, and fear crept back into my psyche. The warm, safe world faded. My heart sped as the blood rushed through me. I took a breath, and until that moment, I hadn't realized how isolated I'd become. How I was taken so far away from myself and so far into Galen that our physical bodies went unnoticed by the people around us. He swallowed me whole, and I never saw it coming.

During training, a soldier is taught the signs of a vampire trying to capture the mind. You are pulled in repeatedly so you can feel the slight flexing of power that emanates before. Some people are more susceptible, but if you're completely susceptible, you can't become an officer, not even behind a desk. It was the only class I aced. My mind is secure. Back then, I had Lord Pune embrace me at random times so I could learn the feel of it. After a while, I could sense when he was going to do it. I can feel it when Romeo tries. It isn't like books or movies. Not every vampire can capture a mind or hypnotize. Some can't even pull in the weak-minded. No young vamp can do it easily. It takes at least a hundred and fifty years to master the art of holding a mind, or to be able to capture passing eyes. To pull a person out of themselves is a remarkable feat, but moments ago I felt nothing. Maybe I was wrong. Maybe he did nothing.

I would guess that at nine hundred, Galen has probably mastered the human mind. My mind isn't fully human so ... was it more difficult? Did he notice? We are told no vampire can embrace the mind without residual effects. Romeo told me the older ones are able to capture without anyone realizing it. I didn't believe it, because that kind of mental power is frightening. Devastating.

My body shook, wondering if he noticed something different about me. I still didn't know for sure that he'd even been in my mind. If he was, I didn't see it coming. I didn't even know I was there. Damn it, it isn't supposed to be that easy. If this was a lesson, I failed.

I blinked, trying to regain myself. I stepped back, a small stumble to put distance between us. He grabbed my arm to steady me, but he was unnerved, untouched by anything other than beauty. That emotionless wall steadied me again. It was as if his touch took my fear and replaced it with his stronger constitution.

"The story of caring for someone and it going wrong is universal. Would you agree to that?"

"I guess so," I said softly.

He talked as if nothing had happened, like there hadn't been a bridge in the conversation. Maybe there hadn't. Maybe I had imagined it. Damn it. Damn him if he did anything. It's illegal!

"There are people we would all fight for."

He opened his mouth to go on when Romeo appeared at my side and took my hand. The skin-on-skin contact broke a mental bubble, allowing me to think clearer. He held my hand in a tight grip and pulled.

"Come on, I have the truck ready." The look on Romeo's face was forlorn, sad, like a threatened boyfriend. He raised his eyebrows and tilted his head to the doors. "I'm ready."

I frowned at him, then at Galen. What were they doing to me? Romeo pulled me another step away from Galen.

"He's impatient," I said, my head too muddled to protest.

"I am late as well," Galen said.

Then he did something very odd. He reached his hand out to me. I thought to do the same, but Romeo jerked me another step closer to the door. Galen watched us. He watched Romeo. Not quite anger, but something.

CHAPTER TWENTY-ONE

ROMEO PULLED ME DOWN the hall and out into the night. He let me go as we passed through the doors. The warm air hit my face and lifted any residual fog from my mind. It was full darkness now. Two large street lamps over the entrance glowed as tiny moths flickered against the glass. The moon was a second quarter waxing moon — about six more days and the night goddess would be brilliant. I jumped into the passenger side of the truck. I put my hand on Romeo's as he made to shift gears.

"I'm not your personal property. Please don't do that again."

"I'm ready so it's time to go." He didn't look at me when he spoke.

What happened with Galen gave me patience I didn't normally possess. It made it a little easier to deal with his tone.

"Don't give me shit because you think you're the boss."

"Here at work, I am."

"This isn't about work, and you know it. And you're hardly in the position to play the jealous boyfriend."

He gave a nasty laugh as if he didn't think that were true, and clear as day, I heard him think, *Whose bed do you sleep in almost every day?*

"You think you own me because we sleep in the same bed? You'd have to do so much more to be called my boyfriend."

"God damn it," Romeo said, banging his fists on the steering wheel. "Stay out of my fucking head!"

"I didn't—"

"You have no business being around him," he said.

"Don't tell me my business, and do you know what's comical? Dacon says the same thing about you."

"It isn't safe for you to be around him, and you know it."

"Dacon says the same thing about you!" He took a deep breath, and I noticed how heavy his breathing was. I put my hand on his arm. The fact that he was worried about me was sweet, but his tactics for protection were obnoxious. "Look, let's not talk about this here. You let me worry about me. I can control 'it' and protect myself."

"Like you did against Jagen?"

"I'm here, aren't I?"

"Not because of your all powerful—"

"Don't say it!"

"I'm right, and you know it."

"No, you're not. This conversation so close to the manor puts me in more danger than my altercation with Jagen. I can control myself. I can't control your thoughts, words, or actions. You're going to get me hurt."

"I'm going to get you hurt?" He tightened his fingers around the wheel. "You do that all by yourself. I didn't have anything to do with you lying to Jagen. What would you have done if Galen and Luise hadn't saved your ass?"

His tone was threatening, so I moved back to put a little distance between us.

"You know I try my best to stay away from Galen, from all of them."

"Answer me. What would you have done?"

"I would have died." He flashed me a miserable look. The way he banged his hands on the wheel had me thinking he might soon rip it off. "Romeo, magik isn't my only source of power. I've never been able to use it, so I've created other avenues. I've built a strong wall of support for times when I can't help myself. You're my strength when I have to be weak. Alivia and Dacon too. And whether he knows it, sometimes I have Galen, because of you. If I have an accident, they'll hurt everyone I know. So I don't have accidents. Jagen or Galen will watch me die before I show that side of myself."

"The closer you are to him, the closer you are to Jagen and the rest, the more danger you're in."

"I know that, and I try to stay out of his way." I touched his cheek. "We were only talking."

"Talking? Do you remember the last five minutes of that conversation?" I couldn't. I had forgotten what we talked about, and what I thought he did to me. "Of course you don't."

"Did he capture me in there?"

"Yes!" He faced me wide-eyed and pissed. "Jesus Christ, you can be thick."

I flinched at that. I hate when he thinks I'm being stupid.

"Why would he do that?"

"Because that's how he gets his rocks off."

I took a steadying breath. If he saw what I am from my mind, he wouldn't have let me leave the building.

"He was in my head," I said, trying to understand what that really meant.

"Not the way you're thinking," Romeo said, grinding the heels of his hands into his eyes. "It's surface stuff, like going into the brainstem, not the cerebrum."

"Oh." I was confused.

"He stares at you like he's never eaten a girl before."

"Livi said that too. That's a new thing, right?"

"Yeah, I guess," he nodded.

"I think you're both making more out of his looks than you should," I shrugged.

"Two people think it, but you still won't listen. I'm not a paranoid person, but maybe he's acting that way because he already knows."

"He doesn't know," I said as much to reassure him as myself.

"You're so sure?"

"If he knew what I was," I sighed, "he'd turn me over to King Jagen. Well, he might tell you first, which is a good thing for me."

"You care for someone that you think would throw you away?"

"You know what? I don't even really know him. How can I truly care for someone I don't know? All these years, he's been nothing but my boss. I've seen him look at me, but you say he notices me. If he does, I'm sure it's barely, and he'll get over it. He probably just wonders what you see in me."

Romeo stared at me and my face got hot, like that moment before you're about to cry. I swallowed and bit hard into the side of my cheek. For a moment, the truck was very quiet.

"You can't even say those words without disappointment in your voice," he said. "You know what's best, but you want him anyway."

"Why can't you let this go?" I wiped a betraying tear that slid down my face. "It doesn't matter. He doesn't care. I don't believe he sees me the way you do."

"He sees you. Believe me, he sees, captain." His tone was mocking, as if the notion that I could be a superior to anyone was ridiculous.

"Why didn't you tell me?" I asked, shoving his shoulder.

"Your dark god beat me to it."

"Are you proud of me?"

"You know I am." He didn't match my smile. He didn't look at me. "If he tastes your blood, he'll know. He won't be like me. He'll know right away—"

"Shh! He won't. You said he doesn't drink people."

Romeo was suddenly so angry that his fingers where white from making such a tight fist.

"If he fucks you, he'll bite you. He won't be able to control that."

"Fucks me?"

"Yes, that thing you do when you have the hots for someone."

"Gods, stop it. That was maybe the fifth conversation I've had with Galen in all the years I've been your partner."

"Only because you can't form coherent sentences in his presence." He touched his fingertips to my cheek. "How can I make them clear if they're not clear to me?"

"What?"

He slid his hand behind my head and pulled me toward him. Our lips barely touched, and I flushed from head to toe. I knew his heart was really pumping, because he exhaled a deep breath into my mouth, and I wanted him so much that I couldn't help but lean into his warmth. I twisted his shirt in my fingers. My hand went into his hair and I kissed him. It was almost as if he were using magik, but I knew my actions were my own. He had a way of making me feel desperate, and I was beginning to hate it. I threw my hands into his chest so hard his back slammed into the car door and my kidneys hit the molded plastic from the opposite force of the push. My hostility surprised us both, but how dare he act jealous when only days ago he turned me down as I practically raped him!

"You blood junkie," I said, my breath rolling in waves of angry heat. As much as we fight, I've never used that racial slur against him. It's nasty, but that's how I felt he was treating me. "You don't want me, but you want me to pine for you. You want me to ignore everyone else, so I'm here whenever you decide you're ready."

His expression changed until he looked guilty, maybe embarrassed.

"If …" He wiped a hand over his mouth. "If you … if you didn't look at him like he was the last man—"

"When I looked at you, you ran."

He opened his mouth.

"Shut up," I said.

He scowled at me.

"I'm not a toy, so stop playing with me." I righted myself in my seat. I was done with this conversation. "Get on the highway toward the turnpike."

❁ ❁ ❁

IT TOOK A MOMENT, but he let it go. I was sure he was sick of fighting as much as I was. Sometimes when we argue it goes round and round. To a small degree, because of what happened a few nights ago, this was different. There was no doubt he'd flirt with me again;

I knew that much. It is who he is. I don't think he even knows that he's doing it. When we pulled to a red light at the corner of 21st and Arch streets, Romeo banged his hands on the dash.

"I'm gonna knock the shit out of him. I swear it."

"What?" I looked up from searching my pack for a copy of McKenney's papers and a map of Pennsylvania. "Him? Who's him?"

He pointed a rigid finger at the right side of the windshield to show me a small crowd of people fighting on the street corner. A newly converted man, Teddy Mastermann, and his human wife, Elaina, have a good fight that usually comes to blows about once every other month. They've lived in our district for years, so we know the gruesome couple quite well. Teddy was a miserable pain in the ass in life, and he's a miserable pain in the ass in undeath. Elaina's no saint. She loves a good row. She's been told that with Teddy's newborn strength, provoking him is a bad idea, but she lives to get him going. Sooner or later he starts knocking her around. She runs to her friends. They call us and the circle goes on.

"Even off duty I've got to deal with his bullshit?"

"No you don't. We're on special assignment. Let someone else handle it." I looked at the time. "Dave and Lucy are out there somewhere. Call it in." He gave me the most wicked grin and flashed his sharp pearly whites. I sighed. He is going to do something dumb because of our fight. I thought that loud and hoped he'd heard it. "It's a domestic. Call it in and we can go."

He pulled the truck alongside the arguing bunch. When he jumped out and slammed the door shut, all heads turned. Teddy must have sensed Romeo's anger because he ran faster than any young vampire I've ever seen move. Why is it always the idiots that get the power early on? Maybe that's why they're idiots. About three-quarters of the way down the block, Romeo had Teddy by his arm and t-shirt. Teddy screamed obscenities before being slammed into the wall of the building next to them.

"Dickhead?" roared Romeo. "Did you just call me a dickhead?"

I didn't hear a thing.

"Mister Mastermann. Are you verbally harassing an officer of the military?"

Teddy shook his head, but Romeo grabbed it. He smashed the younger man's face into the copper sign laid into the brick, and left the names of Smithfield and Basson, Esq. covered with blood. Teddy screamed on his way to the ground.

"You wanna pick on someone," said Romeo, "pick on me, you little fuck."

Oh boy.

It seems sickening to use the word graceful, but when Romeo pulled his foot back and swept his boot into Teddy's side, sending him at least twenty feet up the block, graceful is what it was, like an Olympic event. A perfect ten. Blood flew from Teddy's mouth—a thick, red trail lined the pavement. Romeo stalked toward him. His fingers rubbed against themselves in anticipation. I sighed again. Can you say excessive force?

I made my way to Elaina, who was surrounded by six of her friends—four female, two male. She was sobbing, near inconsolable. Two of the girls had the numbers 1, 2, and 3 stamped in neon green on the backs of their hands. It's a system from Darla's, a local vampire/conferrer nightclub. The color coincides with blood type. The numbers are a way of keeping track of the people who've been bled and how often. Your size and weight determine how many times you can "donate" in one night. To say the two meager, shadowy figures in front of me were able to give blood three times tonight was being seriously generous. One of the guys had a portable vid-phone wrapped around his neck. I told him to call the military emergency number. I really wanted to leave before the situation turned uglier.

Elaina moaned her obscenities. She would've jumped in my face had she been strong enough, but she was particularly beat up. "That's not right, lieutenant. He can't hurt Teddy like that!"

"A vampire doesn't have the same rights as a human; you know that. Any means necessary to subdue the assailant. That's the law."

"He didn't do anything to Romeo!"

"He ran," I said in a tone equal to my mundane expression.

"That's not right." She motioned toward the men. "Look at what he's doing to him."

I turned to the fight, although beating is probably a more accurate term.

"That's the law, and you both knew it before he was converted." I pulled the back door of the truck down so Elaina could sit, and I looked over her wounds. The bites on her neck were swollen, matching older, less tender marks on her wrists and upper chest. The swelling happens when the bite is harsh, he probably forced her. "Is he still in conversion counseling?"

She nodded.

"I think you need to go too."

I pulled a card from my pack with the name and number of a "Partners of Vampires" psychiatrist. Dr. Casey Starr runs a clinic for the abused human partner. Elaina has been "glued," meaning she's a human who has bound her energy or soul, or whatever you want to call it, with a vampire. Some people, mostly vampires, call it bonding, but it truly means Elaina belongs to Teddy, and that can be a good thing in certain circles. Other vampires will smell him on her and leave her alone. It can also make the human a slave, depending on the temperament of the vampire. Elaina will do whatever Teddy tells her, whether she wants to or not. Fortunately, it isn't permanent. That is, it can be broken through separation.

I gave her the card. She wouldn't go, but I had to try. I held her face to the streetlight. She was drawn, skinny, and her skin was ashy white. She looks like a junkie, and she is. Many people, not all weak-minded, become vampire dependent. They let a vampire do all sorts of things to them in return for the euphoria of digging into their mind. It's better than a drug to some, even if the vampire is young and relatively weak.

Romeo says clinics won't work, because people never change. He says in his day people abused drugs, and if today's blood donors didn't have a vampire to leech onto that they would be junkies too.

Maybe, but it's sad all the same. He also refuses to treat Elaina. He doesn't have the patience, and he just plain likes kicking Ted's ass. I think that "love of the fight" attitude is most of the reason we have so many vampires signing up for the military. They are born with innate aggression. The military allows them the liberty to explore that energy under the umbrella of the law.

I pushed Elaina's head up to get a closer look at her scars. Lumpy, soft pink tissue covered her face, arms, and neck, as well as the tender skin near her eyes. Her bottom lip was torn clean through. It was scabbed over, but swollen red with infection.

"That a vampire bite?"

She nodded. "He kissed me and yanked his fang through it."

Thanks for sharing. I used disinfectant from my kit on her lip and a few other bites that were looking rather nasty.

"Haven't you had enough?" I finally asked. "And I swear if you tell me you love him, I'll beat the crap out of you myself."

Teddy came skittering along the sidewalk, careening into the back wheel of the truck. Romeo yanked him to a sitting position by his bruised limbs, banging him into the back end of the vehicle.

"If you touch her when you get out of jail," Romeo said inches from Teddy's face, "I'm going to come to your house and knock every tooth out of your fucking head."

I could hardly believe it, but Teddy started laughing. We've never talked about it, but Romeo has to know that on some level Teddy likes this attention—and probably the pain. Still, I bit my lip for what was to come. He really was one stupid individual. Tears slid down Elaina's face. Her tribe of friends watched like this was the saddest thing they'd ever seen. I doubt that's true though.

"They'll grow back," Teddy muttered past a mouthful of bubbling blood.

Romeo smacked his open hand on Ted's forehead, forcing the back of his head to bang against the truck.

"The point isn't to make you toothless, asshole. It's the price for your predilection for pain. The point is to see how many creative ways I can yank every tooth out of your head with the most amount of hurt. See how much torture you can take, and when you're out of teeth I'll move on to your fingernails."

"He can't do that, can he?" Elaina looked up at me with pleading, wounded eyes.

Romeo smiled at her. He showed a malevolent grin that let you know he was more creative in person than he would ever be on paper. Teddy's pained expression fell, but not in enough time to stop Romeo from sticking his fingers in his mouth. There was a snap as Romeo yanked his hand back. He had ripped out a fang, nerve and all. The young vampire shrieked. He writhed in agony, trying to evade Romeo's grasp and slide under the truck.

Romeo got off his knees but stayed in a squatting position. He callously tossed the tooth over his shoulder and then bent to put their faces together.

"You know that biting without consent automatically gets you thrown in jail with possible fang eradication."

Teddy mumbled something while trying to back away. Romeo smiled at me.

"Eradication means they take them away for good. They pour acid in the root so the teeth won't grow back. But sometimes they do, and it's excruciating, and you'll have to go into the hospital so they can do it again and again."

Elaina fell off the truck next to her husband.

"No, you can't!" She threw her arms around his neck. "You can't do that!"

He hugged her as if she were a never-ending ray of light in his otherwise dreary existence. He'll be executed if he can't get a hold of his temper, but again, he's been told.

Romeo was happy now, quite proud of his lies.

"He'll be like one of those useless old lions at the zoo. No teeth to catch his meal. Spoon-fed by his trainer."

"Stop it," Elaina said.

"No reason to live," he continued.

"Leave us alone."

"You're the trainer, Elaina," Romeo said. "You'll have to heat his blood and pour it down his throat. Watch him wither away if he can't tolerate animal blood. Undead and still alive."

I'd heard enough. I walked to the back of the truck and closed it up. Romeo has a real cruel streak that I can't always abide. It's true that Teddy will spend the next twenty-four hours in a secure cell, and with his rapidly acquired jail terms, there's a chance he'll be banned from human blood. He'll be forced to wear a monitoring collar and drink bottled animal blood or packets of blood substitute from a trade machine, but acid in the mouth? That's just plain stupid.

Another military team pulled up with an ambulance close behind. A female vampire, Lucy, and her human partner, Dave, stepped onto the sidewalk. I smiled to myself. I liked looking at Dave. He's absolutely magnificent. He has light brown hair, spiked like a States' Marine, and deep blue eyes rimmed with lashes so black and thick that it almost looks as if he's wearing mascara. Some people get all the good genes. The female vamps impatiently waited for him to finish training. Lucy lucked out.

I waved, and when Dave smiled at me, I couldn't help but smile back. Romeo rolled his eyes at my behavior. As he passed me, he wiped his bloody hands down the back of my shirt. When he stepped up to the driver's side, he banged the hood of the truck.

"Clock's tickin', Don Juanita."

I caught a glimpse of Elaina explaining to Lucy what happened. She kicked her foot in the air to show what Romeo had done to her man. Lucy's blank stare mimicked my own. I snuck one last look at Dave—that is to say, I snuck a look at Dave's ass before I got inside and shut the door. I was shocked that Romeo waited until the medics got Teddy clear of the vehicle before he moved it. He glanced at me sideways after we pulled away.

"You're naive."

"About what?"

"Dave plays all you girls."

"So do you."

"He knows how good-looking he is."

"So do you."

I looked at the side view mirror as Elaina's friends flocked to Dave as if he were food at a fasting convention.

"He could play me for a while."

"He's a fuckwit," Romeo said. "He's stupid. Literally. Ten cents short of a dime."

"You never approve of anyone I like."

"I'm not jealous," he frowned.

"I didn't say you were."

"The problem is that you have really bad taste in men — and vampires."

There has only been a handful of either in my life, I thought really loud. Of which he is one.

"Can we concentrate on business?" he asked, giving me an irritated glance.

"Whose?" I laughed.

"What?"

"Forget it." I fidgeted with the radio until Romeo brushed my hand away. "You realize they're going to put in a complaint about you?"

"Fuck them," said Romeo. "Let him take me to court."

"To Court? Why? To buy you a drink?"

"What? No, I mean to trial. He can take me to trial."

He sighed that frustrated sigh as if no one in the world understands him. I continued poking the radio so I didn't have to talk. Eventually, he slapped my hand away from the buttons, because I like to listen to classical music when we drive. Romeo likes anything rock and roll or harder. I do too, except when we're working. The fast beat makes me hyper. We were on the highway for about thirty minutes before he spoke two words.

"Stop humming."

WE WANDERED FOR MAYBE two hours, when we came to the Lehigh Tunnel running through the Blue Mountains. I ate two of the apples I had brought in my pack while struggling to decipher the silly little map that probably isn't a map at all. Becoming annoyed at our most recent topic of conversation, I made Romeo pull over so I could stretch my legs. I was beginning to feel strangely claustrophobic around him and his father. They both had a way of making me feel agitated and oversexed at the same time. I wasn't enjoying it. He pulled into an outlook area. There were picnic benches and those magnifying machines you feed money so you can see the landscape, which is definitely worth looking at. The area surrounding the mountains was gorgeous this time of year.

"I don't think strays would use this mountain for safety or anything else really," said Romeo as we left the truck. "There's too much activity with the traffic from the tunnel."

He disappeared into the brush for about fifteen minutes while I stretched, first fingers to toes, then fingers to sky. The stars were like tiny white shards embedded in a tissue of inky darkness. Each sparkle protected the moon like armed soldiers guarding the goddess of the dark. Those are Romeo's words — something I read in one of his poems, and tonight they were appropriate. The sky was beautiful, and I felt poetic under it.

I pulled myself up onto the hood of the truck and let my boots bounce off the grill. Romeo emerged from the bushes holding a rabbit by the scruff of its neck, smelling of pine from the trees he'd walked through. He held the animal close and stroked its back.

"You don't want to admit I'm right," he said as he sat down. "But I am."

"You're not. What you are is so far out of your mind your mouth is talking stupid. The meaning of the story is a girl's — in this case Alice's — ascension into adulthood or womanhood. She goes through the rabbit hole, representing childhood, to come out on the other end, adulthood. All the characters are her childhood playmates, good and bad, which she will eventually have to leave behind."

"No, the rabbit represents a man," he shook his head and held up the gray fuzz in his hands. "And the rabbit hole is the birth canal representing their new life together."

I shook my head.

"She follows him — 'cause chicks always follow the guy — into the hole because she realizes she wants everything that rabbit has to offer." He wiggled his eyebrows and smiled. "All the characters, such as the Mad Hatter, are her possible life and sexual partners. Her fantasies. Every woman digs a guy who's a little mad. And the Cheshire cat? Wouldn't you love a guy who occasionally disappeared?"

My mouth hung open. What was I supposed to say? Besides, I was irritated that he was beginning to make some kind of sense.

"You think everything is about sex."

"Isn't it? One way or another."

"Maybe," I said after thinking about it.

I tapped McKenney's paper and turned my attention back to it. I stared at the grainy picture of trees. It was similar to the view over the outlook railing.

"This part here, it could be those trees." I turned the paper this way and that. "We could be near it." I looked around. "If there's an 'it' to be near."

Romeo clasped both hands around the rabbit. He pulled the hair apart, showing its pink skin, and the animal's feet skittered frantically when he pressed his mouth against it. He whispered for the rabbit to be quiet, and it slowed before it stopped fighting altogether. Romeo closed his eyes before he bit down. He sucked for maybe a minute, and when the rabbit was empty, he slid from the hood and put the corpse back where he had found it. He bounced his way out of the bushes, making a beeline to the truck to get my thermos from my pack. He took a swig, swished the water violently around his mouth, and spit a pink arc into the bushes. He wiped his chin with his shirt-sleeve before he came to me.

"Hey," he said, rubbing his warm hand along my arm. "Do you remember when—"

"Ew, get off me. You didn't wash your hands." I only meant to brush his hand away, but I accidentally knocked him back a step.

He stumbled, exaggerating the movement. He pretended to cry, and I ignored him when he came to lean his head on my lap.

"Don't start."

"You were the one who started when I was at your house last week," he said, wrapping his arms tightly around my waist.

"I was not. You cornered me."

He turned his face up, wearing a familiar look of confidence as if somehow he knew the moon's glow would reflect in the darkness of his eyes. That the images would glimmer like tiny diamonds trying to take my breath away. His arrogance tells him that I'll be his forever, or as forever as I could get.

They shine for you.

I wasn't sure if he'd read my mind or my expression. My thoughts of him were obvious, and I was sure I hated that.

"You know you want what I got," he smiled. "Kiss me, baby."

I kicked him away as I usually do when he opens his mouth.

"You keep harassing me and I'll ask for another partner. It's my right as a captain to be the boss of my own peon. I'll ask for a human, and a girl at that." I pushed around my cloak to find my flashlight on the backseat of the truck.

"Ooh, a human girl. What would you do with her out here in the middle of the woods?"

I ignored him and walked the graveled road going in the opposite direction of the tourist area. Trees by the edge gave way to a deep expanse of woods. I pushed my way through the branches into a vast area alive with darkness. It must have rained recently because the leaves and bark at my feet smelled musty. The air was thin against my skin, but touchable, as if something I could move. It was so different than the city, and I wondered if we were in for an early winter. I could smell a willow tree nearby and sweet alyssum, a faerie favorite. Small diaphanous shapes began to move around the area.

"Who's the first person to say the planet Earth moves?" I repeated. "That's easy, Aristarchus of Samos. And pulsars are the fastest twirling objects in the universe."

The branches moved and cracked behind me.

"What?" asked Romeo.

The shapes were gone. The air was heavy and dense against my face.

"What are you talking about?" Romeo asked as he came up next to me.

"What?" I felt odd, as if I'd been shoved out of a warm bed. "You asked what the fastest object was."

"No, I didn't." He took my hand and pulled me back to the road. He used my chin to tilt my head toward the hanging lamp in the overlook area. "You're eyes are almost black. Are you okay?"

I didn't know. Nothing like that had ever happened to me before. I thought if I stayed in those woods long enough, I could've walked into the Realm. Woodlands are magikal for sure and have always left me feeling connected to my baser self. What just happened was a first and not a welcomed one. I smiled at Romeo to let him know I was okay, and to pretend to myself that nothing was wrong.

"You're sure?"

I nodded, not sure at all.

"I have to get rid of this." He made a sour face and smoothed his fingers over his diaphragm. He walked over to the trash can by a picnic bench. "I think that rabbit had rabies."

With hands on his hips, he leaned over the can and within a few moments, he was relieving his stomach of its contents. When he was finished, he made his way to the truck for my water bottle. While swishing, he pointed behind me to a cluster of tall bushes on the ground by the mountainside. A trail seemed to wrap around the sidewall going up to a more forested area. At the bottom slope, I shone my flashlight into the overgrown weeds and wildflowers spread wide at the base. I pushed the branches aside to guide the light up the narrow walkway, and Romeo was suddenly next to me. It didn't make me jump—not anymore. There was a time that whenever he did the vampire thing, it made me nervous. It's normal now, like everything new eventually becomes.

"So you know, I'm a friend of your boss, captain. You'll never get a new partner. We were meant to patrol together for all eternity."

I started my way up the hill. "I'm not a vampire, so I won't be doing anything for eternity. Gods, especially not patrolling. The best you have me for is maybe twenty-five years."

"You're not a vampire, yet," he said, wrapping his arms around my waist from behind. "Just give me time."

I shrugged him off so I could put my back against the rock wall, keeping the thick foliage in my view.

"Don't try to seduce me," I said as I lowered the flashlight's beam into the broken bushes just above ground.

"You like it."

"Yeah, well, I've had time to reflect." I moved slowly up the path. "It's the chase you enjoy, and no one has given you a longer, possibly more interesting chase than me."

He pulled my belt, yanking me off balance. The shallow steps crumbled and I slid. The rocks rolled against the underside of my boots, and I had to grab the bushes for support. Romeo snatched the flashlight out of the air as it flew from my hand. When I was behind him, he caught my arm so I didn't fall all the way back.

"Jupiter lives, Romeo! If you wanted to go first, all you had to do was ask."

"I would spend your life with you if you would have me," he said, jerking me against his body. "If you weren't in love with someone else."

"We've been through this. You don't want me—full time." The way I want you to is what I wanted to say.

"You have no clue how I want you." He slid heavy fingers down my throat, and his words pulled at me. Not unfairly, not with his inhuman power, but with the man behind the power. I didn't like the scenarios my mind was concocting about the two of us.

"You're a dangerous man, Romeo. If we were together you'd grow bored, and leave me wounded like the rest." I cradled his face in my hands and spoke in teasing elegance. "You run from love, my love. It's never been something you aspire to."

"I don't run from sex," he said as he dragged his fangs across my cheek. "That's a form of love. A form I'm really good at."

"Yes, but there's a whole different side to love than the physical."

"Really?" he asked while scratching his head.

In those quick moments as I was thinking of something witty to say, a dull thud had Romeo's body coming at me with such force the flashlight flew from his hand. He flattened me to the ground, cupping the back of my head before it hit, but it still smacked so hard I saw stars. We slid down to the main road with me pinned underneath his weight. The back of my arms stung from the scraping gravel. A small cloud of dirt engulfed my head, and I couldn't help but gag.

I had a moment to make eye contact with Romeo before a dark-haired man picked him off me. With agility and speed, he heaved Romeo onto the road. That's when I saw all of this guy. He was most definitely a vampire. He was a six foot five monster of a vampire! His hair was short, and he wore blue jeans and a black t-shirt. And then he was gone.

I pulled my gun and fired after him. On burning elbows, I pushed myself up. I faced away from the clearing and it was difficult to turn my head, which was swimming from the hit. I moved slowly and caught sight of another man by the truck. I scrambled to my knees and fired, grazing him in the right side of his stomach. He buckled inward and his black curly hair fell over his shoulders to cover his face. I aimed for his head and fired again. My dizzy brain was off. I only hit the round of his shoulder. He screamed and fell to the ground.

"Stay there or I'll shoot you again," I said.

He took the hand away from his belly, and by the look on his face, I'd say he got very angry with me. Was it too much to ask that this nut be human?

From the corner of my eye, I saw a shadow on the other side of our vehicle. Twice his head appeared at the edge of the windshield, as if he was peeking, but waiting. The next time I saw movement I jerked left and fired my weapon. It was a direct hit to the head. The dark figure fell back. I turned back to the first man. He had already started for me. I shifted my aim and discharged, hitting the right side of his chest. Because I hadn't yet changed my day gun to my night V-Glock, there was no second explosion. Unlucky for me, he kept coming—not unusual for a vampire if you don't get the heart directly. He was nearly on top of me before I could get off another round.

We hit the ground as the rest of his shoulder flew off in a spray of dark liquid and bone fragments. This time he rocked back screaming. On instinct, I slammed my gun into the wound. He shrieked and I yelled as the heel of my palm hit a sharp piece of bone. I kicked him the rest of the way off me, and then quickly shuffled out from under him. Protocol dictated I keep this fucker alive, but I didn't think that was happening. He saw me aim and threw himself back. I missed his heart and blew a hole in the bend of his elbow that nearly severed the arm in two. I kicked him and disconnected his knee from the rest of his leg. He slumped facedown on the ground, blood pouring from his wounds.

I was breathing so hard my chest hurt. I felt the back of my head. My beret was gone, and my hair was wet with blood. My head ached and I knew I was at least slightly concussed. My hand was also dripping red from a small hole made by the vampire's shoulder bone. I was looking for something to wrap around my hand when he caught me off guard. He leapt on top of me, growling like a dog. He dug his fangs through my upper left arm, biting down until his teeth scratched bone. He pulled back with a huge chunk of my flesh, veins, and muscle. He even had a small piece of my shirtsleeve. He spit the wad clean over my head, and all I could think was that he bit me! This motherfucker bit me!

Then the pain registered with such intensity that no sound escaped. My lungs were locked, even though my mouth was wide and I wanted the release of a colossal shriek. Fortunately, or unfortunately, I didn't pass out. I remained quite aware as his assault continued. He smacked me with his open hand. My brain whirled inside my head, and he dropped his weight down, sucking hard and frantic on the wound he'd made. That's when I screamed. I writhed and wailed and tried with unfocused motions to push him away. He twisted my arm at a better angle to feed, dislocating my shoulder and tearing at my skin with his teeth.

I caught a quick glimpse of the devastation. Seeing the ripped skin and the blood smearing his face like red glaze, I panicked. I turned my head away, screaming for Romeo. I saw my gun lying on the ground next to us, and I grabbed it. In that moment, he moved. He shifted his weight until he was completely on top of me, his face hovering over mine. He laughed intimately as if we were friends having a private moment.

"You taste wonderful—better than most blood." He laughed again, only this time it was maniacal, completely nuts. "You're so strong. I'm healing so fast."

He pulled up his arm for me to see the hanging stump, only it wasn't hanging anymore. The two pieces had reattached. I neared the point of passing out. It was an effort to stop my eyes from closing, but the sight of his arm roused me. I could only think of the cruel irony that my fey magik not only speeds my healing, but it also heals my attacker. It didn't seem like it could get any worse.

"You're not normal," said the vampire. "I should take you home."

That was it. It got worse. He said the magikal incantation that evokes blinding panic at the thought of being any vampire's feeding host. It snapped me out of semi-unconsciousness enough to realize my forgotten hand nestled between our bodies. I tried to smile—for dramatic effect. He looked down, and his satisfaction disappeared with his understanding. I saw the beginnings of fear on his face before I pulled the trigger.

At such close range, I blew away a huge piece of his neck and a third of his head. The rain was thick, quick, heavy, and hot, and

I didn't much care that it was full of body bits. He was dead, and that was that. His body glugged and lurched forward. I shoved it off me. My wounded arm was stretched out and at a bad angle, not that I felt it anymore. I didn't feel much of anything. I was going to pass out, and soon.

I wondered where Romeo was, and even in my condition, I got nervous. My gun was still in my hand, and I was tempted to shoot it. I didn't know at what, but I thought maybe I'd get lucky and hit Romeo's bad guy. With another thought, I decided I didn't have the strength. With my third thought, I realized I might shoot Romeo. I lay on the ground more irritated than dizzy or sick. My left arm stuck out. The bleeding veins hung like skinny pipes, leaking red trails onto the ground. I saw bone, and the aching in my head turned to pounding. When two boots came into my view, I pathetically slid my gun from my chest to the ground. The boot came down on the gun and dragged it out of my hand.

Romeo squatted. He leaned over, and not so gently, relocated my arm back into its socket. Somewhere in the close distance, I heard someone screaming. I cursed him until the day he died. He scooped me up, shaking his head.

"Looks like your great wall of support is bailing your ass out again."

I really wanted to spit on him, but I didn't have the energy or the bodily fluid. So I thought "fuck you" really loud.

CHAPTER TWENTY-TWO

I OPENED MY EYES to see Romeo circling a bandage around my upper arm. He pulled it taut; the pain spiked, and I was out. My eyes half opened when the truck came to an immediate stop. Every inch of my body stung as if hundreds of angry wasps were under my skin. My arms were twitching, and I wanted to ask what was going on. As my eyes slid shut, for a vague moment I was pissed at the fact that I was hurt twice in the same week—and really bad at that.

❋ ❋ ❋

ROMEO SAT IN AN uncomfortable chair in the corner of Dru's hospital room watching the nurse add another bag of medicine to her IV. Seeing his partner, his friend, lying in a hospital bed—bruised, broken, immobile—forced his memory back quite a few years—about twelve months after she became his partner.

Throughout the fall and winter of 2056 the Emergency Dispatch Office was clogged with calls reporting violent muggings near a club called the Raven. The police never caught the offenders, and one cold night in February three calls came through the EDO accusing two males—one human, one vampire—of robbing at least four people within five blocks of the club. The perpetrators assaulted the victims and then robbed them of their wallets or purses, jewelry, shoes, and coats. A resident couple walking their dog found two of the victims half-conscious in a back alley five streets behind the club. Romeo's instructions were to stop by, keep watch, and maybe talk to a few patrons.

He remembered being glad for the distraction. Winter can be slow and boring, as people tend to stay inside when the weather falls below thirty degrees.

He and Dru were holed up in the truck for a few hours, and the smell of her was agitating his senses. He wasn't even particularly hungry, and still all he could think about was her blood pouring into his mouth from the hole he would gouge into her neck. And it wasn't just blood. It was her body as well. He wanted to touch it, to feel it in inappropriate ways. He knew he was being irrational, and he couldn't recall anyone making him think such morbid, yet vividly colorful, things. But he liked the way it made him feel when he thought about it, so he kept her talking about procedural detail for visiting dignitaries to keep her from noticing his preoccupied contemplation.

They arrived a little after zero three hundred when the bar was letting out. Romeo parked across the street, and they watched the crowd slowly disperse. When only stragglers remained, they walked around the block to the back of the building. He couldn't fully remember exactly what he was thinking, but Dru was walking in front of him and he had to physically stop himself from rushing behind her and taking what he wanted in the most autocratic way he knew how. It seemed his want of her increased weekly, perhaps only by degrees, but it was enough that he felt powerless against it.

He was so distracted, and so stupid, he didn't hear anything around them before he was slammed from behind and then punched in the gut. He saw Dru turn in surprise just as a smaller man wearing a dark red skull cap knocked her onto the ground.

A tall vampire put his hands around Romeo's neck and was strong enough to keep him immobile and high against the wall. He couldn't gain the leverage to move the bigger man away from him; the vampire's grip was like reinforced steel. Romeo knew he was in deep shit when his windpipe began to give way and crack.

The human in the red cap told the vampire to move, and no sooner did Romeo's boots touch the ground when the small man beat him across the chest and abdomen with a metal pipe. Blood poured from between his lips. He fell, forced to the pavement from repeated blows across his back. Two gun shots boomed, and the clang of the pipe echoed in the alley. A moment later someone hit the ground with a dull thud. Romeo heard more scuffling and he pushed himself to all fours; the blood running from his nose and mouth splattered onto the ground. It was difficult to move, and he was in so much pain he knew his back was fractured. But he could move, no matter how slowly, so he forced himself to straighten in time to see Dru jump on the back of the vampire who had almost strangled him to death. She wrapped her legs around his waist and her arms around his neck. Her face was next to his ear and she bit it, tearing it in two with her teeth. The vampire screamed, backed up, and slammed her against the wall. She cried out, but already had her hands around his eyes. She dug her fingers into his sockets and completely scooped out one of those red orbs before he pulled her hair and coat and threw her onto the ground.

The vampire was screaming and holding his face. He tripped into his dead friend, pitching him into the wall closest to Romeo, who was barely standing. And before the guy could do anything but curse Dru for taking his eye, Romeo pulled the knife from his belt and jammed it into the side of the vampire's head.

The screaming stopped abruptly and the alley was quiet once more. Romeo slid down the wall with the dead vampire, unable to keep balance. He wasn't sure what part of his body hurt more — the space between his shoulder blades, his broken throat, or his chest that ached with every breath his amped-up body forced him to take. But the blood racing through his system was a good thing. He would heal faster with it moving quickly in and around his organs, although he'd lost so much he didn't think there was enough left to heal his entire body. It might be sufficient to keep him alive, but it wouldn't heal his broken bones, nerves, or muscles. So he would concentrate. He would force what little blood he had to mend what he wanted it to. Not every vampire could do that. That kind of healing was a benefit of being Galen's son. And he desperately wanted to be able to move, to be able to get to Dru and help her.

His body slid further onto the ground when a sudden pain, like being stuck in the back with a boning knife, forced him flat onto his back. His hands shook uncontrollably, and he had to swallow the blood that kept glugging into his mouth. It was disgusting, but he needed it. He had to keep it no matter how much his body was trying to get rid of it.

He knew the back had to be first, so he closed his eyes and concentrated very hard, compelling his body to use the blood in his veins to heal the small breaks in his spine. And after what seemed a long time he felt the painful itch of healing begin in his midsection and travel up and out toward his shoulders.

He still hadn't heard a sound from Dru. The weight of that truth, the loudness of it, stung his ears until he was nearly incapable of thinking of anything else. But then footsteps came down the alley, interrupting his desperation. His body tensed, and pain shot down his left leg. He groaned audibly. The sharp stabbing in this throat brought tears to his eyes. The footsteps moved faster until an older man in a suit crouched over him.

"Are you okay?" he asked.

Unable to speak, Romeo tried to put his hand up. The man saw him struggling and took his shaking hand in his.

"I heard shots and called the police and emergency medial. Just try and relax. They'll be here any minute."

Romeo kept trying to move. He finally had the ability to turn his head enough to see Dru next to the dead man she'd killed nearly a lifetime ago. She was on her back. It looked like her head was in a circle of blood. Another person was there, and he was checking all the bodies for signs of life. He looked at the man in the suit and shook his head. Romeo couldn't believe it. He needed to go to her. He couldn't let her die. He would turn her if he had to, but he couldn't let her die.

"Stop fidgeting," said the man helping Romeo. "I hear the sirens now."

Romeo's mind raced. The thought of losing her was surreal. His chest ached. Not from physical pain, but from grief. He'd grown to like the girl.

The paramedics showed up and lifted Romeo onto a stretcher. He watched two others check Dru over, and to his enormous relief, they started working on her and then loaded her into an ambulance. The medics hooked him to intravenous blood to speed the healing process. Upon arriving at the hospital, he was told his partner was conscious when they took her to intensive care. A nurse immediately pulled him to x-ray. She told him to lie flat and still and wait for the doctor, who eventually told him there were rare cases of vampire breaks, especially spinal injuries, that could heal improperly or crooked if the vampire moved too quickly before the healing process was completed. The doctor said limping and perpetual pain were two of the consequences of that and warned him to remain still for twenty-four hours.

After twenty minutes, when Romeo could move, however unsteadily and against orders, he got up and wheeled his infusion pole into Dru's dark room.

Her expression was peaceful, but her right eye and cheek were bruised. He stared at it, getting more and more angry with Galen. This was why he didn't

*like human partners. This was why he liked being alone. He would tell Galen
that he didn't want to watch out for her anymore. He wasn't going to play baby-
sitter to a tiny human girl just to make his father feel better.*

*Dru opened her eyes, and to his annoyance, he had to physically stop him-
self from smiling. They stared at one another for a few moments before her face
crumbled and she began to cry. He pulled his pole to the chair at the side of the
bed and sat down. He lowered the side bar and took her hand away from her
face.*

"What's wrong?"

"You're not dead," she sobbed. "I'm so sorry."

*"You're sorry I'm not dead?" He laughed. "I'm not everyone's favorite
vampire, but that's a first."*

*"I'm sorry." She shook her head. "I wasn't paying attention. You were
behind me and I should've been paying better attention. And when I turned
around, he had you up against the wall, and I couldn't help you because the other
one pushed me. Then he was hitting you with a crow bar ... and I don't really
remember anything else."*

*"No," he said and wiped the tears sliding down her face. "I should have
been paying better attention. It's my fault."*

*"I should have ..." she shook her head. "I almost got you killed. I almost
got the general's son killed!"*

*"Stop," he laughed again and put his large hand on her face to calm her
down. He felt the lump on the side of her head and winced. "Listen to me. It was
my fault. I know better. I wasn't listening to the area. I wasn't paying attention."*

"You must think I'm such an idiot," she cried a little harder.

*"I don't," he said, surprised that he meant it. "Not at all. You saved me.
You get that, right? Those guys kicked my ass, but what you did saved me."*

She stared at him, her anguished expression softening with his words.

"What did I do? I don't really remember."

"You shot the one guy, the human."

"I kind of remember that."

*"You jumped on the vampire," he laughed. "You jumped on his back and
bit his ear off."*

Her eyes went a little wide.

"Yeah, you did that. And then you reached your fingers into his eye sockets and pulled out an eye."

He took her fingers and showed them to her. She cringed at the dried blood caked around her fingertips.

"Yeah, you did that too." He gently chucked under her chin. "You got him off me long enough for me to get my act together, and when he tripped because you blinded him, I got the chance to stab him in the head."

"Really?"

Her look of amazement lightened his mood.

"Really."

"So, you don't want to get rid of me?" She started to cry again. "You won't transfer me for someone else?"

He stared at her, not sure what to say. There was irony somewhere that only months ago she didn't want to be his partner and now she was afraid he was going to dismiss her. And he realized something with those bright eyes staring at him. He would miss her. If he let her go, he would miss her—a lot.

"No," he said quietly. "I won't transfer you."

Her smile made him smile. He stood and pulled at the IV tube in his arm. "Don't leave," she blurted. "I don't want to be here by myself."

"I wouldn't leave you alone," he said, pulling the needle and casing out of the bend of his arm. Blood leaked slowly from the needle he dropped onto the floor. He motioned to the pole. "The bag's almost done, and I'm fine. Your boyfriend will be here within the hour, and when he gets here I'll leave and go to bed. It's nearly dawn."

He sat down and they stared at one another. After a time she reached her arm out to him and opened her hand. He took it in both of his, and her warmth spread up his arms and into his chest. Her energy was almost euphoric; the woodsy smell of her calmed his head. He wondered if she was aware that this was the first time they'd ever really touched. He watched her fall back to sleep, thinking about what they went through. It was harsh, and it bonded them in ways he didn't think he cared for, or would understand for some time.

❀ ❀ ❀

I WOKE UP UNUSUALLY groggy, and in a hospital bed. I knew I was in a hospital because my bedroom doesn't have big machines with heart icons or red lines that blink. I could smell the pungent odor of antiseptic soap. Hurt as I was, I truly didn't want to be in a hospital. A light-haired woman put the finishing touches on the IV in my arm. I watched her hook a cloudy plastic bag with clear fluids — or maybe it was a clear plastic bag with cloudy fluids — on a metal rod anchored to my bed. When I lifted my head it spun with unreasonable nausea.

"Just relax, lieutenant."

"Captain," I heard Romeo say from somewhere in the room.

"You're coming down from a harsh reaction to hydromorphone," the woman said as she gently touched my arm.

"What's that?" I slurred.

"A synthetic narcotic."

"No, what's in that?" I pointed to the IV.

"Oh that. Just normal fluids to replace what your body's lost and strong antibiotics to fight infection. You were unconscious when you got here. Then you had an allergic reaction to two different pain medications."

My right arm had three needles sticking out of it: one in the bend of my elbow, another in the back of my hand, and still another in my wrist. My left arm was strapped at wrist and shoulder to a narrow metal table that seemed to be connected to the bed somehow. The table had a thin, right-angled rod coming from the base that disappeared into my arm at the back of the elbow. Four other rods were at opposite points around the wound. Tiny clamps held the flesh back, exposing the space of bone and other such things. A clear plastic house ballooned over the hole.

"Lieutenant, did you know you were allergic?"

"Captain," said Romeo.

"Allergic," I said.

"Is there anything else we need to know?"

Romeo rose from a chair in the corner. He rudely nudged the nurse out of his way, but spoke in my head. *I think we found the tunnels.*

You think? It hurt to form words in my head, but it was too much effort to speak. *How did I get here?*

He pressed his hands to his chest. "My superior medical and driving skills." I frowned, or I tried to.

We made it to Lehigh Hospital in record time. Then the helicopter transported us back to Philly. About an hour ago.

What happened?

You were on the money tonight. He smiled. *You killed two. A human by the truck and no-head on top of you.*

I had a quick flash of the vampire's body exploding all over me. My heart jolted, and I jumped along with the memory. I opened my eyes to Romeo rubbing my cheek. His fingers skimmed my ear, and it felt strange.

"Stay with me. Roe said the longer you're awake the better."

I touched my ear, but there were no earrings. I felt around for the barbell in the back of my neck.

"Don't worry," said Romeo, and he patted his pants pocket, "I have all your jewelry. They were going to take you straight to surgery, but you had the reaction." He stepped back, continuing our silent conversation. In a broad motion he acted as if he were swinging a bat. *I knocked the complete shit out of the big guy. Eventually. I snapped his neck in hopes he was weak, too young to heal. But he was gone by the time Pennsy Territory Military showed up.*

I caught a foggy glimpse of the nurse circling us. She appeared busy; she knew we were communicating. I think she was trying to listen, or trying to figure out what we were saying.

"So we got nothing," I said aloud.

He shrugged. "Whatcha gonna do? Galen's got people on it."

"Excuse me, captain," The nurse said, coming around the bed and shoving Romeo out of the way. "She's going into surgery in less than an hour. I have to ask her some questions."

It was then that everything the nurse said about the allergic reaction sank in and I realized the severity of what was happening to me.

"Wait, no. Romeo, I don't want surgery."

"Roeanne had a friend take care of you. He said you're going to need surgery to reattach muscles and veins and all that happy crap. But it's bad. They talked about skin graphs and a bunch of shit I didn't listen to."

He'd listened. He knew what I was facing and didn't want to say. A million things ran through my mind—a career-ending disability was among them, but the life-ending thoughts petrified me more.

"I don't want surgery," I said. I pushed up on my elbow only to fall back from the shooting pains.

"Relax. You'll be fine." Romeo leaned down to whisper in my ear. "By the time you're in recovery, the rabies will be out of my system and I'll use my super stud blood on the wound so you won't scar."

"I said I don't want surgery." I pulled at the tubes. I ripped the little plastic house off my completely useless arm. "I want out of here."

"No, no," said the nurse, rushing over to me. "Don't do that."

"Dru, stop it," said Romeo. "Roeanne will be here any minute."

"No! I don't want this."

I kicked him away from the bed. He pinned me down.

"What the hell are you doing? What's gotten into you?"

I wailed from the pressure he put on my arm. The nurse came to stand on the opposite side of me.

"Lieutenant, you'll be fine. You're familiar with Dr. James, and I assure you Dr. Lytel is wonderful." She glanced at Romeo. "There's a sedative in her IV. Try to settle her until it takes effect."

My eyes widened in fear. I pulled the needle from the bend of my elbow with my teeth.

"No!" cried the nurse.

"Jesus, Dru," yelled Romeo. "Calm the fuck down. I'll stay with you."

My head washed in darkness. With my good arm I pulled Romeo by his shirt until we were face to face.

"This will hurt me," I whispered as harshly as I could. "Maybe kill me." I was panting hard, my consciousness slipping away. "Romeo, drugs are bad. They're bad for the kind of … person I am."

He pulled his brows together in uncertainty. He clenched his teeth and then blew a loud, frustrated burst of air. He undid the pale yellow tape at my elbow, wrist and hand and then slid the needle casings out of my arm.

The nurse jumped and then pushed at Romeo.

"Captain, stop. You can't do that!"

Romeo pushed a few buttons on the metal board. The pins painfully disconnected from my wounded arm and then slid silently across the top of the board. He took out the rest of the needles and then lifted my upper body until I was sitting upright.

"Captain Romeo, you can't do this. The lieutenant needs surgery. She's on medication, and she's not in her right frame of mind. You may be her commanding officer, but you can't take her out of this hospital because she says she's afraid."

"She's a god-damn captain," snapped Romeo, probably wanting to holler at me instead. He grabbed a handful of gauze from the stand next to the bed. He flashed the nurse a nasty glance before he bundled me into his arms. The nurse rushed around the bed and out the door; yelling something about calling security. Moments later, we were outside.

"To your house, my royal pain in the ass?"

I nodded.

My home wasn't far from the hospital, but I don't know how long it took to get there, because I was unconscious for the ride. When I woke up, Romeo was giving Livi a quick rundown. He told her he hadn't called Dacon or my brothers yet and to keep watch in case the military showed up. My arm, already covered with fresh gauze, sat neatly over my blankets. Romeo left my room and then came back with a glass of water. He moved around the candles to set it on the nightstand.

A brown stain was growing on the new dressing.

"It's really bleeding. What do you want me to do?" Romeo asked.

What do you think?

"I knew you were going to say that!" He stood up from the bed. "I knew it! But there's rabies in my system. And it's illegal. I could get into a ton of trouble!"

I'm. Bleeding. To. Death

"Now! Now you are!"

"You promised your blood earlier."

"For a scar. I promised my blood for a scar. The amount of blood I'd use would be next to nothing. But that ... that thing is major. It'll take a lot of blood, power, and me!" He sighed, and sat on the edge of the bed. "Why couldn't you just stay?"

The room went dark for a moment or two. Romeo was patting my cheek when I woke up.

"If I were going to take a chance at healing you, I would have done it in the mountains. Don't you think I thought of that? Don't you think I wanted to? But between your weakened body, my blood, and a disease in my system you could be seriously fucked up."

"You won't give me rabies," I said. I didn't have the energy to go into how my faerie blood wasn't susceptible to things like that.

"My blood could turn you, you're so fragile. And then you'd hate me."

I shook my head.

"What? You won't hate me, or you won't turn?" He sighed. "Tell me why you couldn't stay."

Drugs make me ... they exhaust my mind, and I can't hold ... I didn't know how to tell him about my other self. I didn't want to. How could I explain to him that if I were drugged unconscious I could turn into the fey on the operating table, when he doesn't know I can do anything like that?

Drugs affect me differently. My body sees synthetic substances as an intruder. It tries to eliminate the potential hazard. It breaks them down, which is what the nurse called an allergic reaction. The compounds in some human medicine can be deadly to the fey and anesthesia can kill.

Not me, but a part truth would have to do.

He thought about that for a moment before getting seriously pissed off.

"Why didn't you ever tell me? It's definitely something I needed to know. If you never woke up I would've let them do the surgery, and you'd be dead. Damn it, Dru!"

I half-heartedly shrugged. I didn't know what to say.

"Either way I'm screwed. I can't take you back, and if I heal you I risk getting killed by the Grim-fucking-Reaper."

You could leave me here, and let me die.

"You can probably heal it. Why don't you?"

I took a deep, pain-filled breath.

If Galen doesn't feel your energy he'll wonder how I got healed, and he'll ask questions I won't be able to answer.

"Why don't you use nature? You always brag about it like you're special."

"You are nature," I shouted and then started to cry.

"When Galen kicks my ass, I want you there to watch it." He yanked the comforter from the bed. "I want you to cry and moan and act like a real girlfriend." He laid it on the floor with a pillow. "You know what though? A real girlfriend wouldn't let me do this if she knew I would get my beautiful Italian ass kicked." He wasn't gentle when he shoved his arms underneath me. I screamed as the pain shot up my arm, and into my chest. "All right, all right."

"It hurts!"

"I gotta take you out of your little magik ring, don't I?"

I narrowed my eyes at him, hating him for thinking of what I hadn't. He put me on my right side in the middle of the floor. Settling next to me, he spooned my body. He carefully lifted the gauze from my upper arm and tossed it aside.

"It's fairly interesting," he said, studying the oozing hole. "I can see bone. It's chipped, like he bit right into it. I couldn't pull you far enough under for this not to hurt."

"It hurts now, so just do it." My words were coming softer, slower. "I think I'm passing out."

"You'd feel this if you fell into a coma." He slid an arm under me, tightened it around my chest, and then locked his legs over mine. "I'm holding you down so you don't hurt me or throw yourself across the room in a convulsive spasm."

"Ro ... ro ..."

"Yes? What?" He stretched his head up and looked down at me. "Spit it out before you black out."

"Have you ever done this?"

"I've healed through power sharing, but no, not like this. Not this amount of blood."

"I'm afraid."

"I don't blame you."

I nestled my head in the pillow. My arm was burning, but the rest of my body was numb. I couldn't move my hand. Blood seemed to be everywhere. Each time I took a breath, I felt a pain in my upper chest that raced down into my stomach. I was moaning like a woman in labor, and Romeo wouldn't comfort me no matter how many hints I threw his way. Unless I said, "Romeo, I need you to comfort me," which I wasn't going to do, I was out of luck. His hand hovered over the wound.

"I'm afraid," I said, squirming against him.

"I heard you the first time."

I made a pitiful noise when he flattened my left arm across my stomach, holding it there with his hand from underneath my body. When he squeezed me, he forced the air out in a painful sigh; I made a mental note to hurt him when I was healed. He flexed and shook his left hand as if he'd hurt it. When he stopped, a large cut spread across his palm. Blood dripped in front of me. I bit the inside of my cheek, watching the dark drops soak into the threads of my comforter.

"Maybe I should drink it," I said.

"No."

He moved his hand over the wound. The thick, red liquid poured over it and splashed into the gaping hollow in my arm. When it hit I thought a fire was lit inside of me. I fought the pain that drove itself into the chunks of frayed flesh. It seeped into the splintered bone, burst out, and rode the dense hardness to every nerve, muscle, and tendon in my arm and upper body. His potent blood was like a fiery ocean crashing through my insides. It burned my mind from the center to the edge of my skull. I was aware I was screaming, and at one point Romeo's hand covered my mouth. I pushed against his strong frame, forcing him backwards.

As quickly as the smallest thought, I fell into sickness and delirium. I lost consciousness but was cheated the solitude it brings. I was aware of the agony in a warped, third-person way. And even with Romeo's strength around my body, it convulsed. I could feel the pieces of my arm growing and knitting back together. It seemed that long, slimy worms were alive in my body, reattaching the wound. It burned so hot my stomach ached. I lost myself. I lost all sense of anything except ache and nausea and sickness. I tasted bile and blood. I tried to go into the center where I kept the fey magik, but for that I needed concentration, something I had not an ounce of. I was propelled for what seemed hours in a hot, dry, suffocating bubble of pins and needles.

Almost as suddenly as the luridness began, it ended. No more heat. No more electricity. I was left with stinging aftershocks and cold shivers. I was immobile in Romeo's arms, afraid to move. When I was conscience enough I pried my sticky eyes open. I recoiled at the sight and smell of the red vomit on the pillow under my head. The bitter taste lingered inside my mouth. I felt Romeo's heartbeat close, like a part of me. An intense intimacy. My own heart was there, but his overlapped it. It pumped hard inside my chest. And through the nausea I was comforted. With a heavy arm he moved his blood-stained hand to my face, pulling slick strands of hair off my sweaty cheek. He voice was hoarse when he spoke.

"You in there?"

I nodded.

"That was one wild ride. Your body absorbed my blood like a sponge. I've never seen anything like it." He buried his face in the back of my neck. His dry, hot tongue slid along my sensitive skin, soaking in the sweat that trickled down from my head. The feeling was erotic. My body squirmed even though it hurt to do it. His hands groped the front of me, and he pulled off the hospital gown. "Did you see that?" He panted against my back. "The moment I put my hand on the wound we were propelled inward. I saw things from your mind. I saw visions from your past, and your other. I was flying!"

He kissed my back. He was energized, speeding. "But I couldn't see your face. I saw everything as if I were you, through your eyes. My god, I didn't know healing made you feel this way. I want to use every muscle in my body. I feel invincible. I want to fight. I want to do other things. I want to do them to you."

"I feel strange," I whispered.

"It's my blood." He twisted my head and held my face in a tight grip. He swept his tongue across my upper lip in one fierce motion. A drop of blood fell back on my face before his tongue disappeared into his mouth. He did it again, going deeper up my nose.

"My blood's an interloper in your body, healing you, reconstructing your imperfections, preparing the vessel to be vampire. It's incredible, isn't it?"

My stomach lurched. I had to swallow hard to keep it still.

"Oh gods." I used a shaking hand to wipe the blood still running from my nose.

"The pressure," he said as he licked the blood off my fingers, "from your screaming. My blood will fix that too. I didn't give you enough of me to mend all your faults or convert you. I don't know how I know that, but I do. I'm inside you. Traipsing through your body. We're bound together. Dissolving like salt in water."

"Salt? Forever?"

"Don't panic." Romeo laid me flat and topped me. He kissed my lips and then moved quickly to my chest. His tongue smeared our blood over my breasts. His emotions dumped all over me—a confusing mix of lust, anxiety, triumph, and joy. I felt it all as if I were him. He rolled us until he was on top again. It made me nauseous. His large hands pushed the hair from my eyes. He touched shaking fingertips to my face.

"I need to be close to you. You're mine now, and I want to touch you deep inside. It's only fair. I healed you. You belong to me."

His? What? Shit.

I knew I should argue. Letting Romeo have me when he thinks he owns me is a definite bad. But at that moment I wanted him more than I'd ever wanted him. I thought that if we made love we would be one. A great, moving mass of energy, and I wanted it. I wanted to take the leash off my magik and show myself to him.

He scooped me up, and then he put me on the bed so he could strip. When he laid his body on mine, he shoved his energy further into me. I flushed from head to toe. I felt he was stronger than I knew, more powerful than he let on. It impressed me. I was suddenly thrilled by what I perceived a challenge. My wall of mental protection slipped away. I let Romeo's power wash over me. Our strength entwined, creating a rushing tide. I wrapped my sore body around his and I swallowed his power whole. Images of the Fear fey filled my mind, so I filled his. I tore into his metaphysical self, his magik, and I engulfed the force that was him. His concentration broke. His mouth popped away from my neck and his body began to twitch. I guided my hands down his spine to the small of his back, pushing my magik through his skin and into his body until he moaned with unadulterated pleasure.

He turned wild, kissing me viciously, cutting my lips and tongue. He bit my face; I felt his fangs pop through my skin. I pushed him over, putting him on the bottom so I had more control. My blood dripped from my face onto his hard chest, and I smoothed my hands in it, sliding his erection between my legs.

"What happened?" He grabbed my hands, squinting as if maybe he could see me better. "What was that? What are you?"

I wanted to be strong. I didn't want his comment to bother me, but unfortunately I can't always control my reaction the moment my feelings get hurt. There was an unexpected flash of light in my head as the fey magik pushed through me. My body jerked. I fell forward, one hand on either side of his head. I'd gotten carried away and had to pay the price for it.

Since Romeo discovered my secret, I've given him small doses of magik—most of it having to do with witchcraft more than the fey. I was afraid to show him what Livi has seen. I'm still afraid. He was about to witness a revelation—and I was none too happy about it. He was almost as nervous as me, yet nearly too turned on to care. His hands gripped my hips as he slid himself against me. He asked for me to stop torturing him, but I wasn't doing anything but trying to control myself. His own emotions were in a hard fight with fear and pleasure. He pulled me to him for a kiss. He was at the point where reason didn't exist. That feverish vampiric place where even Romeo's control is powerless. When he healed me he invaded my body. His blood mingled and played with my magikal power. He was now desperate to release inside of me, even if he was overwhelmingly afraid. Trying to stop him was futile, as was my metamorphosis.

His hands traced my spine until his fingertips found the bumpy ridges forming the base of my wings. His eyes flew open, red as embers and filled with fear. Horror swallowed his inhuman euphoria, and he roughly pushed me back. I guess your bed partner turning into a faerie right before your eyes was unnerving. Who knew I'd be the person to find the only thing that could penetrate the maddening lust of a vampire?

My skin color changed, as if black food coloring added to clear water, blending quickly, completely. Romeo pushed his heels into the bed, desperate to get out from under me.

"Shit," he said, "what's happening to you?"

His anxiety spiraled around me. The strength of it fed me, dazing my senses as if filtered through every pore on my body. I sat on my knees, struggling to contain my composure. I didn't want to frighten him any more than I had, but my body jerked from trying to hold back the magik. My ears grew. The small black bones formed around my eyes and the line of crystals surfaced along the outer side of my legs. As the fey pushed through me, I had no choice but to cease the fight. I rested on Romeo's legs. I turned my hands palm up so I didn't hurt him with my growing talons.

"Holy shit," he whispered. "You're a shape shifter."

He leaned his back against the headboard, putting extra distance between us. He watched me suffer through the pain. I didn't have to read his mind to know he was horrified. I smelled it. Ingested it. Secretly reeled from it. And yet, moments later, to my complete surprise, he raised his hand past my cheek to touch my ear. He tapped the pointed top.

"Your eyes are fucking weird. Your skin is so … you look like a giant bug."

A man who always knows what to say. At least he didn't cry, or scream, or both. I don't think Romeo had any idea my magik was this strong. He never imagined the fey in me could emerge to exist on this plane. I mean, really, who would? He may have tasted the difference in my blood, but he disregarded my ability, and only now was he seeing what it truly means to be a vessel for faerie magik.

He sat up and put his face close to mine.

"I do love the way you smell," he said, inhaling deeply. "It makes me lightheaded, sort of high."

I shivered from a tremor beginning inside. My hair bled forest green, almost black, growing easily to a raggedy mess.

"My god." His eyes went wide as saucers. "Will you get wings too?"

I nodded.

"I'm afraid of you," he said, his reddish-brown eyes glittering, "but drawn the way the sun draws me. It's bad for my health, but I can't seem to curb the fascination." He quickly rocked his body up and down like a child. "Fuck me now! Please, fuck me now!"

I had to laugh at that. My voice came metallic, and it frightened him.

"Shit," he said, jerking back to the headboard and looking at my mouth. "Say something else."

I shook my head.

"Was that your voice?"

I nodded.

"Come on, say something."

Again, another ache inched up my back.

"What? What?"

I moved to all fours, breathing deeply, using concentration for the pain. I twisted my body to help the stiff, black wings ease their way through the newly grown cartilage that split out of the center of my spine, up to my shoulders, and down the back of my arms to my wrists. The wing itself slid quickly, as if flowers blooming in fast motion. I cried out, tightening my fingers around the sheet. The wings are the most painful part of my change, and though I've learned techniques to keep myself from screaming, it's still quite painful. When the magik had settled, I blew a loud sigh.

He was speechless. His eyes were enormous with the kind of amazement that doesn't have words.

"Oh. My. God."

Well, there are always those words.

I stretched my back, and the flutter rolled to the bottom of the wings like an ocean wave.

"I felt that. I felt that." He tentatively touched the edge of my wing. "There's texture to them like small black leather feathers. They shimmer silver, red, and blue in the light. They look heavy. Are they heavy?"

I smiled and shrugged my shoulders.

"Can I touch them?"

I nodded and he reached slowly.

"Dewy, like flower petals. Kind of. Like velvet, but the weight is light as air." He pushed my arm up, tracing the edge with his fingers. "Why are they tattered here, at the bottom?" He pulled at an extra bit of wing extending past my wrist. "What's this? Does it do anything? Is it like ..." he smiled, "a tissue for when you just have to blow?"

I jerked my arm back as if I were going to punch him. The extra material stiffened with a sharp leather-like snap. It curved over my talon like a long black dagger.

"Jesus!"

Jesus had nothing to do with it, I teased in my mind, and then I wondered if my voice were as sadistic in his mind as it was when I spoke. Romeo didn't move. He didn't do anything, and I wondered if he could even hear me.

I guided the point down his cheek so gently that he shivered. He lifted his head slightly when I moved across his throat, down one long line to his belly button. A drop of blood dripped onto his stomach. His fingers smeared red when he wiped his cheek. He looked at the blood seeping between his legs from the line I'd traced along his stomach and frowned. He put his fingers to his mouth.

"You were so gentle." I rubbed the back of my hand in his blood while his body healed the shallow cut I'd made. "Do the wings work? Can you fly?"

"I glide."

He pulled back again.

"Damn, your voice is like a child possessed. It freaks me the hell out." He tried to bend the natural switchblade. "It's like steel."

"Each is made of hundreds of tiny bones," I said, carefully sliding my fingers down the inside smoothness of one wing. "And when I flex ..." I whipped my hands up over my head and there came another sharp snap, only louder, more metallic, "those bones shift against each other to create a hard structure."

He shuddered, and I tasted his fear in the back of my throat. He forced himself to extend his arm, and he knocked the inside of one wing with his knuckles.

"Unreal. You're less human than I am. I thought faeries were adorable little girls with rainbow dresses riding snapdragons in the forest."

"Some can make you think they are," I shrugged.

"That voice," he said, making me face him by taking my jaw in his hand. "My god, I think I'm afraid of you."

"Trust me, you are. It tastes like food to the starving."

He narrowed his brows.

"I can't help it, Romeo. It's what we are. Try to remember, my voice is one way I keep my enemies at a distance. Try to relax in the fear. We will never hurt you. Not ever."

He watched me for a moment before smiling.

"Good thing fear gives me a rush," he said, pulling me closer, with his hands on my ass. "I think I need your mouth on mine to help me relax in this fear."

I smiled and felt shy, although I didn't know if it came across that way. It made me feel good that he wasn't disgusted by me—at least not enough to not touch me.

"Come on," he urged me on like a teenager trying for third base.

"A few minutes ago you didn't want this. You were afraid."

"I'm completely not caring if I'm drunk on the super mojo, or if I'm pixilated. I want it. I want it now. I. Want. It."

I wrapped my arm around his neck, folding him in wings, and allowing the cooling heat from earlier to surface. He moved to his knees, keeping me in a tight hold.

"You're like a sleek, wiry, scary, beetle. Can I put you down or will it hurt your wings?"

"You can't hurt me."

He laid me back, and I stretched my arms over my head.

"My god, look at your dark, alien face. This is incredible."

"Still afraid?"

"Yes," he said, his head moving quickly up and down. "Yes, I am."

I laughed, and he glided his fingers up my tummy; then he glanced at the tips of them to see if the color came off. He moved about to start some real investigating. Very carefully, he ran a finger under one of my nails.

"I'm confused," he said, licking the blood that fell on my belly, and then moving to the side, with his hand between my legs. "Which you is you? Is this magik?"

"Yes, but not magik the way you're thinking. It's magikal, but I'm not using magik to make you see me this way."

"I didn't think so. I'd be able to sense that. So which you is the real you?"

"They're both me. I was born this way, and I'm equally comfortable in both forms."

"Why were you born this way?"

"An accident, I think."

"Have you ever gone outside like this?"

I watched him a moment before answering.

"Many times."

"Shit. How do you hide this every day?"

"Discipline. Magik. Necessity."

He stared at me as if he didn't know who I was. Part of me felt bad about that, but only a part.

"What would happen if you didn't suppress it? If you didn't use energy to make all this go away? Who's dominant?"

"Neither, really. I have done it. Not here, but when I lived in the States with Dacon. The change is triggered by emotion mostly. Some days I'd shift many times throughout the day. It was exhausting. A little unnerving." I smiled. "Dacon liked it."

He was staring again, so I pulled my claws up to my chest. I was feeling insecure and strangely, a little violated. He smoothed the hair on my head, picking at the wild locks with his fingers.

"I don't hate it. I'm curious, and scared out of my mind," he smiled. "But I don't hate you. How can you be the koolest, unearthly badass and still be such a little human girl?"

"I don't know? What you think is important to me."

"Really?"

"No," I said quickly. "Not really."

He laughed at me, and I hated him for it. He finally noticed my mouth—another reason I don't like to say much in this form. He poked his fingers inside and grimaced.

"Your teeth are pointy like small knives, and there's something on your tongue. Let me see it."

I stuck my tongue out to show him the tiny black stones lining the center. His fingers touched the slightly forked tip.

"Does the split work like a reptile?"

"It's for enhancing my sense of smell, but it doesn't flicker. We have to touch the surface we want to smell."

"You've told me you're a faerie of Fear?" I nodded. "Is this what they look like?"

"The pure Fear have lighter skin. Less adornments, and their wings are true, like a bird. It would seem, for some reason, something gets muddled in the transfiguration. From human D.N.A, or maybe my mind can't understand the entirety of it, so I can never truly be it. Or maybe I don't have enough magik."

"You're stronger than me."

"Much. Older than you too."

"Your human body isn't older than mine."

"Right, but I have old power sitting in a young vessel."

"What exactly does that mean?"

I thought of what the fey elders explained to me and wasn't quite sure how to describe it so he'd understand. I didn't truly understand.

"When I was conceived, an old faerie soul—the energy that is—somehow got stuck to mine. Like a piggyback. Something with the planets and an opened veil when I was born. Like magikal energy searching for a place to land. We share her magik so I can change into this."

"What faerie?"

"No one knows. I can't see her memories or who she was."

"You're separate then?"

"Mostly. We've been entwined for so long. We felt more separate when I was very young. Though lately I've been feeling the magik grow out or maybe, pull away."

"Why you?"

I wanted to give him a good answer, but I didn't have one.

"Your questions hurt my head."

"You must have some idea," he frowned.

"Maybe I am the 'thing' that's supposed to wipe out the vampire. Like Jagen says."

I watched him closely as he thought that over.

"You're not a thing. Jagen said it's the offspring of a human and a faerie. That's not you. Your parents were human."

I nodded.

"You don't feel like the Bringer of Death. Most apocalyptic bullshit is just that. Believe me when I tell you that humans have been foretelling the end of the world every hundred years for the past one thousand." Red dots suddenly popped around the whites of his eyes. His lust rose so quickly it took me off guard. "I wanna know. Will you hurt me when I fuck you?"

"Can you call it anything but that?"

He held my face in his hands and brushed his lips against mine. It felt really good. My wings flittered nervously. Then I was gone. Romeo fell face forward on the bed. I tapped his back and watched him nearly jump to the ceiling.

"How did you do that?" I laughed, and to his credit he didn't seem to notice the voice anymore. "I'm a vampire, and I see things move and breath that shouldn't or don't. Things that look dead to you, to humans."

"Well, I'm a faerie, and I move those things that you vampire see move that shouldn't, and guess what? You've been pixi-led."

He grabbed my waist so I couldn't get away. I could, but who's trying? He pulled me down into his lap. When he kissed me, he rubbed his tongue along the line of pebbles on mine. He felt the wings on my back, lingering on the new sensations.

"In folklore, faeries live long lives, but you seem to be aging as a human."

"Seems so."

"This is the most amazing experience I've ever had," he said, giving a shallow shudder as his control over my voice wavered. "You're beautiful—no, that's not the right word. You are. But that's not what I was thinking. You're ... dazzling. That's it. Yeah, that's a better word. You're dazzling, and I'm petrified. I'd run outta here if I weren't so intent on giving a sacrifice to Venus."

"Give what to who?"

"You know," he grinned, "I wanna thread your needle, plant the seed, do the nasty—"

"Okay," I laughed. "I get it."

"If you don't mind." His eyes drifted from between my legs to my neck. "I'd like to stick you with my teeth as well as my cock." He pulled me close and brushed his lips against my cheek. "I wonder if you taste as good as when you're human."

"You can find out," I said, resting my head on his shoulder. "If you want."

I settled deeper into his lap and cuddled my naked body around his. He shivered again—I think more from being given permission than apprehension. Again, he laid me back, caressing my breasts with his hands, mouth, and tongue.

"Will you let me fuck you every day for the rest of your life?"

"I don't possess the full magik of my namesake, but I'll bet you can't imagine what it's like to make love to a faerie. I can take you to a place where the pleasure will seem to last for days. Indefinitely. You'll beg me to make it stop. And you'll ache for the feeling when it's gone." I grinned. "Ask Dacon."

He was serious now.

"I promise it'll be only you," he said, his eyes nearly the brightest I'd ever seen them. "I won't look at another human or person or anyone you don't want me to look at."

"With your history, Romeo, any proclamation of devotion is on the slight side of empty."

"No, I mean it." He pushed my legs apart and ran his tongue from very low on my bottom all the way up to my belly button. He stared at me through a haze of desire. "I'll follow you anywhere. To … to Faeryland. I'll do whatever you want. I'll cook for you. I'll clean for you. I'll be your slave." He shook his head. "Jesus, I have been pixilated."

I placed a pointed nail under his chin.

"Get over it," I said, gently pulling him up to my face. I'm not your girlfriend, and I'm not your personal pussy."

"Oh please," he begged, only halfway teasing. "It'll be blood and fighting and torture and sex and lust and skin and blood and fighting and torture."

A knock came at the bedroom door, awakening my familiar fears. I was careless, allowing myself to get so wrapped up in my own pleasure that I'd lost interest in my surroundings. I jerked out from under Romeo, and up to the ceiling. I hovered there. Petrified.

CHAPTER TWENTY-THREE

ROMEO LAY IN THE same position for a moment before it registered I was gone.

"Shit," he said, looking around the room. Fine iridescent powder fell from my body, shimmering in the lamplight as it drifted to the bed. He looked up at me. *Is that what I think it is?* He pulled back the hand he'd held up to catch the dust. It bled from many tiny pinpricks. "What the hell?"

I was as surprised as he was. I'd never seen my faerie dust do that before. I suppose I never used it on a vampire.

Mine doesn't make people fly. I thought annoyingly. *It's pure. It's magik.*

It's a weapon, he thought, as if he should have known. He hurriedly shook the blanket out onto the floor on the side of the bed away from the door.

The knock came again, and I knew who it was. I closed my eyes and concentrated. I was strong from ingesting so much of Romeo's emotions that within a few moments my wings and hair receded into my body. I fell like a brick onto the bed. By the time I stopped bouncing I was perfectly normal. Romeo was next to me but was so shocked he didn't even notice Galen enter the room with Livi right behind. They were staring at us because we were both naked, and from changing so quickly I was breathing rather hard. It looked like—well, you can guess what it looked like.

"Modesty, Dru," said Livi, embarrassed for me.

Romeo, holding the blanket in his hand, watched me as if I'd just done something absolutely incredible. I know I did, but he shouldn't act as if I did. I looked at Alivia looking at me, and then at

Galen, who was looking at Romeo, whose eyes were strangely wide. Galen looked at me, careful to keep his eyes off my body. I looked back to Alivia, who was glaring at me.

"Stop it," I said and grabbed the sheet to cover myself. Wanting Romeo away from me, I kicked at him until he fell backwards off the bed.

"Must you be harsh?" Galen asked, bending to help him off the floor. "He saved your life, after all."

"How did you know?" I asked.

"It's okay." Romeo took Galen's outstretched hand. "I was acting like an ass."

"If I hit you every time you acted like an ass," Galen smirked, "you would be brain dead." He muttered something else that ended with, "And you, Andru, are much too physical."

I clamped my mouth closed and gave Romeo an evil squint. Nothing like being scolded by your boss when you're naked with his son in your bedroom. Alivia crossed her arms and leaned against the open door, a beautiful smile indicating her pleasure with the situation.

"How did you know where we were?" Romeo asked.

"I was fairly certain when I heard you had taken her from the hospital," Galen said as he kicked the bloody blanket on the floor to the corner of the room. "I needed only to follow your energy."

I wiped a trickle of sweat dripping down my neck. Morphing so quickly had taken its toll. I was exhausted.

"Perhaps it was not my best idea to come," Galen said. "It appears I am interrupting."

"You're fine," Romeo smiled boyishly, winked, and then whooshed a hand at Galen. "I wish you were interrupting what you're thinking, but I couldn't even pry her legs apart with a genuine act of kindness."

That wasn't true, and Galen had to know it. Romeo wouldn't have to fill me with vampire blood to make me want to be with him. I would've hated to admit it, but willing, I was. I watched both men and had to trust Romeo's mind not to betray me. He has expert control — enough that I don't regularly use magik on him — but this time, if we hadn't been interrupted, I would have. Sometimes when Galen and Romeo look at each other, all the closeness they share drifts around them like some kind of responsive fog, and I have to wonder how Romeo keeps my secret. My brain knows he hasn't told Galen, but still, sometimes I wonder.

Romeo startled me by jumping on the bed. He crawled on all fours and eased me back so he could relax on top of me.

"You owe me about fifty thousand," he said, wiping the hair away from my face and then brushing his lips against the skin on the top of my chest. "Shit," he jerked his head back when he saw the cross tattooed near my heart. He quickly pulled the sheet to cover it. "I hadn't noticed it earlier. I guess I was preoccupied," he said with a small smile.

My heart quickened as did his. He stared, and the way he acted made me feel powerful, like just maybe he was thinking things about me that I've thought about him.

"Okay, yes, I'm going," he said.

I hadn't heard anyone ask, but Romeo rolled off me, grabbed his pants and shirt from the floor, and dressed quickly. My insides were in a knot at the thought of him leaving, and I felt I was going to cry. I was used to wanting his body, but this was different. When he sat on the edge of the bed to lace his boots, I used his shirt to pull him down to me. I slid my hand under the material to feel his skin. We kissed hard, as if we'd never done it before.

"It's intense," he said. "But I have to leave. You don't want to bond anymore than we have. The effects would last a long time."

I stared at him.

"I can't stay."

I kept staring.

I can't, he said silently. *This isn't how you want it to be? All high on the vampire blood.*

I shrugged.

"We'll be banging for months. I mean it. Everywhere we go we'll screw."

"Are you saying," I said, but finished in my head, *you don't want to do that with me?*

"Yes. I mean no." He sighed. "Of course I want that. Do you have any idea how many times I think of it?" He motioned his head to Galen. "He wants me gone. I have to leave."

I glanced at Galen, still in the beautiful burgundy silk. I knew that Romeo had similar feelings toward him; all children were drawn to their sires. So how did they ever get out of bed? It was too unreal. I think more unreal than being a faerie. The invisible cord pulled as Romeo stood and walked away. That metaphysical aura tore from me like untangling tightly twisted electrical wires.

Galen stopped Romeo with a hand on his shoulder before he made it to the door.

"Are you all right?"

"I'm fine." He smiled and scratched his head. "Weak and energized at the same time."

"We will talk later," Galen said, nodding to show he understood. But suddenly Galen's emotions were obvious, his anger unmistakable. "You will tell me exactly what you were doing the moment you were ambushed. You will tell me what was so enthralling you never felt the presence of a vampire, or two, or three. So close they nearly killed your partner. Whatever was on your mind, it must have been important. Because I cannot imagine you would go hunting for strays and be so easily distracted by nonsense."

They stared at one another. Romeo tensed and his expression hardened. Shallow tears pricked his eyes.

"At least," said Galen, "that is my thought. Or was healing her an apology?"

The shame on Romeo's face was clear. How could he tell Galen he'd fed while on duty and felt poorly after contracting a disease, or that we were kissing when we were hit, without it sounding as if we were totally negligent? Because, I suppose we were.

"Galen, I—"

"Later," he said. "You can go."

After a moment, Romeo kissed Galen on the side of his face. Then he left, with Livi pulling the door closed behind them.

CHAPTER TWENTY-FOUR

MY FEELINGS FOR ROMEO didn't disappear when he left, but they became a bit more manageable. I felt I could breath, but it didn't last.

"What are you playing at?" Galen was still standing in the middle of my room, still really pissed.

"What?"

"What. Are. You. Playing. At?"

"I don't know what you mean."

"You don't know what I mean?" he repeated, ridiculing me. "Do you want to tie my hands? Do you want him to lose his job, or be suspended, or arrested?"

"No. Not at all."

"But you were on duty, yes? Looking for the kind of criminal that illegally hauls guns and explosives across borders to hurt innocent citizens through random terroristic attacks."

"Yes," I said, but I was beginning to feel Romeo's shame, and my voice wasn't as loud as I wanted it to be.

"And though it may have been a long shot, you are a captain in your country's military, so I know you were prepared for the worst. I know you were not screwing around with your partner, teasing him the way you do on your off days."

That miffed me a little.

"Why are you assuming we were goofing around?"

His eyes narrowed.

"Because I can feel the guilt rolling off my son," he said angrily between gritted teeth. "Because I feel him trying to shield his mind to conceal what actually happened."

I swallowed. Oh.

"Fucking your partner is completely frowned upon, and I do not have to deal with this behavior from anyone else but you two. Why do you force him to do these things?"

I cringed when he cursed. Galen only curses in American slang when he's fuming and forgets himself. Somehow a European accent spewing profanity sounds even more profane. I sighed, because I guessed we were assuming this was my fault.

"You tease him with your body until he drains you," he said, seeming more agitated than a moment ago. "Have him perform impossible or illegal tasks for sexual rewards. You understand he cannot say no to you? Did you beg him to heal you? Did you promise to fuck him until he was unable to walk?"

"No, I swear." I sat up, holding the blanket to my chest. I was feeling too stupid to keep lying on my back. "No."

"Think about the recklessness of what you have done. How about the illegality of it? What person would ask a vampire who has never healed a mortal wound to do so in seclusion, without the aide of a vampire who is experienced? What person would ask the general's son to do it!"

"I'm sorry. Please don't be angry with him. I asked him to do it."

He shot me a look so cold that I shut my mouth. I didn't think I was getting out of this one with the ease of my last confrontation in the ambulance. The incidents were too close for him not to string me up. He pulled the chair from my desk over to my side of the bed, and we sat for what seemed an eternity with him looking at me, and me doing my best to avoid every part of him. Eventually I felt self-conscious that I might not be totally covered. I looked down at myself. I glanced in his direction. He was still staring. I thought that if he didn't start hollering again I was going to crack into little pieces.

"I am trying to control myself, because being beaten and bitten by a vampire, almost bleeding to death, being dragged from your hospital bed, and then being healed with vampire blood should be punishment enough."

I couldn't help but wonder if he'd read my mind. He shouldn't be able to while I'm on a bed surrounded by magik. Which made me wonder if he were able to feel the magik. And that made me all the more paranoid to be near him. He rested his elbow on the chair's arm, and using his thumb to hold his chin, he rested his index and middle finger on his cheek.

"It is difficult to be without him after receiving so much of his blood, I know. Blood healing is a unique experience, even with the obvious downsides."

I nodded. "This feeling of needing him. It will go away, won't it?"

"I think not. If I were here, I would have controlled how much blood he gave. With the amount in your system, you are bound to him as in the stories of old. You will find it difficult to have relationships. You will be unable to help yourself from hanging on his every word. To lay with him will be blissful, and you will do whatever he asks, even if you hate it."

My mouth turned dessert dry. Panic—yes panic—was the reason I'd forgotten how to breathe. I swallowed hard. Not saliva, but vomit threatening from my sickened stomach.

"No. No. No way." I swallowed the sickness again. Something close to horror filled my insides at the thought of hanging on Romeo's every word, and the happiness it would bring him. "That can't be true. He wouldn't have done that to me. Would he? For the love of the moon, please tell me this will wear off."

"I think now, it is punishment enough," he said. A long, not happy smile spread across his face. Ear to vampiric fucking ear.

My shoulders slumped.

"That was cruel," I said, twisting my hands together to stop the shaking.

"You think?" He leaned forward in the chair, and I moved back on the bed. "I think it was, how should I say, a prank. Much like what you and he pull every time you are together. Listen well and I will explain cruel. Other soldiers will get hurt. Their partners will want to heal them, but they are not allowed, because they do not understand what they are doing. Humans will become sloppy heroes if they think their partner will make it better. Vampire blood is not a quick fix. There can be dangerous side effects, eternal consequences. You feel the need it brings. I will have relationships ending because partners that do not even care for each other are irrepressibly sleeping together. With such a promiscuous attitude, my vampires will be curing hangnails."

I tried to say most vampire soldiers do heal small cuts for their partners, but he waved his hand for me to keep my mouth shut.

"I know what goes on, captain! Never mind the emotional ramifications, if I allow healing to be standard practice, I will also be faced with dozens of unwanted conversions. Because humans and vampire alike are not careful. Conversion is much like human pregnancy. If you know the science of it, it seems you could not succeed unless you were trying. But it only takes too much blood, one time, in a weakened body," he said as he stood up from the chair. "Most of the vampire here are young. They have never healed in this manner, have never needed to. Yet if you and your Romeo are above board, arrogance will force them into helping their partners where medical science would have worked well enough." Galen was now pacing the room.

"Then there is death. Did you think of that? You could have died tonight. The pain could have sent your fragile body into shock. Vampire blood is not a medieval, bloody cure all! You and that vampire have a habit of not thinking before you act. What are you going to say when you show up for work without even a fucking bandage on your arm?"

I was beginning to feel defensive. I wanted to fight back. I wanted to point out that vampire blood actually is a medieval cure all, but I knew what he meant. He was right, I guess, but I didn't like being hollered at.

"I asked Romeo to take me out of the hospital because I was afraid."

"Do not insult me."

"It's true." I sat up. "I was afraid and I asked him to heal me. He didn't want to do it."

He waved me off, again unable to hear me defend Romeo. He fell into the chair, looking far too warn for the responsibilities of the great General of Genesis. I did feel bad about that. It seems that lately we've been pushing our limits, and his.

"I told you I have less patience with officers," he said, rubbing his face with his hands. "I asked you not to do anything stupid."

I pouted. I couldn't help it; I didn't want him to demote me.

"Are you going to take my moons?"

"It would serve you right if I did."

"But you said all the other stuff was punishment enough. Taking my moons would be really harsh."

"Yes, well—"

"And it's not completely fair that I'm the only one getting yelled at." I was being a total female, and if he didn't get sick from it, I was sure I would.

"No, I suppose not. Should I take you partner's moons, then? It would be a just punishment, to be sure. Would that make you happy?"

"Gods, no. Take mine. It was my fault. I'll swear to it."

"Protecting him to the last." He blew out a deep breath. "I do not like how reckless you two are together. I half expect these things from him, and I know you push, but lately ... lately it is out of control. You are an awful, ugly instigator in pretty human clothing."

I blinked up at him.

"Do not think for a minute that I do not know you are not innocent," he said, very seriously. Then he took my arm at the elbow and twisted it gently until the fresh, soft, pink skin showed in the light. He rubbed his thumb over the tender wound. "It looks all right. How does it feel?"

I wanted to say "I was fine until you touched me," but I couldn't speak. My arm was burning, my head dazed. It wasn't the feeling I had with Romeo. It was how Galen always made me feel, but on a grander, more intimate, and somewhat nauseating scale. Something thick and invasive crawled off him. His magik or essence, whatever you want to call it, searched me, seemed to want to take control. I pushed up on my elbows to be closer to him, as he lowered himself to meet me. We were so close my breath came back after it touched his face. I heard his heart pound in his chest. Then I felt the vibration of it on the surface of his cool lips.

I closed my eyes. His mouth rested on mine. Our lips stayed parted, as if a kiss in slow motion. I touched the tip of my tongue to his lips and he jerked back. I cried out from the pain of separation. Like with Romeo, it felt as though an electrical current had been ripped apart. He'd yanked his body and magik, pulled an invisible string from my heart, and staggered to the end of the bed.

I felt exposed, like he'd ripped the sheet away from my naked body. As if he'd taken advantage of me.

"What the hell was that," I managed to say.

"The blood in you." He sounded unsure or troubled, as if he weren't positive he believed what he was saying. He shook his head to clear it. "Sharing so much blood is similar to being scented by an animal. The vampire's blood will taint you for a time, repelling opposing predators."

"You weren't being repelled."

"I know that, but it is as close to that as it is to anything else I can think of. Normally. Only instead of your blood bond pushing me away, I believe it was calling me. Perhaps because Romeo and I share the same blood."

"You were invading *me*," I said, not wanting to be the seducer in this scenario, which was slowly turning into a fiasco. "I felt it."

"No, your body was definitely pulling me in. It could be because he and I are bound so close. With him not here to fulfill your body's needs, it calls to me."

Fulfill my body's needs? My mouth hung open with something ugly waiting to pop out. I was so annoyed at what was happening with these two vampires, and I wasn't even sure what that was. Having Romeo's blood in my body left me high, for sure, and a bond was created, but if something inside called Galen, it wasn't any part of Romeo. His blood might give me courage, but my feelings for Galen have always been there, even if he didn't realize them.

"I did not mean for that to happen," he said, backing away. "I did not know that it could."

He stopped at the door, still talking about blood, and bonds, and how to control them. I think it made him feel better to think out loud. I didn't hear most of it. I didn't care what he said. I turned on my side and watched him. He stared at me from his place across the room.

"Please," he whispered, putting his hand on the doorknob. "Do not look at me that way."

I didn't know what he meant, but I new the distance wasn't enough. I could actually feel his attraction to me, and I didn't think it was something he even truly felt. But knowing he felt it at that moment made me feel good, and it made me feel strong.

"I should go," he said abruptly. "I will tell your Alivia to get you what you need."

"Okay," I said.

"Do you need anything?" he asked.

"No."

"Perhaps I should stay then. I mean, if you need something."

"I'd rather not be by myself."

"No," he said softly, and then shook his head. "I should go."

"Then go."

"I cannot stay," he said as he walked toward the chair next to my bed. Only his tone was beaten, as if he knew he wasn't going to do what he was saying. "It is wrong." Then he pulled the bottom of his shirt out of his pants, and my heart started pounding. "If I am to stay, I should be close to you, yes?"

I didn't know how he drew the conclusion that we should be in bed together, but I wasn't disappointed he did. The shirt slid from his shoulders, revealing his near colorless skin and contrasting ink. His ribs were obvious, his chest slightly depressed. I wondered how long it had been since he'd had blood.

He raised his eyebrows at me, wanting me to move over. Part of me was shocked at the entire exchange, but somehow it seemed right, perfectly normal. Okay, not normal, but perfect. It was like watching a movie, knowing I had control over everything that happened. I'd felt like that a few times before. More when I was young. Once with Dacon, when we were stoned on opium. Galen had the same passive shine in his eyes. The same weakness towards me. My eyes were still wide, and I probably looked as young and naive, and as ultimately dominant as I felt.

"Turn on your side," he said.

I did it, because I wanted to feel his body the way I never had. To touch it without clothing made me near dizzy. The warm air breezed down my backside when he pulled the sheet away from my body, and I broke into a sweat. His cool skin settled against mine. His chest was hard at my back, and he wrapped his left arm low around my pelvis and pulled. The laces of his pants were rough against me. I thought I'd never experienced such extreme sensations, but that wasn't exactly true. The fey emerging was extreme, but I'd never experienced this type of closeness before. It was shocking. I wanted more. I wanted him so close the air around us couldn't get between.

He inhaled, smelling my hair. Romeo scents me all the time, and that thought made me shiver, for both of them. It was at that moment I truly realized how far I'd let this go. How Romeo's blood had influenced me in such a harmful way. I saw what Galen meant about people doing things they wouldn't normally do — things that might hurt them in the long run.

His mouth moved slowly to my neck. His lips stayed soft over the pulse there, the rapid beats echoing into his mouth. His breath was warm but his tongue cool when he touched me with the tip of it. I squeezed my legs together in reaction. The sensation was intimidating. I was suddenly petrified of what he would do to me.

His chest felt warm now. He nuzzled his face in the back of my neck, and it was familiar and comforting. He pushed against me, and I shifted my neck to give him more of myself, a better angle to feed.

The need for him was so strong that my insides were clenched tight, literally hurting. His heart pounded against my back, and I was suddenly very lost. But on top of the lust, even more than the physical passion, there was love. I was so in love with him.

He licked my neck. His mouth worked diligently on my back and shoulder blades.

"I had almost forgotten," he said. "The feel, the scent of ..."

Gods, I had to think. I needed to stop him. If he bit me, even accidentally, he'd taste the truth. And he'd kill me. That thought was enough to bring tears to my eyes.

"I taste Romeo's blood." His mouth trailed down my back until he was at the base of my spine. "Your sweat. Your pain. The way you smell. It is unusual and teasing and upsetting. And ... you are so soft." He grabbed my ass. I startled when he pressed his teeth into my skin.

"Shh," he said and moved up. "I would not ever hurt you."

I couldn't speak. A part of me — a big part of me — didn't want to stop. I gripped the bed sheet, swallowing the swell of hurt pooling inside my chest. The first time, in a very long time, I got what I wanted, and it was too much. He kissed the back of my head, and I made another pained, pathetic noise. He helped me twist my body until I was facing him. He laced his fingers through mine, showing how perfectly comfortable he was with my nakedness, only I shook like a scared human against him. His eyes burned red in the shadows of his face, but his voice was composed. He seemed more in control than Romeo would have been if we were doing the same thing.

"I do not want to stop," he said. "And I will tell you something that distresses me." He glanced away from my eyes. "I should have control of myself, but I am near a point where I will not be able to stop, even if you ask it."

Gods, I was thrilled to hear him say that. But I had to remind myself that even though his actions were passionate and caring, they weren't the emotions he'd allow me to see if he found out I was a faerie. I smoothed a finger over the broad, twisting tattoo on his forearm.

"I can't," I said, nearly choking on the words.

"I have upset you?" he frowned, looking sad.

I shook my head.

"Is it Romeo you wish for? Only natural, for it is his blood at work in your veins."

With clarity, I saw that everything Romeo had ever said about Galen and me was true. It was obvious; I couldn't be with him and expect to live. The unfairness of it completely filled me.

"Confusing me is a hard thing to do. Still, you do it all the same."

I could think of nothing to say, and I knew it made no difference. His words fell empty on the floor, with the knowledge that pain and suffering was all he could offer me.

"This was wrong," he said after a moment and moved off the bed. When he placed the sheet over me, I grabbed his hand, studying his features and burning this single intimate moment into my memory. "You are a puzzle, Andru. So young … and I dinnae understand ye at all." I noticed lines on his face that I had never seen before. Signs of stress, fatigue, or sadness. "If I see Romeo, I will send him to ye," he said, and then he quietly closed the door.

The scent of his hair, the smell of his body, and his magik were all over me. I wanted it to last forever, and I wanted to shower to make it go away. I moved into the spot where he had been. I found his shirt and sobbed into it. I cried until it seemed nothing was left inside.

It was almost sunrise when I felt Romeo reach out before he went to rest. If we're not together, he looks for me. I'm not sure why, and I'm not sure he can help it. This morning, because of the bond we shared, his touch was different. He was as close as if he were in the room. I opened my eyes and expected him to be there. Moments later he fell into sleep, and I had to recover from the loss of him. It was no more pleasant than it had been earlier.

I stared at the shade-covered window. I heard the birds singing in the tree outside. I heard Livi talking on the phone in the hallway, to Dacon, I think. She was going on about the party for me, and what she wanted to do. She was laughing, saying how she loved the idea of having a captain in the family. I wanted to feel my fortune. I wanted to feel how lucky I was to have friends, and my job and family, but I couldn't shake the pain of not only not having Galen or Romeo, but also of feeling alone. I couldn't let go of the utter sadness that fact brought into my life.

For all that I had, I had never felt so empty.

CHAPTER TWENTY-FIVE

I AWOKE NEAR DUSK to a quiet house. A note on the kitchen table was addressed to Nastya, which was strange, but again, I assumed Galen had heard Dacon use the name. I didn't necessarily mind, but I wondered why he thought we were close enough for him to use it. He said I was to stay put for two weeks. He would tell the appropriate people I was injured on duty, and that Romeo took me to a private hospital. For the first eight days I had to stay in, go nowhere, see no one. After that I could go outside, but no work at all. I was out IOD, and we were going to lie about the entire thing. That was his big plan. To lie. Not that I wasn't capable. Lying is something I'm rather good at. Not to mention that being out IOD is better than being suspended. I just thought he would've come up with something a little better than a private hospital. What the hell was I going to do for two weeks?

Boredom and loneliness forced me to the sofa to do nothing but watch the vid-screen and eat. I did, however, do both those things very well. After the first few days, Livi hinted that it would be a good idea if I cleaned out the basement, considering most of the clutter was Wiccan ritual materials and pagan holiday decorations. So there you go — so much for wallowing in my cozy, self-centered pool of hopelessness.

The next Friday, Romeo came to see me. He said he wasn't supposed to, but he missed me, even though he was having better luck picking up conferrers when I wasn't around. He said me staying away for a while was a good thing, as he needed the space. He regretted healing me, and our bond was too much for him. I felt like telling him

I was beginning to regret the entire ten years I'd known him. But it was brought to my attention, several times, that I wasn't going to win any awards for congeniality, so I was trying to be sweet, through silence.

Romeo also said Galen was still angry with him — us — and they were avoiding each other. Avoiding, since Romeo's punishment had Galen tossing him off the roof of a four-story home in the suburbs. I wasn't sure if I believed him. Galen was pissed, but Romeo's always so full of shit. He said Galen told him we needed some time apart to understand what it meant if one of us were taken out of the equation. I asked if that were a threat, and Romeo assured me it was just that. Galen wouldn't separate us. I wondered if there was a part of Galen that didn't want us together. Not because of what happened between him and I; that he would care that much would be wishful thinking, and dread, on my part. No, because Romeo and I don't seem to understand our limits anymore. If what Dacon says is true, and I'm not saying it is, maybe we never have.

The second week of forced vacation, I was freaking out. I was positively bored to tears. Cleaning that isn't personally inspired is a drag, and vegetating in front of the vid-screen gets really old really fast. So I started a new journal. Recording what's happening to me and my other self is crucial. I've kept secret diaries on my metamorphosis since I was a young teenager, at my parents urging. They were both witches and felt I was born with powerful energy. They thought I was a gifted psychic or medium with no certain idea of the truth. I shared my intense, innate understanding of spell-craft with them, while the elders of the Realm helped me with bigger truths such as my physical transfiguration, and how the Faerie Kingdoms were to be kept private at all cost. A hard rule I broke for my brothers, Dacon, and Livi. A decision I regret to this day. Not only because of how they view me, but because I put them in a danger I couldn't comprehend when I was twenty-one and in need for someone to know the truth.

But I was lonely. My parents had died, and my brother, Vincent, left for the States soon after to join Max and Willow in Colorado. I suppose I wanted to share my altered personality in case something happened. A part of me regrets that my parents never saw the fey magik; back then I was terrified of being caught. When I was a child, a dark faerie elder told me that if word got out to someone with any magikal ability—say, a shaman, a dark witch, or a demon—that I was on Earth and unprotected, I would be hunted, tested, or worse. I would bring uncertainty to the Faerie Realm, and if word ever got back to King Jagen or the other vampire lords that I was connected to the fey, they would surely have me killed, because the vampire are paranoid and assume every magikal being is out to get them. Also, they're an industrious lot, always looking for magik to pilfer. Because of that, it took me years to open up; by the time I did, my parents were gone. At times I wish I had the guts to transform on the steps of the manor. To see Galen's face as I unfurl my dark wings. To watch their eyes as I launch myself into the air would be a magik all it's own.

At the beginning of my second week of vacation-imprisonment, Romeo and I used his nights off to watch the area where we were ambushed. He was told that Galen's people found an entrance to an old mine about a half mile from where we'd parked. Our surveillance was secret because I was supposed to be at home recuperating, and Galen had people continuously scouting the area. Besides playing spy, I didn't like being there. The entire area had a strange energy to it. The ground felt odd. I couldn't make my feelings clearer to Romeo, so he shrugged it off. I didn't blame him for ignoring me. That's the price you pay for listening to your intuition. If no one can feel it but you, they aren't going to believe it's there.

Near the end of the week, I stopped by the Realm. Time is different there, slower, so I tried not to get hung up. I wanted more information about what's been happening, the dreams that continue to crowd my head. The fey keep records, but none seem to mention me in particular, or the things that happen to me. The old codices are vague when describing the dealings of the fey and vampire—only to say that, one day, a leader of the spirits will be thick among the undead. Somehow the bringer, or keeper, of death. Not the absolute death of a race—just death. And seeing how that's not me, I figure I'm out of that loop.

I petitioned the High Court of the Dark and was put off. I don't know if they were avoiding or disregarding me. I asked members of my clan to retell the stories I'd heard since I was a child, hoping something more would be remembered. They knew only that faerie energy was bound to me somehow, and they were aware of my existence the moment I set foot on Faery soil. Because I made it through the fabric of realities on my own, even if just with my mind, by fey law that makes me a faerie, and they can't deny me. But I learned nothing I didn't already know—certainly nothing about the dreams. Years ago, when I'd heard of the part-human, part-fey "prophecy" from Romeo, I immediately asked about it. They knew of only one prophecy about the vampire, but none believe I am a hybrid, nor am I the bringer of this prognostication. What I think is the fey version of King Jagen's prediction is a spiritual fable that goes something like this:

"A faerie lamented. A human favored. The destined, timeless sister. Unearth the 'Orb of Paleodeus,' which translates basically to Ancient Deity, and the unraveled ethos will be the triumph of the sister, the venue of reunion for neglected souls, and the final judgment for the guilty, or the lost vampire, and its kin."

I've never understood who is the lamented faerie, the favored human, or the timeless sister. If the faerie and the favored human mate, then who is the timeless sister? I was told the story is about the separation of self to bring the vampire spirit back in line. I don't know what that means, and apart from a few nasty encounters trailing back a millennia there are no other stories of vampires and faeries together.

To me, the whole idea of a prophecy is silly. I don't believe in fixed destinies. No one is born to carry out a specific act. Even if they were, their choices would surely hinder the outcome. This is the twenty-first century; we don't give credence to prophecy any more than we believe the earth is flat. The word alone suggests medieval monk scribblings, and clandestine meetings with the pope. I have neither seen, heard of, nor been a part of any of those things. I did, however, think there were others like me. Maybe not exactly, but there has to be another human born with this kind of power. Surely, I couldn't be the only one with faerie gifts.

But lately, mostly because of the dreams, I feel adrift. It's as if I'm being gently drawn apart. If I am the only person with this magik, why has it been given to me? What am I supposed to do with it? The nervousness at what I am, at least, is nothing new. I am apprehensive with each transition of power, and still nothing has happened to bring me any closer to believing I will hurt my friends, or my country.

CHAPTER TWENTY-SIX

TWO DAYS BEFORE I was to go back to work, a messenger showed up with a note from Galen instructing me to go to his chambers on September 20 for the meeting he wanted to have before I was hurt. That was the day of my birthday party, so my admittedly shallow dilemma was deciding what to wear to the meeting without having to change for the party. I'd wanted to wear something extremely tight, black and leatherish, but doubted that would look appropriate for a business meeting. Besides, I didn't want Galen thinking I dressed for him. I understood he was under the influence of sorts, and most likely didn't intend for what happened to happen, and I'd assured myself it wouldn't happen again, and probably never really did happen. In other words, I tried to be a man about it.

I settled on wearing a white, knee-length shirtdress with buttons up the front and a pocket over each breast. It had long sleeves with French cuffs and a short slit up each side. I finished the outfit with white, heeled sandals that tied up my calf. No stockings. Sexy, but sane. I was painting on dark red, nearly black lipstick when Livi pushed my bedroom door open. She wore only a black slip and jewelry. Her dark burgundy makeup was perfect for her skin and made her eyes stand out like a dark flame. Her curly hair had a slight side part, gently skimming her shoulders.

"Look at you!" she cried. "I love all the extra eyeliner."

"Plain dress, extra makeup."

"I see you got your silver back," she observed, flicking the metal spring in my ear.

"I almost didn't. All of it was in a bag from the hospital, and Romeo brought it back the other night, but he threw it in my bedroom trash can."

She sighed and shook her head, not wanting to talk about him.

"I love your hair," she said as she brushed the short hair on the back of my head. "Blue highlights look really nice on you."

I turned back to the mirror for one last check as Livi took my new black cloak from my closet.

"Wear this. It's chilly."

It would also add a barrier between Galen and me that I was completely comfortable with.

"Is Roeanne coming?" I asked, fiddling with the snap.

"Nope, she has to work a double."

I smiled. Fumbling with the stiff leather at my collarbone, I turned to the mirror so I could see, but Livi grabbed the snap and pulled me to face her. She looped it through and clicked it closed.

"Who invited her to movie night anyway?" she asked.

"Romeo wanted to throw her down."

"Okay," she sighed and nearly rolled her eyes. "You're perfect."

"I'll see you when I'm through," I said, picking up my small pocketbook from the bed. I was at the top of the steps with Livi following me out.

"Don't, you know, do anything with him."

"It's a meeting," I said as I clomped down the stairs. "He doesn't want me."

"Lieutenant Clark got pregnant during a meeting with her boss," She said hanging over the banister.

"Her boss was her husband!"

"Still …"

CHAPTER TWENTY-SEVEN

IT WAS A BEAUTIFUL, cloudy night. My sandals were comfortable, and I decided to walk to the manor. Second shift had begun so only a few soldiers were in headquarters, but the dress was a hit. The attention was confidence building but made me feel uneasy about seeing Galen. When I got to his chambers, I took a moment outside the door, trying, for my own sanity, not to think about the last time we were together. I laid my hand on the palm scanner next to the doorframe, swiped my ID, and punched in my security code. A picture of me, my name, and my identification number ran across the small dark screen along with the date and time. A soft electronic buzz sounded before the large door clicked open.

When the door closed, a large lizard, about two and half feet long, rushed past my feet. It ran across the room to Lord Galen, who was standing at a tall map easel. The lizard leapt to his thigh, gripped its claws into his pants, and skittered up his back. Without taking his eyes off the easel, Galen stretched his arm to a wooden "T" stand bolted to the floor. The lizard tottered along his arm and sat on the flat board.

The room, like the barrack hallways, is subtly lit with electric torch lighting. Movement from the right-hand corner startled me. Lord Cherkasy rose from the large canopied bed, nearly obscured by the royal blue draperies tied to the dark wood posts with black rope, allowing for only a triangle view of the bed on three sides. The sheets were messy and the pillows had been thrown around. I was instantly annoyed and gave myself a mental slap, because it was none of my business.

Lord Cherkasy looked spectacular in a black sheath dress with thin straps. Her lips were the natural bright red of the vampire, and along with thick black eyeliner she had a circle of blushing red smudged around her eyes. Her long black hair rested down her back, likening her to a Kabuki princess. She positioned herself behind Galen, playfully leaning her back on his. I took a military stance to avoid looking at them. It didn't matter—neither said a word to me.

"Will you stop by after you've finished here?" asked Lord Luise. She turned until she rested her front against his back. She was almost as tall as he was naturally, and her shoes put her exactly at his height. "Will you?"

She pulled at the strap holding his hair taut and dropped it. She clawed the strands, fanning the darkness across the back of his white shirt. He didn't respond, and I wasn't sure if he was ignoring her or teasing her. She was quite sure he was ignoring her and after being sufficiently irritated, she pushed him into the easel. The marker he held smeared a long line across the papers. He tossed the pen and straightened as if to stretch his back. He ran fingers through his hair and seemed puzzled, as if he didn't understand how it got loose and in his eyes. He dropped the mass of it over one shoulder.

"Andru . . ." he said when he noticed me.

"Gale!" Lord Cherkasy stomped her foot.

He turned an innocent face to her as if he were noticing her for the first time. In truth, I think he was.

"Did you want something?"

"Yes," she said, and I could see the effort she used to not scream at him, which was eerily reminiscent of how I felt about Romeo most of the time. "Will you come see me later?"

He thought, the way vampires do. A moment of blank staring and no blinking.

"No. I have things to do."

She sucked in a breath and blew it out her nose. She stopped by me on her way to the door.

"Are you the one that killed my Tina's killer?"

I nodded, careful not to look in her eyes.

"She was a good girl." Cherkasy's voice almost sounded normal, no hint of seduction or manipulation.

"Leave her be, Lu," said Galen as he walked to his desk.

Her face puckered with anger and like a flipped switch, her expression changed. She came to me, and damn her, she unfastened my cloak and let it drop to the floor. She brushed both her hands up the short hair on the sides of my head. Her fingers dug into the long hair on the top. She picked at it as if she were arranging it just so.

"Sweet," she said and then flicked the rings in my ear the way Alivia had earlier. "Is it against your code of principles to thank the one who saved your life?"

That is one reason I hate her. She's always so damn caustic. True, I hadn't thought to say anything, but did she have to stand so morally tall? I opened my mouth, but she waved her hand.

"The only reason I used my influence is because your death on the information superhighway would have made us look shocking and masochistic." Too late.

Her energy flared. I felt it crawl along my skin. But her power doesn't surround you the way Galen's or even Romeo's does. It doesn't take time away from you, so you forget who you are or what you want. It enters you as a separate entity. It pushes like a heavy weight inside your head, forcing your will. You do what she asks, but you do it unwillingly, knowing you don't want to. And that makes it all the more terrifying. And she knows it.

I hoped she wasn't trying to get into my head, to find out what Jagen couldn't. She could pry all she wanted, but she'd be just as disappointed. She moved close. She had to bend to put her nose against my neck.

"Your skin," her voice near astonished and lowered to a whisper, "smells like water. Like the lake where I grew up." She wrapped her hand around my neck.

My stomach sank. Jupiter lives, how do I get into these situations? Lord Galen said something quick and harsh in her native

Russian tongue. Knowing enough Russian to speak to my mother and grandparents wasn't enough to understand them. The dialect was too different. Luise answered him and he responded angrier than the first time.

"You can be a pig when it suits you," she said, narrowing her yes.

She looked at me with something like angry fear in her eyes, then turned and clacked on her heels to the other side of the room. When I heard the door bump shut, I started to shake. I truly hated that woman. No sooner was she gone when Lord Galen was in front of me, my cloak in his hand, as if conjured from nothing. I didn't immediately take it because my hands were shaking, so he tossed it on the bed.

"It is hot in here," he agreed, thinking my inaction was my way of saying I didn't want the cloak.

My eyes went wide with agitation. I squeezed my fingers around the purse behind my back. I never know if the older vampires understand how harassing they can be. When they make decisions for you, it's controlling. And with Lord Galen, because of how I feel, it's annoying.

"I like the blue," he said.

I raised a conscious hand to my hair. I smiled for lack of anything witty or sarcastic to say. The silence was agonizing.

"She is hurtful if things do not go her way." He dropped his eyes like a parent taking responsibility for a child's actions. That is an accurate definition, but I don't know how much responsibility you can take for the actions of a six-hundred-year-old child. I guess that depends on the guilt of the parent.

"It's okay." She was easier to deal with than Jagen. "I think I'm getting used to it."

"Getting used to it?"

"Leaders taking liberties to get what they want."

Something in his expression, the way he nodded, made me realize it sounded as if I were referencing what happened between us. I felt like an idiot.

He moved across the room to his desk, gathered some papers, and took them to the easel. He glanced at me.

"Your dress is … pretty." Only the way he said pretty was odd, as if he weren't used to saying it, or didn't like saying it.

"There's a party."

"Yes."

He motioned me over, and I felt like a child next to his height.

"Can I get that stool over there?"

"Unless you would rather sit on my shoulders."

"Jokes," I said and tossed my purse on the bed. "I was told you didn't know what they were."

There, that was normal. A little humor. Just an average meeting with my boss. I set the hunk of metal close to the easel. The stool was small and I had to go on my toes, which was ridiculous and difficult in heeled sandals. Galen moved a few inches away to give me room. He stared at the maps, not at me struggling. It seemed he was being overly considerate.

He pointed to the New York map.

"The territory of Lords Orel, Casene, and King Jagen. Can you go over what you found in the underground clean out last year? You are the only one from my territory that still works here or I would not be wasting your time."

I didn't know what to say to that. It upset me, but what could I do? I didn't think it possible, but it seemed the personal time we spent together made it more awkward instead of less. I guess it was silly to think he and I could be any kind of friends. I pushed those thoughts away because I had to. He wanted to know what happened last year, and I had to think about it.

"Lord Orel's First Captain Regan got an anonymous tip of strange activity in the hills near Canada. A group of humans with guns and homemade bombs were caught digging underground. An old mine was found nearby, freshly opened. Romeo was in Rhode Island so you sent me and that lieutenant from early shift because she had the geology degree."

"You remember that?" he asked, cocking his head.

"Yeah, we talked a lot in the car on the way. She loved rocks," I smiled.

"Yes, she left to pursue that path. Was there anything unusual about the mine?"

"Absolutely. In design mostly. They'd taken over an old shaft mine, but no nest was created. No one was hiding out. And the roaming cow tracked three quarters of a mile altogether."

"Cow?"

"Oh, Lieutenant Carr thought the camera we use to track distance looked like an animal so she glued ears, a tail, and some black and white spots on it."

He didn't laugh, smile, or blink. He nodded, but he looked as though he couldn't understand why anyone would do such a thing.

"Anyway, the main shaft had smaller, narrow passages that branched off but didn't lead anywhere."

"I want to show you pictures of this new find."

I hopped off the stool and sat at his desk while he tapped his fingers on the desktop of the computer. He opened the file and I made my way through the first couple photos of the partially concealed mine opening.

"What do you think they were doing up there?"

"Hard to say," he said. "If I knew who was there it would help, but Romeo's attacker has not been found, and you destroyed the faces of the other two. Neither prints nor DNA were on file. We have checked for recent escaped criminals with no results. The human girl your Alivia assaulted did not know anything. She was interviewed and is now in a coma."

I looked at him.

"Better not to ask."

I was sure that was true.

"What about McKenney?"

"As of the last two years, he is off the grid. We do not know who he was working for."

"If it's terrorists, what could they want now?"

"What do they always want?" he asked, rubbing his face. "The human factions want the death of us. The vampire faction wants to throw us into war and take over the States. The mixed splinters want a full democracy and the death of the royal government for a president. And the religious fundamentalists, including vampires, want peace at the expense of every last vampire in the world."

I couldn't argue. That about sums it up. He leaned over to better see the computer screen. His hair fell forward onto the desk and over my hands. A shiver rolled up my back in a noticeable tremor.

"Sorry," he said quietly, with that drawn English enunciation. "I let Luise take it down, because to pull it back has been giving me headaches." He gathered the hair and dropped it behind his back.

"Really?" I'd never heard of a vampire having a headache.

"No," he gave me a small smile. Then he tapped the computer screen. The pictures were centered, clear, and professional. Most shots were familiar because I'd spent so much time there. Galen reached over me to find something on the desk.

"I hard copied one of those pictures," Galen said as he reached over me to find something on the desk. " I want to know if you can explain it to me."

"It's obscured," I pointed to a section of the computer screen, "but see those small animals off to the side?"

"I had noticed, yes," he said, positioning the large monitor to better see from his higher point of view.

"Stray vampire nests keep a small pen of animals for food."

"The entire area was under watch for nearly three weeks. No one was seen leaving and not a soul came close. If they were residents, they would have been unusually organized to break down so quickly. We were there the night you were hurt. The area was completely dead. It could not have been used to house many. Though I think you knew that."

"No."

He didn't even rattle me this time. He'll never feel it's a lie. He clicked through the pictures, one after the other, until he came to a close-up of the side of my face with brown and green camouflage paint. I was leaning on my crossed arms, sleeping. It was a decent picture of me too. Romeo is such an idiot.

"I gave Romeo my camera. There were probably pictures on it already." I rolled my internal eyes.

He was shaking his head no before I finished the words.

"He must have taken the memory card from my camera and got it mixed up with these other pictures."

"And the paint?"

"Would you believe Samhain? That is, Halloween."

He shook his head no.

"In my defense, if I'm allowed one, you didn't exactly say not to go."

His already wide eyes widened further with incredulity.

"I said go nowhere," his voice rose a notch. "Do nothing."

"But you didn't say do not try to find those tunnels."

"That is the logic of a drowning woman," he sighed.

"Is it saving me?"

"Two," he held up his thumb and index finger. "Two foolish things since your promotion. How much longer will this habit of disobeying go on?"

"I don't think—"

"Exactly. You do not think, and it is grating on my nerves."

"That isn't fair."

"I am thinking," he raised his brows very high, "that what is fair for you is far too subjective when I or my son is involved."

I opened my mouth to speak, shut it, and then started again.

"Well, if Romeo had been thinking when that picture was taken, you wouldn't have found out, and I wouldn't be getting into trouble."

He sighed heavily through his nose.

"I will admit a logic to that. More so, I admire that your brain came up with it."

"And—"

"Do not push it. I have plenty of competent soldiers working for me. You did not have to risk your job just to play in the dirt with him." I kept quiet, considering that was exactly what we were doing. "Was anything else found in last year's tunnels?"

A change of subject. Good for me.

"The supposed leader hinted they were building an elaborate underground system—a district or city, if you will. But I don't believe it. The smaller paths were left undone, dug to a certain point, and then stopped."

"We are solitary. Perhaps they were resting alcoves?"

"No, that's not how strays do it," I shook my head as I flipped through the photos. "These humans and vamps are on the run. They dig caves and tunnels for hiding and sleeping in a group. When the sun comes up, they drop in a lifeless pile on top of each other till dusk. Humans watch over the bodies in shifts." His expression turned sour. I guess the thought of piled bodies bothered him. "I think they were looking for something."

"Looking for what?" he frowned.

"I don't know. But there was something about the way those shafts were dug—the crudity of them, or something. They couldn't use them to become a community. You can't build rooms in a structure as unstable as an old mine shaft with the primitive equipment and materials they were using. The people we interrogated never gave up exactly what they were doing. But no fugitives were involved, only petty criminals. People were fined for trespassing, but not many arrests. The leader stuck to his story about a small commune, but they were finished whatever they were doing. Some of the equipment was packed and ready to be moved."

Galen leaned his butt on the desk next to me and thought for a few moments.

"I would like you involved," he eventually said.

"You want me in charge?" I asked, tossing my spin on his request. "Not that I'm not grateful, but why me? Especially since lately I've not been ... the best listener."

"You have not only dealt with the tunnel situation in New York, but you were also there when the nest was found in West Virginia four years ago."

"Oh yeah, I was at the spring bee festival," I said, remembering how much fun I was having and how angry I was to have to go back to work. "I had to use the last four days of my vacation visa to work on that project."

"Yes, well," he said, pulling his hair into a soft knot. "The Virginias do not like us at all. They would not allow but a handful of our people into the country, so it was good you were there."

"It took me forever to get that visa. They lost my paperwork the first time, and I had to resubmit."

He smiled at my grousing.

"You are in the unique position of being the only person on staff, at the moment, who has had solid hands-on experience with a tunnel search. You will need to be really careful, Ana. We have no idea what has been going on. No idea what we will find inside."

"No one's gone in? They've obviously cleared out. Maybe even left some stuff behind."

"I have been asked by the king to take this slow. He is discouraged in this dangerous time. The attack at the university was less than two months ago. We consider this situation terroristic initiative. We have thoroughly searched the area, but I am also reluctant to go forward."

"Why?"

"I do not know," he said after a moment. "I only mean … I cannot be sure. We need to be cautious."

I nodded. I wouldn't argue with a gut feeling.

"I will need until Wednesday to get everything you will need to move forward. I have a few recommendations for personnel, but for the most part you may pick fifteen soldiers. I assume you will want Lieutenants Kneed and Drake."

"Maybe not Dacon," I said as I clicked to another picture. "He has problems with small spaces, and Alivia's afraid of the dark."

"Excuse me."

I looked up at him still leaning his ass on the desk next to me. He was staring at me again.

"Dacon's claustrophobic, and Livi's afraid of the dark," I said, feeling strangely like I'd gotten them into trouble.

His brows narrowed as he frowned. He half rolled his eyes and would have sighed if he felt like giving it the energy. He looked at the clock on the wall.

"I am through. You can leave, if you want to."

I didn't fully know what he meant by that last bit, but I had to go. The moment was uncomfortable, because I had to step around him, and he didn't move out of my way. When I tried to pass, he put a hand on my face. He turned me to look at him, pulling me closer until I was leaning on him. He did all of this slowly, leaving me the opportunity to pull away if I were uneasy, but I wasn't nervous. I was petrified, and therefore paralyzed.

"Your smell," he said.

The brush of his lips against my cheek made my heart pound.

"I smell?" I asked, closing my eyes and doing my best not to shake.

"Your scent is …"

Please don't tell me, I thought as loud as I could. Please don't tell me. I didn't want to know. There wasn't any way for me to explain it to him.

"It is the scent of scotch broom, and even whin on the moor after a long rain." He pulled back. "Has anyone told you that?"

My eyes were so wide they threatened to fall out of my head. Who would ever tell me something like that?

"I don't think I know anyone who's been to the English moors."

"Scottish," he said.

"Those either."

"Romeo."

"He has?" I thought about that and hated that he'd never told me he'd been there. Sometimes I felt as if I didn't know him at all. That he had this other life he refused to share.

"He cannot smell it?"

I shook my head, but I knew why Galen was the only one who smelled it. Romeo thinks I smell like a wet forest or sometimes fresh cut grass. Dacon's thought is mint tea. Livi's opinion is skin sweating from the sun. And apparently Lord Luise thinks I smell like Russian lake water.

Faerie magik is innate. We have many extraordinary and powerful gifts. One obscure talent, shall I call it, is that people believe a faerie's body scent or odor smells like their favorite thing in the world—be it gardenias or motor oil. Not that they can't tell if we've been eating garlic, but that special smell is from their mind. Long ago the fey used to steal humans to live with them in Faery. Along with wings, beauty, or enchantments, scent was a way to entice and lure potential victims. Most fey can control the use of it. I can't control it any more than I can control breathing heavily while my boss has his face in my neck.

While it works on everyone, some are much more conscious of it than others; that's just the way magik is. One person may be glamoured with a kiss. Some need two, maybe three and a back rub. It's worse if I'm sweating. If I affect you, and I'm perspiring, I'll have as many admirers as the day is long. It's the reason I had so many friends growing up, and why I stayed at home more often as I got older. It's superficial magik, and wrong to know that much about a stranger. I've never liked that particular bit of magik. It's deceitful, and embarrassing. I, myself, smell only skin, hair, and sweat, as anyone does on their own body. Apart from the fey in the Realm, and my family, I have wondered if someone, somewhere can smell just me.

Galen's eyes were bright. Those hollow points fixed on my expressions.

"I have smelled it many times, and wondered how it could be that you radiate that fragrance."

"I've pulled broom from my dedushka's garden when I was a kid, but I don't remember any distinct smell. And honestly, I don't know what whin is or smells like."

"Scotch broom has a clean scent, almost grassy, or like hay, with a slight aroma of honey."

"Oh."

"And whin, it is sometimes called gorse."

"Oh, I know that. That smells like coconut." I frowned. "You think I smell like coconut?"

"I suppose. I have never smelled coconut, or tasted it, that I recall. I do not think it was in abundance when and where I was raised, and food was not a pastime once I was turned."

He smiled, and I smiled back. I wondered what other foods he hadn't tasted. To be alive for so long and have the world become so small, it must be strange to live among foods you've never experienced. We stared at one another until it became serious, and therefore uncomfortable.

"I don't know," I said, looking away. "Probably I don't really smell like those things, just that I remind you of it." I shrugged lightly, trying for indifference. "My perfume or soap or something."

He held my waist, making it hard for me to move. He used his other hand to play with the neckline of my dress.

"Are you still upset with me?"

I shook my head. I didn't understand.

"The other night. In your bed. My behavior was inappropriate, and I apologize. As your boss, your general, it must have been disturbing."

"Oh, no." I started shaking again. "I wasn't angry. I was—"

"Wanting my son."

"No," I said and meant it. "Not that I didn't want him." I gave myself a mental slap. "I mean, I was very confused that night."

He smiled at my verbal clumsiness.

"Can I kiss you?"

"Huh?" My breath hitched.

His closed smile grew wider. I was suddenly agitated. It felt like he was making fun of me, trying to confuse me. I tried to pull away, but he wouldn't let go.

"I seem to have disturbed you again."

"Well, yeah. What are you doing?"

"If you have to ask, I am not doing it very well."

"You know what I mean. *Why* are you doing it?"

"Is it so strange, that I like you?"

"You *like* me?" My head felt like it was going to explode. "What are we, in high school? And what—all the sudden?"

"Not sudden." He shrugged. "We like who we like. Want who we want."

I had no idea whether to be overjoyed, completely suspicious, or absolutely terrified. I'd never noticed this degree of interest. Except maybe the other night on my bed, but that was different.

"You want me?" I asked.

Just a nod, and more of the smile.

"But …" I just couldn't wrap my head around it. "You have her."

"Her?"

"Yes, her."

"Lu? Luise? Lord Cherkasy?"

I frowned. He withdrew then. He pulled back, looked at the floor, and rested his hands on the edge of the desk.

"The situation is complicated. She and I—"

"Belong together. You suit one another."

"You think she and I are alike?"

I saw pain in his eyes; the comparison upset him. I was about to walk away when he caught my hand. I put the other on his chest, so I wasn't leaning on him as before.

"I have to go," I said. "I'm late."

"Is it my son who encourages your distance?" He pulled my hand up and played with it. "You shake when we are together." He smiled. "I like it. Do I frighten you, or are you simply paranoid around all royals?"

All I could hear was Romeo's voice telling me how wrong this was. Dacon's voice saying how wrong this was. My own voice saying, "This is so fucking wrong."

"You do frighten me. I've been told things about you."

"Things?"

I didn't answer.

"From who? My son?" His eyebrows rose very high. "He is perhaps suspect."

"I don't know what to think when you say those kinds of things. You are … who you are, and you can do whatever you want. Why would you want me? Unless you want someone you can force."

"You think I would take what is not given?" He touched my face. "If I was unwilling to wait, I would have taken you already, yes?"

Somehow it was easier when we were in the dark, and I was half drunk on vampire blood. We touched more intimately then, but now, so close to him, a kiss seemed the ultimate intimacy.

"You fascinate me, Andru."

"Fascinate? Will I still? After I've given in to you?"

"Are you offering to give in?" he asked as he wrapped his large hand around my jaw.

"That's the kind of twisting of words I've been warned about." I pushed his hand away. "Truthfully, I don't trust myself around you."

"Then trust me," he said, pulling me towards him until our lips were almost touching.

Oh yeah, sure, okay.

CHAPTER TWENTY-EIGHT

"Hei, hvor er du, Gale!"

My head snapped toward the joyous voice. Galen sighed heavily in my ear before he turned. The very blonde, very tall man was beaming. He stood just inside the doorway. I hadn't even heard the door chime.

"Am I interrupting?"

"Of course you are, James, or you would not have felt the need to ask."

"My deepest apologies," he said, his Norwegian dialect stronger than I'd ever heard it.

Galen moved from the desk, taking his warm presence with him. The far too happy James met Galen halfway into the room. He kissed the dark-haired vampire on both sides of his face, and then his mouth. Galen didn't exactly seem happy to see the taller man, but he rarely seems happy to see anyone. I wasn't at all happy to see James.

"This is Captain Andru Weber," said Galen, motioning back toward the desk. I'd already made my way to the bed, where I picked up my coat and purse. Galen cocked his head. "There is Andru," he motioned to me again. "This is—"

"First Captain James Capone. We've met." I tried to sound matter-of-fact, but I don't think I succeeded.

Galen's eyes flipped from one of us to the other.

"I'm so glad you remember me, Andi."

"Don't," I said, holding my hand up before he started towards me.

"What?" James grinned. "You missed me. You know you did."

"If you come near me," I said as calmly as I could, "I will rip out your fangs while you lay day-cold."

"No," said Galen, confused by my attitude and shaking his hand so I'd stop.

"Calm down, Andi." The amused look on James' face was entirely condescending. "I won't touch you without your permission."

"Don't call me Andi," I said, barely holding onto my anger.

"As you wish," said James, giving a small, stupid bow.

"If I, and I don't know, a hundred other people, had our wish, you'd have burnt to a pile of ash when the sun came shining over that mountain."

"Stop," ordered Galen. "What has gotten into you?"

I did my best to keep what happened between Captain Capone and me private, but I will never forget that day when we were in the mining tunnels of New York. James came on to me and tried to bite me, but I struggled. He pushed me, right into the tunneling equipment the trespassers were using. The fall punctured my shoulder blade, and James stopped hitting on me. As long as he stayed away from me, I was willing to keep it to myself.

James smiled at Galen.

"It's fine," he said, his accent back to what I was used to. "The girl has a healthy dislike for me. It will save her life someday."

I threw myself forward until I was practically on top of him. Anger and loathing outweighed fear.

"Are you threatening me, captain? I dare you to do it. Give me the freedom to protect myself, you priggish son of a bitch."

"Priggish? Me?" He laughed. "What I remember is—"

"Enough." Galen stepped between us. He pushed James in the chest to send him tripping backwards. I was itching to argue, but Galen countered every move I made to get closer to him.

"I'm here only minutes, and already she's panting," James said.

I closed my eyes and took a deep breath. It was my only option, because Galen was holding my arm.

"Yes, James," said Galen, "you are here only minutes, yet you are quickly wearing on my nerves."

A light dawned atop that towhead, and James took a step back.

"Gale, I had no idea Andi was your conferrer," he apologized with wide eyes. "She was displeased with our engagement."

"I am understanding that."

"Just stay far away from me—you got that?" I said, yanking my arm from Galen's grip and heading for the door.

"This will be difficult," said James. "We're meant to work together on these new tunnels of yours."

"Screw that."

"You'll be in charge," assured James. His eyes were on Galen, hoping what he said would appease the stronger vampire. "I'll do only as she instructs."

I practically stomped back to him, too angry to think clearly.

"I thought my instructions were clear enough last year, but my body is scarred by your misinterpretation of, 'No, don't touch me,'" I pointed my finger at him. "And I know it wasn't just me."

James' eyes went wide at Galen's expression.

"I thought she was playing," he said, raising his hands to plead his innocence. "The way she acts. She plays with Romulus all the time! Galen, please, I had no idea she was yours. She didn't tell me."

His use of Romeo's given name annoyed me further. No one uses it. Sometimes Galen, and only when he's trying to make Romeo understand the seriousness of a situation. James uses it because he's a snot, and he likes to think he's closer to Romeo than the rest of us.

"Do you think any soldier protecting the land you live in should have to worry about a ranking officer's repellent behavior?" Galen asked as he moved me out of the way.

James shook his head back and forth.

"Jagen may be lenient with you in the running of his territory, but you will not abuse your power or touch my soldiers in any way."

I was normally opposed to anyone fighting my battles, but unless I shot James, I couldn't win a fight. Which is why my vampire retaliation tactics are so creative. But James being a part of Jagen's personal guard, and whatever else, forced me to bite the bullet and keep revenge to myself. I still didn't feel good about Galen's actions. It seemed cowardly to let someone take care of my problems, especially when I wasn't his conferrer. I wanted him to stop, but I didn't think he'd listen.

"Gale, you have to believe that I didn't mean to upset you," said James.

"But you did not care if you upset her."

"She didn't tell me," said James again, pleading for absolution. "She does it on purpose. She wears my favorite perfume!"

That shook me, kind of. Jupiter, maybe he did think I was playing with him. But I wasn't the only one. James is known for using his position to satiate his greediness.

Galen kept walking toward him, his features changing ever so slowly. His irises turned not red but black. The hollowness under his cheekbones deepened, forcing his fangs to appear large and protruding. I'd never seen a vampire do anything like that. James smacked hard against the wall before Galen's hand reached out. He weaved bony fingers through the other vampire's hair and lifted him slightly off the floor. In one blurred motion, Galen clamped his teeth into the lower part of James' neck. He ripped out a sizable chunk of his throat, and James screeched. I moved out of the way of blood spray, leaving both men's faces splattered red. Galen spit the gob of flesh to the floor as James whimpered and struggled.

"You see, James, I have no sense of humor."

He dropped James and then wiped the blood and things from around his mouth. The blond man grappled at the gushing wound. Blood seeped in thick lines through his fingers while his hand tried to guard the hole in his throat. I watched as labored breath and liquid gurgles bubbled from his mouth. There was a time, before I started this job, that a man struggling to survive would have affected me. Sometimes you learn something about yourself and it frightens you, and sometimes it doesn't. I almost felt bad that I couldn't have cared less.

A buzzer sounded and the heavy wooden door swung open. Romeo stepped inside. Acknowledging the bloody edge of power in the room, he stepped closer to Galen. He looked down at the vampire gasping in pain and was the picture of control. Mostly because he doesn't care. He hates James. Not because of what he did to me—I never told him—but because James is a first-class prick.

"I missed all the good stuff," he said as he looked at me.

Galen spit a mouthful of blood and something else onto the floor. He turned and I could see his face was normal except for the eyes. They were as black and disturbing as any hole I'd ever looked down. He wiped his mouth with his shirtsleeve, and I had a flash fantasy that Romeo would lick the blood away. I checked my smile. It was embarrassing how much I would enjoy that.

"You need him out of here?" Romeo asked, jerking his thumb to the door.

Galen shook his head on his way to the bedroom area of the room. He opened and closed drawers in the small nightstand on the far side of the bed.

"You look beautiful," Romeo said, smiling at me. "White becomes you."

I rolled an approving glance over him as well. He looked too handsome in a deep purple suit. The jacket had no lapels and he wasn't wearing a tie. The shirt was plain, even though I couldn't tell if it had sleeves. He hates sleeves, so if it once had them, it probably didn't now. He wore polished black military boots, because that's all he ever wears.

"You don't like purple," I said.

"Thank your roommate. She's a pain in my ass."

I laughed. "What are you doing here?"

"Livi sent me to get you," he said, stepping over James' outstretched legs to meet me. "She's waiting outside Pune Hall. She's anxious that you're not at your own birthday party."

"This party is for you?" asked Galen. He'd unbuttoned his shirt and slid it over his shoulders. I was mesmerized. I couldn't speak to answer him. Truthfully, I didn't hear the question.

"It's for her," said Romeo.

Galen wiped his face, mouth, neck, and chest with his shirt before he tossed it to the floor. He leaned his butt on the edge of the wooden footboard.

"Why did you not tell me?" he asked as he pulled his hands through his hair, knotting it tightly around itself to keep it off his neck.

The tattoos on Galen's torso were as distinct as jewels in snow. There was a simple Celtic sun on his upper left chest, deep dark blue in color. On his right bicep was what looked like a Celtic boar surrounded by those intertwining lines the Celts were so good at. The cuff around his left arm was as distinct as if the lines were drawn yesterday, and there was one I hadn't seen or remembered. It was Thor's hammer on his lower stomach, on the left side. It was black, but I could make out a few Norse or Celtic symbols etched on the handle. I curled my hands into fists because my fingers itched to touch them, to touch him.

"Captain," snapped Romeo in his official captain's voice. "Speak when spoken to."

The two were staring at me.

"Oh, uh. Yeah. Yes, the party's for me."

"Why did you not say something?" Galen frowned.

"I assumed you knew."

He made an irritated sound as he walked around his bed to the nightstand.

"Livi said everyone knows," I said.

"Jagen knows," said Romeo. "He's here. That's why he's here." He pointed to James and then looked at Galen. "I think your father wants to see you."

James dug his feet into the floor to help push his way up the wall. He made it to a sitting position and stopped. The blood pouring from his neck had slowed, but the hole was gruesome. The muscles weren't attached yet for him to make sound, but he pointed right at me.

"Why does Jagen want to see her?" asked Galen, angrily pulling a shirt from the drawer.

James didn't respond. His eyes closed, and he slid sideways to the floor. It hadn't even dawned on me that if James was here, so was King Jagen. My stomach felt sick with the thought.

"I wish you would have told me," said Galen.

I was confused at why he thought I would tell my boss about a birthday party.

"You never go to that kind of stuff," said Romeo, taking my cloak and purse from my hand to better see my dress. He circled around and then stopped at my back.

"For you," Galen said to me, "I would go."

I opened my mouth, but I didn't know what to say. Romeo slid his hands over the soft material covering my shoulders. He leaned his face to my neck and pressed his fangs against my skin.

"No," I said and smacked the top of his head. He flopped defeated onto Galen's desk.

"Is he escorting you?" asked Galen.

Romeo smiled.

"No," I said, probably a little more indignant than was necessary. "I'm not an escorted kind of woman. When I walk into a room, I'd like to think everyone is looking at me. Not, 'Wow, look at that beautiful vampire.'"

I glanced back at Romeo, who jumped off the desk and grabbed my hand.

"Come on. I wanna get you drunk. I really like that dress ... shirt ... thing."

We passed James, who had just gotten to his feet. Romeo pushed him out of the way, and he fell into the wall and back to the floor.

"Galen," I said. I really wanted to ask him to come, but it was inappropriate and bad for my health. I watched him push his clean shirt into his pants. He waited for me to say something.

Romeo jerked me out the door.

"Let's go. Livi's going to blame me for you being late."

CHAPTER TWENTY-NINE

IN THE COURTYARD, THE cool September air tickled my skin. I remembered my cloak and pocketbook on Galen's desk. I looked back, but I didn't really want to get it. I was much too afraid of that situation.

"You're not going to listen to me, are you?" asked Romeo. "About him. You won't listen."

"I am," I said, feeling worn out. "I'm trying. He's suddenly, persistently interested."

Romeo mumbled something I didn't hear. He took my hand in his. We kept a slow pace through the courtyard, dodging mounted horses and patrol cars on their way out. We were almost at the end, close to the iron gate sectioning off the entrance to Pune Hall, when Romeo stopped me. He moved me to a quiet, dark corner near the military stables.

"You're going to have so much fun it won't matter that he's not there." He hugged me, and it was so comforting to be held that I barely felt the chill dancing up my back.

"If you wore this color more often, I might be compelled to give you another chance."

"You'll give me another chance no matter what I wear," he said, cradling the back of my head in his hand. "You'll not only give me another chance — you'll beg for it."

"You're so vain," I smiled.

"Confident. Am I ever anything but?"

I pushed up on tiptoes to put me at a better angle to kiss him. I barely skimmed my lips against his. I didn't want to ruin my lipstick.

"You know we have a lot to talk about."

"Oh yeah. About what?"

I knew what he meant. He must have sensed I was going to flee because he tightened his grip so I couldn't sneak out of his arms.

"You know exactly what about. I was wonderful enough not to bring this up during your suspension-vacation. I felt you had enough to deal with. But everything's back to normal, and we need to talk—'cause you've been keeping some big, fat secrets."

I felt guilty, but not enough that I wouldn't stand by my decision. I thought it best not to tell him about the fey, and I wished he still didn't know. If I were going to be super honest, I'd have to admit that I didn't fully trust that his fear of what I am wouldn't get the better of him, and he would tell his father.

"You knew I had secrets."

"Not that kind of secret," He said, lifting my chin to meet his very serious eyes.

"What do you want me to say?"

"Jesus, I don't know. Something to make me understand why you allowed me to know that you were *special,* but only in the fact that you had great witch's intuition, and that maybe you could hypnotize yourself into some other place."

I shushed him, because even though he'd pulled me to a corner, I was afraid a passerby would hear our argument.

"In the all too elaborate explanation of what you are, never once did you say, 'Oh by the way, I can change my body to look like a giant flying scarab. And I'm so foreign my internal organs can't withstand human medication.' And, 'Oh yeah, when I turn into this Fear faerie, I can make you so afraid that if you have the capacity to shit yourself, you will.'"

The sarcasm wasn't a surprise. The way he manhandled me was. He'd wrapped his hands tightly around my upper arms. I kept my mouth shut until the people walking through the courtyard moved passed us.

"First off," I whispered, "I never *allowed* you to know any of it. I never told you I was different. You *raped* me," I spat. "You found out on your own, remember?"

His grip tightened. My breath came out in a groan as he lifted me off the ground.

"Don't," he said.

"It's true."

"You would have fed me sooner or later, and I would have known."

He dropped me, and I staggered, but I didn't fall.

"When I joined the military, I never dreamed that six months out of training I'd become a first captain's partner. I couldn't imagine I'd be working this closely with Lord Galen and the others. But if I were honest, I didn't want you to know the truth, because I didn't want Galen to hurt you for being disloyal if he ever found out."

Part truth.

He made his way to the tall iron gate. He wanted away from me, and it showed in every facet of his body.

"Why would you come here knowing you were so different?" he asked. "And that Jagen might want you dead?"

"I only knew vampires disliked faeries, but I'd been around them all my life. I didn't know about that dumb prophecy until you told me. I didn't know my blood tasted different until you came into my room and took me without permission."

"You should be glad it was me," he yelled. "That I found out and not someone less sympathetic."

"I am. But I could have gotten you in almost as much trouble for the way you found out."

"Stop changing the subject," he demanded, pointing his finger at me.

I was irritated that he'd brought this up now, but it was too late to pretend we weren't fighting.

"I certainly didn't know your father would be interested in me, or that I'd have to choose between what I want and what's best for all our lives. And damn it, most of all, I didn't tell you because you're his son, and a vampire. I didn't know if you would tell him. I didn't trust you. I couldn't. Not about this."

"You didn't trust me with your life?" He tightened his fingers around the scrollwork on the gate. "Something you've put in my hands every night since we've met."

"This was different." My shoulders fell in sadness. "No, I didn't trust you."

"If I'm the bad guy, then why do I feel betrayed?"

"Holy Jupiter, Romeo, I'm sorry. I never intended to hurt you."

"You never intended for me to find out." He stared at the gate, chewing his bottom lip like he does when he's upset or trying to figure something out. He motioned with his head to the entrance to Pune Hall. "Do they know?"

It took me a moment to answer, which gave him the answer.

"You had them lie for you?" The hurt, and probably shock at the fact that he'd never read it in either Dacon or Livi's mind, was all over his face. "All's fair in love, war, and eternally damning prophecies, huh?"

"I'm sorry. I am. But let me ask you, would you have gone to your father if I'd shown you that part of me when we first met? When you hardly knew me?"

He was suddenly in front of me. Way too close. I backed up to the stone wall, into the deepest corner of the courtyard. He came forward, putting a hand on the wall next to my shoulder, and one next to my head.

"Don't make me chase you," he whispered.

It was a simple enough statement, so why did it scare the crap out of me? What do you do when you don't want to be near a vampire, yet running away will make him want you more, or make him want to hurt you more? I was finding myself in this situation a little too often.

He held his hand close to my face but didn't touch me.

"The way you look at me, the way your body reacts to mine, and the way your 'other' scares the living hell out of me, adding a chase to the mix would be a real bad thing."

I agreed. Only I wanted to reassure him that I was still a loyal friend. The same Andru he knew and cared for. As if he'd read my thoughts, he smoothed the back of his hand down my cheek. I reached up and touched his face, uncomfortable with the way he stared so directly in my eyes. My fingers traced his lips and then brushed lightly over his sensitive chin.

"No," he said, pushing my hand away. "Don't start that. You honestly don't want to know the awful things I want to do to you right now. You don't want to know the pleasure it would give me."

He was so right. An angry vampire imagines torture or full submission. Things like pain, terror, and dread can all be aphrodisiacs for the kind of sex that doesn't really resemble sex at all.

"Do you pixilate me all the time?" he asked. "Is it glamour that makes me see you like this? Is that what makes me feel the way I do when I'm around you?"

I wanted to ask, "See me like what? How exactly do you feel around me?" And I wanted to tell him to stop being so insulting.

"No," I said. "I'm a regular person, Romeo. I have no glamour in human form."

"Yes," he said very quietly, "you do."

He moved even closer. He put his hands around to the back of my neck. I felt something cold slide down my throat, and I reached up to grab it. The necklace was small—a white gold faerie charm with her wings extended. It was an abstract piece. From far away it would probably appear to be a butterfly. She had a small green stone in the center of her belly.

"I know we don't do the gift thing, but it's a promotion, and a milestone birthday."

I ran my fingers over the cool metal and smiled up at him.

"The stone's aventurine. It's supposed to help your body center or strengthen independence. Not that you need that."

"I can feel it," I said. "I'm impressed. Romeo the vampire buying stones for their metaphysical properties."

"Yeah, well."

"Hokey bullshit are the words you used."

"It is," he said, his posture stiffening.

I threw my arms around him and kissed him hard. Forget the lipstick; he deserved it.

"Every time I see you two, you're kissing," said Dacon, hanging on the gateway, drunk. "If you're gonna bare it, you should share it."

His suit was almost identical to Romeo's in style, but the color was midnight blue—my favorite for him. Dacon staggered to the corner to get closer. He pulled us apart and leaned in, taking a good look at me. I started for him, and he shook his head.

"Nah. I was talking to him."

He quickly seized Romeo's head for a kiss. Romeo didn't fight it. He likes this kind of ride. He put a hand on Dacon's back to hold him close. Their mouths moved slowly and confidently. I watched their bodies, and again I was embarrassed by how I wanted to be in the middle of it.

They parted and Romeo said, "It's her birthday."

"Her who?"

They laughed, and I couldn't help but think they truly enjoyed making me feel bad.

"Why are you harassing me?" I asked, punching Dacon in the back on my way to the iron gate.

"Because it's fun," Dacon laughed. Romeo must have cut him, and the blood on his lip gave a picture of what he'd look like as a vampire. "I'm sorry," he slurred. "C'mere, and lemme see if I remember how you like to be handled."

I started toward the club's entrance. I didn't think I wanted a kiss from him. His intoxication level was a bit disgusting.

"What's gotten into you?"

"Bastard's rum."

"Never heard of it."

"I've never had it before. I like it."

He made a move toward me, but I moved away. I bumped into Livi, who looked great in a tight black satin cocktail dress. I pulled her in front of me to use as a shield.

"She'll do," said Dacon.

He motioned for her to come forward. Livi shook her head,

but I pushed her into him anyway. He grabbed her, and I hurried around the bend to the entrance to Pune Hall, where Romeo was waiting for me.

"She won't mind," Romeo smiled. "I didn't."

"Dacon is a lot more than useless in that department," I grinned. "Even drunk, if I remember correctly."

"I'm understanding that," he said, touching fingers to his lips. "Why does he have a faint smell of the beach? Like suntan lotion?"

"He puts it in his hair—has for years. I can't believe you've never noticed it."

"Me either."

"Says it attracts girls."

"Men too."

I grinned at him.

"That guy does not lack confidence," Romeo said. "I'll give him that."

"You've kissed him before."

"It's so rare, I forget. I'm going to make it a point to remember."

"He's even better sober," I said.

Romeo's eyebrows jumped. Livi pulled Dacon up the walkway. He pawed at her, and she slapped his hands. She was thoroughly enjoying herself.

"Did you ask him?" Livi questioned.

"No," I said, not wanting to talk about it in front of other people.

"She didn't have to," Romeo said and he grabbed me from behind, "because I sent Galen a note that said, 'If you like Dru, check this box.' And can you believe it, he did!"

Livi flipped him off, but directed her words at me.

"I know you shouldn't, but that's not why you didn't. You're a coward."

"Whatever," said Romeo, pulling me by my hand.

I let him take me to the entrance of the club. I didn't want to hear anything else Livi had to say, especially seeing how she hadn't told Dacon how she felt. Besides, I couldn't pretend I only wanted sex from Galen. I looked at Romeo's hand forged around mine — the pain in my ass with a beautiful face. I didn't think I could pretend with him anymore either. Crap. Suddenly I wanted to go home. Dealing with vampires was exhausting.

Romeo pulled me into the queue that had formed. We waited for the door attendants to check identification and jackets. Livi said hello to Kwan, a tall, dark-skinned man with dyed brassy hair. He smiled and nodded. He was wearing a white tuxedo with gold trim, which matched the tall blonde female standing next to him wearing a gold tuxedo trimmed in white. She patted the girls while Kwan checked the men. She stamped me, imprinting a red fluorescent circle with the number 30 on the back of my hand. I was anxious, because so many people were here for me. And I was nervous — the dreading kind — because King Jagen might at some point ask to see me. I took a breath as I went through the metal detectors and into the long foyer.

We stood for a moment, waiting for Dacon to finish drunk flirting with the female attendant. I noticed a man standing by the bench outside the bathroom. He had short, shaggy brown hair and wore an old brown suit. He talked to a man whose appearance was neat, maybe even orderly, with short black hair. The conversation was animated, almost an argument, but they were too far up the hall for me to hear. The one with brown hair looked vaguely familiar. Blackie handed him something and then walked up the corridor to the solarium, where other members of the party had congregated.

"Hey, over here."

I smacked Romeo's snapping fingers out of my face.

"I have to compete for your attention when he's around. Now I come second to men you don't even know?"

"Shut up. Does that guy look familiar?"

Romeo huffed, but turned. They were both gone.

"No," he said, yanking me toward the club.

CHAPTER THIRTY

I WALKED INTO A blast from the past — the very distant past. A page out of Louis the XV's life, with a few modern amenities. The cavernous club was dimly lit yet strangely bright from walls billowing with sheets of white satin. Dacon took off for the oval bar directly in the center of the room, a huge showpiece of wood and brass that was a replica from New York's old White Horse Tavern. He leaned on the bar rail to pester the female bartenders decked in frocks of white brocade, elaborately embroidered with rich, fancy golden thread. They matched the serving staff in high white stockings, gold trimmed white knickers, and powdered wigs. The opposite side of the bar had a white and gold checkerboard dance floor facing the rounded alcove for the nightly entertainment. To the right was a long table filled with food. Two-seater tables were scattered about the area, decorated in the same white material.

To the left of the bar were even more small tables. Most were occupied, making it hard to see that on the very far wall, across the room, was another alcove, longer and deeper than the band area. That space was always decorated black with red furnishings. It has a strange awning built onto it. It's guarded on both ends and is reserved for the lords when they come to the club. Lords Jagen, Pune, and Cherkasy were among the many people already there. It made my muscles tight to be this close to our king.

Large white and gold pillows were thrown about the perimeter of the room. If you wanted to get cozy, you could drop where you stood and do so.

"I don't know what to say, Liv. It's incredible."

"You really like it?"

"Of course. It's beautiful."

"It was my idea, but Pune did the decorating. He wasn't going to let me do a half-ass job after he found out King Jagen was going to be here. He said I'd have to change the date or I could get five times what my money paid for if I shared the space. Open bar, all night. All the food we can eat. And a royal show."

I frowned.

"I know you hate them, but many of us little people love to hang in the same room with the upper crust. They won't even know you're here."

I laughed, not wanting to hurt her feelings. I thought, *yeah sure, who wouldn't mind having the vampire that nearly killed her at her birthday party?*

Romeo guided me to the food table.

"I don't know how you stay alive. I really don't," he said, his expression evidence of his discontent.

"I know you're lacto-ovo, but there are quite a few vegans here, and I knew you wouldn't mind, so it's all vegan, " Livi said proudly. "And no one asked you to eat it," she said to Romeo. "Or look at it."

"Why don't you go away so I can enjoy this?" I said to Romeo. "It's not everyday someone goes through all this trouble to make me happy."

He gave an irritated laugh, knowing what I was hinting at. Dacon bounced back with drinks, including a cup of fermented blood wine, a true delicacy for the undead, served only when royalty is present and only to a certain few. He shoved the cup into Romeo's hand and then gave Livi and me a cup of something else.

"This is disgusting," Dacon said, referring to the food. "Where's the meat?"

"Oh, be quiet." I stared into my glass. "What is this?"

"It's the drink I told you about."

"Bastard's rum," said Livi, and she smelled it. "What's that mean?"

He shrugged and took a big mouthful from his cup.

"Looks like bits of raw meat at the bottom," said Livi.

"Pork," I said, smelling inside my cup. Together we set our glasses on the table.

Dacon turned to Livi. "You should have peanut butter." He nudged Romeo with his elbow. "Peanut butter is an incredible food, am I right?"

Romeo nodded and swallowed a big gulp of his wine. He wiped his mouth on his sleeve, leaving a dark smear to soak into the cloth. Livi led me to a small table next to the buffet. She shoved a sandwich of grilled peppers into my hand and left to get me a real drink.

Lord Pune, being the serious flirt he is, had me up for the first slow dance. I'd have felt special if he didn't do it to absolutely every female. If Romeo's a player, Pune's a mentor. A true Casanova. He's from Scotland, around the sixteenth century, but he doesn't sound like it. Not to me anyway. At five foot eight, he's the perfect height for us short girls. He's got wavy black hair and clear blue eyes. He wasn't nobility or anything like that. He was a farmer. What makes him royalty is that Jagen is supposed to be his father, but one time when I was working security at one of his gala events, he made a droll reference to himself being a bastard, meaning the vampire that sired him left him for dead. I asked Romeo about it, and he gave me some long song and dance about indirect lineage that ended with references about ducks. I figured everyone was lying for the guy, which is fine unless the general public finds out. All the royals can be traced back to Jagen, and that fact allows them to hold office. People may not be so kind to a vagrant vampire running a nation.

I don't care. I like being around Pune. He loves to talk and party, and, of course, have sex with military personnel. He's the only royal that truly cohorts with us commoners. Don't misunderstand, he enjoys his title, but he also likes being one of the people. Probably because he is. I think Galen tolerates his behavior because they share a territory, and he can keep an eye on him, and maybe because he sees how everyone loves the guy.

Pune inhaled the air around me and smiled.

"Don't you dare say I smell good!" I cut him off before he could say anything.

"I was going ask if you kissed your partner," he said, wide-eyed.

"What? Why would I do that?"

"I don't know," he smiled, leaning his head to my cheek to smell my skin close up. "You …" He drew back quickly. "You smell of the Lord of War."

"No I don't," I said.

"You do."

I turned my head, embarrassed. No, not embarrassed — defiant.

"It's not what you're thinking." That wasn't entirely true. "He wanted to talk to me."

"Talk? Yes, of course."

I narrowed my eyes at him.

"Andru …" Pune's eyes glittered with joy, his mock French accent exaggerated to the point of silliness. "Are you turning into a RoCh?"

"I am not a Royal Chaser," I said, slamming my hands into his chest and laughing, but trying to be angry. "Nobody kicks me around. You got that?"

"Okay. Okay," he said. "I'll never insinuate something like that again."

"I don't really smell like him, do I?" I asked as he led me back into the dance.

"Barely." He nodded toward the V.I.P area. "Your queen was going on about the frail human girl with the white dress in Galen's chambers — another one of her father's misfit soldiers that he's ridiculously protective of, even though she's a strange-faced girl with blue hair."

I slumped my shoulders.

"Would I have repeated it if it were true?" he clicked his tongue at me, the way some European men do when they want to tell you you're being foolish. "She rarely gets his attention. You know she rants and raves until he can avoid her no longer."

I didn't know that. I eyed him suspiciously, because royals never say anything bad about each other. It's an unwritten, very spoken rule. Pune shrugged.

"I trust you won't start rumors. Besides, it's the truth." He danced my tense body to a dark corner of the room. "Must I tell you how wonderful you are? Because I will. But not here. My room is better suited."

I giggled. No, I didn't. I laughed.

Pune and I have a tiny history. It was so fast it wasn't even a blip on radar. Livi knows, but no one else. Especially not Romeo. He doesn't think twice if I'm with a human, but he gets obnoxious if I'm with a vampire. He would hit the roof if he knew I'd had sex with Pune. I'm not exactly sure why apart from it being against policy—and just possibly, it would hurt his fragile ego to think of me with a higher-ranking officer.

I didn't let Pune get too far into his spiel before I bailed. I didn't want to hear the things he wanted to do to me. The problem with men like Lord Pune is that they're sincere when they're with you. A big part of them believes what they're saying, so you start to believe it as well. But out of sight, out of mind. Suddenly you're no longer his muse, and it feels like the sun has shriveled up and died.

AFTER FORTY-FIVE MINUTES THE house music stopped and the band began to play. The drummer was Dacon's bassist back in college, so I assumed he arranged for them to be there. When my drink was empty, Romeo appeared out of nowhere with another and disappeared just as quickly. Loki arrived with his partner, Danielle. They gave me a drink and when Loki turned away to talk to friends Danielle opened her mouth wide, pointed to Loki then made an obscene hand gesture to let me know they were sleeping together. I laughed so hard I nearly spit my drink onto the bar. I had a thought that Galen was wrong about Romeo and me being the only inappropriate partners at the manor. Although I doubted Danielle and Loki were kissing in the high turret.

Sara and Lucas showed up before their shift for "free eats and booze." At most parties Luc and I are designated dance partners, and he wanted me on the floor. The problem was, dancing with him is more of an indoor sport than anything else. He loves to bounce in the pit and normally so do I, but I hadn't planned on it with the heels and dress, so I promised him we'd go out soon.

Lord Brasov, our Justice Lord, who heads the manor in Maine, stopped at the bar to see me. Jupiter lives, was the entire Royal Calvary here? Brasov's a sweet undead guy. He's the youngest lord, a few years over three hundred, and I believe the oldest when converted—around sixty-five. But vampire genes do wonders, and he doesn't look a day over fifty. I've worked with him only once on a special project in his territory. He's one of the nicer lords, like Pune. Not quite like Pune, but congenial. He gave me the usual pleasantries and a small kiss on the cheek before he joined Jagen in the cove of the undead. So many people were with the king that I began to feel as if it were his party and not mine. It made me sick—which is why I tried not to think about it. Tried not to dwell on the fact that he was there with a bunch of his cronies huddled in a corner, talking about how he tried to kill the birthday girl a few weeks ago. And how fun it would be to watch her squirm a second time—to watch blood drip from all the wrong places.

I shivered so hard some of my drink spilled over the side. I made my way to the food table, because food is comforting, though not as comforting as the drink Romeo handed me.

ANOTHER TWO HOURS GONE. Luc and Sara wished me luck, giving me a creepy kiss on the cheek at the same time, and then left to start their shift. It's amazing how time flies when you're having fun or you're really drunk. When I was feeling quite un-sober, Dacon found me and went on about how polluted he was, and how if we fucked behind the stage neither of us would remember, so what would be the harm? It made sense, even though I had the feeling I wasn't the only person he'd propositioned. I declined, and in my inebriated state decided to crowd surf, in my dress, to the band's remake of the Nine Inch Nails' classic, "Head Like a Hole." It seemed reasonable until my clothes were nearly torn. I escaped with my dress in one piece, my wits, and my shoes. I realized that I had to stop drinking. There's a big, black faerie reason I don't drop my inhibitions in public. I don't know what I was thinking.

"I'm taking you home tonight," said Romeo. "You're not sober enough to drive."

"I didn't drive." I tried to frown, but it felt weird. My entire face felt weird. Romeo handed me another drink. "No," I said, putting the glass down. "Dacon made me promise I would take him home, so you'll have to escort us both."

"Sweet. I'll go see if Alivia is too drunk to drive or walk, and we can all go together."

Gods, why did he have to be such a deviant? I pulled him back by his jacket. My body smacked against his and I hurt myself. He smiled at me.

"Tell you what," I said with a slight slur that made me uncomfortable. "Leave them out of it, and I'll let you do whatever you want to me."

"Anything?" He looked down my body. "Because I want to do a lot of things to you, and some aren't so nice."

"Yep, however many times you wanna do it."

His brows went high and his smile was ear to ear.

"If you win at rail standing."

He burst out laughing.

"With you?" He pushed my shoulder, and I nearly fell over.

"No, stupid. With Dacon."

He glanced over to Dacon, who was hanging all over Livi and her friend, Tia.

"You got a fuckin' deal."

He hopped off like a child to challenge Dacon. But Dacon always wins at rail standing because Romeo distracts himself by doing tricks. I looked at my drink and then stared straight ahead, wondering why I'd just made that deal. I didn't need anyone to take me home. Livi was right; I needed to find a man who didn't manipulate me the way he did. I certainly didn't need to be high and alone with that confusing, obnoxious vampire. The thought of us together actually made me drool a little. But I had to stop. My life was odd enough. Why would I start a relationship with a vampire who'd admitted he didn't want one? I needed fresh air. I made my way through the crowd to the entrance of the club. I passed Kwan and headed for the solarium at the end of the foyer. There was a group of people lingering in the hall, but no one in the cool, indoor garden.

Pune designed a section of the lower tower to resemble a garden with a long pebbled path and small trees and bushes. The glass walls stretched from the main stone building, with a sloped roof overhead. The air was filtered and slightly sweet. During the day, the sun lights the room. In the fullness of night, however, the solarium is romantic. Tall pillar candles sit in the wall, and small solar lights line the path. Five benches are strategically placed for optimum romance. I picked one on the opposite side of the room, in a darkened corner by the glass wall. The view of the woods circling the manor was lopsided, and I prayed to Bacchus my head would stop spinning.

A few cadets walked past. I was partially concealed, and I couldn't hear them laughing, but I saw it. They seemed less complicated than anything I was going through. They were normal—something I didn't think I'd ever be. I understood that having the fey with me made me special, but it was unbearably lonely. My home in Faery is amazing, but my life with humans and vampires is good too. It seems I am forever split, always looking for where I belong. I knew though, that if I fit anywhere, by Galen's side wasn't the place. How could I have a close relationship with an expert mind reader? How could I be with a man who thinks I smell like his fondest memory, which happens to be a place I've never been, from an era I didn't exist? The playing field is not anywhere close to even.

"Fuck me," I said, kicking a few pebbles at my feet as tears pricked my eyes.

"Give us a moment. I get shy in a crowd."

I jumped, a hand on my thigh reaching for a gun that wasn't there. Galen stood on the path, unexpectedly close. One of the few times I've thought of the fey and Galen inside the manor, and behind me is a quiet, deadly mind reader. I swore to myself; I would never drink in public again.

"Will you please stop sneaking up on me? If I'd had my gun, I might have hurt you."

"You were in deep thought. I did not want to disturb the view."

He leaned closer, extending his arm to hand me my cloak and purse. I set it on the bench, hoping he didn't notice how off balance I was. Would he be so friendly if he'd heard my secrets? Did he just imply he was enjoying the view?

"Thanks. I remembered, but I didn't want to go back. Oh, I mean, I didn't ... not that I didn't want to ... it's just you had James and I was—"

"I understand," he smiled.

I plopped down on the bench, trying to remain focused. But it was difficult while I was drunk. His smile, his gestures, made my body stand at attention, even while the voice in my head was screaming. He'd left his hair down, which had parted itself on a high side and settled by his face before falling over his shoulders. His dark lashes framed his pale eyes like kohl. His lips were red, but not intensely so; I knew he hadn't fed in weeks, maybe six or more. He and Jagen are good at that type of discipline. He looked a bit disheveled in the type of clothing I seldom see him wear, unless he and Romeo are traveling to one of the other territories. He wore blue jeans, so old they were baggy, worn white at the front, and the pockets were frayed. The brown thermal shirt was snug, also faded, and thin from washing. He'd lost his black boots for a pair of dark brown work boots, and the extra lacing dragged on the floor.

"You came," I said.

He smiled, white gleaming in the moonlight. Fangs have a way of turning even the happiest smile into something menacing. And it did frighten me, but I was too drunk to care.

"I was summoned," he said.

"Yeah." My stomach churned. "You think he'll want to see me too?"

"I apologize," he said, shaking his head. "I came for you. I would like to finish our conversation."

"I'm almost positive what we were doing *wasn't* having a conversation." I crossed my legs, trying for sexy but getting maybe as far as slightly coordinated.

"Your leg," he said. "It seems to have healed completely."

I felt my face drain of color. I stared at him for a moment or two. That the wound on my leg would still be healing, or that I'd have a scar, had completely slipped my mind.

"Oh, yeah." I automatically put a hand on my calf to conceal what wasn't there. "I'm a good healer."

"Vampire blood also heals well."

"Excuse me?"

"Romeo's blood. I would imagine it healed any cuts or wounds you may have had at the time."

"Oh yes. Right. It did." I brushed my hand over the once injured skin. "Good as new."

"Yes," he said. "Lovely."

I didn't think my legs were long enough to be lovely, but I stretched them out, not caring that I was partially flirting. He smiled a moment before I felt a sort of buzz inside my head. I remembered the feel of his personal energy, and I took a deep breath.

"You know what?" I shook my head, using every ounce of will I had to speak before he captured me completely. "I thought I imagined you beating against my brain."

He smiled wide, almost embarrassed. Almost.

"You have a nasty habit of pulling me under without my consent." I wagged a finger at him and was sure I looked sober doing it.

"I thought a vampire lord was supposed to be noble and uphold the strict laws of his territory. If our leaders don't respect the laws, how can they expect anyone else to?"

"You think I am noble?" he grinned. "Common sense implies it would have been foolish to convert the royal or the rich. Embracing either position would bring untoward attention. Suspicion would surely surround a royal that never aged, attending only evening engagements."

"That's not what I meant by noble, but I suppose someone would notice."

"They did. However irrational the speculation of demons or vampire, there was always a pestering faerie to feed the flame of inanity."

My eyes widened a touch at the word faerie.

"The fact that the vampire did exist made the faerie not so pestery, and the speculation not so inane. You've done an excellent job at changing our original topic," I said. "Especially the bit about common sense. Insults to put me on the defensive are a good trick. If I weren't so drunk, you may have gotten me."

"Gotten you?" he smiled.

"I'm led astray much easier when I'm sober, because I get angry at the things people say. Being drunk keeps me focused. Not that I am — drunk that is."

"Does it?"

"I think it does," I said. "What were we talking about?"

His full smile deepened the lines around his mouth and showed maybe not his age, but the centuries of knowledge that has aged him. My stomach felt sick with a flood of emotion, and it was hard not to act on impulse now that he'd made his feelings clear. I wanted to touch him, and I knew I could because he wanted it too. He wasn't doing it because I was filled with vampire blood, and it wasn't my imagination. As deadly as that fact was, it was what I wanted.

"I cannot remember," he said.

"Doesn't matter." I stood and smoothed my dress. "I was just leaving."

"Oh?"

"Maybe." I bit my lip and smiled, because I was nervous, and because I wanted to flirt. "Romeo wants to take me home."

"I bet he does."

"He says I'm too drunk to walk."

"Will you be letting him carry you then?"

I was sure he was referring to the fact that I didn't let him carry me home when my leg was hurt, but I couldn't tell if he was amused or agitated.

"I haven't decided."

"I cannot let you go," he said.

"You can't stop me."

"He is not worth it."

"Oh no?" I questioned, taking in the recent parallels. "He says the same about you."

"I know he does." He shifted his weight from one leg to the other, and his warm energy pushed me. He was suddenly inches away, and I hadn't seen him move. Damn it. I backed up into the glass wall. He closed the steps between us and rested a hand on either side of my head, palms flat against the glass.

"No," he whispered. "No running."

This scene was too familiar. His lips parted, acicular fangs waiting patiently inside his mouth. His eyes closed and he lowered his head.

"You're going to kiss me," I whispered in a panic.

"Oh, aye," he said softly. "But first ..." His lips scarcely grazed my own before he moved to the side, running his nose along my cheek and neck. He inhaled one long deep breath. "He has been close to you."

Here we go again.

"Look, why don't we—"

"Quiet," he said. "Let me concentrate."

I didn't like that. Not at all. He straightened his arms and hung his head between us. After a silent few moments he raised up, eyelids heavy, pale irises bleeding red like endless spider cracks on broken crystal. He leaned in, licking my neck. Not with the tip of his tongue. Not delicate or teasing, but flat against my skin. He moved from my collarbone up to the back of my ear. It wasn't sexual exactly—more like he was tasting his dinner. I shivered, a little more from fear than anything else.

"Whin," he said, and I thought he'd forgotten my name. "Remarkable."

The words seemed to stumble past his fangs and out over his lips, sounding much too close to the old movie version of Count Dracula than was comfortable. Still, I wanted him. I was drunk, and stupid, and my libido was in overdrive. I wanted the polished predator, unearthly, and somewhat cold. I was lost in what was, for me, a desire so intense it scared me as well as set my senses on edge. Saying a quick prayer to Artemis for strength, and for my life, I set a shaking hand on his stomach. I smoothed my fingers up the soft, worn fabric of his shirt, until I was over his quiet heart. His eyes changed completely as lust drained the last of his humanity.

He took my face in his hands. I flinched the moment his heart chose to bang against my palm and he kissed me. In his breath I caught the rush of his blood lust. First cold and then warm. The energy was different from Romeo's, but it was blood lust, and I was coated with it. Saturated with emotions so heavy I lost my footing. He grabbed me, wrapping an arm around my back and one around my neck, almost in a headlock. His arms tightened, and he pinned me against the window with his body. His tongue explored my mouth, and I pawed at his shirt, twisting the fabric around my fingers.

He shifted and his hands took hold of my head. With effort, he pulled his tongue from my mouth and his blood lust pushed again; heated currents passed from his open mouth to travel like smoke down my throat and into my lungs. I choked on the invisible thickness. My legs gave out again, and he pushed harder against my body to keep me standing. His warm lips moved along my jaw, behind my ear. I panted with not only my desire, but also his hunger. My body thrummed with his loss of control. I had an overwhelming urge to run. I wanted him to rip me open. Somewhere in my mind I knew these were his desires, but it was difficult to fight that dominance. My own frenzied, drunk feelings were heightened beyond reason.

His mouth pushed against mine. He grabbed my lower lip with his teeth. I felt pain. The metallic taste of blood washed over my palate, and I jerked my head to the side. His motivation sharpened from the smell of blood. He pushed so hard I thought we'd break through the glass. I kept fighting. He took hold of my face, and I shoved at his chest. I pushed his face with my palms, which only fueled the fire; he enjoyed that I fought him. He took both my hands in one of his and pressed his cheek against mine. He situated his leg between my thighs, which made it impossible to struggle. He'd outmaneuvered me. To the outside point of view, it probably looked like rape. It sort of looked like rape from an inside point of view. A strange rumble reverberated inside his chest, unlike anything I'd ever heard from a vampire.

"You tease me," he groaned.

"You don't drink human blood."

He put my wrists against the glass, this time over my head. His breath came in shaking waves. In his eyes I saw the tiny black pupils burst. A thin, dark horizon line shock waved across the center of the crimson background. I choked low, pitiful noises, catching a glimpse of the raw power behind his carefully constructed walls of humanity. I saw exactly what Romeo meant by teetering on the brink of destruction. And it excited me. He took a few deep breaths and then set his forehead on mine. When he was slightly more controlled, he let my arms go, but he pulled at my thighs until I wrapped my legs around his waist. His large hands squeezed the backs of my thighs, and he kissed the side of my neck.

"If Romeo had gone that far, he wouldn't have stopped. I've never felt blood lust like that."

"You are not safe," he said, and the cadence of his voice shifted. His words were harder, cut off. "I have not fed for many weeks, and I am long away from harmless. But I use control, because although I know you want me, you push me back." He shook his head lightly as if to clear his brain.

"I'm sorry," I said, sifting my fingers in his hair.

"You are confusing, Nastya. Like a little girl. Still so young, with the changing temperament of a child."

I didn't know how to explain my behavior so I kissed his cheek in apology. He gave a small sigh, so I did it again—only this time I grazed my teeth gently over his jaw. When my fingers played along the back of his neck, his hands gripped my rear end and he rocked himself between my legs.

"You are small," his words came on a shiver. "Your hands, your face. But the power you hold with these immature things can be most unbearable. You are frightening in your ability to rule my thoughts and actions." I stared at him—the man I'd wanted for so long. I wondered what fantastical door I stepped through to wind up in Alice's Wonderland. "You do not believe me. Have you never noticed my attention?"

"How long?" I asked. He put his mouth close to my ear.

"Always."

"Stop it." I pushed at him to let me go. "Don't say things like that. Don't act like Romeo."

"I have done the appropriate thing." He was slightly angered. "I have never offered more than I was able to give. I have kept a distance from your inexperience. Until now."

"Gods, I'm too drunk for this," I said. Knowing I needed space to clear my thoughts, I pushed against his chest with shaking hands. "I want Dacon to take me home."

"I cannot let you leave." He touched his cheek to mine. "Not with him."

I wanted to get away, and I wanted to have my way with him. The fact that he was distressed at my leaving made me feel good.

The stinging of my lip prevented us from kissing, so I bit at his ear and down his neck.

"Lately," he said in a voice that shook just a little, "you have my constant attention. At work. Off duty. And I am wondering if I will ever be spared the constant interruption of my thoughts—the persistent contemplation on the warmth of your skin and what you feel like inside."

I sucked his neck hard enough to leave a mark, and his desperate noises tightened everything between my legs. I was practically wearing his anxiety as a coat. It tasted so good on so many levels I shouldn't be comfortable with. I wasn't just okay with it; drinking his tension was near orgasmic. I wanted to wring him out. I wanted to pound his buttons until every emotion poured from him like a faucet.

"No lass, dinnae push me." He punched the window next to my head. "You are no' safe. I was no' speaking melodramatically or merely cautious when I told ye so."

I didn't stop. I didn't think I could. The alcohol pushed me like a tornado whirling out of control. I pulled his shirt up, sliding my hands against his skin. My needs were so raw I couldn't help but touch, and lick, and suck any part of him I could get into my mouth. Like son, like father, I wondered as my tongue slid along his jaw to his chin, and I gave it a soft sucking kiss. I bit his neck so hard my teeth nearly broke skin.

"Please, no." He pushed me back with a hand on my neck. "You canna do these things and expect nothing in return. If ye dinnae stop, I will take ye whether you are offering or no'."

I nodded as if I'd understood, but my mind was fractured. I did expect something in return, just not bloodletting. I wouldn't let him bite me, but I would let him fuck me. He didn't release his hold on my neck, which was good, because I wasn't going to stop.

"Ask me something," he said.

The request was insane. My mind couldn't process anything so linear. I leaned in to kiss him.

"Please," his fingers tensed around my throat. "I want to obey your wishes of abstinence." He furrowed his brows. "Help me do it."

"Not blood, but we could fu—"

"No." His eyes widened. "I canna do that. Not now."

I wasn't going to get what I wanted, because he couldn't control himself. I was given an out and I needed to take it before I got hurt or worse. I took a good, long breath. I pushed at his hands to let me down because I needed to be able to walk away. He stood over me, eyes on fire, one hand still on the window over my head, when I grumpily decided to think of something else for us to do. Like talk.

"Galen!" Lord Cherkasy's voice boomed in the room. It wasn't that she screamed; I just hadn't realized how quiet we'd gotten. "Why are you in here? I want you to come see this."

My heart barely had time to sink from another interruption when Galen straightened and stepped back. He blinked, shut his eyes for a moment, and when he opened them they'd changed to their normal pallor. Change isn't the right word though—not fast enough. It happened with such speed that if we weren't so close I'd have missed it. I was confused that he could withdraw in those small seconds. The command he had over his body made me nervous. It also made me angry. He took another step away and I felt awkward, as if we were doing something wrong, something behind her back.

"Come," she demanded. "Stop playing and come with me."

Playing?

I wanted him to tell her exactly what he was doing with me. I wanted him to tell her to get lost. And I probably wanted him to slap her. He smoothed his shirt in place, and when he turned to her he took everything that was between us. He looked back, his eyes so bright they seemed like tiny moons set in the stillness of his face.

"I'll go and allow ye to rejoin your guests."

"Oh," said Lord Cherkasy, a bit annoyed. "Stop speaking that way. You know I hate when you do."

Galen put his fist to his mouth as if he were going to cough—a formal gesture—and he gently cleared his throat.

"Is this better?" He smiled at Luise. His accent was polite, a professional British accent. No hint of the stronger, yet more relaxed accent of a few minutes ago.

She smiled and then gave him an overall look of disapproval.

"What were you thinking when you dressed? You look like a laborer. You can't change, but do something with your hair."

"Right," he said, and jumped as if he'd meant to put it up but forgot.

He pulled a leather strap from his back pocket and before he could use it, Lord Cherkasy grabbed it, walked behind him, and tied the leather in the middle of his back. She moved to his side and linked her hand around his upper arm. When he covered that slender hand with his, I thought I'd lose my mind. So he was going to go with her? Just like that? How about, "Screw you, Lord Luise." How about, "I'm not leaving this room with you, you skanky blood junkie."

"I don't know the human's name, but he's standing on the rail of the bar with your son. They've been at it for almost ten minutes."

"Dacon," I said, my tone clipped and disrespectful.

"What?" She acted as if she only now noticed I was in the room, or better yet, like I was something horrible she was forced to deal with when she'd had no intention of acknowledging I existed.

"His name is Dacon," I said.

"I've never seen Romeo act so ridiculous," she said as she pulled Galen towards the door, "but I do like the look of the other. Do you think he enjoys women and men?"

My heart pounded like a wild dog. I had to blink to keep my eyes secure in their sockets. I pressed my back against the window and swallowed a violent scream. I felt stupid, and used, and a little more stupid. How could he let her do that? That was one of the rare moments I'd been truly embarrassed, and it had to be in front of her. In one brief conversation she managed to take every man from my life. Just uttering their names somehow made them hers.

I truly hated that woman. I should have told her where to go. I have never waited for a man to save me, and the first time I did? I drowned.

CHAPTER THIRTY-ONE

I TWISTED THE ACHE in my chest to something much more tolerable. Anger. Loathing. I flung the solarium door open and pounded like a storm down the hall. Only when I was near the entrance to the club did I think better of going inside. I touched my lip and realized I needed to go home before anything else happened that I couldn't control.

Through the glass doors, I watched everyone having a good time. The scene seemed like a metaphor for my life. I would forever be on the outside. Happiness happened all around, but not to me. Never to me. Because I wasn't allowed to show who I am. I couldn't walk around as the fey anywhere, but especially not here. Maybe my brother was right and it was time for me to move to Colorado. I was feeling really sorry for myself when I turned and banged into someone

"Jupiter! I'm so sorry." I steadied the man before he stumbled. "Excuse me. I didn't see you there."

"It was my fault," he said.

"No, I wasn't paying attention."

It was the shabby man in the brown suit I saw at the beginning of the evening. He had big brown eyes, a pointy nose, and thin lips. A regular guy, and yet familiar to me at the same time. I tried to open the door for him, and we both went for the handle at the same time. His hand covered mine and I had a second to notice the dryness of his fingers. The pads were white and calloused as if he worked in clay without washing.

"Sorry," he said, giving me what I think he thought was a small smile. But it was as if he didn't want to do it, or didn't know how. He moved his hand to a free space of door handle and pulled it open. "Please, you go."

The whole thing was incredibly awkward, and I didn't want to make it more so by declining. I headed inside, intending to leave as soon as he walked away. The music hit like a hand, and Livi came rushing to me before the guy was out of sight. She limped, holding one high-heeled shoe in her hand. Her arms circled me and she put her mouth next to my ear.

"Oh thank Jesus, you have to help me."

I shrugged and widened my eyes, not wanting to compete with the music.

She dragged me to a slightly quieter corner of the room and pointed to the crowd at the bar behind her.

"Dacon has to win. I can't lose the bet I made with Romeo."

I widened my eyes further.

"It's your fault," she said, "for saying you'd go home with him if he won at rail standing."

"I told him to leave you out of it."

"Well, I'm drunk, and the limits of the bet kept getting wider and wider. I need you to do something."

"I can't. I'm leaving."

"Oh no, you can't go."

I pointed to my lip.

"Who did that?"

"Never mind, but I have to go."

She shook her head.

"Please. You're the only one that can distract him enough to lose."

"That's not true."

"Offer him your blood," she said, nodding anxiously.

"No! He distracts himself by doing tricks. If you wait long enough he'll fall trying to do some dumb stunt."

She shook her head.

"Dacon won't last that long. He's totally smashed. You know he is."

Her eyes pleaded, and it worked because I did feel partially responsible. I didn't think it would be too difficult. Only his appetite for blood eclipses Romeo's sexual appetite. I could ruin this wager and be home within the hour. I nodded, and we headed to the large gathering of people at the left end of the bar. I pushed my way through until I was on the edge of the circle that had formed around the two exhibitionists. As miserable as I was I had to smile. What Romeo wouldn't do for sex and attention was probably a short list.

The men were about seven feet apart. Dacon was in his bare feet, balancing on the brass rail surrounding the bar—quite well, considering. He was concentrating really hard, but it was only a matter of time before he fell. Romeo had just leaned sideways to reposition himself in a handstand. His fingers curled around the rail, his body poised straight up in the air. In my short heels, his face and mine were nearly the same height. Livi was busy looking anxious while handing five notes to Tia, who was writing on a notepad. A path in the crowd of people led directly to Jagen's secluded section. I couldn't see our king, but Lord Cherkasy was sitting on the arm of a big chair. Galen stood behind her, leaning against the wall.

Romeo had already lost his jacket, so all I needed was a knife. The bartender handed me scissors, thinking I was too drunk for the former. I wasn't sure her choice was much better, but I was sure I wasn't drunk enough to be doing this. Leaning into Romeo's ear so he could hear me wasn't necessary, but some human habits die hard.

"Can't you just let this go," I asked.

"Not on your life." He laughed and tried to connect our mouths in a kiss. I pulled away and he almost fell. The crowd of people sighed in unison, and then cheered when he didn't fall.

"Please," I said, moving back to look in his eyes.

He shook his head no, grinning like he knew a secret.

"This isn't fair. Dacon's too drunk."

"That's why I'm on my hands and he isn't."

"C'mon, for me?"

"I am doing this for you."

I frowned and opened the scissors so I could cut my wrist open.

"No, no! What are you doing?" He carefully balanced his weight on his right hand, getting a round of applause, and he tried to take the scissors from my hand. "Blood is not fair!"

"Why not?" I jerked my arm back and he almost fell.

"Because I can't say no to that," he whined, his boots rubbing against each other in anticipation.

"Sure you can. I've seen you refuse blood before."

I have never refused blood from you, he thought to me.

I grinned. I made to cut my wrist again, and he yelled again for me to stop.

"You're chest," he finally said, face sobering, eyes becoming focused. "I'll accept if you cut your chest."

I cringed. I really didn't want to do that in public. But Dacon was wavering, even though Livi was doing her best to distract him. She looked at me, her expression desperate. I took a deep breath. Fine. I unbuttoned one button of my dress and pulled it a bit wider. I used the scissor's edge to quickly slice a deep cut into the fleshier part of my chest. The noise in the room dropped a touch as my blood filled the senses of the nearby vampire. I caught the seeping blood on my finger and stepped close to Romeo.

"This is so unfair." He shook his head, rolling his tongue over his lips.

I smeared a thick red line across his upper lip. He twisted his face and sniffed really hard to pull the blood into his nose.

I bent to his ear.

"This is free of charge. Today only. Right now."

"You don't give me anything for free," he said, wiggling his nose and coaxing the blood down.

I had to laugh. The truth is the truth. I leaned to his ear again.

"How many times have I given you blood without you having to beg for it? I can tell you right now, I'm not having sex with you even if you win. So if you don't hurry all this thick, red, clean blood will soak into my dress."

I watched him closely, and when the *fuck-it* look passed over his face and his boots hit the floor, signifying he'd lost the bet, I quickly turned around.

"I changed my mind," I shouted. Then I took off, using the only path open to me—a straight line toward Jagen's cove. Definitely not where I wanted to go. I glanced back, only to have darkness engulf me. The force hit me, and the air hissed around my head as I tumbled toward the pillow-covered wall at the foot of Jagen's den. Cheers boomed inside the room. Half of the crowd, probably the vampire half, chanted his name. "RO-ME-O! RO-ME-O!"

We came to a stop, with his body tangled around mine, protecting my head and neck. There was a short pause before I was disencumbered and flipped onto my back. I glanced above my head to one of the vampires that was guarding King Jagen's area. He'd moved closer. Romeo pulled hard on the collar of my dress, breaking off a button.

"God damn it!" He banged the floor with the side of his fist. "You're unbelievable!" He yanked the fabric down, exposing more than just the wound, but careful not to show the cross tattoo on the other side of my chest. "You're giving it up. I mean it! I'm taking it!"

"It's already healed," I yelled, beating at his shoulders, slightly amused with my tactics. "It's healed!"

"It isn't!" Again, he banged his fist on the floor. "Damn your games!"

I hit his chest, completely understanding where his raging adrenaline was coming from. He slammed my arms to the floor and clamped his mouth over the oozing slit. He sucked as though he'd pull my lungs through that three-inch line. His tongue snaked inside, causing a tremendous amount of pain. If I had to be honest—which I'd rather not—but if I had to be, something in my body clicked, and shouted. A hot sensation born from his mouth and tongue sliding viciously over my skin. Something that, for me, had nothing to do with blood.

"Don't," I said, my voice turning weak. "Stop."

I bucked underneath him, which only served to excite him more and make it look as if we were having sex on the floor. When he finally raised his head, he wore a wide, cruel smile. He blew air from his nose like an angry bull. My blood was all over his teeth, as if he'd been punched. A string of reddish spit dripped slowly toward me. I felt it hit my chest, warm and wet between my breasts. I swallowed a mouthful of saliva.

"I think I'm going to be sick." I turned my head away. "Get off before I vomit."

"It's just … it's just so good." He kissed me hard, forcing me to taste my own blood. *I'll use my blood to heal it if you let me suck on it for another minute.*

I knew he'd beg me. Okay, so he's not begging exactly, but he is asking nicely. For Romeo that's a lot like begging. The cut stung as he diligently sucked, pulling more blood from the wound. But when the surrounding tissue burned, I knew he'd mingled our blood. And damn it all, it was too soon. Only weeks since he'd healed me. It wasn't enough time for our blood bond to have broken completely. He moaned so loud I was glad the music was blaring. I realized I was holding him too tightly for it to be innocent, and I forced myself to push at his shoulders. I wanted him off me. I was hot, and aroused, and so tired of the blood dynamic I was stuck in with this vampire.

I pulled hard on his hair to bring him to his senses, and he jerked back. He was startled but knew better than I what was happening. He stared at me for a few moments before slowly standing. He tentatively offered me his hand, as if he wasn't sure he wanted to touch. I ignored it and while righting my dress, I looked into the royal party cave. The room was small but crowded. A few celebrities had shown up including the glamorous vampire, Reese. A buxom Syrian beauty, she wore only a red string bikini with multicolored tatters of cloth hanging from the strings. She held the handle of a linked chain leash, the collar locked around the neck of a young woman of maybe twenty. At the back, three men sat at one of the fancy white tables. The chairs were pulled together, allowing the two on the outside to feed from the wrists of the man in the middle.

I saw Lord Brasov on the opposite end talking with Lord Pune. Lord Luise was chatting up a few men in uniform. A waiter carried a tray of champagne through the crowd and toward us, the clearest path. Romeo wiped the blood on his face and grabbed a glass off the tray. I smiled and held out my hand. Throwing his head back, he dumped the bubbly liquid into his mouth. He swished it back and forth before spitting it back into the small glass. He narrowed his brows as he slid the glass into my hand.

"You want this?"

"Ick. Not anymore."

I saw Jagen coming our way, with James a few steps behind, like the sycophantic reptile he is. He'd changed his shirt, but he hadn't showered so he still looked disheveled and grimy. Jagen caught my eyes and held the gaze. His white hair swayed like a virginal bridal veil, and if I thought the blue outfit he'd worn in the park made him look stunning, the red satin shirt was a shock to the system. It was ugly, tacky even, but he wore it magnificently. With one hand holding a silver chalice, he came forward. He looked like—well, he looked like a king.

I nearly dropped the champagne glass onto the half wall. My heart pounded, and I would have turned away if I weren't paralyzed with fear. Jagen reached out and took my hand. A wave of nausea passed over me as it had that night in the park. I'd thought the sickness was from my injury. Maybe I was wrong. I did my best not to look revolted, and thank the moon for Romeo because if he hadn't taken my other hand, I think I would have fallen. Jagen bent slightly. He kissed my hand in true regal fashion. As if he hadn't tried to kill me a few weeks ago. Come to think of it, that probably is true regal fashion.

"You appear to have healed nicely."

It took me a moment to understand he was talking about my leg.

"Oh, um, yes."

"I wanted to see you, to congratulate you on your promotion. If my general feels you are superior enough to promote you, who am I to disagree?"

There was no mistaking the sarcasm. He obviously wouldn't have promoted me to head janitor. It didn't hurt my feelings. I didn't care what he thought, in that regard, but I couldn't meet his eyes. And they say if you can't look in someone's eyes you should look at their nose, but that's too close to his eyes. So I looked at his mouth. Jagen's mouth has very sharp teeth, so I glanced at the floor like a child.

"Thank you."

"It would appear you have many friends." He motioned to the chaos behind me. "And your tantalizing show, quelle joie."

He smiled, his eyes on Romeo. It's no secret Jagen likes men only, and Romeo is at the top of his list. As it stands now, and has always from the best of my knowledge, Romeo would die first. I can't deny the utter happiness that brings me.

"Romeo," said Jagen, "you hunt like the dark panther. It is beautiful to watch."

Talk about nauseated stomachs. Jagen reached over to wipe a thin streak of blood from his mouth. He knew Romeo didn't like it, and normally Romeo wouldn't have allowed it, but we were in public, and I think it took him by surprise. Giving thanks to Odin, he didn't put it in his mouth. The blood didn't even show on the hip of his jeans.

Lord Cherkasy strolled over. She positioned her rotten self next to Jagen. It was then that I noticed a not so happy Galen still against the back wall, arms crossed against his chest the way Romeo does. No one was near him. He looked lonely. He looked angry. Cherkasy asked Romeo if he was going back to Jagen's suite after the party, because every time Jagen visits a manor the visiting suite becomes a haven of debauchery—a den of iniquity, if you will. The events seem to take on a legendary status among the participants. Not that that's common knowledge for the papers. Just a perk for me that I work with someone close to the royals.

She leaned herself against the low dividing wall and nearly pawed at Romeo's chest. I was taken aback. I'd never seen her flirt before, and certainly not with Romeo. It made me ill. She slid her fingers along Romeo's waist while speaking in his ear. As if I wasn't standing in front of her holding his hand. Not that we're a couple. Not that it would have mattered to her if we were. When she put her hands up to his face, I'd had it. I tried to pull away, but Romeo wouldn't let my hand go.

"No," he said and moved away from her. "I won't be there. I'm spending tonight with my ... the woman of the evening." He showed them our folded hands while discreetly pushing Luise away. He turned his attention to King Jagen. "I hope you have good nights while visiting, my King."

His words were pleasant and respectful but left no room to wonder if he'd ever join them. He looked past them to acknowledge Galen, whose expression had changed from angry to downright pissed. We were back in the crowd when Romeo swung me in front of him.

What do I get for that?

I gave him a giant smile, and he yanked me up into his arms. I wiggled my butt against his hands, lost under my dress. He kissed me, sucked my split lip into his mouth, and reopened the wound.

"I know you saw my father. His death is all over you." He put his nose against my shoulder. "Christ, did he suck on your clothing?"

I stared at him. I didn't know where to begin.

"Shit." His eyes opened wide. "Did he ... did you and he? Wait, when you left, did you? Where would you have? How could you?"

"No, we didn't do that."

Romeo's entire body relaxed. I should've corrected him sooner, but I was kind of enjoying the silliness of jealousy.

"Is that why he's angry? You turned him down?"

"Not exactly." I glanced at Galen, almost too far away to see through all the roaming people. I tightened my arms around Romeo's neck. "I don't know what his problem is. You and me maybe—I give you blood, but not him?"

"You think?" He licked the cut on my lip. He sucked on it, and I let him until he hurt me.

"Stop it!"

"I swear to Christ, I'm so horny I could …" He bounced me in his arms. "Stick your tongue in my mouth. Let's give him something to be angry about. Then let's fuck in the bathroom — or hell, let's do it right here and really give him a show."

"Hey!" I jumped out of his arms when his fingers did more than brush between my legs. "You have to stop."

He wiped his mouth in frustration. He knew he was out of control from our blood bond. He just didn't want to admit it. He stamped a foot on the floor, which reminded me of Dacon. "You're a pain in my ass, and everywhere else on my body."

"You're the one who can't keep his fingers off me."

"Make up your god-damned mind. You either want me or you don't."

I knew it was wrong to smile, but I couldn't help notice the irony in his words, or that I liked how much he wanted me, or that he was jealous.

"You're a friggin' tease. If we weren't in public—"

"You'd what? Turn up the heat until I was about to pop and then find another lame excuse to leave me hanging?"

If looks could kill, I'd be dead.

"I swear," he said, "you are so lucky."

"Am I ever anything but?" I grinned.

He made an angry sound before a cheer came from behind me. I spun around to see a circle of people backing up from the bar. It widened until Dacon was the only one standing in the middle, swaying. Now vomiting. He was hunched over, hands on his knees for support. More liquid came out of him than I thought possible. It pained me to see someone so sick, and to think of the staff member that had to clean it up. When he was finished, Livi took his arm and guided him out of the club. Probably to the bathroom. Again, I saw the guy with the brown hair. He was by himself at the other end of the bar, uninterested in joining in the laughter coming from the crowd around him. I tugged Romeo's belt loop to get his attention.

"Do you know that guy?"

He ignored me. He was staring at a woman — no, at Roeanne following Dacon and Livi.

"I thought she wasn't coming," I said.

I jerked his belt until he swayed, but he kept staring.

"Don't read her mind," I said, pounding him in the chest.

He turned to me, unfazed by my attack except a slight frown.

"You don't even like her."

"Shut up. Leave her be. How do you know I don't like her?"

He shook his head like I was annoying him and pointed to a tall, dark-skinned woman sitting at a table in the far corner, in back of where Roeanne had been standing. She was just his type. Pretty face, all legs.

"That's what I'm looking at. That's what I want."

"Yeah, whatever." I bent my head toward the bar. "Do you recognize that guy near the end?"

"Brown hair, strange eyes? No, should I?"

"I don't know. I think I know him."

"He's at your party. Chances are you know him from somewhere."

"Yeah, I guess."

He wiped the blood from around his mouth and then rubbed his hands on his pants. He started toward the woman in the corner. I looked at Brown Hair and then back at Galen. I couldn't see much as the undead party had about tripled its human volume. I stood there looking from one end of the club to the other. People were dancing, and eating, and drinking, and laughing. Except me. I felt like I had nothing to do, and no one to do it with. It was time to leave — right after I checked out the guy at the bar.

I moved to the dance floor, pressing my way through the thick wall of sweaty people. I didn't know what I was going to say, but I was determined to find out who the guy was. I shoved two people out of my way and popped out of the mob, emerging, only slightly beaten, on the other side. I took a deep breath and put on my friendly face. When I got to where I saw him sitting, he was gone. I looked at the other end of the bar where I'd come from. I searched through the people at the food table. It was as if he'd vanished. He wasn't a vampire though. At least I didn't think so. The glass he left on the bar was full of wine. I flopped onto his barstool, and then thought that was rude and would be awkward when he returned, so I sat next to the one he was sitting on.

My mind flashed to when I bumped him at the front door—his sadness, his worn appearance. I was sure I'd seen that face before. I closed my eyes. I remembered it was hot. I remembered there were other people. A party? I remembered him looking at me … before … before he and his buddies took off, leaving Brian McKenney stuck in the car.

Shit.

I jumped off the barstool and then climbed back onto the stool for a better look around the room. It was too difficult to make out faces in the shadowy light. I ran to Kwan. He was on break when Brown Hair and I reentered the party, but he did remember him from earlier in the night. He hadn't seen him leave. I made him check the bathroom and solarium and then call for more security. I raced around the room, one eye checking for Brown Hair and the other for Romeo. I found Romeo at a corner table entangled in the arms of that beautiful woman.

"Hey." I smacked his shoulder, still searching the room. "I know where I've seen that guy."

Romeo pulled his mouth away from the woman and shoved her over to one leg. He tilted his ear to me as if he were straining to hear.

"He's one of the guys that ran from that car. The Psycho. The car with the guns in it!"

He stood with the woman, who kissed his neck until he gently pushed her away.

"You're sure?"

"Positive."

"Where is he?"

"I don't know. I lost him."

He glared at me with wide eyes.

"I know! I know!" We quickly made our way to the bar where Brown Hair had been. Romeo pushed a man who was about to sit on the stool. He set his hands on the back and smelled the air.

"Is he human?" I was nearly jumping in place.

"Hard to say with so many people. Yes, I think. If he were the last person to sit there."

"I was the last person to sit there!"

"Then I don't know," he shrugged.

We heard a sudden percussive boom that was so loud my entire body startled. I felt the rumbling vibration under my feet.

"Kali lives! What the hell was that?" I looked at Romeo staring at the front entrance. There was a single moment of quiet, where everyone in the room stopped talking, moving, or breathing. Romeo put his hand on my arm and as if on cue, another deep boom sounded. Louder. Stronger. Romeo pulled me to him and down to the floor. The room filled with smoke. I heard muffled crying and yelling. Romeo turned my head up to him. I saw his mouth moving, but I couldn't make out what he was saying. My ears were ringing. He pulled me to my feet, and very quickly we were in the hallway facing the exit. People rushing through the door pushed us aside.

Romeo turned me toward the room to face him.

Get DeFarr, emergency medical, and Freck and his bomb squad.

I nodded, and then he was gone. I could see the hallway now, smoky and ruined. The bathroom where I'd seen Brown Hair and Blackie arguing had been blown up, along with half the solarium. The wide hall was covered in dust and debris. People were staggering, limping, coughing, and wiping blood off their faces as they made their way to the exit as fast as they could.

I was about to turn away, do what Romeo asked, when I saw Blackie walking through the crowd toward the solarium. I had to follow him. I didn't have a weapon, but I just couldn't let him get away like Brown Hair. I pushed myself against the sea of people desperate to leave the building. My sandals slipped on a fallen hunk of drywall, and I fell to my knees. When I finally made it to what was once the solarium, I didn't see the black-haired man, or anyone else. I waved my hands to clear the dusty smoke, when I remembered Livi and Dacon leaving the party. My stomach dropped with the thought that they were in the bathroom when it blew. I immediately turned to make my way back, but the man I was looking for was less than six feet in front of me.

"Oh," I said unintelligently. "We have to leave the building. Are you hurt?"

I was slammed from behind and practically flew into Blackie's arms. He helped me stay upright as I was headed toward the ground. He took hold of my shoulders with hands that were a little too rough. I found my balance, and as soon as I did, Blackie yanked his large arm back. The last thing I saw was his fist headed for my face.

END OF PART ONE

The second book in the Anastasia Evolution Series will be released in Summer 2016

To Odin, for keeping my children under your watchful eye

Made in the USA
Middletown, DE
03 May 2016